RISE OF THE PENGUINS

STEVEN HAMMOND

ROCKHOPPER BOOKS

RISE OF THE PENGUINS
Copyright © 2016 Steven Hammond
All rights reserved.
ISBN-10: 0-9965424-6-9
ISBN-13: 978-0-9965424-6-3 (Rockhopper Books)

First Edition

Edited by Murphy Rae with Indie Solutions
www.murphyrae.net
Cover art by Pablo Fernandez
Formatting by Tanya Adams

Exclusive content at:
riseofthepenguins.net

Dedicated to

All of us who have had to battle forces greater than ourselves.

ACKNOWLEDGMENTS

I would like to thank everybody who helped me along this path and helped make this possible. My wife, Joy, for her continuous love, friendship, support and for never letting me give up on myself; my kids, Abby and Kevin for giving me the motivation to show them that if an unemployed former construction laborer can write a book then they can do whatever they set their sights on; my granddaughters for giving me hope; my good friend and fellow author John Daulton, without his help and encouragement I would likely still be trying to figure this stuff out. And Buster Dog, who knows when I need a break better than I do.

THE RISE OF THE PENGUINS SAGA

RISE OF THE PENGUINS

THE WARLORD, THE WARRIOR, THE WAR

CROSSCURRENTS

WHISPERS OF SHADOWS

THE ROYAL CREED

ORDER OF KINGS

THE GREAT AUK WAR (Coming Soon)

DRAMATIS PENGUINIS

Supreme Commander Liutites-Royal Emperor

General Diutes-Royal Emperor

Antaean-Royal Emperor, Overlord of the Southern Realm

Mearna-Royal Emperor

Ceocilus-Royal Emperor

Lieutenant-General Lavour-Chinstrap

Captain Mevoule-Chinstrap

Lieutenant Trevot-Chinstrap

Corporal Meuseaux-Chinstrap

Captain Nok-Rockhopper

General Treeg-Rockhopper

Sergeant Cort-Rockhopper

Corporal Trarck-Rockhopper

Keerka-Rockhopper

Leepoh-Gentoo

Lantot-Gentoo Elder

Colonel Kimmer-King

Commander Kiley-King

T'Cuh-Ka-Magellanic

Cuh-trük-Magellanic

K'K' Ru-ki-Emperor

Kra K'K' ki-ro-Emperor

Pìn-Blue

DRAMATIS PERSONAE

Gina Rosedale-Climatologist

Randy Lee-Photographer

Dan Alcorn-GT expedition leader

Lawrence Redeniek-GT base supervisor

Ferdinand Davis-GT base hand

Jack Freeman-GT base resource supervisor

Vance Lyons-President/CEO GT

Alejandro Varela-Poacher

Manuel Rojas-Poaching boss

RISE OF THE PENGUINS

Prologue

T HE PENGUINS WERE RELENTLESS. They kept coming and coming. Like arrows launched from a company of archers, they shot from the surf near a small California coastal town. The screams were deafening; along with braying and bleats of the invaders they created a din of unimaginable horror. Beach goers enjoying a late spring afternoon were taken completely unawares. The carnival-like atmosphere of the day turned to carnage. Men swatted at the diminutive horrors with boogie boards, umbrellas, or whatever they could find, hoping to give their families a chance to escape. The last beach combers made it to their SUVs, mini-vans, or, for the less fortunate, convertibles. The exodus of cars clogged the streets and traffic grinded to a halt. The penguin beaks clacked away at car doors and windows and overcame their occupants. The local sheriffs arrived and the deputies laid down suppressing fire to cover those who still had the ability to escape. Some made it, most didn't. Twenty officers repeatedly fired into the penguin incursion, but as one went down, three replaced it. The officers were soon overwhelmed and had to make a hasty retreat. A single police dog remained, shaking an invader by the neck, tossing it around like a play thing. The attack seemed to incense the birds. They advanced on the courageous shepherd with hatred burning in their eyes. A patrol car returned, parking between the dog and angry avian. The deputy fired his shotgun at the flightless terrors then opened the door, calling his furry companion. The K-9 heeded his master's call and they fled. With that, the battle was lost. As the sun disappeared into the horizon, an ominous red sky ushered in the darkness and an unthinkable reality . . . the penguins were here.

CHAPTER 1
ONE YEAR EARLIER –

FORWARD COMMAND ONE: A penguin burst from the sea, slid on his belly, and stood to approach a larger penguin. He offered a salute by lifting his beak high and then spoke. "Sir, a report from the Falkland Islands," the lieutenant announced to the commander.

"What is it?" the commander asked impatiently.

"The Magellanics have organized and are awaiting further instructions."

"Excellent. Have the Chinstrap inform Pack Ice Command at once. We now have all the clans with us and there'll be nothing to stop us," the commander said, clicking his beak after each word as if he were warning anyone who would challenge his assessment.

It was March and early fall in the southern hemisphere. Forward Command One sat on the edge of the ice floe and was in constant flux because of the changing weather conditions in Antarctica. The ice jutted far into the Atlantic Ocean, making it the perfect station from which to send or receive information from Pack Ice Command. Forward Command was simple in design. A two-meter ridge surrounded a central area of about two thousand square feet. To one side of the central area were three seal holes in the ice floor, with ten-foot furrows directly in front of and connected to them, called slides. The slides were there for the messengers to come to a sliding, but safe, stop after popping up through the holes from the aquatic abyss below. This was an efficiently designed outpost. It could be easily defended or abandoned, and it was far enough away from Pack Ice Command and the rookeries that, if there were an attack, there would be time to give a warning so that they could mount a defense.

The commander, General Diutes, a Royal Emperor, stood nearly four feet tall, slightly larger than a common Emperor penguin. His head was black with yellow markings and looked like most other Royal Emperors, save one feature; his right eye was blood red. This gave the general a fearsome, if not gruesome appearance, and the twenty-five other penguins under his command made sure to follow his instructions to the tee. He ran a tight station. No energy was wasted on trivial matters, and there was no dereliction of duty. Diutes and his subordinates were bloodthirsty and ruthless, and soon, very soon, their thirst would be quenched.

^^^

PACK ICE COMMAND: PIC, as it was called by the penguins stationed there, was a huge ice compound buried deep within the ice shelf where the Weddell Sea met the continent of Antarctica. It began as natural caverns, but through the ingenuity of the penguins, there were passageways large and small that crisscrossed and led to various chambers, antechambers, and command centers. Intricate etchings of swirls and dots with diagonal lines marked each entrance. Air holes came down from the surface and branched off to provide ventilation for the entire complex. The rookeries and learning centers were on the upper levels where natural light and warmth was most plentiful. To provide light in the lower levels, tunnels led to the exterior with a fixed layer of clear ice left on top to act as a window of sorts. The sunlight flowed through these windows; reflected by mirror-like polished ice, it was angled to every room. When winter's darkness fell upon PIC, lamps and lanterns, liberated from human camps, substituted for the natural light.

Everything had a blue-white translucency about it, and all of the light eventually reflected into the main hall where a giant ice crystal stalactite hung in the center. The warmth generated from the hundreds of busy penguins scurrying about caused meltwater to drip slowly from the end of the stalactite monolith into a frozen pool below. The stalactite absorbed the light beams and refracted them into a prismatic beauty which bathed the room in ever-changing color.

^^^

A Chinstrap penguin, Lieutenant-General Lavour, approached Supreme Commander Liutites after entering the main hall. The Supreme Commander was intimidating in his stature. Standing a full four feet tall, he was large, much larger than the common Emperors, which were the largest of the penguin races known to man. Liutites, however, was anything but common. He carried a deadly black beak and penetrating black eyes, which looked as though they could peer into your very soul. Yellow stripes flowed down from the corners of his beak, giving him a perpetually angry frown, and a gold crest on the back of his head added to his imperial appearance. Red stains on his chest bore witness to his violent ascent to Supreme Commander.

"Sir, a message from General Diutes," announced Lieutenant-General Lavour.

A large flipper struck the unsuspecting Chinstrap across his beak, sending him flailing to the ground.

"This is not a social gathering. You will address me as Supreme Commander and wait for me to acknowledge your presence before you speak! Is that understood, Chinstrap?" Liutites angrily proclaimed, adding an evil, condescending tone to his rebuke.

"Yes, Supreme Commander," Lavour shakily replied as he struggled to his feet. "Please forgive my eagerness."

"You are forgiven, Lieutenant-General," Liutites said evenly. "Now, what is this message from General Diutes?"

"He said the Magellanics are ready and await your instructions."

"Is that so?" the Supreme Commander hissed as he looked away, as if focusing on some unseen object in the distance. "Then the time has come," he said to no one but himself. In a sudden motion, he turned back to Lavour, inspecting the Chinstrap. "Go to your quarters and preen yourself. Then return here. You will accompany me to the Overlord's chambers and deliver this information to him yourself. Tell no one of this news."

"Y-yes sir, Supreme Commander, sir," Lavour stammered. He offered a high beak salute and shuffled away insecurely.

As Lavour slunk away, Liutites inwardly smirked. He was no fool. He had not achieved the rank of Supreme Commander on brute strength alone. He knew if the Overlord, for whatever reason, was somehow displeased with the message, someone would have to bear the brunt of that displeasure. That someone, unfortunately for Lieutenant-General Lavour, would not be the Supreme Commander.

CHAPTER 2

Lavour traveled the corridors back to his quarters, pondering the possible outcomes of his future meeting. "Why should I be so worried?" he asked himself quietly. "The information I brought seems like good news. All of the clans are united now. That's what we've always strived and hoped for—a united penguin state, for the good of all penguins, to defend ourselves from the human encroachers," he babbled to himself, repeating a penguin mantra.

Lavour silently berated himself for, as he saw it, having acted cowardly. But in the back of his mind, a thought occurred to him. *If it is for the good of all penguins, then why do we fear the Overlord so?* He decided this was a question best left for another time.

When Lavour arrived at his quarters, he was greeted by a cacophony of honks and bleats that echoed throughout the icy cavern. His quarters were not private; he shared them with at least one hundred fifty other Chinstrap penguins who had been sent to PIC as part of the Penguin Defense Alliance. The Chinstraps are smaller than their Emperor cousins. They stand on average eighteen to twenty-four inches tall and have a white face with a black stripe that runs across the cheek, accounting for their name. Although they are small in stature, their numbers are great and they make up a large retinue in the PDA.

"How'd it go?" a slightly shorter Chinstrap named Mevoule, asked

Lavour as he approached.

Lavour straightened himself to his full height of two feet. "As well as one could expect when dealing with the Supreme Commander," he responded and looked away out of embarrassment.

"Indeed, I can see by the swelling around your eye," Captain Mevoule said.

"Yes, yes, a slight breach of etiquette," Lavour replied. "He sent me here to preen myself for my visit to the Overlord's chambers."

"You're going to see the Overlord?" Mevoule asked in disbelief. "This must have been some message," he followed up, almost questioning Lavour.

"It is, but I can't discuss it just yet," Lavour answered as he started to preen himself, picking away loose feathers and rearranging barbs and barbules. "Now if you don't mind, I have to prepare."

Mevoule nodded. "I understand," he said and turned to leave.

"Wait," Lavour said, lifting a flipper to stop him.

"What is it?" Mevoule asked.

"Mevoule, you and I, we've been friends since we were hatchlings," Lavour said then paused as he thought. "And I trust you like a brother, and you trust me, right?"

"Of course," Mevoule said sincerely. "What's bothering you—your visit to the Overlord?"

"Partly, and . . . I don't know. Something just doesn't *feel* right. I mean we are becoming united, which is good, but it's just . . . the Royal Emperors— their methods are, well, ruthless."

"I know, I know," Mevoule said with resignation. "Though it is their leadership that has brought us this far. And they will help us broker an end to the destruction of our homes and lives at the hands of the humans."

"You're right. I know you're right," Lavour said, without feeling reassured. Something in the way Mevoule spoke bothered him. It was as if he was reciting the propaganda taught in the learning centers. "Just do me a favor."

"Anything for you, my brother," Mevoule answered lightheartedly.

"Keep alert for anything that might be . . . unusual. All right?" asked Lavour, choosing his words carefully.

"You mean besides a great penguin alliance?" Mevoule joked.

"Yes, besides that," Lavour said apprehensively. "Anything though."

"I will. You know you can depend on me." Mevoule replied, taking a much more serious tone.

"I have to go. I don't want to *upset* the Supreme Commander again," Lavour said mockingly. "Wish me luck."

"May the spirits of the Ancients be at your side," Mevoule intoned, reciting the penguin blessing to his friend.

The two friends looked at each other for a moment in silence. They gave a nod to acknowledge their reverence for one another. Lavour turned away and exited the Chinstrap quarters.

CHAPTER 3

Supreme Commander Liutites stood talking to a King penguin when Lavour returned. The King's eyes stood level with the blood stains on Liutites's chest, forcing him to stare at bloody reminders of his power. Lavour watched the orange-lipped beak of the King chatter something about the Order of Kings demanding something. He paid it no mind and paused for a moment before he spoke, "Supreme Commander, sir."

Liutites slowly turned from his discussion and looked down at the little Chinstrap

"Yes?" he sneered.

"Lieutenant-General Lavour reporting as directed, sir," he announced with confidence.

The Supreme Commander stared down at the Chinstrap and let the silence hang for several seconds. When Lavour remained steady beneath his heavy glare, he snorted. "Very well, Lieutenant-General, follow me." Liutites excused himself and directed Lavour toward an archway at the rear of the main hall.

The archway had similar, but more intricate, etchings as found over other entryways. Beneath the arch, Lavour's eyes followed a long curving corridor, leading to the Overlord's chamber. Several bas-reliefs, representing the eighteen penguin races, adorned the hallway. The light became a darker shade of blue, and the azure eventually faded into a hazy violet near the end of the corridor. The passage opened into a large oval room which suggested the interior of an enormous egg. A bluish-purple mist hovered near the floor, flowing between short ice pedestals arranged in two rows of three in the center of the room. The violet light appeared to emanate from the nearly twelve-meter high walls.

The Overlord stood in the shadows near the back of the room, and Lavour saw what few had seen. He emerged from the darkness revealing a frame nearly twice the mass of Liutites and a foot taller. A large black head supported a massive beak glimmering with an odd metallic tip. Yellow stripes drew back from his beak into a perpetual devilish grin. Golden feathers draped from the back of his head, carrying an iridescent glow and adding to his supernatural visage.

Lavour tried not to stare, but the rattle of a necklace made of sinewy strands strung with Leopard Seal teeth pulled his eyes toward the large penguin. The Chinstrap's gaze travelled down, resting on the Overlord's thick flippers which bore rudimentary grasping hands. Six guards stood by. Each had the same grasping flippers as the Overlord, holding long staffs with spear tips made of teeth.

The Overlord sauntered forward. His guards stepped back, raising their beaks high in salute. Lavour followed the guards' lead. The Overlord stood before them and gazed down with piercing black eyes. "What brings you to my chambers, Supreme Commander?" the Overlord asked, each word carrying the hint of threat.

"My lord, I bring you this messenger, just returned from Forward Command One," Liutites announced.

The Overlord's gaze fell on the Chinstrap. "Lieutenant-General Lavour. What is this message so urgent that the supreme commander saw fit to come to my chambers unannounced?"

Lavour forced himself to calm beneath the Overlord's gaze. "My lord, the Magellanics of the Falklands have organized and await further instructions."

The Overlord stared down at Lavour for a moment, turned away, took a couple of steps, and stopped. "This is *most* excellent information, Lieutenant-General Lavour . . . most excellent." He pivoted toward Liutites, "Supreme Commander, send messengers to the clans informing them to send a representative accompanied by a full regiment."

"Yes, my lord," Liutites answered, but he made no motion to carry out the order.

"Go—now. The time has come, and there is not a moment to waste. I want them here within thirty days. You are dismissed," the Overlord told him, waving his flipper as if shooing away an irritant.

Liutites offered a salute and turned to leave, throwing a malevolent glare at Lavour before shuffling from the Overlord's chambers.

Lavour disregarded the Supreme Commander. There were other things to worry about now that he had been left alone with the Overlord. He tried to push the rumors he had heard from his mind—rumors about the Overlord's violent and malicious nature, that he brutally punished penguins for even the slightest breach of decorum.

The Overlord loomed over the diminutive Chinstrap, letting the tension hang like a physical thing. "Lieutenant-General Lavour, your message finds you in good favor. You are fortunate to bear witness to a day that will be remembered by all. This is the beginning of the end of our oppression by the human encroachers. You should be proud to know you have done your small part. We are at last united."

"Thank you, my lord," Lavour said, trying not to sputter, thankful he hadn't upset him.

"Now go to your quarters and rest easy. Prepare yourself and your Chinstrap companions. In thirty days, there will be a gathering of our kind, the likes of which has never been seen. We will unveil our plans to end our oppressors' domination. You are dismissed," the Overlord said in a surprisingly calm voice.

"Yes, my lord." Lavour offered a high-beak salute and waddled out, relieved to be free.

CHAPTER 4

Lavour returned to his quarters, and the familiar calls greeted him once again. He searched the room for Captain Mevoule, finally finding him near the back, engaged in an intense conversation with a Chinstrap sergeant. When Lavour approached, the captain offered a formal salute.

"Lieutenant-General, sir," Mevoule said, unusually formal for the relaxed atmosphere of the Chinstrap quarters.

"Is there a problem, Captain?" Lavour asked, sensing the stress within Mevoule.

"Sergeant Gereaux just informed me that one of our corporals has gone missing."

"Missing?" Lavour asked the sergeant. With the Overlord's plans about to be unveiled, this wasn't the time for mishaps.

"Yes, sir. It's Corporal Meuseaux. He was summoned to the main hall for cleaning duty and hasn't returned," Gereaux told him.

"When was he due to return?"

Mevoule looked to the sergeant and back Lavour. "Yesterday."

"Yesterday?" Lavour said, nearly shouting. "Have you informed General Devét?"

"No, I haven't told the general yet. He's in a meeting with the Gentoo and Adélie commanders. The sergeant has sent three teams to search for

Meuseaux. It is possible he is just lost. PIC is enormous, after all."

"Possible, Captain, but not likely. Who assigned him to cleaning duty?"

"One of the Royal Emperor commanders," Mevoule said. "You don't think the rumors of the lower reaches are true, do you?"

"I'm not concerned with rumors, Captain." Lavour leaned into Gereaux. "Sergeant, take two Chinstraps and assist the others in the search. And don't bring any attention to yourselves. I don't want to arouse anybody's curiosity."

"Sir, shouldn't we ask for help with the search?" Mevoule asked, sounding confused. "There are thousands of penguins here. Someone has to have seen him."

"Captain, in a moon's time the greatest gathering in penguin history will take place here, and how would it look if we have Chinstraps strolling around, getting lost?" Lavour asked. In truth, that was only part of it. After dealing with the Supreme Commander and from his time spent at Forward Command under General Diutes, he no longer fully trusted the Royal Emperors, and he had a feeling of dread he couldn't explain about Meuseaux's disappearance.

"What are you talking about, sir?" Mevoule asked, now sounding exasperated.

"The message I brought to the Overlord, that's what it's about. The Magellanics have officially joined the PDA. The Overlord has sent summonses for all of the clans to send representatives here. They'll be arriving in the next thirty days. If Meuseaux *is* lost, we can't let anyone know about it. We can't show signs of disorder or weakness right now." Lavour looked to Gereaux. "Sergeant, you may go now. I want everyone back by night."

Sergeant Gereaux saluted and hurried off.

Mevoule watched the sergeant leave. "All right, he's gone now. Tell me what's wrong."

Lavour studied his friend for a few seconds, unsure about how much to tell. "I don't know. It's just something I overheard during my time at the outposts." He paused for a moment, watching other Chinstraps go about their business. "From now on, nobody goes on any detail alone. If anyone, and I mean *anyone*, inquires as to why, tell them that we're doubling our efforts for the greater good of the PDA."

"You're making me feel uneasy," Mevoule told him.

"Not uneasy enough," Lavour said, looking again at the crowd of Chinstraps.

"Are you going to tell me what you overheard?"

"Later. Right now, you need to focus on finding Meuseaux, and I need to talk to General Devét. Do you know when he's supposed to be finished with his meeting?"

Lavour's question was answered by the chorus of Chinstraps.

Mevoule nodded toward the general entering the quarters.

Lavour started to walk away, but Mevoule stopped him. "You are going to let me in on what's troubling you, right?"

"I will. Let me inform the general of the Overlord's orders and we'll talk." Lavour rushed away.

Mevoule watched Lavour walk away, his eyes narrowed, studying his friend.

CHAPTER 5

Surf pounded an island south of the Falkland Islands known to the penguins as Rockhopper Colony 23. A Chinstrap messenger sent from Pack Ice Command crawled from the sea and traveled up the rocky coastline, hoping to find a member of the Rockhopper ministry. "Hello?" the courier called to the deserted coastline. The wind blew across the rocky landscape, leaving his calls unanswered. He heard the trickle of falling gravel behind him and spun around but saw nothing. "I am an envoy of the Overlord. Is anyone here?" I'm not here to cause trouble. I—"

"Shut up," a penguin called from somewhere beneath an outcropping.

The messenger looked but didn't see anybody.

"Down here," the impatient voice said.

The Chinstrap looked a little closer and spotted the yellow plumage of a Rockhopper penguin between two boulders. "Ah! There you are. I am—"

"Quiet," the Rockhopper said in a hushed voice. "Are there any more out there?"

"Are there anymore *what* out here?" the confused Chinstrap asked, looking around.

"The humans—poachers."

"I saw no humans when I arrived, but the fog is thick," the alarmed messenger told the frazzled Rockhopper. "I am Lieutenant Trevot, from PIC, and I have an important message for your commander."

A foot-and-a-half tall Rockhopper clambered out of his hiding place, keeping a wary eye on the surroundings. "I apologize for my tone, Lieutenant," he said, offering a casual salute. "But this is the second raid by those filthy, featherless snookers in as many weeks. We're all a bit tense right now." The Rockhopper remembered his manners, ruffled his long yellow head feathers, and stood upright. "I'm Captain Nok of the RHC 23 Defense Ministry."

"Snookers?" asked the amused Chinstrap.

"Huh? Oh . . . sorry," said Nok, somewhat embarrassed. "Just trying to be polite in present company and all."

"Well, Captain, not to worry, our fortunes are about to change," the upbeat Trevot told him. "Where is your commander?"

"I believe General Treeg is back in the warrens. At least I hope he is. I haven't seen him since the battle began. He organized a counter attack this time, and we overwhelmed them and drove them away," Nok told the lieutenant with pride, walking toward the warrens. "Over there is where our forces took out three of those, um, guano heaps. Would you like to see our enemy up close?" He indicated the spot with his beak.

Having never seen a human up close, alive or dead, Trevot hesitated. But not wanting to appear cowardly in front of the captain, he accepted. "All right, but quickly."

The two penguins walked about fifty meters over rocks and through the island's abundant tusset grass. They stopped, and Trevot spotted the bodies of three dead humans surrounded by several dead Rockhoppers. Dried blood speckled the rocks, giving testimony to the violent struggle.

Trevot struggled to maintain his composure. Seeing dead humans was one thing, but he hadn't expected to see the dead penguins. "What happened here?"

Nok's gaze drifted away to the ocean's horizon and sighed. He looked back to Trevot. "We were about to go on our morning feeding run when several of the human craft came to land, just north of here. Nobody had spotted the ship. The fog hid it. They came in a rush, about fifteen of them. They immediately started blasting us with their . . . guns. Yes, I believe the humans call them guns. They slaughtered forty of us before we made it to shelter. General Treeg decided on a counter attack. We made a diversionary attack from the east, over there." Nok pointed to the rocky cliffs in the distance.

"They certainly weren't expecting an attack. That's for sure," Nok continued. "About fifty others, myself included, headed to the south cove and swam here to attack from the west, which put them in complete disarray. During their confusion, these three got separated. And that was our chance. Once they realized they were surrounded, they panicked and started firing their weapons madly, but my squads overtook them and buried their beaks deep in their stinking hides. I regret that I didn't get the opportunity to share in bringing them down. If you haven't noticed, their eyes and throats are particularly vulnerable," Nok said, indicating the dead men's wounds. "Anyway, after it dawned on the guano heaps that their lives were in danger, they fled back to their little boats. But they kept shooting at us during their retreat. Sergeant Cort and his company swam out after them and managed to turn over one of their boats. They don't do so well in the water, those humans. The sergeant's group dragged seven of them to the bottom of the sea until the air ran out of their heartless chests. After the humans were gone, the colonel sent me to search for survivors. That's when you showed up. I thought you were one of them, so I took cover." After Nok finished his tale, he just looked at Trevot in silence.

Trevot took in the scene surrounding him. He had heard stories of the humans' brutality. The Royal Emperors had drilled it into them at the learning centers, but he had never before seen the consequences. His heart ached for the fallen Rockhoppers. At the same time, he felt a cold indifference, almost disgust, for the dead humans. But he was amazed. He had never heard of penguins, of any race, defending themselves in such a way.

"Well, let me take you to the warrens. That's where the ministry is," Nok finally said.

Trevot stood in silence for a moment longer then gathered himself and followed his guide.

The pair traveled up a sloping hill and over increasingly larger rocks until they reached a rocky cliff. Trevot could see waves crashing against rocks near the bottom of the sheer wall. The rocks staggered upward, with curious grooves etched by millennia of Rockhopper claws climbing to their nesting grounds and warrens.

"All right, up we go," Nok told Trevot.

"What? We have to go up?" Trevot asked. Chinstraps were decent climbers, but they usually only climbed icebergs, where they could sink their claws and beaks into ice. He had never attempted to climb anything as formidable as a mountain.

"It's the only way," Nok informed him. "Why do you think we're called Rockhoppers?"

"Why couldn't they have asked me to deliver the message to the Macaroni penguins?" Trevot mumbled to himself.

Trevot struggled over each rock for what felt like hours while Nok bounded ahead effortlessly, occasionally hopping back to check on Trevot's progress. They arrived at the entrance well after dark. A small fissure in the rocks marked the opening to the warrens. Once inside, they confronted a rocky stairwell, leading down to the warrens proper. A faint glow emanated from the bottom, rousing Trevot's curiosity. When they reached the bottom, several passages branched off in different directions, but an unnatural light brightly lit only one of the passages.

"This way to the Defense Ministry," Captain Nok told Trevot, hopping toward the passage.

The Rockhopper Defense Ministry was brilliantly lit by an assortment of strategically placed torches and lanterns perched on rocks, wedged into crevasses and natural fissures. Trevot squinted against the light. "Oh my,

I've never seen anything quite like this. PIC isn't nearly as bright. How?"

"Ah yes. These are compliments of a human ship that ran aground. Their loss was our gain."

"But how did you—"

"General Treeg," Nok interrupted, spotting the old Rockhopper.

Captain Nok hurried off to his general and Trevot, still dazzled by the variety of lights, struggled to keep up.

"General Treeg," Nok said, offering a salute.

"Captain Nok, how did the search go?" Treeg asked.

"Currently incomplete, sir. This messenger from Pack Ice Command arrived," Nok said, waving his flipper at Trevot. "By the way, it is good to see that you survived."

"Thank you, Captain," Treeg said, turning to the Chinstrap. "And who are you?"

"I am Lieutenant Trevot of the Chinstrap company, Penguin Defense Alliance. I am stationed at Pack Ice Command, and I have an urgent message from the Overlord."

"Well? Let's hear it," Treeg said impatiently.

"The Overlord has announced that all clans are now fully united, and he requires a representative and one full regiment from each clan to come to PIC immediately," Trevot said, reciting the message very formally.

Treeg and Nok looked at one another. "This is outstanding," Treeg proclaimed. "Captain Nok, gather the First regiment and inform them that we'll be leaving at first light."

"Yes, sir," Nok said, eagerly acknowledging the general's command. "It was good to meet you. I hope to see you back at PIC," Nok said to Trevot, rushing away.

"Lieutenant, this message means everything to us. With the clans united as part of the PDA, we can finally aid and assist each other. We can direct resources where they're needed and mount sufficient defenses against humans, Sea Lions, Orca or whatever else wants to hunt us, eat us, or steal our eggs," Treeg said with relief. "Now, Lieutenant, I hope you'll stay until morning and enjoy our hospitality. We've been through a lot today, but we would be honored if you would stay."

"Thank you, General, that is most gracious of you," Trevot said, intending to decline.

"We have food and plenty of it," Treeg added.

This was different, and Trevot thought about it for exactly one second. "Well, I am feeling a bit peckish."

Treeg let out a hearty laugh. He took Trevot on a tour of the warrens, showed him the food stores, and explained to him the workings of the Defense Ministry. He even went as far as showing him how to operate the lanterns. Trevot enjoyed the feast with extreme gusto. After several hours, Treeg showed Trevot to the sleeping quarters, which was the most welcome of all the sights.

CHAPTER 6

A couple of hours before daybreak, Trevot woke to the sound of Rockhoppers calling an alarm. He quickly cleared his head and ran into the crowded corridors. He spotted Nok approaching Treeg and scrambled to catch him.

"General, sir," Nok said breathlessly. "The humans have returned."

Treeg stared thoughtfully at Trevot, whose eyes went wide with horror. "Which direction did they come from this time?" he asked in a calm tone.

"The southern shore, near where their dead still lie."

"Good," Treeg said, looking up the passage leading out of the warrens.

"Good, sir?" Nok asked, sounding confused.

"Yes, it's good. Send a warning to the Gentoo on the north shore, and then I want you and Sergeant Cort to take a squad. Go out the southeast passage. Each of you take a stick of fire. I will lead a direct assault from the east and draw them in. When you hear the cries of battle, go to their boats and burn them. The flames will be the signal for the forces in the west and north to attack. What are their numbers?"

"From what I gathered, twenty or more. They all appear to be carrying guns."

"Twenty thousand Rockhoppers will taste human blood before the day is over. It ends this morning. Enough is enough! No human will be allowed to leave here alive. The petrels will feast on their remains and we will nourish the sea with their corpses."

^^^

An approaching storm had blown away the previous day's fog. Moonlight from behind gathering clouds faintly illuminated the rocky landscape. Nok and his squad made their way to the small boats, taking the long way to avoid their torches being spotted in the darkness. Nok carefully put down his small torch and turned to Cort. "We'll need to send a scout ahead to make sure none of them are keeping watch. If we don't hurry, the coming storm will douse our torches before we get there."

"Corporal Trarck, you heard the captain. Go now, and hurry," Sergeant Cort ordered. The corporal set his torch down and ran ahead. "What will we do if the rain gets here first?"

"We'll hop across that stone when we get there. In the meantime, let's stay low."

After several minutes, Corporal Trarck returned from his scouting mission. "All clear, sir," the burly Rockhopper reported.

"All right, let's move," Nok ordered.

The squad moved across the rocky coastline, clinching the tiny torches tightly in their beaks. They reached the boats just as the cries of attacking penguins erupted in the distance, followed by gunshots and shouts from humans. Nok and the others rushed to set the torches on the boats. Nothing happened. The Rockhoppers stared at the slowly dying torches in disbelief.

CHAPTER 7

"Manuel, listen to me, we must go back. The birds on this island are mad," a bearded, middle-aged Hispanic man exclaimed as his companions made their way across the dark landscape. "The others did not survive our trip because of them."

"Don't remind me, and quit making matters worse, Alejandro. Blaming your mistakes on your idiotic superstitions won't change a thing," Manuel responded. Manuel, a nondescript man in his early forties and the foreman on the latest expedition to the island had already made two trips to the island this season. He had come back for a third forage before the penguins headed to sea for the winter. "I don't know how you convinced the others to go along with your lies."

"I'm not lying," Alejandro insisted.

"Enough already," Manuel said, irritated. "We're going to have enough explaining to do once the boss finds out what happened, and this asinine story of yours will make it that much worse. This is the last I want to hear of it."

Alejandro shook his head and gripped his gun tightly. No amount of talking would change Manuel's mind.

"All right, everyone, keep spread out and let's see if we can find any survivors. And check your safeties. We don't want any more mishaps."

With flashlights on and weapons holstered or slung over their shoulders, the men continued at five-meter spreads. They had heard the survivor's tale, and they moved in nervous silence. Although most of them dismissed it as lunacy, they were a superstitious group, and the disappearance of ten of their colleagues unnerved and fanned their superstitions.

The men, from poor villages in Argentina or Chile, had come along for quick money. They would take a few hatchlings and adult Rockhoppers they could sell on the underground live animal market. The men had to capture large numbers of Rockhoppers because only a small percentage would survive. They would sell some as taxidermal trinkets in local markets or online. The eggs were considered to be a delicacy, and dead birds were ingredients in stews or other dishes. Beaks were ground into a fine powder, which some believed to hold a medicinal power, and yellow head-feathers made fine additions to opulent women's hats.

Most of them earned only meager pay, and the conditions on the ship were even worse. The bosses and poaching kingpins took a lion's share of the profits, and their search for a better life would continue.

"Manuel, if we find no one, why must anyone know? Nobody pays attention to us," Alejandro said, stepping close to Manuel.

"The bosses do," Manuel snapped. "We've lost time and equipment, and that means they've lost money. And don't forget about the families of those missing. If they come searching for them, we'll have a whole new set of problems. If the authorities get involved, bribes will cost even more. We don't want that. But the bosses will want answers, and if you go off with your insane story to them—I'm not even going to guess what will happen."

"It's not a story, it's the truth," Alejandro said a little too loudly, the fear making him do things he wouldn't normally do.

"Spread out," Manuel told him.

Almost as if affirming Alejandro's insistence of the truth, a faint penguin call came from somewhere in the distant gloom.

All of the men stopped, listening intently, only hearing the waves to their backs. The sound of guns being drawn and safeties being released came from the line of men at once.

"Don't be cowards. It's just a bird—a stupid, fat little bird that can't even fly," Manuel shouted, turning back to Alejandro. "Do you see? Do you see what your stories have done? The men are nervous. Nervous men don't think clearly. They get jumpy, and when nervous men get jumpy, people get hurt."

"They should be nervous. I'm telling the truth. And now you'll see for yourself." Alejandro started to walk back to the boats, but appeared to think better of it.

Manuel stared at Alejandro and drew his gun. He holstered it and let out a long breath. "Let's just see if we can find the others, alive or dead, and then we'll be on our way. Okay?"

Alejandro stared at him for a moment. "Are you saying you believe me now?" he asked suspiciously.

Manuel scratched his head under his cap. "I believe something happened, something that frightened you and the others. And we're going to find out what happened and deal with it. Now, are you good enough to continue? I need everyone working together. Besides, if it's like you say and it is *penguins*, I think we brought enough firepower to handle them. We'll be fine." Alejandro nodded, and Manuel patted his back with an exaggerated show of patience. "Now let's get moving."

A drizzle came, and Alejandro followed the group through the gloom. They traveled inland for nearly fifteen minutes, and the drizzly mist seemed to thicken, further obscuring their sight. They started up a hill, stumbling over clumps of tusset grass, and caught sight of a dark mass moving toward them in the dreary early morning light.

Manuel squinted through the mist, peering over his flashlight. "What the hell is that?"

"It is our doom!" Alejandro yelled, turning to run back toward the boats.

"What?" Manuel asked, watching Alejandro flee.

His question was answered by the battle calls of ten thousand Rockhoppers.

CHAPTER 8

Sergeant Cort paced in front of the zodiacs. "We have to do something."

Nok matched his pacing, looking for a solution. "I know, I know, I know." Hearing the sound of battle added to his anxiety. He looked at the back of a boat and pointed. "There, what's that?"

"I think it's the . . . the thing that makes it move," Cort answered, adding his nervousness to Nok's.

"Try to burn it. Grab your torches and try to burn the thing at the back of the boat," Nok said, hoping for a miracle.

The squad picked up their torches and moved on to the engines, but still nothing would receive their flames.

"All right," Nok said, finally giving up on burning the craft. He turned to two members of the assault squad. "You and you, go to the others waiting for our signal on the north and west points. Tell them to attack. Hurry." The little penguins hurried off and Nok watched them go, thinking. He whirled back to the others. "If we can't burn them, let's tear them apart so they can't escape."

The penguins converged on the boats, taking out their frustration, pecking at anything they could get their beaks on. They tugged, pulled at wires, and ripped fuel lines.

An explosion three boats down sent penguins scattering. Nok scrambled to his feet, looking for the source of the blast. He spotted a boat engulfed in flames. Two Rockhoppers, who were too close when fire met the leaking gasoline, lay on the ground. One was dead, the other gasping his last breaths. Nok and Cort rushed to his side.

"What happened?" Nok asked, hoping it wasn't an attack.

The Rockhopper trembled, trying to maintain his pride. "Underneath," he said through a cough. "Liquid, like the lights in the warrens. It smelled strange. It touched the fire. We watched the fire climb back. Didn't know this would happen, or else we would've moved." He tried to laugh but only managed a gasp.

Cort turned to the others and instructed them on how to destroy the boats, warning them to stay clear after setting the fire.

Nok leaned in close to his fallen comrade. "You did well, my friend. You just saved a lot of Rockhoppers' lives."

The wounded penguin nodded without speaking.

"Now, you just hang in there. We'll get you out of here and find some help." Nok looked at the boats, watching them burst into flames. "We did it," he said, looking at the wounded Rockhopper. But he didn't respond, and Nok watched the life fade from his eyes.

With the boats burning behind him, Nok stared at his dead compatriot. His heart ached for the fallen hero. The loss of another Rockhopper suddenly became more than he could bear. As far back as he could remember, the humans had been coming. Every season it was the same; they took penguins and the eggs of those who couldn't nest in the warrens. Year after year, week after week, and now day after day, they had taken life after life. Rockhopper families were torn apart; parents were taken, leaving their hatchlings alone.

A wave of anguish washed over Nok, and he remembered the day his parents were killed.

He heard his mother calling for his father when the men dragged her away, her screams coming to an abrupt stop. His father, badly wounded and lying on the ground, told him to run to the warrens. Nok didn't want to go, but he did as he was told. He ran. He reached the base of the warrens and heard a gunshot. He turned to see his father struggling to stand despite having been shot. Their eyes met and his father pleaded for Nok to go. But he couldn't. His feet felt embedded in the stone, and he could only stand and watch. He flinched at another gunshot and saw his father's struggle end. Nok hid in a crag, watching the men gather the bodies of his family and friends and stuff them into bloody bags. That day, cold fear and fiery hatred planted their seeds in him, and they had been growing ever since.

The seeds, planted years ago, finally blossomed. The fire burning the boats crept into his soul, fueling a white-hot rage. He let out a horrific scream which cut through the misty air. Nok looked at his companions, his eyes filled with hate and yearning for the blood of man. Nok twisted away, gathered his breath, and rushed toward the battle.

The others stood for a moment, shocked by Nok's display. Cort puffed his chest and ordered the squad to follow their captain.

CHAPTER 9

"Lieutenant," General Treeg called out. "Move the rear lines forward to join the assault. Nok's team should've signaled the others by now. Send messengers to the north and west points and tell them to attack. Hurry, we haven't a moment to lose."

The rear lines moved in swiftly, and the penguins pressed the men into a hasty retreat. The men ran, firing back at their attackers but with little accuracy. They stumbled and tripped over rocks and clusters of tusset grass. The sheer number of attackers meant that some of the wild shots found their targets, but despite the occasional loss of a comrade, the Rockhoppers continued their pursuit.

Several of the men stopped and met their pursuers with a wall of gunfire. A dozen or more Rockhoppers fell, but the penguins were undeterred and kept charging. A Rockhopper found its way through the hail of bullets and launched itself from a rock. With clawed feet forward, wings spread wide, and beak open, ready to bite, it landed on the kneeling shooter's face, making the man fall back.

Countless Rockhoppers moved in on the fallen human. The man tried to fight back, but the penguins pinned him to the soggy ground, viciously stabbing and slashing at the man with deadly sharp beaks. Another man fired at the mass of ravaging birds. Several fell, but the rest left the dead man and pursued the shooter.

Nok charged toward the battle, undeterred by the sound of gunfire. The long-simmering rage within his heart coursed through his blood and thrust him onward to the clash with the demonic men. The crack of more gunshots echoed across the island, closer now, but still he sped on.

The gunfire erupted once more and he could hear the shouts of men. And then he saw them running back toward their boats. The man leading the way stumbled over rocks hidden by the darkness. Nok firmed his resolve and charged toward the faltering man, letting his rage engulf him. In one motion, he hopped onto a rock and leapt through the air, crashing into the man with a satisfying thud. The force of the blow knocked the man to the ground, smashing his head against the rock which had tripped him. Nok pressed his advantage and stabbed at the man in a blind fury. He attacked the eyes and face repeatedly, undaunted by swinging arms as the man haplessly tried to protect himself. He winced at the blood-curdling scream the man let out when his left eye was torn away. He didn't flinch when he removed the other. Nok found an opening and plunged his beak deep into the throat, ignoring the gurgles when he tore through the windpipe. He continued to peck and stab long after life had left the man's body, releasing years of pent-up anguish and hatred, making this one man pay for the sins of his kind.

The sound of men and penguins fighting to the death continued on behind Nok. The gunfire became sporadic, and the men's death cries became fewer and fewer. The sound of the victorious penguins filled the morning air, but Nok remained oblivious to all.

Sergeant Cort stood back and watched Captain Nok unleash his rage. He had been there when Nok's parents were killed and had become his brother when Nok became an orphan. Another minute passed and Cort approached him. "Captain."

Nok continued his assault on the long-dead human, oblivious to Cort.

"Captain Nok," he said louder.

Nok still struck at his victim.

"Hey!" Cort said, resting a flipper on Nok's back.

Nok looked up, blinded by hatred and blood. He stared at Cort, not really seeing him. His breath came in rasps until at last he shook his mind clear. He looked at the ground and then at the dead man. His gaze followed the pool of blood and up to Cort. The years of hurt shone in his eyes.

"It's all right," Cort told him. "Come now. It looks as if the battle is nearly over. Let's get back to the warrens. You'll be all right."

With his yellow feathers pinned against his head from blood and drizzle, Nok nodded. He felt strangely liberated and hopped off the body, not looking at the corpse and damage he had inflicted. He stepped away from the carnage, but movement caught his eye. A bloodied man lying on the rocks aimed his gun at Sergeant Cort. "No!" Nok cried, and the weapon fired.

Cort's body slammed into Nok, knocking him to the ground. He stared into Cort's lifeless eyes, another family member gone. He got up, gently rolling Cort to his back. He turned and found the man looming above with his weapon aimed at him. The man muttered something that Nok couldn't comprehend. He pulled the trigger and Nok accepted his fate, but death didn't come. The gun made a click, followed by two more. The man uttered something and threw the empty gun at Nok, which he easily avoided.

The angry human reared back to kick Nok, but the kick never came. A pack of Rockhoppers leapt on the man, knocking him to the ground. Nok stood and watched the man's flesh get torn away by the rampaging Rockhoppers. They left in search of another victim, and Nok went back to where Sergeant Cort's body lay and he was once again overtaken by grief.

CHAPTER 10

Alejandro scurried over the rocks, searching for a place to hide. He trembled from fear, exhaustion, and the biting rain. He spotted a would-be hiding spot and shouted out with excitement. He quickly looked around, hoping there hadn't been a penguin within earshot. He pulled the flare gun from its box and fired it into the rainy morning sky, then crawled inside a recess within the rocks, tucking himself in his sanctuary. He could only sit and wait, and hope someone aboard the ship saw the flare and would send help before the penguins discovered him.

^^^

"What is that?" Lieutenant Trevot asked, watching a light fly toward the clouds.

"I'm not sure," Trarck said. "General?"

Treeg slowly raised his eyes toward Trarck.

"I am sorry, sir, but what is that?" Trarck asked, pointing his beak at the dissipating flare.

Treeg watched the flare fall away, then returned his gaze to his son's body. He stood in silence for a moment, considering what he had seen. "A human still lives. It's signaling its comrades. It must be found," he said to Nok, his voice coming through in a hiss. The general spun toward the others. "A human has survived. Find it. Hurt it. Hurt it badly. Make it rue the day its wretched hide came to be. But do not kill it. I repeat, do not kill it. I want it alive and with sight. Bring it to me, and it will scream for death long before it's released from its intolerable existence."

The Rockhoppers scattered off, searching for the man and informing the others of the general's orders.

Treeg turned to Captain Nok. "Captain."

"Yes, sir?" Nok responded slowly.

"I need you to do something for me. Are you up to it?"

Nok straightened, presenting Treeg with a puffed chest and firm resolve. "Yes, sir."

Treeg eyed Nok for a moment, both understanding each other's grief and their sense of pride and respect for all Rockhoppers. "Take Corporal Trarck to North Shore and ask the Gentoo for help. They have a stake in this as well. Tell them about what took place this morning, and the risks to us all if the humans are allowed to leave. Go to the ship, slip aboard, and destroy them all. You know as I do, if they escape and they return before our hatchlings have fledged, more penguins will die."

Without saying a word, Captain Nok left to go in search of his squad.

Treeg looked to Trevot, who stared back with concern in his eyes. "Lieutenant, go now, and have no fear. Your path is safe now."

"It is not me I fear for. I fear for us all," Trevot said.

Treeg held Trevot's gaze until the Chinstrap turned away and headed to sea. "As do I, lieutenant. As do I."

CHAPTER 11

Hiding in his cramped nook and waiting for a sign of rescue from his hell, time slowed for Alejandro. He couldn't remember when he had last slept. He sat contemplating the events of the day, trying to keep his mind busy and awake. Free of the icy Atlantic wind, his thoughts drifted away. Listening to the breaking waves, his eyelids felt like magnet and steel. He couldn't resist the pull and he slumped over.

^^^

Alejandro twitched awake. How long had he been asleep? A minute? An hour? He didn't know; he only knew something had awoken him. He sat quietly, letting his hazy head clear. He stared through his narrow field of view—still daylight. He hadn't been asleep long, then. A quiet trickle of a pebble caught his attention. He strained to hear above the waves and wind. Something was out there, just beyond his sight. He leaned forward and heard it, the scratching of clawed feet scraping the ground nearby. His breathing became shallow as he tried to stay still for fear of giving away his position. His head bobbed with each pounding heartbeat.

He heard menacing little feet scurry by just outside his hole. He pulled his eyes away from the opening long enough to glance at the flare gun lying at his feet. One flare left. The scratching of claws returned, followed by soft, barely audible calls, sounding like a whisper. Alejandro wondered if penguins could whisper. He dismissed the thought, knowing they couldn't.

Whatever they were doing, they were close. The sound of the surf seemed to intensify, nature herself allying with the penguins to mask what noise he could hear. Something moved, and he caught a glimpse of black, white, and yellow hopping across the opening. Alejandro pressed his back against the wall of his shelter, bracing himself. As he slowly reached for the flare gun, another wisp of motion dashed and Alejandro froze, his hand inches from his prize. He waited another moment and then snatched the gun, clumsily inserting the cartridge.

Gravel trickled down from somewhere just beyond his view. He could hear it, *click, click, click.* He raised the gun, locking the barrel in place and wincing at the noise. He pointed the flare gun forward, trying to keep his hand steady. He had seen and heard how the others died and knew his death would be painful and slow. Three more Rockhoppers darted across the opening. He tensed, nearly pulling the trigger, but held back as they'd already passed. Alejandro stared with wide, unblinking eyes, straining to hear anything above the din of the ocean. Panicked noises escaping with each breath, he tried to force himself calm.

Click, click, tick. More pebbles and claws came from somewhere beyond sight. "Go away, just go away," Alejandro whispered, hoping death would leave him be.

Click, click, click. Like a clock ticking away the seconds of his life, the noise continued. Webbed feet smacked against stone, followed by more chatter. Alejandro stared at the opening, eyes wide, anticipating an attack, his breath coming in raspy gasps. He rested his finger against the trigger.

Nothing happened. No attack came.

His eyes remained glued to the world outside, expectation replaced by hope. "Maybe they didn't see me," he mouthed through a breath. His eyes burned from the cold, but he feared to blink. He relented and squeezed his eyes shut for half a second. He opened them, taking a second to refocus. It took another fraction of a second to spot the Rockhopper staring at him. Alejandro blurted a pathetic half-scream, and the penguin replied with a better one. He reflexively pulled the trigger of the flare gun, and the luminous projectile hit the small bird square in the chest, sending it flying back several feet. Alejandro clambered out of his hideaway while keeping a careful eye on the dead penguin with the flare still burning in its chest, and then he ran.

He staggered over the rocks to escape, and a leaping Rockhopper hit him in the chest. The force of the hit knocked him off balance, but he managed to stay on his feet and continued to run. Another leaping attack came at him from the left, but it was only a glancing blow, ripping his down-filled jacket. He pressed on and saw a flat stretch of beach about fifty meters ahead of him. He knew if he could reach the smoother terrain, he would be able to outrun his pursuers. They had the advantage on the rocks, but they wouldn't catch him on the flat beach.

Another attacker came at him from the front, and he managed to grab the leaping penguin out of mid-air and slam it on the rocks with all of his strength. Although the bird no longer moved, Alejandro stomped on its head to make sure it would never move again. He made his way over the rocks, desperately trying to get to the open beach. He leapt over one of the rocks with a little too much exuberance, stumbled, fell, and banged his knee solidly. He swore out loud and struggled to get back on his feet. As he stood, he saw three Rockhoppers appear on the rocks ahead of him.

Alejandro and the Rockhoppers stared at one another, each waiting for the other to make the first move. He went first, ignoring the pain in his knee, juked left and right. Two of the Rockhoppers had already committed themselves to a leap. One missed entirely, and the other brushed his shoulder and spun out of control. The penguin, unable to right itself, crashed into the rocks, landed beak first, and let out a scream of pain.

He tried the same tactics as before to evade the third penguin, but the angry Rockhopper wasn't fooled. It jumped and struck him hard on the upper body. He anticipated what was coming and had braced himself for the assault. The undeterred bird clung tightly to his coat with its sharp claws and slashed at his face with its beak, opening a two-inch gash on his cheek. Blood instantly began to pour from the wound. He grabbed the penguin by the wing, twisted it, and swung the bird away from him. Alejandro heard a hollow pop of the breaking flipper as he flung the bird to the ground. The penguin squawked in pain. He took a step toward it, but the Rockhopper had already righted itself. It gave him a threatening hiss, and hopped away.

Alejandro stopped to catch his breath and to see if any other would-be attackers were nearby. It appeared to be clear; nevertheless, he kept his guard up.

His adrenaline began to wane, and his legs and arms felt heavy. He ripped off a piece of his torn jacket and pressed it to the wound on his face. The blood had already begun to congeal in the cold air, and he could feel its stickiness against the hood of his jacket as he pulled it over his head. The open beach was before him now. He walked toward it and took his first tentative steps onto the coarse, black-brown sand, feeling it crunch beneath his boots. The beach stretched for nearly a half mile ahead of him. With rocky hills to his left and the sea to his right, he felt that the open shoreline gave him the best view of potential attacks. What troubled him, though, was what to do when an attack came.

Exhaustion haunted his every step as he scanned the beach. With no penguins in pursuit at that moment, Alejandro took a deep breath and felt all of the injuries he had sustained overcome him. An assortment of cuts, scrapes, and bruises covered his body. The gash on his face stung like hell, but what concerned him the most was the pain in his knee. It was aching and throbbing severely, and he was convinced he had at least fractured the kneecap. The little finger on his left hand was swollen and unmovable, most likely broken. He thought it was strange he hadn't noticed it before.

His thoughts drifted to the men who had died. He wondered if anyone else had survived, but remembering the swarm of penguins he had seen as he was running away, he dismissed the notion. None of them really liked him, anyway. They were co-workers at best and didn't respect him as a boss. *Good riddance*, he thought spitefully but then regretted thinking it. Most of them had families, and they hadn't deserved to die.

He gingerly let himself down to the sand and stared off at the waves, feeling the rain intensify. He pondered what could have made these penguins so aggressive and concluded that they must have been diseased. Or—an alarm went off in Alejandro's head—*a person has to have sabotaged the boats! Someone has to have trained these birds!* The thought of a person having caused this didn't set his mind more at ease than if it had been diseased birds; in fact, it had the opposite effect. The penguins were just mindless beasts, but a person causing this was a different thing altogether.

He looked around warily, wondering if someone was watching him. Nothing could be done about it, and he was too tired to search. Alejandro had a hopeful thought. Maybe this person could be reasoned with, and maybe he would let him go. Alejandro's body sagged. He knew it was wishful thinking and he probably wouldn't get off of this island alive. There was nothing for him to do now except sit, wait, and hope someone on the ship, or elsewhere, saw the flare and would send help.

CHAPTER 12

"It's just over these hills," Nok told his squad as they came ashore. Nok and the others had swum around the island to the Gentoo stronghold, known as Gentoo Rise. It received its name from the way the hills suddenly rose up just beyond the beach. The Gentoo penguins made their home on the second set of gently sloping hills.

They lived in a vast system of underground burrows. Unlike the Rockhoppers, who had only a couple of escapes from the warrens, Gentoo Rise was littered with openings. The difference had kept them safer from the poachers. Also, the Gentoo, with their sleek, torpedo-like bodies, were nearly double the Rockhoppers' size, making it harder for the men to carry Gentoo back to their boats.

The Gentoo were more loosely organized than their Rockhopper counterparts and, at best, had only half of the Rockhopper population. They were generally good-natured and enjoyed a life of solitude, preferring to keep to themselves. After the initial formation of the Penguin Defense Alliance, they opened up a bit to share ideas on how to avoid poachers and what not, but they still had very little interaction with the Rockhoppers.

"Hello," Nok called out from the bottom of Gentoo Rise. He waited a minute to see if he would get a response, but none came. "I am Captain Nok of the Rockhopper colony."

After a few minutes without an answer, Nok turned to another

Rockhopper. "Corporal Trarck, it looks as if we're on our own. Let's move out."

The group started to leave when a Gentoo scrambled out of a burrow near the base of the second hill. "Hey! Where're you rushing off to?" it asked. "It takes a minute or two to squeeze out of these holes, ya know."

Nok appraised the Gentoo as it bumbled its way down the hill. "I apologize. It's been a long night and we're a bit pressed for time."

"So I've heard," the Gentoo replied. "My name is Leepoh. What was your name again?"

"Captain Nok."

"Captain, huh?" Leepoh asked as he looked the Rockhopper over. "Well, Captain Nok, what brought you to this side of the island—romance, mystery, or perhaps just a walk on the wild side?"

"What?" Nok asked in confusion.

"What . . . do . . . you . . . want?" Leepoh asked slowly.

"Oh," Nok said, shaking his head. "I need to speak with whoever is in charge. We are in need of your help."

"And what makes you think I'm not in charge?"

"What? I don't understand," Nok said, not sure of what to make of Leepoh.

"Why don't you think I'm in charge?" the Gentoo asked as he turned away.

"Well, for one, you don't have a rank, and second, you don't seem very—commanding," Nok told him, becoming more and more irritated.

There was a long pause as the two penguins stared at one another.

"Hah!" Leepoh finally bleated out a laugh. "You sure got that right! I'm barely in charge of my own bowels, especially after eating spring squid. Nasty little buggers, those are, spring squid. Bah! They're not quite ripe. Fall squid! That's what I like! *Mmmm—mmmmh!* Do you like fall squid? Nice and seasoned, aren't they?" he asked, without giving Nok a chance to answer. "As for ranks. Bah! We don't really have *ranks* on this side of the island. Oh, we work together, and we all know our duty—who does what, what needs done, watching out for humans and all of that. But we don't need ranks for that. I thought a smart penguin like you would know that."

"I'm sorry, I . . . " Nok said to the rest of his squad for answers. They shook their heads, not knowing what to do. "I'm not really a diplomat. Are you all right?" Nok finally asked.

"All right?" asked Leepoh. "I'm not all wrong, if that's what you're implying. You can't be right all of the time—wrong either, for that matter."

"Excuse me, but is there somebody else we can speak to?" Nok interrupted. "We really are in a hurry."

"Somebody else?" Leepoh asked as if surprised. "Sure, there's lots of somebody else's. But I suppose you want to speak to somebody who is *in charge,* right?" Leepoh asked, again not giving Nok a chance to answer. "That somebody else would be Lantot. He's sort of the Elder of our community. He has the final word, based on how the other penguins feel, and we all pretty much abide by it."

"I see," said Nok, not really paying a lot of attention to the Gentoo.

"Do you really? Remarkable!" Leepoh said with heavy sarcasm. "So do I. I guess that's because we have eyes, huh? Or maybe that's why we have eyes. Hmm. Well, come with me. He's in the top burrow."

Nok turned to his squad. "Corporal Trarck, you come with me. Everybody else, wait here."

Leepoh led the way, walking about ten feet ahead of the Rockhoppers. Nok leaned in to Trarck. "Keep a sharp eye. I don't think this Leepoh is right in his head. I've never really been around the Gentoo, but if the others are like this one, it might be better if we handle this on our own," Nok said in a hushed tone.

"I understand, Captain."

Leepoh stopped and waited for the pair. "Better keep up," he admonished.

"Right. Sorry," Nok said, looking at the burrows dug in the hillside.

"This is an impressive community you've built here."

"Bah! We didn't build it, or dig it for that matter," Leepoh snorted.

"Well, where did it come from, then?" asked Nok impatiently.

"What—you don't know? Humph. Rockhoppers," said Leepoh, as if he were reprimanding the whole species. "Always scrapping and fighting and not learning your history."

Nok had had enough. "Listen, I'm not in the mood for your nonsense. We had an extremely vicious battle with the humans this morning—during which many Rockhoppers died, including my dearest friend, who died by my side. So I am not willing to listen to your babbling any longer." He lambasted the Gentoo then turned to Trarck. "Let's go, Corporal. We'll leave this idiot to his fate." The pair began their descent from the rise.

Leepoh watched the Rockhoppers for a second, and then he rushed to stop them. "Wait!" he called. "Just hold on. I apologize, not for me—I am who I am—but for my words."

Captain Nok stopped and growled. Even the Gentoo's apology didn't make sense. Corporal Trarck seemed to concur.

"I know of your fight with the humans. We all do," Leepoh told them. "We heard it, and some of us saw it as well. The Rockhoppers are admired by the Gentoo more than you know. Humans . . . humph!" he snorted. "Guano—all of them, if you ask me. Well, most of them, anyway. You gave them what they deserved." In an almost malevolent hiss, he continued. "I hope they suffered long."

Nok waited for a moment before he answered. The sudden venom in Leepoh's voice startled him. "They did," he finally said. "Though the one I killed went far too quickly."

"You killed a human?" Leepoh asked as they began to climb back up the hill. "So how many did it take to bring it down?"

"Just me," Nok answered without looking at Leepoh.

"You, by yourself?" Leepoh asked, disbelieving.

"Yes, just me by myself," Nok said, reflecting on the incident. "I guess

I just lost control and went mad for a bit." He wasn't sure just why he was telling this stranger what he felt. Maybe he needed to get it off his chest.

"It sounds to me like you took control and released your mad," Leepoh told him in his strange way of saying things.

"What do you mean?" Nok asked him, a little puzzled.

"You took control. You didn't lose it. You gave the humans what they have deserved for so long. You didn't *go* mad, you already were. You just sort of . . . let it out."

The statement caused Nok to pause and think. He thought about his life and about how events had shaped him into the penguin he was today. "I can't believe I'm getting sage advice from someone like you. But you know, maybe you're right—maybe."

"Maybe I'm all right?" Leepoh asked.

Nok looked at him. "I wouldn't go that far," he deadpanned.

"Hah!" Leepoh laughed at the insult.

CHAPTER 13

The three penguins continued to trudge up the slope while Leepoh continually rattled off about myriad subjects. When they reached the top of Gentoo Rise, they looked back at the rain-shrouded vista.

"This is some view," Nok stated. He noticed he could see all the paths that lead from each burrow. "Was this planned—with the elder's burrow having a view of all of the others?"

"I don't know. Maybe, maybe not," Leepoh told him. "That's what I was going to tell you before those wrong words came out of my head. The burrows were already here. We just expanded what we found. The Magellanics built this place. They are magnificent artificers of holes," he added pompously. "When they left, for whatever reason, the Gentoo moved in and made it their own. It was a lot of work, digging, digging, and more digging. Magellanics aren't much bigger than your kind."

"Well, it seems to have helped keep the humans away from you."

"Yes and no. It's not really that much different from your warrens. We just have a better view of the coast, and that gives us more time to get to safety. Also, they can't dig us out too easily. You have one place to hide. We have many."

Nok was surprised to know Leepoh knew of the warrens and how the Rockhoppers lived. At first he thought the Gentoo was insane, but now he saw him as a near genius in comparison to himself. He wondered if all of the other clans knew as much about each other. Nok had always busied himself with the day-to-day matters of evading humans and other predators, feeding runs, and so on. Then the duties of being a captain in the Defense Ministry occupied his thoughts, and it never occurred to him to ask the senior members of the ministry about the other clans.

Then Nok had a troubling thought. It seemed as if his life, since his parents were killed, had been spent on survival, his own and that of the other Rockhoppers, and nothing else. He had never even taken the time to find a mate or nurture friendships. He pushed the thought away; it was a thought best left for another time. Survival was why he had come to this side of the island, not only for the Rockhoppers, but for the Gentoo as well.

Trarck came along side of Nok. "Can we meet with the Elder now?" he asked.

Leepoh looked at the corporal then turned his head and let out a loud, bleating call.

The sound jerked Nok out of his thoughts.

"He'll be here shortly," Leepoh said, eyeing the Rockhoppers. "Now, let me tell you about the etiquette when speaking with the Elder. First of all, don't speak. Unfamiliar voices frighten him. Second—"

"Unfamiliar voices?" asked Nok disbelievingly. "What's wrong with him? Is he blind?"

"No, no. He's just strange that way."

Nok shook his head incredulously. "Your calling somebody strange is like . . ."

"Like what?" Leepoh asked.

"I don't know—the river calling the ocean wet."

Leepoh looked at Nok but didn't respond right away. He let out his one-vowel laugh. Nok couldn't tell whether it was a genuine laugh or sarcasm.

"Second," Leepoh continued, "You tell me what you want to say to him, and then I'll tell him."

"Wait a second," Trarck said. "Won't Captain Nok's talking to you frighten the Elder as well?"

"Very astute, my little Rockhopper friend. It will, so he must speak quietly."

"Cripe," Nok said in exasperation.

At that very moment, Nok spotted a grizzled old Gentoo as it ran toward them. On a glance look, he saw a Gentoo chick following close behind.

"Go away!" he heard the old penguin yell. "I don't have anything. Now leave me alone!" The old Gentoo dodged and weaved in an attempt to lose his pursuer but to no avail.

"What in the . . . " Nok started to say something profane as he and Trarck watched the comical sight of a fluffy gray check chasing down the Gentoo Elder.

"It's an old ritual of the Gentoo," Leepoh explained. "When we came back from our feeding runs, other Gentoo chicks, as well as our own chicks, would chase us around and try to get a meal. We feed only our chicks, but the others would always try to get a free meal before their own parents returned. We've recently outlawed the practice, but apparently this one is a slow learner."

Nok and Trarck exchanged looks and shook their heads in disbelief.

"Go on!" Leepoh yelled at the chick when the two penguins approached. The greedy little chick nearly stumbled trying to stop and stared wide-eyed at Leepoh. After a few seconds under the hard, angry glare of Leepoh, the chick bowed his head and slunk away.

Watching the scene, Nok was surprised by the sudden aura of authority that Leepoh exhibited, and wondered if perhaps he had underestimated the Gentoo.

Lantot the Elder approached the group warily, and Leepoh offered a deep bow with his head extended forward. Lantot returned a similar bow. "Lantot, I present to you Captain Nok and Corporal Trarck from the

Rockhopper Defense Ministry." Leepoh then turned to the Rockhoppers. "This is the Gentoo Elder, Lantot."

"Greetings, Elder Lantot," Nok said quietly to Leepoh, leaning close so as not to be overheard.

Lantot was the same size as Leepoh and carried the same markings: a black and white body with white streaks behind the eyes and a red-orange beak. His bushier tail feathers and duller coat distinguished him from Leepoh.

"We have come here in need of the Gentoo's assistance. We fought a great battle against the humans. We were victorious but at a tremendous cost," Nok continued.

Leepoh put up a flipper to stop Nok then turned to Lantot.

After hearing Nok's statement, Lantot looked at the Rockhopper. "Captain Nok, the cost will always be high when war is waged."

Nok once again leaned toward Leepoh, but Lantot stopped him.

"You may speak directly to me," the Elder said.

Leepoh looked nervously back and forth between the two. The Gentoo Elder had not spoken directly with an outsider in years.

"Yes, sir," Nok said with uncertainty, looking to Leepoh for affirmation.

Leepoh threw up his flippers in the penguin equivalent of a shrug.

"As I said before," Nok continued. "We took great losses during the battle, and those who weren't wounded are caring for, gathering those who were. The rest are either searching for the dead or hunting for a human that managed to escape. This leads me to why we came here." Nok paused as he noticed Lantot was shuddering nervously. "Would you like me to stop? I can see that I'm making you uncomfortable."

"What? No, no," Lantot replied, appearing to be a little embarrassed. "If the little Rockhoppers can face down an enemy as terrible as the humans, I can surely tolerate my phobic mind."

Leepoh, who had been quiet—for once—since Lantot had begun speaking, interrupted him. "Lantot, you don't have to do this. I can speak for him."

"Bah!" Lantot blurted out. "I'm tired of living this way. This is nothing. What Captain Nok and the Rockhoppers endured was something. Now, my friend, you may continue."

Nok looked to Leepoh, who gave him the go-ahead, then continued. "Well, as I was about to say, there is a human ship just off of the south shore, and we believe it is the one that brought them here. If it is allowed to leave, we are sure they will return with even more humans. If they do come back, it will certainly mean the destruction of us all—not just the Rockhoppers but the Gentoo as well."

Lantot still shuddered nervously, and Leepoh appeared to be rather solemn as they looked at each other. "Why would the humans attack the Gentoo?" Lantot asked. "After all, we didn't attack them."

"He has a point," Leepoh added.

Nok disagreed. "The humans don't care. They're indiscriminate killers, ruthless and evil to their very soul. When they return, and they will, they will kill all who remain. If you had ever encountered them, you'd know that."

"He also has a point," Leepoh said to Lantot.

"But I have encountered humans before. They did nothing to harm us. They just sat and watched us for hours, looking at us through strange devices," Lantot replied.

"He has a point as well," Leepoh remarked to Nok.

"That may very well be true, but these are not those kinds of humans. These *will* kill us. Of that I'm sure," Nok said sternly.

"He has a point too."

"Shut up!" Nok and Lantot told Leepoh in unison.

"Well, then," Lantot said, looking at Leepoh who stared at the ground. "It appears as though the time has come for the Gentoo to *fully* integrate ourselves with the PDA." He turned toward Nok. "How many humans do you believe are on that ship?"

"It's difficult to say, but they lost several during the raids. There can't be too many left. Though to be honest, we don't know."

"I don't think there is a need or the time for a council meeting about this," Leepoh said to the Elder.

"I agree. Gather the males who are able, and inform the females to gather the chicks into the burrows. The Gentoo are going to battle," Lantot said.

CHAPTER 14

From the top of Gentoo Rise, Leepoh called out. "Attention all Gentoo. Gather to the summit immediately!"

Lantot the Elder informed the captain that gathering the entire clan would take a while. A thought occurred to Nok as he waited, and curiosity got the better of him. "If you don't mind my asking, why is Leepoh addressing the Gentoo? Why not you, Lantot?"

"Huh? Oh, that. Well, you see, he kind of oversees things around here," the Elder answered in his nervous voice.

"What—him?" Nok exclaimed in surprise. "Why, that lying . . . He told me that if anyone was in charge here, it was you."

"That's only half true. Leepoh was assigned here several seasons ago by the PDA. But I *am* the Elder of this colony."

"I suppose the next thing you're going to tell me is that you have ranks?"

"No, not yet—not us, anyway—but Leepoh is a general."

"A general—you are joking, right?" Nok asked in continued bewilderment.

"No. You see, when the Penguin Defense Alliance was formed, General Leepoh came to us to help organize. We had our nesting grounds further up the shore, and when the Magellanics left, he had the idea to dig out the burrows for us to have a safer place to hide from men and other predators. I believe he got the idea from your warrens."

"That is amazing," Nok said in disbelief. "And I thought he was teetering on insanity."

"Oh, he is a little eccentric. But aren't most of us just a little bit flippy?" Lantot asked.

Nok wasn't quite sure if he meant only the Gentoo or if Lantot was including him under the description of flippy. What he did know was they were running out of time. He had seen human ships before, and knew they didn't stay close to the island when storms were near, and the rain was falling heavily now.

"Sir," Trarck said to get the captain's attention.

When Nok turned around, he was taken aback by the sight of over three thousand Gentoo penguins standing just below the brow of the hill. They had arrived in near silence. Nok was impressed. "Am I more tired than I think, or did a few thousand Gentoo just walk up behind me without my hearing them?" Nok asked Trarck.

"No and yes, sir," the corporal answered in a somewhat less-than-serious tone.

Nok did a double take in response. "You've already been around this Leepoh too long," Nok said dryly but then turned serious, his eyes narrowed. "This is perfect. If the Gentoo can move this quietly on the ship, we should be able to catch the humans completely by surprise."

General Leepoh let out a loud cackling noise, which cut off any further discussion. An immediate response by the thousands of Gentoo who had gathered sounded through the low hills.

"Gentoo," Leepoh started after the calls grew silent. "I have learned that we face an immediate threat to our existence. As most of you must surely know by now, the Rockhoppers engaged in a furious battle with the humans last night. Nearly all of the humans were killed." He paused to let the chatter die down. "But there is a human ship just off of the south coast. If this ship is allowed to leave, it will mean the destruction of us all, as they *will* return in greater numbers. "

"The courageous Captain Nok and his troop of Rockhoppers have warned us of this threat and call on us to help them eliminate it. As members of the Penguin Defense Alliance, we will answer their call. All able-bodied males and females without chick will join me in destroying the humans who remain on the ship. The young and the elderly will stay in the shelters. Today, we will dance on the lifeless carcasses of the invaders, and we will end their terror on this island once and for all. Come now, Gentoo! We shall march to war!"

Led by General Leepoh of the PDA, the usually docile Gentoo formed into ranks and turned to face the sea as the other Gentoo looked on. All knew if the attack failed, they would have to head to sea prematurely, before their chicks would be ready, or face annihilation. As the Gentoo headed toward the shore, a cacophony of calls erupted and the Gentoo began to sing:

> *To the human ship we go today.*
> *With their lives, they will pay.*
> *From the ocean, comes their doom.*
> *In their ship, will be their tomb.*
> *Death to the humans is what we call.*
> *To dance in their blood as they fall.*
> *Terror will strike them when we arrive.*
> *Another day, they'll not survive.*

When the penguins reached the shore, all twelve hundred stopped on Leepoh's command. Leepoh approached Nok, who was now reunited with his squad. "Captain Nok."

"Yes, sir," Nok snapped sardonically as he turned to face him.

"Hah!" Leepoh blurted out. "Captain Nok, I consider you my friend. Just because you uncovered my little ruse doesn't mean you have to call me anything but Leepoh."

"Yes, sir, General Leepoh, sir," Nok said in perfect military cadence and with a strong dose of sarcasm. "There are a few other things I can think to call you, but they will have to wait for now."

Leepoh went into a tirade of laughter but stopped as abruptly as he started. "Now, about this ship; how do we get aboard?"

"Well, we had a chance for only a quick reconnoiter on the way over, but it appears as though the rear of the ship has the lowest sides. If we get up enough speed, we should be able to clear the sides and from there—" Nok paused and looked more intently at Leepoh, "—we kill everything that doesn't have feathers."

"Sounds sound," said Leepoh with his usual mirth. "May I suggest after we get within range, you let us lead the attack? The Gentoo are faster swimmers, and I think speed will be of the essence in this situation. Plus, we're not already fatigued from a night of fighting."

Nok pondered the notion for a moment. Normally he would have been affronted by the suggestion, but it had indeed been a stressful night *and* morning, and in a vast understatement, it wasn't over yet. He wondered when it would ever really be over. Nok nodded in agreement.

"Very well, Captain Nok, lead the way," Leepoh told him.

Captain Nok faced his squad. "Rockhoppers, let us, the *united* penguins, finish this!"

The penguins, led by the Rockhoppers and Captain Nok, went to sea. The water churned as more than a thousand penguins waddled into the calm of the northern shore. The huge flock headed to their fate and flew through the deep, hell-bent on destroying their enemy.

CHAPTER 15

Alejandro sat and stared at the water. He was waiting—waiting and hoping against hope for a rescue. He knew his chances were slim. Odds were nobody aboard the ship saw the flare, and he had used his last one killing one of the *pingüinos demonio*, as he called them—the demon penguins. His hopes rode on somebody aboard taking notice of not hearing from the landing party, but the problem was they were still within the allotted time to return.

A thought then occurred to him. *Manuel had a phone!* He jumped up with excitement, forgetting about his injured knee, and fell back down just as quickly as he'd stood. It would have been a fool's errand to try to find the phone anyway, he decided. Manuel's body was lying back in the killing grounds, which were, more than likely, still crawling with the pingüinos demonio.

Alejandro gingerly stood back up, being careful not to put too much weight on his hurt leg. The cold made his body stiff. He figured it was better to do something rather than nothing. He gathered rocks from the beach to use for defense against the penguins if they returned. *No, not if, but when they returned,* he reminded himself.

Hobbling his way along the beach and away from the water's edge to where the larger stones were deposited, he looked back at the sea. The sky had grown even darker, and portentous gray clouds held the promise of continued rain. Alejandro's hope grew dimmer when he realized that, with the storm getting worse, the ship couldn't stay anchored close to shore.

Alejandro limped to slightly higher ground and faced the sea. He could see the Caracara in the distance, but something else held his attention. He saw strange movement in the surf. At first, he thought it might have been the waves crashing, or perhaps the heavy rain was distorting his vision. It took him a minute, but then he realized what it was. He dropped his handful of rocks out of shock. Hundreds of penguins were porpoising in and out of the water as they swam, and it was obvious they were headed to the ship anchored on the horizon.

"No!" Alejandro screamed out. "You God-damned little bastards—no!"

He spun around, not knowing what to do. The penguins were about to take away his only hope of escape. He paced back and forth, ignoring his pain and feeling helpless, anxious, and frustrated by his own impotence. Then another and even more horrifying sight caught his eye. A Rockhopper stood on a rocky dune not quite twenty meters away. The lone sphenisciform was soon joined by another, then another, and then several more. Before long, the dunes were covered with penguins. They stood and watched Alejandro, making quiet cackling noises amongst themselves, waiting for the moment to attack.

With nowhere to run and a ship that soon would be overrun with penguins, Alejandro fell to the ground and wept. The prospect of his imminent death stole his remaining strength. He picked up one of his fallen stones and weakly lobbed it at the line of penguins. A few of the Rockhoppers fluttered agitatedly as the rock fell well short of its intended target.

"No," Alejandro whispered. The Rockhoppers moved on him.

CHAPTER 16

The penguin assault group bobbed in the rough waves about two hundred meters from the human's ship, waiting for their leaders to finish discussing the final plans for the attack.

"All right, here it is," said Leepoh. "Twenty others and I will go on board ahead of the assault and do a quick reconnoiter. After we give the go-ahead, the rest will come in waves of one hundred. The initial attack will be eight waves. We'll hold four waves in reserve to call if needed."

"They will not be expecting anything like this, so we should be able to catch them completely unawares," Nok said to the group of selected wave leaders.

"Right," Leepoh concurred.

"As soon as we receive word from your group, we'll begin our dive. The plan, as you say, 'sounds sound,' but I'll be coming aboard in the seventh wave. I want to be there to witness the final destruction of these beasts," Nok informed the general.

"I would expect nothing less from you, my friend," Leepoh replied.

Nok was about to say something else on the subject when one of the scouts popped to the surface. "General Leepoh, Captain Nok, sirs," the breathless Rockhopper said. "We completed ten trips around the ship. As near as we could tell, all of the humans are inside, though one came outside briefly and breathed smoke."

"Thank you," Leepoh told him. "Go inform the rest of your squad the attack will commence shortly." He looked to Nok as the Rockhopper sped away. "We're going to have to find a way inside if we want to win this."

"Create a distraction," Nok told Leepoh. "Tap on something with your beak. They're curious creatures. One of them is bound to come out, and then you'll get in."

"Good idea, now let's get started."

^^^

General Leepoh of the PDA and Commander of the Gentoo on the island of RHC 23 swam to the front of wave one. He was accompanied by twenty other Gentoo, who would be the first to board the human ship.

"Dontah," Leepoh addressed another Gentoo. "Make sure the others stay in their assigned ranks, and when the assault begins, remind them the humans are most vulnerable from the neck up. Good luck."

Leepoh and his group headed under. They dove deep as they bulleted through the water. Once they reached the appropriate depth, they angled upward, flapping their flipper wings to gain more speed. They rose from the depths, looking like tiny torpedoes as the contrails of air bubbles streamed from their sleek bodies. When they neared the surface, they flapped even harder, which gave them the final boost to explode from the water and clear the side of the ship.

The 120-foot-long ship, a cutter-type fishing boat and cargo hauler, was capable of handling the rough seas of the South Atlantic Ocean. Its aft section had low sides with winches starboard to bring in the boats with their illegal harvest. Medium-sized cargo containers held down by chains and straps crowded the deck. Toward the bow, two stairways sat on either side of a three-tiered top deck, wherein lay the bridge. The ship easily could have held a crew of seventy-five or more, but to save money, they set out with significantly fewer.

The ship was named the Caracara, after the bird of prey that regularly fed on penguin chicks, a fact that was lost on most of the crew who worked aboard her. It seemed the poaching bosses or even the kingpin himself was arrogant, almost boastful about their illegal work.

The ship had seen better days. Rust bloomed on nearly every surface, and the blue and white paint of the hull had faded, orange streaks cascading down it. Profit was more important than safety, as the Caracara didn't carry a transponder, beacon, or RFID of any sort. The officers relied on GPS and satellite phones for communication with the mainland so in case it wrecked, there would be no connection to the owners. In the middle of the deck was a hatchway, where the harvest could be brought below. It remained open in anticipation of the landing party's return, and the wails of captured penguins were just audible above the howling wind and the increasingly violent sea.

Leepoh and his group waddled and slid across the deck with their webbed feet, trying to find purchase on the wet steel as the ship rocked in the roiling sea. They finally took up a position behind one of the crates.

"Everyone is accounted for," Leepoh said, looking at their faces. "Now we need to find a way inside that up there," he said, gesturing to the bridge with his flipper. "We need to create a distraction, something to get their attention, so they will come out and we can get in."

A penguin cry came from the cargo hold below deck. Leepoh asked, "Was that a Rockhopper?" The others responded with silent, affirming nods. "Wait here," he told them and skidded his way to the cargo hatchway. He peered into the dimly lit area below, and was overtaken by the stench. Even through the rain and salt air, he smelled waste, death, and fear. Without hesitation, he leapt down into the chasm.

When his eyes adjusted to the gloom, he saw a cage to his right with seven Rockhoppers inside. They were alive but terrified. The penguin prisoners were huddled in the back corner of their pen with their faces turned away. To his left, Leepoh spotted a large container with its top open. He walked to it but hesitated, not wanting to see what was inside. But he had to look. He hopped onto a nearby crate and looked over the container's edge. Leepoh stood in shock and horror at what he found. Inside were the remains of an undetermined number of Rockhoppers, all of them butchered beyond imagination. He hopped off the crate, weakened by what he had seen. He looked at the caged penguins, who were still facing away from him, seemingly unaware of his presence.

"Sir, are you all right?" a Gentoo called from the hatchway above.

Leepoh looked up to the voice but didn't respond.

"Sir?" the Gentoo called again.

As Leepoh stood in contemplation of the situation, a fury ignited within him, a fury like he had never felt before. His body trembled with anger and hatred.

"Sir, are you—" the Gentoo began to ask again, but Leepoh cut him off.

"Send a message for all groups to attack now!" Leepoh told the other through a clinched beak. "All groups attack now! That will be our distraction."

"Yes, sir!" the other acknowledged then disappeared from Leepoh's view.

Leepoh turned back to the caged Rockhoppers and took a few steps toward them. He heard a metal door swing open from somewhere above and behind him. Leepoh froze. His mind raced as the clank of heavy boots tramped down the steel stairwell. He looked to the caged penguins for some sign of acknowledgement, but the Rockhoppers only pressed themselves tighter into the corner. The heavy footsteps reached the bottom of the stairs. Leepoh looked up at the hatchway above him and spotted six concerned Gentoo faces staring down at him. He was suddenly struck with inspiration. He shook his head at the others, telling them not to do anything yet. The man spotted him.

"Hey! How did you get out?" the man said as he tried to maintain his balance on the rocking ship.

Leepoh waddled toward the cage and waited for the man to arrive.

"You're a smart one, aren't you? You know where you belong, don't you?" the man said.

Leepoh pretended not to understand. He looked up and made eye contact with the other Gentoo. "Get ready," he told them. To the human standing in front of him, the command sounded like a quiet warble.

"Well, back in the cage with you," the man said, fumbling with his keys.

When the man finally opened the cage, Leepoh calmly said, "Now!" and the waiting Gentoo immediately leapt down behind the man, landing with a wet thud.

The startled man turned to the sound of the Gentoo. "What the hell?"

With the captor distracted and the door to the cage open, Leepoh called to the frightened Rockhoppers.

The group turned slowly to look at the newcomer.

"Let's go! Let's get you out of here," Leepoh told them.

The surprised Rockhoppers hesitated at first but then seemed to realize what was taking place and happily obliged.

"Hey!" the man said yelled when he turned and found the last of the Rockhoppers exiting the cage. He turned back and saw a dozen Gentoo advancing toward him menacingly. "What's going on here?" he said to no one. His eyes darted between each penguin, and horror fell across his face. "Alejandro was right." He took a few steps toward the Gentoo, and they hissed at him.

"Rockhoppers, I'm General Leepoh of the PDA. Do you have any strength left in you to fight?"

The Rockhoppers ruffled their feathers in indignation. "Of course we do," one of them answered.

"Are there any others?" Leepoh asked.

"None that we know of, sir," another answered.

Leepoh looked at them appraisingly and then nodded. "Well, then, now is your time for vengeance."

The man seemed to think better of standing and fighting. He made a fast break to safety. A Gentoo jumped in front of the man as he ran past, tripping him up. He hit his head squarely on the first step of the stairs and slumped to the floor. He tried desperately to stand but managed only to roll onto his back. The Rockhoppers and Gentoo descended upon him. He opened his mouth to scream but never got the chance.

Leepoh stood back and watched the carnage with grim satisfaction.

One of the other Gentoo called him from the hatchway. "Sir, is everything all right down there?"

"Everything is perfect. I believe we have found a way inside," he said, looking up the stairs at the still-open doorway. "When the others arrive, instruct them to make their way up the two stairways. We'll flush the humans out."

"Very good, sir!" the other replied eagerly.

Leepoh approached the penguins, who were standing around the body of their victim. "We still have work ahead of us," he said without preamble. "These steps should lead us to the rest of the humans. We're going to have to flush them out to the attack group, which should be here in moments. We're going to have to get them to open their, their . . . "

"Doors, sir," a Rockhopper chimed in.

Leepoh looked at the Rockhopper blankly.

"Doors, huh?" Leepoh responded. "Thanks. We'll go up here." He indicated the stairway. "That will, hopefully, take us to where the humans are. If any of the *doors* are closed, we'll tap on them with our beaks. The noise should be enough to arouse their curiosity. Once the *doors* are open, we'll overtake whatever is inside and chase out whatever we don't overtake. Now let's get moving."

The penguins hopped up each stair, trying to keep upright from the sway of the boat. They went down the hall at the top of the stairs, and entered the first open room. The room was devoid of people. All they found were a table and chairs. In the upper corner was a TV and VCR mounted to the wall. The images of an old black and white Western movie flickered across the screen silently. Either the volume had been turned down or, more likely, it didn't work. All of the penguins stopped to stare at the image, mesmerized by the sight.

"What is it?" one of them asked.

"I have no idea," Leepoh answered. "It looks like some sort of cave or opening," he said as he walked underneath and looked up and around the TV curiously. "But it doesn't lead anywhere. Look, there are little humans inside of it. They're riding some sort of beasts and killing each other—very strange." Leepoh studied the room and noticed two open doorways on either side. "But that is not our objective," he said sternly. "Let's keep moving. We may see many things we don't understand, so let's try to keep focused." He walked to the nearest doorway and heard muffled voices not far away. "This way."

Leepoh and the others hopped up another flight of stairs. Once they reached the landing, they came to their first closed door. One of the Gentoo moved to the front of the crowd and began to tap on the door repeatedly. The plan worked perfectly. Within seconds a human opened the door.

"What's wrong? Did you forget how to open a door, you—" The human's words trailed off as the marauders immediately rushed him. Another man witnessed the attack and ran up a nearby stairwell.

Leepoh noticed the man flee and called to his squad. "A man ran up there!" he shouted and pointed. The penguins had already dispatched the man who was caught off guard and hopped up the stairs in pursuit.

CHAPTER 17

Five men were sitting around the bridge of the Caracara, and another was looking through binoculars at the increasingly rough sea.

"Any sign of them?" the captain asked. The captain was in his late fifties and carried a large potbelly, barely contained by his coat. His face was grizzled by age and the years spent in the company of the sea, drink, and nicotine. Gray stubble, which covered his double chin, accented his dark skin.

"No, Captain, no sign of them," the man with the binoculars answered.

"The storm is becoming too strong. We're going to have to pull anchor and wait it out on the north side of the island." The captain looked through a window of the bridge and sighed. "I hope they didn't try to come back in these waters. Any luck reaching Manuel on the phone?"

"Nothing," one of the men answered.

"Well, keep trying. Ortiz, pull anchor," the captain said to another.

Ortiz, who was large framed with a closely cropped haircut, stumbled his way to the controls.

"Start the engines," the captain barked out. "I'm going to step outside for a smoke before we get underway."

The captain swung the door open, allowing the cold rainy air to blow into the bridge. A latch on the back of the door snagged its receptacle on the wall outside and kept the door from slamming shut. He stepped into the cold, wet and windy air, ducked back inside to light his cigarette, and then strolled off to get his fix before they cast off.

While the rest of the crew waited for the captain, one of the men stood by the door leading below deck and continued to try to reach Manuel on the satellite phone.

"Nothing still," he said, just as the man who had escaped the attack below rushed through the door and slammed into the man holding the phone, sending it flying across the room.

"Alejandro was telling the truth!" the escapee shouted breathlessly.

"Damn it, Rico. What's wrong with you? You could have broken this," Ortiz reprimanded the man while picking up the phone.

"I don't care! The penguins are here!" he told them in exasperation. "Alejandro was right."

"What are you talking about?" someone asked.

Rico saw that the door was still open and rushed to close it. "I saw them. They killed Ronaldo in the galley."

"What? Who did?" Ortiz asked.

"The penguins, damn it!"

"I told you we were telling the truth," one of the survivors from the first landing party said. "That's why you can't reach Manuel. They're all dead."

The other men looked at each other. "Okay, let's go get some weapons," one of them said after a long pause. Rico had been on their crew for several years, and they knew he was not prone to telling wild tales or believing in omens the way Alejandro was. They could tell Rico was genuinely frightened.

"I'll go get the captain," Ortiz said. "You get the weapons," he told one of the crewers. The crewman walked to the door and reached for the handle when Rico realized what he was about to do.

"No!" Rico shouted, but it was too late. The door opened, and nearly twenty penguins rushed across the threshold.

^^^

The captain walked along the walkway, which wrapped around the bridge. The rain began to fall even harder, making it difficult to have a smoke. "So much for enjoying my cigarette," he said in disgust as he flicked it into the sea.

The past twenty-four hours had been a nightmare for the captain. Most of Alejandro's landing party was lost. How he had gotten the survivors to go along with that asinine story was beyond the captain's comprehension. Alejandro was incompetent at best, but he was the second most experienced at grabbing the birds—second only to Manuel. Manuel had taken the bulk of the crew back to the island to investigate what had really happened, and now neither of them had been heard from for nearly twelve hours.

This trip had been a bad idea from the beginning, the captain thought. There were too many greenhorns this time. In large part, that was thanks to the superstition of someone from the last trip. According to that person, as they were leaving the island only a couple of weeks prior, he was looking through binoculars and saw an omen, a portent of death. Instead of seeing barren rocks upon departure, as was usual, he saw the penguins standing on the rocky coast, watching them leave. Why that was an omen was beyond the captain, and once he thought about it, he surmised that that probably was what fueled Alejandro's fantastic story. Regardless, since then, the locals had taken to naming the island *La isla de los Pingüinos de la Muerte*, the island of the death penguins. "Humph," the captain snorted as he pulled a whiskey flask from his coat pocket.

He was beginning to take a drink as he walked back to the bridge when he heard a strange noise coming from behind him. He stopped, held on to the railing to keep steady, and swore that, through the wind and waves, he heard the sound of slapping, wet feet. He spun around and caught a fleeting glimpse of something moving behind the rear wall. The captain was briefly startled. He knew his crew should be preparing to leave. No one should be on deck.

He walked toward the movement, and for a moment, entertained the thought that it might be Manuel and that he had made it back somehow. But the idea was quickly quelled when reached the end of the walk and saw an extraordinary sight. It chilled his blood and caused him to tremble. He saw hundreds of penguins milling around on the deck, the stairways, and the walkway in front of him. Still more were coming aboard by the dozen as they flew from the roiling sea, onto the deck.

The captain and the penguins locked gazes for less than a heartbeat. He heard the scream of one of his crew on the bridge, and the moment of indecisiveness was ended when the man turned and ran. The penguins moved in pursuit and quickly overtook the old captain of the Caracara. With their first attack underway, the Gentoo rushed the walkway, over the fallen body of the captain, and made their way to the bridge.

^^^

The screams and shouts of man and penguin reverberated off the walls of the bridge as the two species engaged each other in a fight to the death. The penguins were down to a dozen, and all of the humans were still standing. One of the men threw off an attacking penguin, cussing all the while. The penguins huddled into the corner for defense.

"Look what they did to my face!" one of the men exclaimed, holding his hand against several deep gashes on his face that were bleeding profusely.

"Get ahold of yourself," Ortiz told the frantic man. "We have them now. Rico, go below and get the guns. We're going to want to make sure we kill them all. Antonio," he said to the man who was holding his face. "Go make sure the captain is all right. He has been gone way too long." Antonio started to leave, but Ortiz stopped him. "On second thought, wait until Rico gets back with the weapons. We'll need you in case they attack again. Get going, Rico!"

Rico carefully sidestepped the penguins then sprinted down the stairway, closing the door as he left.

CHAPTER 18

Leepoh and his group weren't planning to attack again anytime soon. With three of the rescued Rockhoppers already killed and five Gentoo as well, he knew they couldn't defeat this group of humans on their own. *The reinforcements should be here at any moment*, thought Leepoh. Then he heard the scream of a dying man and the calls of his own kind. He looked to the open doorway and Gentoo flooded through. The humans barely had time to react as the penguins overtook them, and the men's screams were extinguished along with their lives.

Rico rushed through the door carrying an armful of weapons but was dumbfounded by what awaited him. The bridge was wall-to-wall penguins. He quickly regained his wits, dropped all of the guns but one, and fired into the mass of birds. After killing several, he endeavored to make his escape below deck, but the incensed penguins brought him down before he reached the stairs.

^^^

Nok and the Rockhoppers boarded the ship and found a thousand or so Gentoo milling around the deck. Apparently the battle was already over, and the Gentoo were the obvious victors.

"Excuse me, where is General Leepoh?" Nok asked a passing Gentoo.

The Gentoo indicated the top of the stairs then scurried off.

"This way, I guess," Nok said. When they reached the top, Nok was overjoyed as he saw four Rockhoppers making their way toward him, down the walkway. "Tog, Seck?" he called out with excitement. "Melk, Lydeck! Am I glad to see you! We thought you were dead."

The four Rockhoppers looked at Nok, their eyes still burning with hate.

"Captain Nok?" Lydeck finally responded.

"Yes, it's me. Are you hurt?"

Lydeck and the others were covered in blood but not their own. "We're all right, sir, but three others did not make it," Lydeck answered.

Nok looked at them solemnly. "I understand. As you can see, we are fighting back now, and we'll not let this happen again. We've already taken care of the humans who came ashore last night."

The four Rockhoppers looked around the ship and pondered the meaning of it all.

"I hate them," is all Lydeck could say.

Nok watched them silently for a moment as he remembered his own hatred for the humans. He thought it strange, however, that even after killing one of them himself and seeing their destruction, he still was not relieved of his hatred. "I know, my friend, me as well." Nok instructed Trarck to take the squad and see the survivors back to the warrens. Then he headed off in search of Leepoh.

Nok continued along the walkway, hopped over the body of a dead fat man, and noticed another lying across the threshold of a doorway. As he approached the bridge, he saw a red haze on the windows and heard singing and joviality coming from within. A piece of something sinewy and bloody hit the ground in front of him, and Nok cautiously peered inside the room. What he saw nearly made his stomach lurch. The Gentoo, led by General Leepoh, were dancing and singing on the deceased humans. One of the deadly seabirds stood on his victim's chest and slashed violently at its stomach, flinging bits of flesh with each peck of his beak.

Captain Nok was appalled, but then he remembered that had been he only a few hours before as he'd taken out years of frustration and anger on a would-be killer. Though he had not acted with such glee. Leepoh stopped his dance and locked gazes with Nok. The general's black and white feathers were no longer visible, and only his eyes could be seen beneath his crimson suit. Nok gave Leepoh a simple nod, and the gesture was returned.

As Nok prepared to depart the doomed ship, he thought this may be a turning point in penguin history. They were the victims no more. They now had the power to control their own destiny, and things were forever changed for the penguins. He left Leepoh and the others to their jubilant, if not somewhat twisted, victory celebration and leapt into the sea, feeling a small sense of freedom.

CHAPTER 19

After the attack on the beach, Alejandro was surprised to find himself still among the living, albeit regretfully from the amount of damage he had sustained. He was hurt and hurt badly. Uncountable wounds covered his body. Some were bleeding worse than others were, but he was still alive. The penguins had stopped short of killing him and left his eyes intact. For a while, he just lay on the beach and waited for them to continue their assault and for death's release. But death never came, and he eventually found the strength to get to his feet.

The number of penguins seemed to have doubled since the attack began, but they all stood off to one side and just watched Alejandro as he stood on his wobbly legs. He tried to walk away, but the Rockhoppers quickly cut across his path. He went toward the water, and they corralled him again. He finally began to walk toward the rocks that had first led him to the beach, and the Rockhoppers didn't try to stop him. Alejandro guessed they wanted him to go that direction, so he limped on.

He gingerly climbed over the rocks back to where he had started. Every time he deviated from the path, the penguins were there to stop him. All along the way, Rockhoppers appeared on the rocks, either to keep him on track or to intimidate him. Alejandro couldn't decide which and figured it was both. When they arrived at the tusset-grass-covered slopes where the bodies of his companions lay, the penguins appeared by the hundreds and watched over him silently. The Rockhopper shepherds kept him away from the bodies of the fallen men so that he would not be able to grab one of their weapons. Alejandro briefly entertained the notion of making a run for it to find Manuel's body and phone but dismissed the idea as he had before, knowing he would most likely not survive the attempt.

After a long and painful trek, Alejandro arrived at the base of the rocky shelter the Rockhoppers called home. To his left, Alejandro saw the much rockier coast where the Rockhoppers attempted to escape when landing parties arrived. That was the place where the first attack had happened. He still wondered whether any of those men had survived, but he didn't feel guilty about having left them behind. It was a matter of survival—something Manuel hadn't understood until it was too late.

Only the day before, when the first attacked happened, they'd thought it was just a fluke. Penguins fought back only when they were caught, and at worst, it was only a painful bite. This was different. They swarmed over their first victim. The other two men tried to help, but they too were attacked. Alejandro, having heard the stories about the last journey, and the omen, had fled and never looked back. He and a few others who had followed wasted no time, got back in the boats, and motored back to the ship. He'd briefly seen the other boat as it plowed its way through the surf, but he'd lost sight of it and never saw it again.

Once on board the Caracara, Alejandro had told his tale to all those who would listen and was continuously rebuked. No matter how many times he recapitulated the events, nobody had believed him. When Manuel and the captain had decided they should send a search party, Alejandro warned them once more and begged them not to make him go back. But he'd failed on both counts.

None of that mattered any longer. What mattered was that there was a rocky cliff wall in front of him and countless Rockhoppers behind him. There were two paths. One led to the warrens, and the other to the top. One of the Rockhoppers bounded ahead of Alejandro and jumped from outcrop to outcrop, and one behind Alejandro pecked him sharply on a wound on the back of his leg. He flinched in pain, took the hint, and looked at the penguin climbing the cliff wall ahead. He wondered whether he had the strength to climb the nearly 200-foot monolith. He had to try, he thought. He still had a faint hope that the penguins were leading him to the master who had trained them and that his life had been spared for a purpose. He clung to that tiny hope and began to climb.

The strong, bitterly cold wind chilled him to the bone as it cut through his tattered, blood-soaked clothes. Two-thirds of the way into his climb, he nearly lost his grip, but even in his weakened condition, he somehow found the strength to hold on. As Alejandro watched the Rockhoppers easily hop from ledge to ledge, he realized again that if they had wanted to, they could have killed him with a quick bite to his hand. So, despite the broken bones and wounds that still bled, he struggled upward with the hope of finding the answer to the madness.

When he finally reached the summit, the rock tapered into a more gradual slope, and Alejandro rolled over the precipice and lay on his back, too exhausted to stand. For a while, he just lay there and let raindrops fall on his face. After what felt like just a few seconds, the Rockhoppers prodded him to his feet and began to chatter excitedly as he limped forward. He stopped to get a look at his surroundings. If it had been a clear day, he could have seen most of the island. He saw a rocky vista, and to his right he saw that the rocks gave way to rolling hills. To his left and behind him, the tumultuous sea crashed into the rocks far below.

From this vantage point, he could almost see where the boats had come ashore, and as he let his gaze drift out past the waves, he caught sight of the Caracara through the misty veil of rain. His heart sank as, even from this distance, Alejandro could see that the ship was drifting listlessly and perilously close to the shore. It was obvious no one piloted the doomed vessel.

A sharp peck to his calf brought Alejandro back to the matter at hand.

He turned from his view of the sea and saw a mass of Rockhoppers standing only ten meters away. The penguin horde began to separate, and they created a path between them. Alejandro's heart pounded with anticipation. He thought this would be the moment when the phantom person behind all of this would reveal himself and would explain what in the name of God was happening on this forsaken island.

Much to Alejandro's dismay, it was not a man who came forward but another Rockhopper. He looked beyond the penguins to the rocks to see if there was somebody in tow, but there was no one.

The other Rockhoppers stood motionless with their beaks held high in salute as the newcomer languidly strolled toward the human. This penguin looked very nearly the same as all of the rest but slightly more podgy. It projected an air of authority, which was obvious even to Alejandro. It waddled toward the man and stopped a meter before him. Then, General Treeg of RHC 23 of the Penguin Defense Alliance raised his right flipper and stood motionless.

With the appearance of General Treeg, Alejandro surmised that there were no human controllers of these beasts. He understood that his time had truly come and it would be unmerciful. *The ship,* he thought. *If I can find a way to the ship before it hits the shore!* He spun around and peered through the heavy sheets of rainfall just in time to see the Caracara, his last hope of salvation, smash into the rocky coastline. He stood and watched the shipwreck breathlessly. Even though he knew there was really no hope of escape from these savage birds, seeing the wreck of the Caracara was confirmation of his plight and more than he could bear.

He watched the sea claim the ship and pondered the *ifs* of his life. If he hadn't tripped and hurt his knee . . . If they would've listened to him and never returned to this place . . . If somebody would've seen the flare . . . If he had never taken this job. If it weren't for these things, he wouldn't die here. *So this is how it ends?*

Treeg lowered his flipper and the Rockhoppers attacked. Alejandro tried to fight them off. He flailed his arms and let loose a guttural scream, but to no avail. The penguins overwhelmed him and brought him to the ground. He thrashed about wildly as the frenzied birds slashed furiously at every part of his body. General Treeg halted the attack and the Rockhoppers became silent. All that could be heard were the distant crashing of the waves, the steady patter of rainfall, and Alejandro's quiet whimpers and moans.

In a sudden burst of energy, Treeg ran and leapt onto the fallen man's body and drove his beak into an already opened wound. "For my son!" he shouted in the language of the Rockhoppers. Alejandro writhed in pain, causing Treeg to hop off him. "For my family!" he yelled and attacked again. The human screamed in agony and tried to swat the Rockhopper off, but Treeg held firm with his claws and beak. "For the Rockhoppers!" cried Treeg, and then he tore at the man's face.

Treeg hopped off the man and walked a few feet away. He was breathing heavily, not from physical exhaustion but from releasing his pent-up rage and hatred. The Rockhopper watched Alejandro carefully as the man somehow managed to get to his hands and knees and crawl toward the edge of the cliff to attempt an escape. Treeg marched up to the man calmly and stared at him for several seconds. Alejandro returned a blank gaze.

The Rockhopper general then leaned in close to the man and in Alejandro's own language, said, "Now *I* will take *your* life."

Alejandro shook his head in shock and fear. "¡*Vos sos existe el Satanás—el demonio enviado desde el infierno, a tomar mi alma!*" "The Devil does exist!" He scurried away on his hands and knees, no longer giving a care to his injuries. His only thought was to escape this demon. He crawled, lunged, and tried to get his feet, whimpering all the while. He looked behind him to see the Rockhoppers, led by General Treeg, advancing on him. He got to his feet and faced the devilish birds. He panicked, turned to run, slipped on the wet rock and plunged down the cliff.

Treeg stood and looked over the edge as the man fell. "Good enough," he said and then walked away.

^^^

Captain Nok watched from the shore as the human ship slammed into the rocks. General Leepoh waddled alongside of him, panting and complaining all the while. Corporal Trarck leapt from the crashing waves and landed in front of Nok and Leepoh.

"All penguins are safely off the ship, sirs," Trarck reported.

"Thank you," Nok said. "Go back to the warrens. I'll be along shortly."

"Why don't you penguins find an easier way in and out of the water?" Leepoh asked, watching the corporal hop away.

"We are *Rockhoppers*," Nok replied mordantly.

"Hah! That you are."

"Outstanding work on the ship, Leepoh. I can't thank you enough," Nok told him seriously.

"Bah! It was our pleasure. We sure showed those humans a thing or two, didn't we?"

"Or three," Nok answered, and the pair enjoyed a stress-relieving laugh. "Well, General Leepoh, what's next?"

"Squid, squid, squid, squid, and more squid—and then maybe a few itty-bitty tiny fish. I am *starving*. After that, I have to go to Pack Ice Command and report on what took place here."

A scream from high atop the cliff wall caught their attention. They looked up and saw a man falling and flailing his arms wildly. The man hit the side of the sheer cliff wall, bounced off, and continued to fall, limp and silent. He landed against the rocks with a sickening smack just a few meters from where the duo stood.

"Looks like they found that missing human," said Leepoh unaffected.

"Looks like," Nok replied then looked back at Leepoh. "Well, thank you again. Maybe I'll see you at PIC, if General Treeg sees me fit to go there."

"I hope so," Leepoh said with all earnestness.

The two parted company with a respectful nod.

CHAPTER 20

Antarctica: Approximately 50 kilometers east of Forward Command One, "Gina!" a man called out through the blustery wind. "Gina!" A woman came trudging up an icy slope toward the voice, pulling her hood over shoulder length dark blond hair.

"Hurry—come here! You have got to see this," the excited man told her then turned and ran further up the slope.

"I'm coming. I'm coming," she said, breathless from the cold. "What could you possibly want that's so damned urgent?"

"Over there," he said, wiping his perpetually frosty beard. He pointed to something she couldn't see. "About a hundred yards from here. Come on!" He ran back down the hill, grabbed her by her gloved hand, and led the way.

"This had better be good, Randy," Gina threatened him, not bothering to pull her hand away. "I just found toboggan tracks for the first time since we got here."

Randy flashed her a smile, which she had learned from working with him side-by-side over the past five weeks, that he was about to say something close to nonsensical. She wasn't disappointed.

"Gina, we've known each for how long now? Ten, twelve years?" He asked

"Um, I think it's been closer to three or four months since we first met." She smiled at seeing a mock frown form beneath his scruffy beard. She held her gaze on the beard a moment longer. They had had far too many conversations about the beard. He hadn't trimmed it since arriving in Antarctica and insisted it added to his roguish good looks. She said he looked more like a derelict than a rogue.

Gina and Randy had come to Antarctica as part of a research group, which was funded by Global Threat, or GT as it was known, an environmental-monitoring, non-profit entity that studied the effects of human impact and global warming on the Polar Regions. During the five weeks since they had arrived, they had yet to see a single penguin in their area. This had caused great alarm among the researchers, since one usually could expect to find vast numbers of Antarctica's primary inhabitants.

"They're right over the next slope," Randy said excitedly, pulling his ever present wool beanie cap over his ears.

"Who is?" Gina asked, sounding both annoyed and amused.

"You'll see. Just be quiet when we get there. I don't want anything to disturb what you're about to see."

"Okay, but what am I trying not to disturb?"

"All right, get down. We'll have to crawl to the top," Randy told her, ignoring her question as they reached the top of the slope.

"Randy?" Gina said, never being one to enjoy a surprise.

"I know. But what you're about to see is something I couldn't possibly describe."

"And you're going get your book published?" Gina asked sarcastically.

"A photography book, and besides, I'll have some help. You're the one with Master's degree from Berkeley," he said in reference to an offer he had made to Gina for her to write the captioning.

"My degree is in natural science. I'm a climatologist, not an English professor," Gina replied with a sardonic tone. "Besides, Red, you can't afford me."

"I told you, it's not *red*—more of a strawberry blonde. And after you see this, you won't be able to resist helping." He pulled his cap down more, hiding tufts of hair.

"Strawberries are red," Gina replied teasingly.

When they reached the top of the hill, Gina gasped.

"Here," Randy said quietly as he handed her his camera. "Zoom in to get a better look."

Fifty meters from where they lay was a procession like none any human had ever seen. There was a vast assortment of penguin species. Some were walking. Some were sliding on their bellies, known as tobogganing, in large columns, and all were headed inland. They were escorted by larger than average Emperor penguins and common-sized Chinstraps. The parade stretched as far as Gina and Randy could see in either direction.

Gina was astounded. "This . . . but . . . it can't be. Don't some of these species live only in the sub-Antarctic regions or even further north?"

"Exactly. This is something completely unheard of," he told her. He took back his camera and began photographing the anomaly. "This will change my life—and yours. I can't believe my luck. First, GT calls me out of nowhere for a chance of a lifetime, and then I come across what could be the discovery of lifetime. Plus I get to work next to you. Which isn't so bad."

Gina coughed a laugh. It was as close to flirting as Randy had ever gotten. And it was probably nothing more than a compliment veiled by a joke. But she knew he carried a lot of respect for her and would never do anything to make her feel uncomfortable. She appreciated it; especially being the only woman in a research station full of men. "I'm sure somebody at GT saw your work in NatGeo. That's why you got the call."

"Maybe," Randy said. "Plus I work cheap."

Gina rolled eyes and brought her attention back to the penguins. "What I want know is, what are they all doing *here*?"

"I have no idea. But look, there are Gentoo and Adélie. The Emperors have returned. And of course, there are the Chinstraps. Look," he said exuberantly. "There are Rockhoppers, Magellanics, and if I'm not mistaken those are Macaroni. But they look almost like Rockhoppers, so it's difficult to tell."

"But these species rarely interact, right?" Gina asked. She didn't know as much about penguins as Randy did, as he was practically a penguinologist, but she did know that some of the named species were not even native to Antarctica.

"Yeah, that's what makes this especially amazing. I don't know of anywhere in the world, besides maybe a zoo, where you can see a King side-by-side with a Snares Island Crested."

Randy continued to snap shot after shot while Gina watched. "Something doesn't *feel* right about this. I wonder whether some sort of intense environmental pressure has caused them to behave so oddly."

"Hard to say. Maybe it's some sort of mass migration that happens only once a millennium or something. I don't . . ." Randy stopped talking and stared into his viewfinder intensely. "What in the world?" he said in astonishment as he lowered his camera and looked at Gina. "Those are Yellow-Eyed."

"So . . ." said Gina, who didn't know what was so extraordinary about this one species among all the others they were seeing.

"*So*, they're native to the southern, forested area of New Zealand's coast and are the rarest of all the penguins. To see any outside their native environment doesn't bode well for their species." He continued to watch and photograph the Yellow-Eyed penguins. With their yellow-feathered crown, blue-gray backs, and yellow eye stripes, the two-foot tall penguins were unique.

"This doesn't make sense. How are they surviving in such a radically different environment?"

Under his heavy coat and layers of clothing, Randy gave an almost imperceptible shrug. "I'll tell you what," Randy said with a hint of circumspection. "Why don't you take the crawler back to camp and grab

Davis and the video equipment?”

“No, no way, Randy,” Gina said sternly. “You know that no one is allowed to be out alone. Besides, Davis will chew me out up one side and down the other if I show up alone.”

“Then he won’t have a choice but to come with you. I’ll be fine. We have the radios and that GPS whatchamacallit. We really need to get this on more than just stills.”

“Why don’t you *call* Davis and have him come out to meet us with the equipment? You can record with your camera too,” Gina proposed.

“There’s not enough memory on my cards to video it. Plus, we need to record and photograph simultaneously. And I did call Davis, before I called you. But no one was available to come with him, so he refused.”

“Well, then, he’s smarter than you or me.”

“I’ll take that as an insult, thank you. Does that mean you’ll do it?”

Gina hesitated a bit longer.

“You *know* this is important,” Randy urged.

“That guy makes my skin crawl, so you’ll owe me. Are you sure you’ll be all right?” she asked with concern.

Randy smiled at her. “Of course. I have my camera, my radio, and the GPS thingy—and there’s a wildlife phenomenon happening right in front of me. What else could I need?”

Gina looked to the sky. “Well, at least the weather looks good—for now. Okay, I’ll go. You stay safe and don’t go very far. As a matter of fact, don’t go anywhere. Stay *right* here, and I’m planting a marker flag so I’ll know if you strayed. It’ll probably be at least thirty minutes before I get back,” she said, still unsure about the risk.

“I’ll stay right here, I promise. Now get going, woman,” he said, knowing it drove her nuts for him to call her *woman*. “Oh, here. Take this.” He slipped off a glove and fumbled to get the memory card out of his camera so he could give it to her.

“Don’t you need this?”

"I have another," he said, already fishing it out of his bag. "This way if something *does* happen . . . to my camera, at least I know these shots are safe."

"This is that important to you?"

"You know it is," Randy said.

"Okay, I get the hint. I'll get outta your hair" she joked. "Be careful."

"I will, I will. Get going," he said, flashing a toothy grin.

She shook her head in amusement and disbelief at what she was about to do. She trotted back to the crawler.

After watching Gina climb into the crawler and letting his eyes linger on her a second longer, Randy resumed his work. The procession seemed never ending. He pulled the camera away from his face to check his battery, and when he looked back through the viewfinder, he saw what appeared to be an odd-looking Emperor and Chinstrap facing each other. "Weird," he said aloud. It appeared to him as if the two penguins were engaged in conversation. He continued to snap his pictures. The Chinstrap made a gesture with its head and hurried away from the march. He zoomed in his camera on the Emperor and saw the penguin turn its head toward him, just slightly, almost nonchalant, then turn back. Randy pulled the camera away quickly and looked down at the penguin with his brow furrowed, feeling perplexed and a bit disquieted. "Weirder," he said. Then he shrugged it off and continued with his work.

CHAPTER 21

Chinstrap slid on its belly to a pair of penguin squads made up of Royal Emperors and Kings. It immediately hopped to its feet and raised its head in a high beak salute. The squads were on their way to witness the trek of the penguin clans. General Diutes was given permission by Supreme Commander Liutites to see the event since those stationed at Forward Command One were not going to attend the Grand Gathering, as it had come to be known. Liutites's orders were two-fold: one was to boost morale for those stationed at the outpost, and the second, more important order, was to assist in guarding the procession and report anything that might appear to be out of the ordinary. It now seemed almost visionary that the Supreme Commander allowed such an action.

"General Diutes, sir," the Chinstrap said with precision.

"Yes, Chinstrap?" the general asked in his usual condescending tone.

"Sir, Lieutenant-General Mosthelus has an urgent message."

"Very well, Chinstrap, out with it," said Diutes, never failing to speak without sounding insulting.

Learning from experience while serving under Diutes, the Chinstrap remained impassive at his treatment by the general. "He said he has spotted humans near the procession."

"What? Humans?" the general barked out. "Where and how many?"

"As near as the lieutenant-general could tell, there were two who were watching them from an embankment. But one departed, leaving the other behind."

Diutes looked off in the direction of where the procession was taking place and pondered the information. He was as opportunistic as he was cruel and was forever trying to find ways to get in good favor with the Overlord. "How unfortunate for that human," he said sinisterly. "This is *outstanding*. Go back to Mosthelus and tell him we will be right behind you. Inform him to speed up the procession and *not* to lose sight of that human."

"Yes, sir," the Chinstrap snapped and hurried off to perform his duty.

"Colonel Kimmer!" Diutes called out at a King penguin standing nearby.

"Yes, sir?" the gruff King asked.

"We have an unprecedented opportunity before us. I just received word that a pair of humans have been spotted near the procession and that one left the other behind," he said with a disturbing giddiness.

"A human . . . alone?" asked Kimmer, somewhat surprised. "That would make a fine trophy for the Overlord."

"Indeed, Colonel Kimmer. It would be a gift beyond compare." Diutes paused for a moment as he thought about his strategy for capture. "Take your group north, around and behind it. Lieutenant-General Mosthelus should be keeping watch on it, so you'll know the location. I'll take my squad and go directly at it, thereby creating a distraction for you to subdue it. But remember—do not kill or seriously wound it. Go now and move quickly, before more humans arrive."

"What if the thing has weapons or if this is a trap? It is very unusual to see one of them by itself. After all, they are hardly fit to survive alone," Kimmer said.

"No, Colonel, there is no reason for it to be a trap. They couldn't possibly know our intentions. And if it does have a weapon—well, Colonel, we must all make sacrifices for our cause," Diutes said as he stared down the

King penguin.

General Diutes watched Colonel Kimmer depart then called for one of the Chinstrap messengers, who were always close by. "Go back to Forward Command and relay a message to PIC. Inform them that we have encountered a human near the procession, and tell them to make the necessary arrangements for the possible arrival of a human captive."

"Yes, sir!" the Chinstrap acknowledged then hurried away.

Diutes called to his fellow Emperors and felt the thrill of the hunt course through his body. This would not be an ordinary hunt for fish, squid, or krill; this day man was the prey, and that man had no idea of what was in store for him.

ᴧᴧᴧ

That was easy for Diutes to say, Kimmer thought. He and his group were just the distraction, while Kimmer and his would have to face the beast. Colonel Kimmer dismissed himself and began a hurried march to the procession. Along the way he pondered just what *sacrifices* the Royal Emperors were making for the cause. He silently reprimanded himself for his treasonous thoughts and began thinking of a plan of attack for his squad against the human.

CHAPTER 22

Randy continued to watch and photograph the wide assortment of indigenous and non-indigenous penguins. After what seemed like just a few minutes, the Chinstrap, which had left so suddenly, returned to what Randy began to think of as the penguin guardian. The Chinstrap made the same odd gesture with its head as before and then once again appeared to communicate with the Emperor penguin.

"I can make an entire book just with *these* pictures," Randy whispered.

The Chinstrap lifted its head high once more and departed. Seconds later, the Emperor let out a loud, strange call that Randy didn't recognize as an Emperor penguin call. The procession came to a sudden halt and turned to face the caller. The Emperor continued to let out squawks and clicks until the mass of migrating penguins turned and started to waddle and slide away as quickly as they could.

Randy was absolutely astounded by what he had witnessed. "These penguins *are* communicating with each other," he said aloud. He quickly grabbed his radio. "Gina. Do you copy?" He felt foolish saying things like that, but he didn't know what else to say. Outside of his camera equipment, he was completely uncomfortable with any tech stuff, regardless of how primitive it was.

"That's a big 10-4. I'm here, good buddy," Gina said, mocking his awkwardness after a second of static.

"I'm fine, thanks for asking," he said in response, knowing she was probably enjoying a laugh at his expense. "Where are you? I just saw the most amazing thing," he said with no trace of bitterness.

"We're just now leaving. Davis is driving. What's happening?"

"It's incredible! These penguins are communicating with each other," he said excitedly.

"What's so amazing about that? I thought all penguins communicated with each other."

"No. Not like this. You don't understand. This is *species-to-species* communication," he informed her. After no response, Randy spoke again. "Did you hear me, Gina?"

"Yeah . . . Are you sure about that, Randy? This is really incredible if you're right."

"I'm positive. I saw it. I heard it. And one of the Emperors called out to the others. They stopped and turned toward it. Then they. . . " Randy stopped mid-sentence when it dawned on him that the Emperor that had glanced at him was the one that ordered the procession to speed up. "Stupid," he berated himself.

"Randy?" Gina's voice came through to break him out of his thoughts.

"I'm here. Just hurry. These aren't normal penguins," he said with all seriousness.

"We are. What -o you -ean by not -mal?" asked Gina through increased static on the two-way radio.

"I'm not sure. It's just . . . I don't know," Randy told her, honestly not knowing the answer.

"Not normal like those Gentoo that you told me about?"

"Kinda, but not really. Those just had different nesting behaviors. I've only heard of Magellanics nesting in burrows, not Gentoo."

"-ell wi-," Randy's radio started to become filled with static. "-romental pressure, I'm n- surprised."

"Gina, you're really breaking up," he told her.

"We'll -there in -ty minutes, -refuel."

"Okay, hurry then," Randy said. He didn't know what "-ty" meant, but he was hoping it meant twenty minutes and not forty. He put the radio in his coat pocket, turned his attention back to the oddity, and saw the parade making a quick exodus.

"Damn it!" he said in frustration then looked to his left and saw the end of the line hurrying along. Most of the birds were sliding on their bellies, pushing themselves along with clawed feet. Some, like the Gentoo, were running, and those like the Rockhoppers were hopping along hurriedly. "Crap! No!" he said, exhausting his vocabulary of cussing. This once in a lifetime opportunity was scrambling away from him, and he was powerless to stop it.

He watched as the last of the spectacle passed him by. He briefly entertained the notion of following them but thought better of it. To venture off alone on the barren ice fields would be foolish, and Randy knew it. He was already taking an extreme risk by sending Gina to get the video equipment. Anything could and probably would happen. A sudden windstorm could pop up, which they often do, and create blinding, whiteout conditions. Best to stay put, Randy reasoned. He decided to wait for Gina, and then they could track the migration from the safety of the crawler.

The last of the penguins were gone. He snapped one more picture of their distant backsides. When he pulled his eyes from the camera, he was surprised to see nearly twenty of the strange Emperors on top of a hill, directly opposite where he stood. The pack of penguins stood and watched him back until a slightly larger Emperor that stood in the middle began making a braying call and giving peculiar gestures with its flippers. The others then spread out along the ridgeline.

Randy got an uneasy feeling as he watched the penguins. There was nothing overtly threatening in their actions, but something just didn't seem right with the way they moved. It was obvious to him they were communicating on a level never before known, and the way the big Emperor gestured, it was as if it had given the others direction. His uneasiness turned to concern when the picket of penguins began coming toward him. He snapped a couple one-handed shots with his camera and pulled the radio from his pocket with his free hand. "Gina, Gina, do you copy?"

After a moment of static, she replied. "I'm -ere."

"Where are you?" he asked, not taking his eyes off the advancing lines of penguins.

"We're on our way, -e -ad a -blem with the fuel pump. Are you -right? You seem a -tle uptight."

"Um . . . I think you'd better hurry. Something's not right with these penguins—they seem a little . . . aggressive." That was the best way Randy could describe them. Some penguins were curious and would sometimes approach a human, but this was definitely not curiosity.

"You're -aking up—did -uo say -essive?"

"Yeah—listen, I'm going to start making my way back in your direction. You two just double-time it here."

"Okay. -old tight, -be there -ortly."

Randy watched as the strange Emperors tobogganed down the opposing slope, and he decided that prudence required him to stop taking pictures and get moving. As they got closer he noticed they had a plume or a crest on their heads. Definitely not any Emperors he'd ever heard of. He turned away from the unusual specimens and stopped. In front of him was a group of King penguins staring at him menacingly. "Uh . . . Gina?" he said into his radio. "Tell Davis to speed it up a bit. There's a group of Kings standing right in front of me, and they look a little pissed," he told her for lack of a better description.

"How can a penguin looked pissed? What do you -ean by -issed?" Gina asked, a little confused.

"I mean pissed! You know, angry, livid, incensed, irate, mad. Just hurry!" Randy turned to go back the way he had come only to have his path blocked by the Emperors. "Great," he said as the penguins advanced. "Gina!" he yelled into the radio.

"Hold tight, Randy," Gina told him. She waited a few seconds, and after getting no response, she called again. "Randy?" Still no reply. "Randy!" Silence was her only answer.

CHAPTER 23

If they had been driving on asphalt and had tires instead of tank-like treads, the crawler would have come to a screeching halt when they arrived at the spot where Randy was supposed to be. Gina flung the door open and dashed from the crawler.

"Randy!" she began to call repeatedly. After they lost contact with him, she frantically tried to reach him on his radio to no avail. The ride from the base had seemed excruciatingly slow, almost as if Davis was trying to reprimand her for leaving Randy alone.

Ferdinand Davis was a stocky man in his mid-forties, with dark skin, an unpleasantly protruding brow and near perpetual halitosis. On his best days, Davis, as he preferred to be called, was unpleasant. On his worst, he was profoundly horrid. In the several weeks Gina had known him, she had learned to detest him. That didn't matter to her now. All that did matter was that she had to find Randy.

Davis, who was strangely enough having one of his best days yet, lumbered his way over to where Gina was standing. "Anything?" was all he asked her. He was not a man gifted with verbid expression.

"Nothing," she answered despondently. "We were right here. I told him to wait right here. He wouldn't have just wandered off."

"How do you know you were right here? The landscape looks pretty much the same for twenty miles," Davis said.

"I'm sure of it," Gina answered Davis's lengthy—for him—inquiry. "Look, there's the marker flag," she said, pointing to the bright orange flag now lying on the ground.

"Didn't he say he was headed back in our direction?"

"Yeah, but we would've seen him," Gina said as she spun in circles, scanning the area for a sign.

"Maybe he followed those penguins?"

"No. He would have told me."

"He sounded scared," the suddenly talkative Davis stated, as if he was enjoying her panic and liked feeding it.

"Yeah. I don't know. He said the penguins were behaving oddly—that they were agitated."

"He said they were pissed. So what I want to know is what could piss off a bunch of penguins?"

The two of them stared at each other for a minute, both knowing something was amiss.

"We have to find him," Gina said urgently.

The two spread out and continued calling for Randy. Davis called loudly while Gina used her radio.

When she approached the slope where Randy had been when she left him, she heard a faint sound. "Randy?" she called into her radio once again and heard her own voice coming back to her. She was confused for a moment until she realized it must have been Randy's radio. She walked further along the slope, calling into the radio until she spotted two dark objects against the colorless backdrop. She sprinted to them, and her heart sank as she found Randy's radio and camera lying in the snow. "No," she whispered as she fell to her knees.

Davis walked up to her without saying a word.

"He's gone," Gina said as she turned to him. She could say nothing else. An overwhelming feeling of helplessness threatened to overcome her, and it took all of her strength to pull herself off the frozen ground.

"But how . . . how could he just disappear?" Davis wondered, not bothering to lend her a hand as she stood.

They surveyed the area, looking into the bleak surroundings. Davis spotted something. "What's that?" he asked, pointing to a dark lump on the ground about twenty meters away.

Gina looked, and a feeling of dread came over her. She ran to the object, which was a quarter buried in the snow from the ever-increasing wind. Davis followed her but with less urgency. She was relieved to find that it wasn't Randy lying in the snow but a dead penguin. Still, the dead penguin disturbed her, but she did not know why. "That's odd," she said as Davis approached.

"Just a dead penguin," Davis said, stating the obvious.

The two of them took a quick look around to see whether there were more; there were none.

"Its neck is broken—look," he said as he hunched over and flopped the partially frozen penguin's head around. "Do you think Randy did it?"

Gina stood, staring at the bird, and had a sinking feeling that it did, indeed, have something to do with Randy, but she couldn't see how. "No, Randy loves these animals. He would never do anything to hurt them."

"Well, there's nothing else around, and how's a penguin gonna break its own neck? Slip and fall?" he said, rapidly turning into the more unpleasant version of Davis. He surveyed the surroundings, surreptitiously feeling for something under his coat as he did.

They began searching for some sort of a clue or sign that could give them a hint as to where Randy could have gone. But with the wind constantly rearranging the surface, their task was extremely difficult.

"Here!" Gina shouted, pointing to the faint outline of a boot print in the ground a few feet from the dead penguin. "Well, it looks as if he might have come into contact with the penguins."

"How could you know that, and really, what does it matter? It still doesn't explain what happened to him," Davis said, becoming increasingly fouler.

Gina dismissed his testiness as the effects of stress. She presumed he must have had some sort of position as security or safety, though she'd never actually inquired about it. "I know, but at least it's *something*. Maybe he saw the injured penguin and got close and . . . Oh, hell, I don't know."

Davis looked at her with a hard glare. "I'm gonna call Lawrence and get a search and rescue started," he said then stomped off.

While Davis called Lawrence, the team leader, Gina continued to search. The wind was steadily increasing, and she was becoming more and more worried. The environment in Antarctica was harsh enough on a perfect day, but with nightfall rapidly approaching and the strong wind getting stronger, she knew that if Randy wasn't found soon it wouldn't matter. If he wasn't found soon, he wouldn't survive. As she tried to keep those thoughts from her head, an idea came to her. "Poachers," she said to herself and ran to Davis. "Maybe it was poachers."

"Huh? Hold on a second," Davis told the person on the other end of his conversation.

"Maybe when he got closer to the penguins, he came across some poachers and that's what spooked the penguins—and that's why they were agitated." Once she said it, she knew it was a stretch.

"Seems a bit far-fetched, don't you think? Poachers don't go this far inland or even this far south. It costs them too much," he told her impatiently.

"It's something at least. Maybe he took their picture and they . . ." She stopped herself from saying any more, knowing she was clinging to a false hope. Chances were that he followed the damn birds and got himself lost. "I just want to find him."

"We'll try. The rest of the team are on their way here now," Davis told her.

She tried not to pay attention to his use of the word "try," guessing it was as close as Davis could get to giving her words of encouragement.

"Why don't you take his stuff back to the crawler and drive it up here," he said, not looking at her.

Gina hesitated, feeling that she was being dismissed.

"I know you two have a thing, but . . ."

"We do not have a *thing*," Gina snapped at him. "He is my friend."

Davis threw up his hands in mock defense.

Gina turned away and stomped back to the crawler, suddenly very happy to be dismissed.

CHAPTER 24

PACK ICE COMMAND: Lieutenant-General Lavour walked along a corridor with Lieutenant Trevot, discussing the events that took place at RHC 23.

"That *is* incredible," Lavour said. "And what was the Supreme Commander's reaction to the news?"

"That's what was strange. He just glared at me for a minute, said I was dismissed, then spun around and waddled off as fast as he could," Trevot told him. After his long journey back from the island, he immediately reported to the Supreme Commander before anything else.

"Well, that doesn't surprise me. The Supreme Commander has never been one to practice any social skills. What does surprise me is that penguins actually went on the offensive against the humans. As far as I know, it is entirely unprecedented."

"It was a shock to say the least. But I have to say I am more than a little concerned. If any humans should find out what took place there, it might put us all in jeopardy."

The two penguins nodded in silent agreement. They had been indoctrinated on the evils of all humans, but up until Trevot's experience at the Rockhopper colony, none of them had ever experienced any of that evil.

"I'm not sure, but I think that might have something to do with why the Overlord has ordered this gathering. When I met with him, I got the impression he might be devising some sort of defensive plan," Lavour informed him.

"You met with the Overlord?" Trevot asked in amazement.

"You didn't hear?"

"No. I've been gone for a moon's time. You met with him face-to-face—what's he like? I've never even seen him." Trevot continued to sound amazed. The Overlord was not a social penguin. Few had ever seen him, let alone had a personal audience with him.

"Yes, I met with him and he is . . ." Lavour paused for a second to find the right words. "He's different, very big and very intimidating. It was the only time I've ever seen the Supreme Commander's bravado waver."

"Different? How so—I mean besides being huge?" Trevot asked, now even more intrigued. "Is he like the guards?"

As the two continued their walk, Lavour described the Overlord and his meeting with him. The description kept Trevot riveted. "What makes you think he has some sort of plan of defense against the humans?" Trevot asked Lavour. This was one of many questions he had asked over the course of the conversation.

"Why so many questions?" asked Lavour when he realized something was bothering Trevot.

"I don't know. Honestly, it's just that, after what I witnessed on the island, I'm beginning to wonder about this leadership that we have all entrusted. Don't get me wrong," Trevot quickly added, "I think the PDA is wonderful. We're all working together for the good of penguin kind. It's just the violence and loss of life that took place there, on that island. I'm worried that is our future, and if so, is it the future we want?"

Lavour studied him for a minute. He had his own reservations about the Royal Emperor leadership. "I understand what you're saying," he finally said. "There have been certain things that have taken place that seem, well . . . odd," Lavour told him, trying to remain ambiguous in case he was overheard.

Trevot's curiosity was piqued, and when Lavour didn't elaborate, he had to ask him, "What's been odd?"

"Corporal Meuseaux, for one thing. He's been missing for weeks now, without a trace. And there's the fact that we weren't allowed to go home for breeding, and now the season has passed," Lavour told him angrily but in a hushed tone.

"Wait, what do you mean by *missing*? Nobody knows where he is? Have you asked the Royal or King's security details?"

"That's the last thing we want to do right now. With the Great Gathering upon us, it would look very bad on our part if it appeared as if we couldn't keep track of our own. He's been gone so long now, we have to assume he either defected or died." Lavour stopped for a second and looked around to see if anyone was paying attention to the conversation. "Besides, I have a feeling there's something more to it."

"More to what?" Trevot asked. He sensed uncertainty in the way Lavour was speaking.

Lavour inhaled deeply and let out a long breath. "I'm not sure, but now that you're back in PIC, don't go anywhere alone until we get this sorted out. Stay in a group. And keep this among the Chinstraps only."

"This doesn't sound good."

"It might not be, or it could be nothing. I'm hoping the latter."

"What do you think is going on?" Trevot asked.

Before Lavour could answer, Captain Mevoule came rushing toward them. "Lieutenant-General, sir," he said breathlessly then looked at Trevot. "Hello, Lieutenant, welcome back."

"What is it, Captain Mevoule?"

"Just come quickly," Mevoule said excitedly.

"What is it? Did you find Corporal Meuseaux?" Lavour asked hopefully as the two Chinstraps started to follow the captain.

"Unfortunately, no, but this is big. General Diutes just arrived with a group of Royal Emperors and Kings from Forward Command," he told them as they rushed down the corridor.

"I thought he was watching over the arrival of the contingents," Lavour said, inwardly irritated at the Royal Emperors' freedom to do as they pleased.

"They are, or they were. They came here with a prize for the Overlord—and not just an ordinary prize—but a human . . . a *live* human!"

Lavour and Trevot stopped. "What?" the two asked with equal shock.

"A living human—are they insane?" Trevot continued. "What could they possibly be thinking? Do they have any idea inside their intolerably egotistical minds how dangerous those things are? If it gets loose, there's no telling what kind of damage it could do!"

"Relax, Lieutenant," Mevoule told the extremely disconcerted Trevot. "I don't think the Overlord will let it wander about and escape."

"You don't understand. I've seen them and I've seen what they're capable of. They're cleverer than you think, and they're dangerous and violent. If a member of their flock goes missing, they don't just leave it for dead. They'll search for it, and if it is dead, they'll want to know how it died and why," Trevot ranted on.

"I'm sure that's not true for all humans," Mevoule said, trying to placate Trevot. "Besides that, there's no way that they would suspect penguins would take one of them," he said, looking to Lavour for confirmation.

Lavour shook his head. "I don't know. I've never actually seen them the way Trevot has."

"Exactly," Trevot agreed. "They might not have suspected a penguin was capable of that. But if they find out what happened on RHC 23, they will suspect us. And they'll come looking."

"I have to agree with Trevot," Lavour interjected. "It seems like poor judgment on the general's part."

Mevoule looked at his friend with mild surprise. "Hey, I didn't do it. I was just letting you know about it."

"I know," Lavour said to his friend. "We're not condemning you for their stupidity."

"Well, do you still want to see it?" Mevoule asked.

"Of course," Lavour answered quickly.

"Let's go, then, before they move it."

The three Chinstraps hurried on their way. When they had gone, a tiny Blue penguin poked its head out from a small, shadowy crevice at the base of the ice walls. It looked to where the Chinstraps had been gathered just moments before, then to the direction they were headed, and ducked back inside of the cranny.

CHAPTER 25

After realizing he was being attacked, Randy had snapped the neck of one of his assailants. The last thing he remembered was falling backward over a penguin, followed by a very large Emperor penguin falling on his face. Other penguins had fallen on top of him, pinning him to the ground. No matter how hard he'd struggled, he couldn't release himself of his burden. Eventually, everything went gray, then black as he faded into unconsciousness from the lack of air under a nearly 120-pound penguin. He had a vague memory of sliding down a steep incline. Upon regaining consciousness, he found himself in a vast ice cavern.

He tried to shake off the haze of nearly being suffocated to death and saw that he was surrounded by penguins. The penguin group was made up of four different species: the odd Emperors, King, Chinstrap, and Adélie. In front of the avian mass were six penguins that, like the others he'd seen, appeared to be Emperors. Upon closer inspection, however, Randy saw that they were clearly not any Emperor he had ever heard of. Each one stood at least four and a half feet tall, which was taller than the average Emperor by at least half a foot or more. But that feature wasn't what caught his attention. The most significant feature Randy saw was their jointed flippers that ended with a grasping, hand-like appendage and gave them the ability to hold objects—objects like the spears they were pointing at him.

Unsure about what his next move should be, Randy chose to remain sitting. His head was aching tremendously, and he realized he had several small puncture wounds from his fray with his captors. He sat and took notice of the room. Above him was a huge domed ceiling. Along the walls and on the ground floor were several archways, and above those were similar archways, which stood behind ledges. The room was filled with the diffused blue light that was universal within PIC. Behind him was an upward sloping tunnel, which explained to him his earlier feeling of sliding downward.

Above and to his left, three Chinstrap penguins caught Randy's attention as they came through an archway and stood on the ledge. He watched them as they did the same back. He was astonished to see them turning their heads to one another as if they were conversing. *They really are talking to each other*. Communicating is one thing. Most animals communicate. But not all converse, and Randy was thrilled at the prospect of it all. If they were talking to each other, the next logical step would be for them to communicate with another species—humans, Randy hoped.

He instinctually reached for his camera before realizing he no longer had it. "Wonderful," he berated himself. "The second great discovery of the day, and I've lost my camera." He had hoped his earlier pictures would gain him some *real* recognition. It wasn't that he wanted to be famous. He just thought it would be nice to pay the bills. That didn't really matter to him now though. He had no doubt that he would eventually escape from this improbable situation. The trouble was, how?

Randy shook his head disbelievingly and was disgusted with himself for not being able to photograph what he was seeing. A sharp jab to his back brought him out of his self-admonition. One of the odd Emperor penguins was poking at him and making an upward movement with its spear. Randy took the hint and shakily got to his feet. A nervous chatter arose from the penguin spectators as he stood on his wobbly legs. Another Emperor guard, as Randy thought of them, called out and a group of Adélies moved away from one of the archways. After another prod by a spear, Randy was motivated to move in that direction.

They entered the opened passage, and Randy found that the ceiling was just high enough for him to avoid ducking his six foot frame. He saw several markings etched into the wall, and it didn't take him long to figure out what they were. "Oh my God, you can write too?" Randy asked one of the guards, not expecting an answer. This elicited a rather solid jab of a spear from behind. As enthralled as Randy was by what he was witnessing, he decided it was best not to try and speak to them for now.

Randy was pushed and prodded along the corridors, giving the guards sideways glances every time he was jabbed. He briefly considered trying to overpower his silent sentinels but dismissed the thought, guessing at least one of them would call out in distress, which would most likely send hundreds of penguins descending upon him. He didn't know how right he was in assuming that. He did know they could have killed him back on the ice plains if they had wanted to. They had kept him alive for a purpose.

Traveling through PIC, Randy saw several entryways that led to various chambers and halls, each with dozens of pairs of curious eyes staring out at him as he passed. He didn't entertain any ideas about there being a person behind the penguins' unusual behavior. He accepted that they were more advanced than anyone previously could have imagined. They passed through another archway and entered the main hall, where all of the corridors converged and where the monolithic ice stalactite hung. Randy marveled at the structure as they passed by, unable to take his eyes from it, and bumped into a guard who had stopped in front of him. Within a second, half a dozen spears were pointed directly at him. "Accident," Randy said, putting his hands in the air. After a tense few seconds, the guards seemed to be placated and slowly lowered their spears.

Two of his guards approached another pair standing underneath an arch with more intricate etchings across its crown. Randy looked at the arch and the plain ice wall behind, concluding it must be a doorway. After finishing a conversation among themselves, the two guards stationed in front of the door turned and inserted the butts of their spears in holes on the abutments of the archway. A few seconds later, Randy heard the grinding of ice, followed by the door sliding smoothly down to reveal another passage.

The guards prompted Randy forward, and he moved into the corridor beyond the opened door. The light inside darkened into a deep azure but remained bright enough to see by. He began to get an uneasy feeling to go along with his sense of wonder as he looked at the reliefs carved into the wall. Something about how advanced the penguins actually were didn't sit well with him. It had nothing to do with a human superiority complex but more of an eerie sense of foreboding. Entering into the Overlord's chamber did nothing to quiet his uneasiness.

A near-luminescent, violet mist hugged the ground and silhouetted the short columns in the center of the room. Randy's sense of foreboding turned to a feeling of genuine alarm as he looked at the columns. Each column was topped with the skull of one animal or another, displayed like a hunter's trophy. He saw the skull of a bird of prey, most likely that of a Giant Petrel that feeds on penguin chicks. He saw the skull of a seal of some sort. The likely candidate was a Leopard Seal, notorious penguin killers. There was what looked like an Emperor penguin skull, though why, Randy could not imagine. What struck him with fear was the familiar grin of a human skull staring back at him. The skull was devoid of its fleshly veneer, and whether the penguins killed the unfortunate person or merely found his remains on the ice did not matter. Randy now knew that the penguins viewed him as an enemy.

Beyond the mist, in the darkened back portion of the chamber, Randy fixed his sight on a large dais, not for its construction or to marvel at the penguins' ingenuity in building it, but for the creature that stood on it. Randy witnessed the largest penguin he had ever seen, the Overlord. It was larger than the guards that surrounded it and stood nearly as tall as Randy.

At the foot of the dais were two of the large Emperors, one slightly larger than the other one. Another nudge in his back got Randy moving toward the intimidating birds. As he moved closer, he recognized the smaller of the two Emperors by its one red eye. It was one of his attackers. When Randy got close to the dais, two of the guards crossed spears in front him, preventing him from moving any closer.

The Overlord brought himself to his full height and slowly approached the man standing before him. He glared into his eyes for a long moment, and then Randy was given an enormous shock.

CHAPTER 26

After the guards passed in front of the Gentoo quarters with their prisoner, Leepoh stood in silence, contemplating what he had seen. He quickly turned to another Gentoo. "I've seen that human before."

The other Gentoo was taken slightly off guard. "Excuse me, sir, but don't they all look alike?"

"No—similar, yes, but not alike. I'm sure I've seen it before." Leepoh stopped talking and stared at the ground in concentration. "RHC 23, that's where—or maybe before."

"I thought all of the humans died there?"

"No, this was a while before that. It wasn't one of them." Leepoh reflected back on when he had seen Randy. "This one was there some time before those. It would sit in the distance and watch us. It would arrive in the morning from its ship and spend the entire day looking at us through some sort of device."

"Was it a weapon?" the other Gentoo asked with a hint of concern.

"No. I don't think it was. If it was, the human never used it against us. It came close to our colony on several occasions and seemed genuinely pleased to be among us. I don't think it was a killer like the others. It was there when . . ." Leepoh's words trailed away and he thought about it for a minute longer. Something didn't feel right about this human being there.

He wasn't sure if it was the coincidence of seeing the same human twice in a lifetime or if it was something else that bothered him. "What will they do with it?"

"I'm not sure, sir. I'm not sure if this has ever happened before. It appears as if they're taking it to the Overlord."

"*Then* what will they do with it?" Leepoh asked the other Gentoo, who gestured as if to say, "Who knows?" He was becoming slightly irritated with the chatty general. For another minute or two, Leepoh thought about what to do and why it mattered for another.

"Sir, you may want to ask one of the Chinstraps. I've been here only a short while myself, but from what I have seen, they appear to be the keepers of tasks around here," the other told Leepoh, either trying to be helpful or trying to get rid of him.

"That's right!" Leepoh exclaimed loudly, causing the other to jerk in surprise. "I forgot. It has been awhile since I've been here. I don't seem to remember it being this big though. Do you suppose they know where the Rockhoppers are quartered?" The other Gentoo opened his beak to answer but never got the chance. "Of course they do. All right, I'll be back." Leepoh quickly exited the Gentoo quarters, leaving the Gentoo he was speaking *at* to catch his breath.

For some reason, seeing the human captive troubled him when he knew it shouldn't have. After the battle of RHC 23, his last thought should have been compassion for any human, but he felt this one was innocent. Killing an innocent would bring them down to their level. Maybe it was something simpler or something more complex. He wanted to find out whether his new friend, Nok, had come and get his perspective, even though he already knew what it would be. So he hurried down the corridor, a penguin with a purpose.

^^^

"I still think it was unwise to bring a human here. This place is our one safe haven from any kind of predator," Trevot argued to Mevoule.

As the three Chinstraps watched the human from their second-story balcony, it looked anything but threatening. It lay on the ground passively even after regaining consciousness. After watching it be led away to the Overlord, Trevot once again complained of the folly of bringing a human to Pack Ice Command.

"We are the Penguin Defense Alliance. That implies that we were formed for *defensive* purposes. This is clearly an aggressive move on General Diutes's part," Trevot ranted.

"I thought you said humans were dangerous, violent creatures. If it was found near the procession or PIC, that would justify capturing it," Mevoule responded, if not for any reason other than just to be argumentative.

"I'm glad you're finding this amusing, but you don't understand," Trevot said. "The humans have weapons of unspeakable power. I've seen it. On that island, the Rockhoppers killed probably not more than forty humans, but the Rockhopper's losses were in the hundreds. I would hate to see that kind of power brought to bear against PIC. Regardless of how hard they try to indoctrinate us into hatred, I fear the humans and what they're capable of. The costs are too high."

"I doubt that will happen, Lieutenant. This land is far bigger than RHC 23, and even if the humans search for their missing comrade, this area is just too vast. They would eventually give it up for dead."

Lavour decided the debate had gone on long enough. He knew Mevoule was just goading Trevot and Trevot was obviously troubled by the events he had witnessed. And Lavour knew that powerful emotions stemmed from trauma. "Mevoule may be correct. We can't find even one Chinstrap in the PIC, and the ice fields and mountains are far too immense for them to search entirely," Lavour said, looking at Mevoule. "But I do think it was reckless for the general to bring a human here. This just reaffirms my concerns that the Royal Emperors are becoming far too bold."

Mevoule looked at Lavour out of the corner of his eye. "They must have their reasons. They have brought us together, united as one. So it must be for the good of all penguins for them to be 'so bold,' as you put it."

Lavour stared at Mevoule. He was his oldest and dearest friend, and Lavour was surprised at the tension he felt between them. He held his gaze until Mevoule turned away. A call from down the corridor broke what tension remained.

"Excuse me," a lone Gentoo said.

The three Chinstraps turned to the newcomer, happy for the distraction. "Can I help you?" Lavour asked.

"Yes, I'm General Leepoh, and I'm trying to find someone."

At hearing this, the three Chinstraps exchange furtive glances and hoped the newcomer wasn't experiencing the same thing they were.

"I'm Lieutenant-General Lavour. This is Captain Mevoule and this Lieutenant Trevot," he said, indicating the others with his flipper.

Leepoh studied Trevot for a moment. "Have we met?"

"I don't believe so, sir," Trevot said as he looked to the other Chinstraps, a little surprised.

Leepoh studied him a little longer. "Were you on RHC 23 recently?"

Trevot was now more than a little surprised. "Yes, I was. I delivered a message to the Rockhoppers. I'm sorry, but I don't recall meeting you, sir."

"No reason to be sorry, Lieutenant. You didn't meet me. I observed the initial confrontation from a distance, and a lone Chinstrap stands out against a sea of Rockhoppers."

Trevot stood in silence, remembering the events. "How did it end?"

"Violently," Leepoh said and looked back at Lavour. "Speaking of which, I'm looking for the Rockhopper quarters."

"The Rockhopper quarters are back this way," said Lavour. "We'll show you the way."

The group headed down the corridor. After a minute of silence, Lavour looked at Leepoh. "What did you mean by violently?"

"I was wondering that myself." Trevot jumped into the conversation. "I left just after General Treeg's hatchling was killed, and the Rockhoppers were searching for a missing human."

"Oh, they found their missing human." Leepoh paused, averting his eyes for a moment. "And it took quite a nasty fall. But before that, Captain Nok recruited us—the Gentoo, that is—to help overrun the human ship. We had a magnificent party aboard. That is, after we defeated them."

"A party?" inquired Mevoule, confused as to why anyone would want to have a party after fighting humans.

"Yes, Captain Mevoule, a party. There was singing and dancing and joviality beyond belief."

There was a hint of malevolence in the Gentoo's voice, and Lavour and the others decided it was a subject best left alone.

"By the way, where are they taking that human?" Leepoh asked casually.

"To the Overlord, I believe," said Lavour.

"A bad idea in my opinion," Lieutenant Trevot interjected.

"Why is that, Lieutenant?" Leepoh inquired.

"Oh, here we go," Mevoule said, throwing up his flippers in exasperation.

Trevot gave Mevoule an annoyed look. "Why do you ask, sir? I'm surprised you'd even have to ask. They're violent, dangerous, and extremely intelligent. You know this."

"I do know this, Lieutenant. I've fought and killed some of them, but this one is different. I don't believe it's like the others. I've seen it on the island."

The three Chinstraps stopped and faced Leepoh in astonishment. "Wait, wait, *wait*," Mevoule said. "You've seen this very human before? How can you be sure?"

"I recognize the eyes. I'm sure of it. And you're correct, Lieutenant Trevot. This *is* a risk that should not have been taken," Leepoh told them, not bothering to explain his reasoning.

"If you *have* seen it before, perhaps it was a good idea for them to capture it," Mevoule said in a tone that wasn't overly insistent, almost as if he was playing the devil's advocate.

"Explain," Lavour told the captain. He too thought it was odd that General Leepoh should see the same human twice.

"Well, General Leepoh, what if it's a scout or a spy? If it *was* at the island, then showed up here, that might indicate that the humans already know about the PDA and are looking for a way to stop it."

"That is precisely the reason it was a bad idea to bring the thing here," Trevot said sternly.

"No, it's all the more reason for it to have been captured," Mevoule replied in kind.

Lavour had heard enough of the debate. "Why don't you two take your discussion back to the quarters, and keep it down, will you? We don't want anybody thinking there are dissidents within our ranks."

Mevoule and Trevot obliged. They saluted Lavour and Leepoh and headed down the hall, still bickering, albeit more quietly, as they went.

"All right, let me show you where the Rockhopper quarters are," Lavour said, shaking his head as the two Chinstraps disappeared.

"It's good to see that the Chinstraps care enough for the Penguin Defense Alliance to engage in such heated conversation over what's best for us," Leepoh said.

"We Chinstraps welcome all opinions, but sometimes it's better not to voice those opinions in the open while inside Pack Ice Command." Lavour looked around as he told Leepoh that piece of information. Something had been creeping about in the back of his mind, a feeling of not being alone. He dismissed it as paranoia or just plain fatigue, but it still came up, especially at moments like this.

Leepoh scrutinized the Chinstrap for a moment. "Why would that be? I thought *all* penguins had an equal voice on matters concerning the PDA. Have things changed that much since I've been away?"

"That depends on when you left. It appears as if some penguins have *more* of an equal voice than others." Lavour went silent, contemplating how much he should say. He thought he may have said too much already, but

Leepoh was an outsider and he continued to vent his frustration. "Things are just a bit tense within our company, if you hadn't already noticed. We were called to stay on for another season and missed our breeding time."

"That is a little unusual. Was it put to a vote?"

"No, more of an edict. There's more. But we've reached our destination, and I've probably said too much already."

Leepoh continued to scrutinize Lavour. "I'm not even sure if the penguin I'm looking for came here. I'm just assuming he did. Come on, Lavour, I'd like you to meet him—if he's here, that is."

Lavour was happy to accompany Leepoh. The thought of traveling alone through the corridors was unsettling, even though the halls were bustling with newcomers. It made him feel that much more foreign in a place familiar to him. Corporal Meuseaux's disappearance was trying on his nerves.

CHAPTER 27

"We've been searching for hours, and now the wind has really picked up, Gina. I'm sorry, but it's near whiteout conditions. We have to return," Lawrence Redeniek said as he closed the door of the crawler. Lawrence, faithful servant of Vance Lyons, President and CEO of Global Threat, was the base leader. Nothing happened, or was supposed to happen, at the base or camp without his permission or direction. He pulled off his hood, rubbing his gloved hand through thick dark gray hair. "I know you two are close. Hell, we all really like Randy. It's just there's nothing more we can do right now."

Tired to the point of exhaustion, worried and upset, Gina didn't bother trying to refute that she and Randy had a relationship. She looked out the window of the snow crawler and tried to make out the faint outlines of the others walking through the blowing snow toward the vehicle. She knew she had no right to ask for them all to keep looking for Randy in these conditions.

The sudden windstorms, which kicked up loose powdery snow to create blinding whiteouts with zero visibility, were common in Antarctica. The wind constantly reshaped the landscape, effectively erasing any tracks of any living thing that could survive in such a harsh environment. Because of the risks involved in traveling to a place such as this, all of those who agreed to come on this expedition signed waivers, releasing GT of any liability should anything happen outside of the company's control. Everyone who signed knew those risks.

Gina couldn't leave without exhausting all efforts. "No, Lawrence. He's still alive. I *know* he is. We have to keep looking. We can't just leave him for dead."

"Gina, we can't risk anyone else's life. He knew the risk he was taking, and so did you when you left him alone. Even if he isn't dead and is just lying unconscious out here, we run the risk of not seeing him and running him over. We have to get back while we still have some visibility," Lawrence told her in his authoritative voice, tinged with a hint of compassion.

Gina looked away in silence as other team members climbed in the vehicle. She knew Lawrence was right, but it still didn't make leaving any easier.

"Listen, we'll go back out as soon the storm dies down. I'm sorry."

Gina lowered her head, turned away and looked out the window. "I'm sorry too," she said quietly.

ᐱᐱᐱ

Randy stood before the Overlord's dais, surrounded by guards as the Overlord approached him. The Overlord looked him up and down in a disdainful manner. "Human," he said in a voice nearly as plain as Randy's, and with an unmistakably condescending tone.

Randy was staggered. He felt as if he had been hit in the gut and had lost his breath at the shock of it all. "Y-you can talk?" he stammered.

"Humph," the Overlord sneered. "You humans are so arrogant in your belief that the world belongs to you and you alone—that no other beings on Earth can match you and your intelligence. You think you have the right to take what you want, what is not yours to take, and from whomever you please."

Randy didn't know what to say. He felt like he was being accused of the sins of all humanity. "Some, yes—but not all."

"Silence!" the Overlord bellowed.

Two of the guards moved on Randy with unexpected speed and cracked their staffs across his back and on top of his skull. He fell to the ground, stunned by the attack and by their surprising strength. As he lay on the cold floor, trying to clear his mind, he tried also to think of a way to reason with this creature or escape it.

"You will speak when I say you can speak, human, or your time here will be short."

Randy bowed his head in a display of respect as he stood.

"Now, human, what do you have to say for yourself before I decide your fate?"

Randy hesitated. He knew now that he was indeed the one who would be made answerable for his kind's transgressions and he would have to choose his next words carefully, for his life hung in the balance. "First of all, I apologize for speaking out of turn, as I am not familiar with your protocol. Second, I understand your anger with my species. I am angry at it as well. But not all of us are as you say. I am here, in your land, to study penguins and educate others of my species, so that they can appreciate your kind and stop any future destructive behavior."

"So, you say you study us?" the Overlord hissed, taking a few steps closer to his prize.

"Yes, some of us are here to find out why some of your populations are decreasing."

"Your very presence here is why our populations are decreasing!" the Overlord roared with hostility.

"You are correct, it's just . . ." Another sharp smack to the side of Randy's head cut off his remark.

"Of course I'm correct! You and your kind have defiled our homeland long enough. You say you are here to study us, do you? *I* say you are a spy, sent to bring about further destruction. I know your plans and your deception. I am through with talking to humans. Take it away." The Overlord waved his flipper in dismissal and turned his back on Randy.

Several elite guards moved on Randy. "Wait! Please, now that we know that we can communicate with each other, maybe we . . ."

"Silence it!" Supreme Commander Liutites ordered in the penguin vernacular from the Overlord's side.

Another blow came at Randy, but this time he was ready for it and grabbed the staff from the surprised guard's grip. "We can work this out and find a solution," Randy pleaded, attempting to keep the guards at bay.

A hard hit to the back of his legs, followed by another to the back of his head, and Randy fell.

"The elimination of your kind from our realm will be the solution," the Overlord hissed. "Take this thing from my sight."

The guards held their spear tips to Randy's throat and directed him out a passage at the back of the Overlord's chamber.

The Overlord watched the human until he was gone. "Supreme Commander, make sure the human is secure and that he remains alive and functional. He will make a fine bargaining piece, if it comes to that, or a tremendous sacrifice."

"Yes, my lord." Liutites saluted and followed the guards.

"General Diutes, return to Forward Command One and bring a company of Chinstraps with you. Double your patrols. The humans will no doubt be looking for their missing member. This human was an excellent gift, General Diutes. For your initiative, you now have direct control over your region. All humans that enter your area of command are to be eliminated. You will follow the example of the Rockhoppers. Show no mercy."

"Yes, my lord. Thank you." General Diutes offered a very proud high beak salute and exited the Overlord's chamber.

CHAPTER 28

Leepoh and Lavour meandered through a crowd of Rockhoppers until Leepoh said he'd had enough of it and stopped one passing by. "You there—do you know if Captain Nok came with your contingent?"

"Oh, yes. Yes, he did," the Rockhopper said. "He should be back at any moment. He had a meeting with the Supreme Commander."

Lavour inwardly cringed at the mention of the Supreme Commander. He knew just how brutal Liutites could be. If Captain Nok's first impression of the PDA is Liutites, that could prove disastrous for the unity of the clans. The thought of the Supreme Commander flamed a bit of anger inside Lavour. It was anger he had not realized he had.

"Thank you," Leepoh said, turning to Lavour. "Let's wait by the entrance."

Eager to be away from the noisy braying of the Rockhoppers, they decided to wait outside to catch Nok before he entered.

"So, tell me. How do you feel about not being able to return home to your mate?" Leepoh asked, putting aside all pretense of appropriateness.

Lavour paused before answering, not because he was offended by Leepoh's frank way of asking. He wanted to be careful in the way he answered. "Frustrated, I guess you could say. We came here with the understanding that we would be relieved in time to join our mates. But that time has come and gone, and we're still here with no explanation as to why."

"Ah, nothing worse than an amorous penguin."

Lavour looked at Leepoh and snorted a penguin chuckle. "It's not like we have a lot of time to think about it. It seems we have more than our fair share of the duties."

"You sound a little bitter."

"Bitter? No, not bitter. It's just trying on us—on me. My first hatchling has grown, and it's difficult to send other Chinstraps to clean the Royal Emperor's rookeries when . . ." He caught himself mid-sentence as he realized that he did indeed sound bitter. He was, he admitted to himself. He was bitter, frustrated, and angry. "You're right, I do," Lavour conceded. "I've said more to you than I've said to anyone. You have a way of getting me talking."

"Bah, I'm just a fresh face to complain to. Sometimes that's all you need."

Lavour was getting ready to respond when a call from down the corridor interrupted him.

"Leepoh!" exclaimed Nok as he came upon the pair.

"Nok!" Leepoh replied, mimicking Nok's tone. "Glad you could make it."

"General Treeg thought it would be a good idea to send me along with our contingent. I was wondering if you had anything to do with that."

"Me?" Leepoh asked incredulously. "Bringing down a human all by yourself can make you quite a celebrity in the PDA. So it's no wonder he sent you."

"You're the Rockhopper who did that?" Lavour chimed in, a bit surprised to meet the penguin that most of those in the PIC were speaking of. Word had spread quickly of the Rockhopper and Gentoo's success in defeating the poachers, and the exploits of a Rockhopper that took down a human alone was already reaching the point of legend.

"Oh, let me introduce you. Captain Nok, Lieutenant-General Lavour.

Lieutenant-General Lavour, Captain Nok."

"I deduced," Lavour said sarcastically to Leepoh.

"Good to meet you." Nok lowered his head in a casual greeting. "And yes, that was me, but there were many others who were much more heroic than I was—like the general here. Honestly, I don't know what all of the fuss is about. We were just defending our home. But I guess General Leepoh enjoys the sound of his own voice, so now every penguin from here to the Galapagos knows."

"Bah! I just like to brag about all of the important penguins I know. Besides that, Lavour here was doing all of the talking."

"I find *that* hard to believe," Nok remarked while looking at Lavour.

"He just got me on a subject I couldn't let go."

"He's annoying that way."

"You know him well, then?"

Leepoh snapped his head back and forth between them in false indignation. He opened his beak to speak but closed it in mock indecisiveness.

"Let me go check in with Commander Khik. Then we'll talk some more."

Lavour watched Captain Nok hurry off. "He doesn't seem like a man-killer."

"None of us do, do we?" Leepoh asked with a morose tone. "Where do you think they will take the human after the Overlord is done with it?" he asked, changing the subject after a few too many seconds of silence.

"It's difficult to say. I was wondering the same thing."

Leepoh looked around the corridor then to Lavour. "Let me ask you something."

"What is it?" Lavour asked with a touch of suspicion.

"Could I trust you not to tell anyone if I were to take a look around for the human?"

"After the way I spilled my gripes to you, I should be asking if I could trust you. And yes, you can trust me—as long as I can tag along. I'm looking for someone myself."

"What's all this talk about who can trust whom? I've never heard of penguin spies," Nok cut in from behind Leepoh, startling the both of them.

"You're right, Captain Nok, but the longer you're here, the more you'll get this feeling of a . . ." Lavour paused, choosing his words carefully, "an undercurrent of mistrust."

Leepoh and Nok looked at Lavour, not believing what they'd heard. Leepoh and Nok exchanged glances. "How so?" asked Leepoh.

"I can't say exactly, nor do I really know. It's just a feeling."

"Perhaps it would do us well to have our conversations in more private surroundings," Leepoh suggested.

"If there is such a place," Lavour commented. He looked down the corridor. Something was giving him the feeling of being watched, but he couldn't place what or how. He dismissed the feeling and changed the subject. "Now, about this human . . ."

"What? What human?" Nok asked with a mix of venom and anxiety.

"Relax, my friend. It's not like the kind from back home. It's different," Leepoh reassured his friend. "You didn't hear about its capture?"

"I've been busy. And how do you know it's not like the others? It has been my experience that *all* humans are evil, soulless creatures that should be eliminated from our homes," Nok insisted with a little more anger.

"That's true most of the time. This one is different, and I've seen it before."

"Doubtful," Nok snorted, his anger somewhat quelled by his friend's reassurance.

"Perhaps, but I have to know for sure. I have to see it, and hopefully speak to it."

"Why?" Nok asked.

"I have to. That's all," Leepoh said, uncharacteristically abrupt.

"If you say so, that's good enough for me," Nok said.

"Good. Lavour, let's see if we can learn what has become of this human. Shall we?"

"We shall," Lavour replied.

"Are you sure about this, Lieutenant-General?" Nok asked as they began their search.

"I'm sure the human will be under the tightest security," Lavour answered.

"Not that. Are you sure you want to be seen with this Gentoo?"

"I was once on guano duty for a week. How much worse could it be?" Lavour wasn't sure why he found it so easy to insult the Gentoo. He knew only that he enjoyed it.

"Oh, it gets worse. Trust me."

CHAPTER 29

The elite Royal Emperor guards pushed and shoved the semi-conscious Randy along a lengthy corridor. A guard inserted its staff into a keyhole and a door began to slide slowly down. Randy stared at it blankly. His mind was unable to process information, even something as mundane as a door opening. He saw a darkened room beyond the arched doorway, and the guards shoved him inside. They hit him across the back of his head one more time for good measure. Knocking him to the ground, they left him in the gloom.

Randy crawled to his feet as the door closed behind him. He gently touched his head, thankful he still had his wool beanie cap. Without it, the damage might have been worse. His head spun as he surveyed the room. The room itself was circular, as all of the rooms in Pack Ice Command were, with a domed ceiling. A halo of light around the top of the dome was just enough for him to see by. There wasn't much to see besides a few very old wooden crates, a couple of fifty-five-gallon steel drums, a pile of assorted items, and a very tattered British flag still mounted on its pole.

Randy's head throbbed from the repeated blows he had received from the guards. He sank to the ground. He had awoken this morning secure with the knowledge that human beings were the only civilization on Earth, but that illusion had been shattered into a million tiny shards. Nothing in the world made sense any longer. Nothing felt real and nothing felt right.

After lying on the very cold ground for several minutes, Randy sat up but immediately wished he hadn't. His head throbbed worse than before, and he was dizzy and nauseous. He tried to get his mind off of what probably was a concussion, and his thoughts turned to Gina. He began to worry for her. He worried not only for her safety—he knew she was on her way back and didn't know her fate. He also worried because he knew inside that she cared for him, and because of her tenacious character, if she *was* safe, she would stop at nothing to find him.

The chemistry between them was undeniable. Recalling the playful banter and the stolen glances when she didn't think he was looking made Randy long for her. Now, here, when his life was going to meet an unlikely end, he understood just what she meant to him and how much he truly cared for her. Maybe it wasn't love, not yet anyway. But if it wasn't, it was as close as it could be. He made a vow that if, by some chance or miracle, he found a way to survive this ordeal, he would get past her aloofness and tell her how he felt. "If I survive," Randy said quietly.

Ever the optimist and with a renewed purpose, Randy stood up, and, ignoring the swaying feeling, began to do an inventory of useful objects. He started with his pockets. He was glad to find that the penguins, despite their cleverness, failed to do a diligent search of his person. He found his small pocketknife, a couple of energy bars, a mini LED flashlight, and a cold weather lighter. Because GT thought them too expensive for every member of the team to carry, Randy didn't have a personal locator beacon, which would have given a search party his location within a hundred yards. He wished he still had his radio. The thought of the radio reminded him of Gina and the last thing he'd heard from her—a panicked voice calling him from the radio. "God, I hope she's all right," he said, lost in thought again. "Okay, stay focused."

He turned his attention to the items that were strewn about the room. The room itself was obviously used as a storeroom for various forms of bric-a-brac that the penguins had gathered from the ice fields. He rummaged through the crates, finding various old tins and other refuse from years gone by. One crate did yield a very old and ragged pup tent, a backpack of equally poor condition, and some very used gloves. Randy propped himself against one of the crates, disappointed that his search hadn't been more fruitful. He could use the old tent to wrap himself in for warmth, however.

The condition of the room told Randy the penguins didn't usually take prisoners, or at least weren't expecting to. Their putting him in a storeroom indicated there were no prisons in this place. He didn't know if that was good or bad. He decided to try and bust up one of the crates and burn it. When he dragged a crate away from the wall, he heard a slight scraping sound, even after he stopped dragging the box. He disregarded the sound, telling himself he was hearing things because of his fatigue.

Another scuffle-scratch sound grabbed Randy's attention. He stared at the steel barrels. He was sure he'd looked behind them earlier. It had been a grueling day, and he didn't want to see what was scratching around back there, but the persistent noise left him no choice.

He slowly reached for his pocketknife, extended the blade to its less-than-impressive length of two inches, and told himself that if he ever made it home he would buy a bigger knife. He crept to the drums and cautiously peered over the top. Nothing was behind the drums except a few scrapes on the ice floor that indicated he had indeed checked there earlier.

He let out his breath and turned to break the crate when he heard the noise again. This time it was more distinct, as if it was scratching against metal. He began to tap on each of the drums, attempting to elicit a response. As he tapped on the last of them, he heard a muted warble come from within.

Randy took a deep breath, grabbed the edge of the barrel, and spun it toward him. A hole was cut out of the other side of the drum. He stepped back and squatted down with his barely offensive weapon at the ready. He looked inside. A sharp screech, followed by a Chinstrap bursting out of the hole, startled Randy. He let out a quick yell, stumbled backwards, and fell to his seat. He looked around, trying to see where his pocketknife had landed. The blade was lying just out of reach, so he sat still, not wanting to provoke an attack.

The Chinstrap watched him carefully. After a minute or two with each of them watching the other with a fixed gaze, the Chinstrap looked around then back at Randy. He noticed the penguin relax a bit, almost as if its shoulders slumped a bit. Randy followed suit. Not sure about what to do next, he decided to say something to the penguin. "Hello, little fella. Do you talk as well?"

The penguin perked up a bit but just continued to stare at Randy.

"You don't, huh?" Randy put his hand out in a friendly gesture, and the little Chinstrap lowered its head slightly and took a step toward him. "I'm not gonna hurt you," Randy said softly.

Even though Randy's treatment by the penguins had been somewhat less than kind, his deep affinity for the birds had not been diminished. After all, that was what had brought him to Antarctica, to be part of a research team and photograph its chief inhabitants—the penguins. He gave it some thought and figured Gina was probably correct in surmising that the penguin's behavior patterns must have been adversely affected by intense environmental pressure. By some astounding and unheard of means, these incredible and highly intelligent creatures were responding to man's constant invasion of their habitat. He'd seen the penguin leader's point when it said humans were the problem. He couldn't change the past, but he could affect the future, so he went to work on befriending one Chinstrap penguin.

Randy kept a careful eye as the penguin watched him warily. "I wonder if you can understand me," he said, more to himself than to his companion. The Chinstrap continued to stare at him curiously until it abruptly swung its head toward the door. It ruffled its tail feathers and raised its wings in alarm. Randy noticed one of its wings appeared to be broken.

The Chinstrap watched the door then let out an angry hiss and ran back to its hiding spot. Randy looked at the door then at the penguin, his tired and befuddled mind not letting him put two and two together. The telltale sound of grinding ice let him know that someone was coming, and it dawned on him that the Chinstrap didn't want to be found. He quickly tucked away his knife, stood up, and spun the barrel around so that the cutout could not be seen.

Supreme Commander Liutites entered the room, followed by four elite guards. Randy backed away.

"The Overlord has decreed that you should remain alive for now, human," Liutites sneered in lisping, but otherwise near perfect, English.

Randy decided to try a little diplomacy on the imposing bird. "My name is Randy. Do you have a name?"

"My name is unimportant to you, human," he snapped back and called the guards forward in the penguin language.

Two guards came forward, each carrying an old wooden bucket and tossing its contents of dead icefish at Randy's feet.

"Enjoy your meal, human," Liutites said with disdain and left the room.

Randy stepped over the pile of fish, not wanting to think about how they'd caught and transported them here. "Your Overlord is most gracious, *penguin*," he said, mocking Liutites as he left.

The Supreme Commander spun around, glared at Randy from outside the doorway, and made a low, evil clicking noise as the door shut in front of him.

"I have got to work on my penguin skills."

CHAPTER 30

Darkness had settled in, and Gina stared out the small window of her room. There was nothing to look at. The wind had intensified since they'd called off the search, and visibility was down to zero. After returning to camp, Gina closed herself in her room to change and spend some time alone with her thoughts.

The research station was made up of several portable buildings adjoined to one another. There was a separate garage and fuel shed, which stood fifty meters away. They had two crawlers and four snowmobiles they could use to carry out the search, but the weather conditions rendered the snowmobiles useless. Dan Alcorn, the field supervisor, informed Gina they had been in contact with McMurdo, a U.S. settlement in Antarctica, and they too were turned back by the deteriorating conditions.

"I should've taken the snowmobile back. I could've gotten to him faster. No, I should never have left him," Gina lambasted herself as tears began to flow down her face. A knock on her door made her look away from the window, but she didn't respond. A second, more insistent knock followed by Dan's voice made Gina pull herself together, wipe her face, and open the door.

"Hi, Gina. How are ya holding up?" Dan asked quietly, sticking his head through the door.

"How do you think, Dan?" she bit back, unintentionally harsh but too tired to give a damn.

"I figured as much. Listen, Gina, I'm sorry. Randy was a good man—a helluva nice guy," he said, not knowing what else to say. "This *is* unfortunate."

"He might still be alive, you know. Don't talk about him like he's already dead."

"Gina, we have to face the reality of the situation . . . It's more than forty below out there, not including the windchill. He has no shelter."

"What if he's not out there?" Gina said with a glint of hope in her voice.

Dan was a practical, straight-forward man. He didn't entertain flights of fancy or nonsense. He shook his head.

"He said he had encountered penguins, and they looked angry."

"What does that have to do with anything? And how does a penguin look upset?" Dan asked her with a hint of annoyance in his voice as he turned away.

"I really don't know how, but what if they were agitated by poachers?" Gina had concluded there was no way Randy could have just disappeared in the short time she was gone. Somebody must have taken him.

Dan took a long breath and ran his hand down his face. "Davis told me you mentioned something like that. It's a bit far-fetched. Poachers no longer come here. This isn't the 1800s. Nobody harvests these birds for oil anymore. Did Randy say anything about poachers? Did you find vehicle tracks?"

"Well, no," Gina admitted. "But if he took pictures of them, they could have taken drastic measures and kidnapped him." She knew she was reaching, trying to grab hold of something that in all likelihood wasn't there.

"Listen, Gina," Dan said in an even voice. "If there *were* poachers out here, we would most likely know about it. And even if there were and Randy came across them, poachers aren't the type of people who take prisoners. And about the penguins, if what he said was true and they *looked* upset, then that may mean that they were diseased or something," he said, looking away.

Dan abandoned his attempt to bring Gina back to reality. And completely out of his character, he made amends. "That's neither here nor there. Jack is going to download those pictures. Maybe they'll tell us more about what happened."

"I have to hold on to hope," Gina said in a small voice.

"I know you do." Dan looked at her and quickly looked away once again.

Gina thought she picked up on something in the way Dan averted his eyes but dismissed it as frayed nerves.

"Let's go see if those pictures are ready yet," Dan suggested.

Eager to know whether her theory was credible, Gina agreed to go have a look. She left the solace of her room for the common area where everyone had gathered.

^^^

"So, Lieutenant-General, why don't you tell us where you're from?" Leepoh asked as they traveled through the seemingly endless corridors of Pack Ice Command. Their attempt to find where the human captive was being held had, so far, been a fruitless endeavor. Every penguin they asked either didn't know or wasn't telling, and Leepoh's request of secrecy from Lavour became a moot point as they had inquired with a good portion of the penguins in Pack Ice Command. Leepoh asked those in the upper echelons, the Royal Emperors, and the Kings, but received the same silent stare Nok did when he asked an elite guard. It didn't make sense to them. Someone had to have seen it.

"I make my nest in the archipelagos," Lavour answered

"Do you know where they took the human?" Leepoh asked a passing Adélie, who answered by shaking her head no. "Do you have a mate?" he asked Lavour.

"Yes, though I've been away for so long now, I'm sure she's found another." Lavour lamented having been away from Lannera, his mate, for so long. His hatchling had grown, and he had missed it all while being stuck in the service of the Overlord's Penguin Defense Alliance.

"Chin up, Chinstrap," Leepoh said with his usual mirth. "You'll see her again."

"Technically I don't have a chin. And I do hope I'll see her, but I have a feeling I'll be away for a lot longer still."

"What makes you think that?" Nok asked. He had remained silent until that point, listening to Leepoh's annoying line of questioning rather than have the Gentoo start asking him personal questions.

"Just rumors and rumblings I've heard."

"What kind of rumors and rumblings?" the ever-inquisitive Leepoh asked.

"It's more of a feeling around here than anything definitive, like something big is on the horizon."

"Chinstrap!" a commanding voice thundered from behind the trio, cutting off Lavour's words.

Lavour's heart skipped a nervous beat at hearing Supreme Commander Liutites's angry voice. He immediately spun around and snapped his head up in salute. "Yes, sir."

"I understand you have been inquiring of the whereabouts of the human prisoner." It was not a question.

"Yes, sir." There was no need to lie about it. It was obvious now that Liutites had his sources, but Lavour didn't feel the need to elaborate on his answer.

Liutites glared at Lavour. "Might I be privy as to the reason why, Lieutenant-General?"

Before Lavour could answer, Leepoh stepped in. "It was on our behalf. Mine and Captain Nok's—whom I believe you have already met."

Liutites looked down at the two heroes of the battle RHC 23. "What would be your purpose?" he asked slowly, carrying an air of suspicion.

"I want to see it," Leepoh matched his tone, not intimidated in the least by the Supreme Commander.

Liutites studied the Gentoo for a minute. "*If* I were to allow you to see it, you wouldn't damage it, would you?"

"Bah. Not at all, nor will my companions."

Liutites and Leepoh locked stares, and after a few strangely tense moments, Liutites broke first. "Very well, General Leepoh, you may go. Do you speak human?"

"Some."

The answer drew a quick, surprised look from Captain Nok.

Liutites turned his attention to Lavour. "Chinstrap, escort these two to the west passage outside the Overlord's chambers. I will inform the guards to expect your arrival. They will escort you the rest of the way. Remember this, Chinstrap, I am only allowing you this privilege because you have found yourself in good favor with the Overlord *and* our esteemed guest."

Liutites glared at Lavour for a second longer and abruptly departed.

Lavour watched the Supreme Commander leave. Leepoh nudged him with his flipper. "Got in good with the Overlord, eh?"

"I guess so," Lavour said, distracted, watching Liutites turn the nearest corner and disappear from sight. "All I did was bring the Overlord the message about the Magellanics finally joining the PDA."

"Well, if that's all you did, you should be a full general in no time," Nok put in his sarcasm. "And aren't you a penguin that's full of surprises?" Nok asked Leepoh. "Why didn't you tell me you speak human?"

"You didn't ask."

Nok shook his head in a gesture that bespoke, *I should have known better than to ask.* "Is there anything else I should know about you?"

"Well, I can fly," he answered straight.

The trio shared a chuckle as Lavour led them away.

After the group departed, Supreme Commander Liutites peered from around the corner. "Keep an eye on those three, and inform me of anything unusual."

A tiny Blue Penguin, standing just over a foot tall with a white belly and bluish-gray feathers covering the rest of its body, snapped a salute and ducked into a hole.

"A Chinstrap in good favor with the Overlord . . ." Liutites grumbled and then tramped off.

CHAPTER 31

With the door shut, the Chinstrap crawled from its hiding spot once again.

"You don't like him either, huh?" Randy asked as the penguin passed by him to investigate the pile of fish. It looked at the fish then up at Randy. "Are you hungry?" The penguin repeated the motion of looking at the fish, then at Randy. "Okay." Randy picked up a couple of fish and held them up to the Chinstrap. The penguin made a motion at them but stopped to look at him once more. "It's all right. Go ahead. I'm not a big fan of sushi."

The Chinstrap hesitated a second longer then snapped the icefish from Randy's hand and greedily gobbled them down.

"Wow! How long has it been since you've eaten?"

The penguin didn't respond but instead turned its attention to the other fish strewn about the floor. It looked back at Randy for permission. "Go ahead," he said, waving his hand at the fish. "Just save me a few in case I get my fire started. Speaking of which . . ." Randy busied himself with busting up one of the crates, all the while watching the Chinstrap in amusement as it hungrily devoured the icefish.

After the penguin finished its meal, it waddled to Randy and looked up at him. "Too long, since ate."

Even though he shouldn't have been, Randy was surprised once again.

He had assumed since the Chinstrap hadn't spoken to him initially that only the large Emperors had the ability. He worked to decipher what the little Chinstrap had said to him. Because of its broken speech and its heavy, almost parrot-like enunciation, it was difficult to understand. "You can speak too?"

Then penguin shook its head. "Tiny."

"Tiny?" Randy repeated, a bit puzzled. "Oh, you mean you speak only a little bit."

"Yesss," the penguin said, dragging its "S."

Randy smiled to himself. He realized this was the opportunity of a lifetime. Not only that, but this could also prove to be the biggest discovery in the history of the world. Humans were not the only sentient creatures on Earth. Suddenly feeling like the fictional doctor who could talk to animals, Randy carried on with his conversation. "Do you have a name?"

The Chinstrap cocked its head, puzzling over the question then nodded.

"Can you tell me what it is?"

"Not know to, your ssspeak."

"Okay," Randy said while decoding the jumbled words. "What are you doing here? In this room, I mean."

The Chinstrap tilted its head again as it processed the question. "Hide."

"Hiding from what?"

The Chinstrap shook its head. "Not a what—a who."

Randy remembered the little guy's reaction when that unpleasant Emperor had shown up. "You're hiding from the big one?" he asked indicating its height with his hand.

"Yesss."

"Why? I thought he was one of your leaders."

The Chinstrap thought the question over for a minute, and then replied almost angrily, "Not mine leader. Not more. He want me to be eat, by Phocid."

"Phocid? What the hell is a Phocid? And why?" Randy asked, thinking he'd misunderstood.

The Chinstrap held up its broken flipper. "No good. And reason other, too."

Randy had to take a second to make sense of what he was hearing—not because of the Chinstrap's speech. He was already growing accustomed to that. It was the whole feeding to a Phocid thing that was bothering him. "Hold on a minute. You mean to tell me they'll feed you to some creatures just because you broke your flipper? Surely you've found a way to treat injuries?"

"Not only because broken." The Chinstrap thought about how to say what he meant. "Give to Phocid, make happy. And punish."

Randy again had to let the meaning of the words sink in. "You're telling me they were going to *sacrifice* you to whatever a Phocid is because you did something wrong?"

The Chinstrap just nodded.

"My God," Randy said, dumbfounded at the brutality of these penguins. "You must have really done something wrong."

"Now you know why hide."

"Yeah, I would too." After a period of silence in which Randy just watched the penguin, he asked, "Can you tell me what a Phocid is?"

The penguin thought about the request then fell on its belly and began to undulate on the floor.

Randy watched in confusion at the bizarre game of charades taking place until he finally grasped what the bird was trying to convey. "A seal!" he said, a little over exuberantly. He helped the Chinstrap get to its feet, which it seemed to appreciate. "They were going to feed you to a seal." He knew Leopard Seals were at the top of the food chain in the Antarctic waters. So in an odd way it made sense to Randy for the penguins to try to appease them.

"If you don't mind my asking, why are other penguins more fluent in my language than you are?" It was a blunt question, but he had been curious as to whether there was a difference in abilities between the species. He hoped he hadn't offended the penguin in asking.

"Learning not done," the Chinstrap said plainly. If it had been offended, it certainly didn't show any signs of it.

"You have penguin *schools*?" Randy asked incredulously.

"If 'schoolsss' mean learning place, yesss. But I speak better from hear you."

The weight of everything he had learned today made Randy a little weak in the knees. Penguins learning, talking, and living in vast communities under the ice—and penguins kidnapping, plotting, and sacrificing each other in a strange appeasement ritual—it was all more than he could have imagined. Then there was this Chinstrap's learning capacity. He had read stories of animals with remarkable cognitive abilities, like dolphins that could learn a word on a single command or a border collie that did the same, but this was phenomenal. The Chinstrap had undeniably made improvements in its syntax during their brief conversation. He kept expecting to wake up and discover that this was some bizarre dream, but he knew it wasn't. This was most definitely real.

Randy decided to make the best of what he had. What he had was a penguin that trusted him. "My name is Randy. Have you figured out how to say yours yet?"

"Clossse to,"

"Okay—well, what is the name of the big one, the one you hid from?"

"He iss called Supreme Commander Liutitesss."

Randy stared at the penguin blankly. "Supreme Commander? You have ranks?"

"Yess, uss that are here," the Chinstrap answered with his "S" dragging beginning to lessen.

"Of course you do," he said disbelievingly. "And what is your rank?"

The penguin pondered the answer for a bit. "Corporal, believe I."

"Corporal? This really is a lot to take in."

The Chinstrap cocked its head while it studied Randy as if it were trying to grasp what he was saying. "Meuseaux," the penguin blurted out unexpectedly.

"What?" Randy asked him, a little puzzled.

"Meuseaux, iss my name in your speak."

"Oh!" exclaimed Randy. His tired mind was a little slow on the uptake on that particular piece of information. "Well, I am pleased to meet you, Corporal Meuseaux."

"Me as well to meet you. All I hear here, alwayss 'humanss are evil', never anythi—"

Meuseaux stopped and turned his head sharply toward the door then scrambled back to his hiding spot. "Pleassse, tell not."

"You got it," Randy said as he spun the drum around to better conceal the hole. Just as he finished spinning the drum, the door opened and two elite guards marched in with their staffs at the ready. Behind them followed an unlikely trio of penguins: a Gentoo, a Rockhopper, and a Chinstrap.

^^^

Supreme Commander Liutites waddled along a corridor, lost in thought about how best to deal with the Chinstrap who had begun to annoy him, when a Blue penguin called to him from the shadows. The Blue penguins, or Blue Fairy penguins as they are also known, were the smallest of all penguins in the PIC and, as such, were easily overlooked, which is why they suited the Supreme Commander's needs perfectly. They were the eyes and ears of the Supreme Commander and the Overlord, and only the Royal Emperors knew of their existence in Pack Ice Command. Because the Blue penguins lived in isolation from other penguin clans, very few had ever heard of them.

"Yes, my tiny friend?" the Supreme Commander asked the Blue as they ducked into a side passage so as not to be seen. Because of their status as informants, the Blue penguins commanded respect, even from Liutites.

The Blue spoke in a series of whirrs and clicks that were decipherable only to Liutites and the Overlord. This was an added security benefit. If no one knew their language, no one could know their purpose.

"Is that so? Very good. You have done well. Thank you." Liutites pondered the information and then called out in a low-frequency voice that only other Royal Emperors could hear. First, he summoned General Diutes and then told the elite guard to bring Lieutenant-General Lavour to him at once.

Within minutes, General Diutes came tobogganing down the corridor with great urgency. "Yes, Supreme Commander," Diutes said, clambering to his feet.

"General, I am pleased that you have not left."

"We were just on our way to the main entrance when you summoned me, sir."

"I take it, then, that you have assembled the company of Chinstraps as the Overlord directed?"

"Yes, sir."

"Good, but you will be bringing one additional Chinstrap along." Diutes cocked his head in question, but Liutites answered it before he asked. "This Chinstrap has become a problem. I want him given the most grueling duty. Put him in the forward scout position, and have him cover vast areas with no messengers available. He is to report directly to you. After he returns from scouting put him on watch, with minimal rest between shifts. Feel free to come up with new duties. I'm sure you can be inventive in that manner," he suggested in a fiendish tone.

"Yes, sir." Diutes matched the Supreme Commander's tone. "If I might ask, if this one has become such a problem, could he not just disappear? The Phocids are restless, and there is always the one who dwells below."

"No, not yet. He's an officer, and it would be noticed if he were to go missing suddenly. Go and wait for him. He will join you shortly." Liutites dismissed the general.

Diutes snapped a high beak salute and slid away.

CHAPTER 32

When the three penguins entered the makeshift holding area, Captain Nok instinctually and immediately lowered and extended his head while letting out a growling hiss. The man backed away a few steps.

"Easy, Nok," Leepoh told his friend.

"I hate them—all of them," Nok replied, watching the human carefully.

"I know. We'll be here for only a little while. All right?"

Nok gathered his composure. "Not all right. Only a little right, and only for you."

"You know, you're starting to sound familiar," Leepoh joked.

"Bah!" Nok responded to mock the Gentoo.

"If you two are done, you should get on with your questions for the human," Lavour interjected.

"Oh, lighten up, Lavour," Leepoh chided him.

"I'm light. I'm just a little nervous," said Lavour, defending himself.

Randy stood in front of the threesome. Not sure of what to make of them, he decided to sit down to make himself appear less threatening.

"You see," Leepoh said to Nok, "this one isn't like the others."

"Maybe, or maybe it just knows it's trapped here and there's nothing it can do *except* act submissive," Nok replied doubtfully.

Leepoh stared at Nok. "You sure said a beakful there."

Nok looked away in exasperation.

"Anyhow, let's find out what kind of human he is. *Hola, humano, saludos*," Leepoh said, turning to Randy.

Randy looked at Leepoh in disbelief and began to laugh. "You speak Spanish? We're going to have some trouble communicating because I hardly speak a word of it—at least nothing appropriate."

Leepoh looked at his companions in mock chagrin. "Wrong language," he said sheepishly and turned back to Randy. "Hello."

"Hello. I don't know what to say." He was caught off guard once again by the penguin's intellect. It was one thing for them to know how to speak one human language, but two was totally unexpected and left him flabbergasted once again. "My name is Randy. What's yours?"

"I am Leepoh."

Randy was curious about their ranks but didn't want them asking any questions about how he found out they had ranks. "And the others?"

"This is Nok and this is . . ."

"Chinstrap!" an elite guard barked from outside the door. "The Supreme Commander demands your presence at once."

"Do you have no manners?" Leepoh reprimanded the guard, which induced an angry glare.

"Now?" asked Lavour incredulously. "I am in the middle of something very important."

"His orders are not debatable."

"Very well," Lavour gave in, knowing he didn't have an option.

"Can't this wait?" Nok asked Lavour, figuring the more penguins present the better.

"I'm sorry, but no. It is not wise to upset the Supreme Commander. I'll find you later. If not, find me," he said, looking at Leepoh and holding his look a few seconds longer than necessary in hopes that Leepoh would catch his meaning.

Leepoh held his stare. "Don't worry. Of course we'll find you."

"Where is the Supreme Commander?" Lavour asked for the benefit of Leepoh.

"In the main hall," the guard snapped.

With that said, Lavour took his leave.

"What was all that about?" Nok asked Leepoh.

"I don't know for sure." Leepoh turned his attention back to Randy. "Well, Randy, this is quite a predicament you've found yourself in."

"I didn't find it. It found me."

Leepoh took a second to digest Randy's sarcasm. "Hah! I like it already. We'll be fine, my antsy friend," he said, turning to Nok then back to Randy. "So, tell me, how did you come to be here?"

Randy looked at the Gentoo, pondering his motives. "I don't know exactly. I was taking some photos when a group of Emperor and Kings . . ."

"Wait a moment, please," Leepoh said, stopping him. "You'll have to pardon me. My human is only so good. What are photos, and how or why would you take them?"

Randy took a breath and then went into a lengthy explanation about photography. All the while Captain Nok stood at the ready—just in case the human should try something. He was oblivious to their conversation, not having taken the time to learn the human language.

"Amazing. Have you taken these photos other places as well?" Leepoh said, sounding enthralled at Randy's explanation.

"Yes, I've been to a couple of islands to photograph penguins over the past several years. As a matter of fact, I photographed Gentoo at both islands I've been to." Gesturing toward Nok, Randy added, "One had his kind as well."

"You see? This *is* the human I saw before," Leepoh said, turning to Nok excitedly.

"How can you say that for sure? And no, I don't see. I only hear a bunch of babbling gibberish," Nok replied angrily.

"Sorry, I forgot you are linguistically challenged. But he is the one I saw at our home." Leepoh stopped and got a faraway look. "And once before that, I believe." He turned his attention back to Randy. "I've seen you before, at our home, and now I find you here. How do we know you're not here to do us harm?"

"Are you from the Gentoo colony that nests in burrows?"

"Yes, but you didn't answer my question."

"Oh no, I would never harm a penguin." Randy thought about his attackers. "Well, not unless I was defending myself. I do apologize for that, however. Even through all of this, I feel terrible about what happened, but they did attack me."

Leepoh's demeanor had changed after hearing that Randy had visited more than one Gentoo colony, and he began talking in a more direct manner to the man. "That was unfortunate. But humans are not to be trusted. And as you humans say, 'as a matter of fact,' not long ago a large number of humans came to our island and killed several of my friend's kind." He indicated Nok with his flipper.

"When you say 'several,' how many do you mean?" Randy asked, afraid of the answer.

Leepoh studied Randy for a minute before answering. "A hundred or more," he said.

Randy's shoulders slumped in remorse for the Rockhoppers and for what could be a lost opportunity to build an interspecies relationship. "I am truly sorry," he said, looking at Nok.

"Why do you apologize? Did you have something to do with it?"

"No," Randy said resoundingly. "I'm sorry for his loss and for the fact that there are those of my kind who would commit such an atrocious act."

Leepoh looked at Randy long and hard. He knew in himself that humans were no longer the only beings capable of such a deed. "Don't worry. I don't think they will be troubling us again."

"What do you mean?" Randy asked suspiciously, getting a sudden uneasy feeling from the way the Gentoo spoke.

Leepoh didn't bother to explain. "Thank you for our talk. It was enlightening. I must be leaving now." He turned to leave. "Come on, Nok. I'm through here."

"Wait!" Randy said, trying to stop them. "What about me? When can I leave?"

Leepoh turned back to him. "I'm sorry. I truly am. But that is not my decision to make."

"But can't you do something?"

The closing door cut off his question.

CHAPTER 33

Lavour stomped down the corridor, slapping his webbed feet against the icy floor with emphasis. He was inwardly fuming at being called from his meeting with the human. But such was life under the command of Liutites, whose orders were to be acted upon immediately and without deviation. Deep down inside the Chinstrap, a tiny spark of resentment and anger had been ignited. It was a spark that, if left unchecked, might burst into a fiery hatred. He saw Supreme Commander Liutites standing at the end of the corridor, waiting for him. Liutites stood there, so grandiose, so smug. The tiny spark grew into a glowing ember.

"Supreme Commander, Lieutenant-General Lavour reporting as ordered, sir," he snapped out as he approached.

Liutites eyed Lavour, saying nothing, letting the tense silence hang in the air before responding. "Lieutenant-General, prompt as always."

"Yes, sir," Lavour said with a touch of defiance.

The Supreme Commander watched Lavour for a second longer. "Go and tell Lieutenant Trevot that he has been permanently reassigned to Forward Command One under the direct command of General Diutes and he is to report to him immediately."

Lavour was taken aback by the order. "Now?" he asked, putting aside all pretense of formality.

"Yes, Lieutenant-General. Diutes awaits his arrival at the main exit."

"But sir, Lieutenant Trevot has only just returned from extended messenger service."

"Those are my orders, Chinstrap."

Lavour was desperate to prevent him from leaving. He knew something was amiss. "I understand, sir. It is just that I fear he is not properly rested and will not be of proper service to General Diutes."

"Are you questioning my wisdom, Lieutenant-General?" Liutites asked, the menace in his voice apparent. "Perhaps you would like to take his place or join him?"

Lavour stared at Liutites. He was not questioning his wisdom but his motives. "No, sir. Has General Devét been informed?"

"Of course he has," Liutites answered with a touch of twisted amusement.

"Then why didn't General Devét inform him? Surely he . . ."

"Because I ordered *you* to do it. General Devét is far too busy to be bothered with such trivial matters."

"But . . ."

"That is all!" Liutites snapped. "General Diutes awaits. Further delay is unacceptable. You are dismissed, *Chinstrap*," he snarled, saying the name as if it were beneath him to speak it.

"Yes, sir," Lavour said as he huffed away.

The glowing ember grew.

ΛΛΛ

When Lavour returned to the Chinstrap quarters, he was not greeted by the customary calls, as the entire group was asleep. His heart was heavy with worry for Trevot. That was obviously the Supreme Commander's intended effect. He thought about the conversation between Mevoule and Trevot and about Trevot's displeasure with the direction of the PDA and wondered if, perhaps, somebody had overheard that conversation. If so, who was it and how? It was plain as the beak on his face as to who it was. The question was how had he found out. He looked at Trevot as he slept and knew he couldn't put this off any longer.

He made his way to Trevot, let out a deep sigh, and woke him. "Lieutenant Trevot."

Trevot opened his eyes with a start. "Lavour? What is it, sir? Is everything all right?"

Lavour looked at his friend with concern, wanting to do anything other than tell him. "I'm afraid I have some bad news, my friend."

"What is it?" Trevot asked, fearing the worst.

"The Supreme Commander has reassigned you to Forward Command One, permanently."

"What? Why?"

"I don't know for certain, but General Diutes is waiting for you right now."

"What do you mean? I have to go right *now*? But I've only just returned." Trevot was livid and for good reason. It was customary to give messengers a few weeks off from service before giving them another assignment.

"I know. I strongly disagreed, but there was nothing I could do."

"This is unacceptable. Why me, when there are a hundred others who could go?" Trevot fumed on, causing a stir among the sleeping Chinstraps.

"I'm sorry, Trevot," Lavour told him sincerely.

Trevot took a breath, trying to calm down. "I know you are. It's not like we have much of a choice anymore. Please do me a favor and lodge a complaint with General Devét."

"I intend to. Before you go, however, I have instructions that are to be kept between you and me only. Is that understood?" Lavour said quietly. "Do not speak any disagreement out loud."

Trevot looked at him intently. "Do you think our conversation today had anything to do with this?"

"It might have, but I don't know for sure. If anything should happen to make you feel threatened in any way, by anyone, return to our nesting grounds. Do not hesitate. Do not return to PIC. Go home and stay there. Do you understand?"

Trevot held Lavour's eyes. "Yes. You're making me feel uneasy about this reassignment."

"I feel the same way. Just remember what I told you."

"I will. I would have liked to have been able to see the Great Gathering though. Tell me about it when we meet again."

"I will. You'd better get going, and be safe." Lavour watched Trevot leave and worried about his friend. Something wasn't right. There were too many strange things happening. It couldn't be mere coincidence. His thoughts drifted to Corporal Meuseaux, and he began to worry even more.

^^^

"You can come out now." Randy turned the drum around to expose Meuseaux's hidey-hole.

The Chinstrap poked his head out for a quick check.

"Don't worry, they're gone," Randy reassured him.

"Caution does not cause harm."

"That's true. It doesn't," he said, chuckling at the penguin's sensibility. "Do you know the others who came to see me?"

"Not all. They are newcomers, I believe."

"What about the Chinstrap?"

"Yes, I believe it wass Lieutenant-General Lavour."

"Do you think he knows about your situation?"

"I assume he knows I gone. Not probably how much."

It took Randy's tired mind a minute to process the penguin's jumbled speech.

"Lavour is a good. He could help if he knew," Meuseaux added.

"Help you or me?"

"Us, maybe. He iss, well . . ." Meuseaux searched for the word. "Respected among my kind, although he iss not up on the command."

"Well, then there is hope for both of us, my friend," Randy said as he pulled himself up from a crate. He looked at his watch. It was 12:15 a.m. He had been awake since 4:30 a.m. the previous morning, and the fatigue was pulling heavily on him. He lit his lighter and watched it flicker to make sure there was a draft, and there was, so he knew there was ventilation for his fire. He pulled a lidless drum to him, threw the pieces of the crate into the bottom, and started his life-saving fire. He un-rumpled the old tent, wrapped himself in the Union Jack, and lay down. He looked at the penguin, who was watching him curiously.

"I am with question. Are you true in ssaying you my friend?" Meuseaux asked in his odd way of speaking.

Randy smiled at the bird warmly. "Yes, I am. Though I'm afraid if I don't find a way out of here, I won't be alive long enough to build on that friendship." He smiled inwardly at finding this unexpected ally, pondered his future, and slipped into a troubled sleep.

CHAPTER 34

"These pictures are incredible," Dan said, sounding astonished. "Have you ever seen anything like this?" he asked Davis, who was sitting next him.

"No. But that's not what I do, is it?" Davis answered, disinterested and in his usual unpleasant manner.

"Randy was just as surprised," Gina answered before anyone could ask. "He was so completely amazed by what he saw. That was why he wanted to film this." She briefly stopped talking, not wanting to relive the events.

"This is something completely unheard of, then?" Dan asked her, exchanging looks with the others.

"As far as I know. Some of those penguins are from New Zealand, so it's really odd."

After a moment of consideration, Dan looked at the others. "Who all knows about this?"

"Just us . . . and Lawrence. I don't think David or Ron knows yet," Jack Freeman said.

"Okay, then," Dan said. "We need to sign a non-disclosure. Nobody outside of the base knows about this. Understand?"

"Wait a second. Don't we want people to know about this?" Gina asked, surprised. "I mean if there's something affecting an entire species, we should let people know."

"That's exactly why we shouldn't let anyone know. This could be GT's break. If GT gets credit for the discovery, it would mean a lot more funding."

"But we don't know the reason for this yet. There's a lot of research to be done," said Gina.

"I know, but this is *our* discovery, and *we'll* be the ones to do that research," Dan said.

"That is why we're here, I guess," Gina said with her thoughts focused elsewhere. She knew Randy would have loved to be part of that research, and the thought made her heart ache. Dan and Davis exchanged looks, and this didn't escape her notice. "What?"

Dan looked at Davis and Jack and then sighed and looked at Gina. "Gina, as you know, the ship will be leaving in a few days."

"I know that," she said suspiciously.

"This isn't easy." He paused as Gina watched him. "Gina, you're going to have to be on that ship."

"What? That's ridiculous! Who's going to do my research? And with Randy still out there, I'm not leaving," she said defiantly.

"We'll still be searching for the next couple of days. We've already contacted the American and French stations, and they'll be aiding in our search. But realistically—if we don't find him in the next twenty-four hours it's probably too late. Hell, it's probably too late now. You know that. I'm sorry, Gina, but you broke protocol, a rule that you signed and agreed to before you came here."

"I know, but . . ."

"There are no buts," Lawrence said, walking into the room. "I've already talked to Vance Lyons back home. It was his decision."

"You can't just fire me, Lawrence. Besides that, what would you have done if it was already winter and the ship had left?"

"We would have flown you out. If you leave now without any problems and sign the non-disclosure agreement, your name will still go on the discovery. Believe me, I don't like this any more than you do. With the loss of Randy and now you, we'll be down two people on an already small team."

"This is unbelievable. I can't just *leave* with him still missing," Gina said pleadingly.

"I'm sorry, Gina, but the decision is final. There have been accidents on other expeditions. We can't take chances. We'll still be searching, and if we find him after you've gone, we'll let you know. His loss affects us all and not just personally. There's the lost research you were supposed to do. I had to argue with Vance to keep him from pulling the plug on us completely. Hopefully this discovery will make up for it."

Gina looked at Dan, then Jack, who turned away. She looked at Davis, who met her eyes with a non-committal stare. "He asked me to come back."

"I know. He took a chance. You took a chance, and we all lost," Lawrence told her.

"I'm sorry," Gina said while trying to keep her emotions from welling up. She looked at Dan and then left the room.

Once he heard her door slam shut, Dan looked at Davis. "Make sure she's on that ship one way or another. We can't afford any more trouble."

CHAPTER 35

All of the penguins awoke to the sound of shrill calls that echoed throughout Pack Ice Command. *The Great Gathering will commence today*, the message said.

Lavour ruffled his tail feathers in an attempt to wake up before General Devét approached.

"Lavour, the day is upon us. All of the clans have arrived, and the assembly will take place in four hours in the grand auditorium," Devét said without preamble.

"Yes, sir. This is quite exciting. I have never encountered most of these clans," Lavour said, trying to sound enthusiastic. But in the back of his mind, his thoughts were already on Trevot *and* Meuseaux.

"It's more than that," Devét said without elaboration. "Make sure everyone is assembled in time for the gathering. I have some business to attend to with the Adélie general." Devét rushed off without returning Lavour's waiting salute.

Lavour called on Mevoule and delegated some of the duties to him. At the end of the discussion, Mevoule asked about Trevot. "Who decided he should go to Forward Command?"

"The orders came straight from Supreme Commander Liutites himself," Lavour informed him, disgusted.

"Well, maybe it'll do him some good," Mevoule said, looking at Lavour out of the corner of his eye as he turned his head away.

"Good? It's not good, Captain," Lavour snapped back, noticeably using Mevoule's rank instead of his name. "Trevot had just returned from extended messaging duty and needed the rest. I fear for both his health and safety at Forward Command."

"I apologize, sir. All I meant was he has been a bit outspoken on certain issues as of late and has not been very sensitive of the Rockhoppers' troubles. Therefore, the assignment to General Diutes might instill some discipline."

Lavour couldn't believe what he was hearing. It was as if his friend was purposely trying to bait him into disagreeing, and despite this, Lavour took the bait. "What has gotten into you, Mevoule? You know Trevot is as dedicated to the PDA and to all penguins as anyone. And if there *were* discipline issues, it would've been up to me to deal with them. My loyalty is to the Chinstraps under my command and then the PDA, in that order. If they needed more bodies, they should have sent the Adélies. We are being taxed enough as it is. We are not servants to the Royal Emperors."

Captain Mevoule was stunned by Lavour's rant. "That kind of talk could get you into trouble around here. You know that, don't you?" he asked as he looked around for dramatic effect.

"I know." Lavour stopped himself from saying any more. He was no longer sure he could trust Mevoule. "I don't know," he said more calmly. "It's just that we missed the breeding season, and we haven't been off duty in so long. Plus, Meuseaux is still missing."

"Corporal Meuseaux had a tendency to mess things up a bit. He probably just got lost. Or maybe he, too, got reassigned, and nobody gave us the message."

"Maybe, but I doubt it. He's been missing far too long to have just gotten lost, and I'm sure somebody would have told us if he had been reassigned. I am still in charge of duty assignments, regardless of recent events."

"Oh, or maybe Lord Saeson snatched him up for a meal," Mevoule joked.

"That's not funny. It could've happened."

"Sir, if you don't mind my saying so, you worry way too much."

"Actually, I do mind you saying so. But, I seem to be hearing that a lot lately," Lavour said. "However, there's a difference between concern and worry."

"Well, concern *or* worry, you needn't do either. We're part of the Penguin Defense Alliance, and with us all united, there's nothing we can't accomplish, including finding Meuseaux," Mevoule told him proudly.

"What are we defending ourselves from?" Lavour asked absently, thinking about Trevot's reassignment.

"From anything or any threat," Mevoule answered, reciting a mantra he learned in his indoctrination. "Look what the Rockhoppers accomplished, initially without the aid of the Gentoo."

Hearing Mevoule mention the two penguin clans caused Lavour's mind to switch to the human captive. "And what if the threat comes from within?"

"What do you mean?" Mevoule asked him suspiciously.

With a heavy heart, Lavour looked at his oldest friend. "Nothing. I have to take care of a few things—make sure everyone is preened and in good order in time for the gathering. I'll be back."

Mevoule watched Lavour leave with a strange look of satisfaction in his eyes, and then he turned his focus to his duties.

Lavour meandered through the bustling corridors, troubled by Mevoule's attitude of intolerance. It all seemed very imperial to him. *Maybe that's the way things are now in the PDA,* Lavour thought. *Maybe I'm falling behind in my way of thinking, or maybe I just need to take a break and go home.*

ΛΛΛ

"There's enough food here to eat for a month!" Leepoh said enthusiastically, hopping in front of a trough carved from the ice walls and filled to capacity with squid, small fish, and assorted other penguin delicacies.

"Do you mean for everybody or just you?" Nok asked, slurping down a squid.

"Hah!" Leepoh laughed after swallowing a fish. "You're not one to talk, my plume-headed friend. You're eating like you have a dozen hatchlings to feed."

Nok's tail feathers bristled with indignation. "I haven't had a meal in some time. I'm accustomed to catching my own food. A penguin sure could get used to this."

"Just be glad you didn't have to catch all of this."

Leepoh and Nok looked at each other and shared a laugh at the expense of PIC's food gatherers.

"You seem to be enjoying your meal a little *too* much," a familiar voice said from behind them.

The two turned around to find Lavour.

"Gesh ish qui diyishous," Leepoh said indecipherably through a beak full of fish.

Lavour shook his head at Leepoh and then snapped up a couple of icefish. "How did your meeting with the human go last night?" he asked after swallowing.

"Good and bad, I suppose," Leepoh said and then grabbed another squid in his beak. "The good is that I was right about its being the one from the island. The bad is that it *is* the one from the island."

Lavour looked at Leepoh blankly and then, for clarification, to Nok, who just threw up his flippers, indicating he didn't know.

The Gentoo decided to elaborate. "What I mean is, although I don't get the impression it intended to do us harm, it seems more than coincidental that I should find him both there and here."

"So do you think it's a spy or a scout?"

"I don't know. Could be. I mean we've all been told for so long to distrust humans, and from what I've seen, I more than agree. It's just unfortunate that the truly innocent get caught in the middle. Even if the human is guiltless of any subversion, the result of its being here will be the same—death."

"Were any of us less innocent?" Nok put in.

"No. It's just that, if these rumors and rumblings are true," Leepoh said, looking at Lavour. "Neither side will be innocent."

Lavour stared at Leepoh. "So what did *you* hear?"

"Probably the same things you have," he answered as he grabbed another squid. "That there might be some kind of push to keep the humans away from our territories."

"That's outstanding!" Nok chimed in again. "Now it won't be only one colony defending itself from the humans. Look what *we* did. Now, imagine with twenty or more colonies standing together. The humans would be out of their minds to try to occupy any of our nesting grounds. And as far as this one human being innocent, that may very well be. But when I witnessed my parents being murdered by those rancid beasts, my innocence died with them. My good friend Cort did nothing to them, and I looked in his eyes as I watched him die, killed by one of those creatures. I would've been killed myself had fate or luck not intervened. So if this one supposedly *innocent* human *is* killed, it's only because its entire species is guilty of atrocities most of us could not imagine."

Lavour and Leepoh stared at Nok with their beaks agape, shocked by his lengthy spiel.

"You are right, of course," Leepoh finally said. "It really is a shame though. It seems this human genuinely wanted to establish communication with us. But I have tasted the bitterness of their blood, and I am sure that before my life ends, I will taste it again."

Lavour looked at Leepoh and Nok silently, while thinking back to his conversation with Mevoule. He began to think that maybe Mevoule was right in saying Trevot wasn't sensitive to what the Rockhoppers had faced, and perhaps he was guilty of the same insensitivity. "I apologize to the both of you. I shouldn't sound like I'm against any kind of military push, especially since I haven't gone through what you have."

"You haven't said anything of the sort," Leepoh said.

"But I was thinking it," Lavour admitted.

"Don't fret, my friend," Leepoh said before Nok could snap a moody retort. "Nobody ever wants to experience what we have. We had to. The choice was made for us. Besides, you and all of us may experience the same thing before long."

"That's what I fear," Lavour said solemnly.

"Speaking of things to come, I have a meeting with some of the other generals before the gathering begins. So, if you will excuse me, we'll get together after the gathering," Leepoh said, plucking yet another squid from the trough as he left.

Lavour and Nok looked at each other, both feeling a little awkward without their mutual and very vocal friend.

Captain Nok finally broke the silence. "Don't feel bad, Lavour. If I had to do it all over again . . . Well, I'd do it, but I still wouldn't want to. You have to remember, to us Rockhoppers, the humans have been exceptionally brutal and ruthless. We have suffered much because of them. In my opinion, they got what they deserved."

Lavour looked at Nok with a new respect. He felt sorry for the suffering he had endured and felt like his own troubles were trivial by comparison. "You know, Captain, I like you. I hope that, after you leave here, I can find the time to pay you a visit. I would like to see your home. And who knows, maybe even say hi to that Gentoo."

Nok snorted derisively. "If you're so desperate for a friend as to visit him, you're welcome to it."

Lavour nodded in agreement. "I'll walk with you back to your quarters, and you can tell me the parts he left out about the visit."

Nok didn't object, seeming to be happy to have a guide through the maze of corridors in Pack Ice Command.

^^^

"General Leepoh, good of you to join us," a King penguin, General Manes, said derisively when Leepoh entered the chamber of commanders.

"General Manes, good of you to notice," Leepoh bit back in response.

"General Leepoh, before you arrived we just received confirmation from the Supreme Commander that, at the gathering, the Overlord is expected to announce that we will indeed begin a push to remove the humans from our territories," General Devét informed him.

Leepoh nodded his head as if he already knew. "Does this mean *everyone's* territory or just the Royal Emperors'?"

The statement caused a rustle among the birds and an exchange of capricious glances.

"Everyone's, of course," the Adélie, General Kuyuki, said after calm returned. "But from what we have been informed, the push *will* begin here."

"We'll know more after the Overlord makes his announcement," General Butiewy of the Blackfoot penguins added.

"If you had been here when you were *supposed* to be, we wouldn't have to be going over this again," Manes admonished Leepoh.

"Bah!" Leepoh blurted out while looking at his newfound antagonist. "With a belly full of fish and squid, I'm *supposed* to be at the latrine. Instead, I'm here listening to you blabber on. And let me tell you, the company is comparable."

"General Leepoh!" Manes barked out. "We are at a pivotal point in the history of all penguins. I would hope you would take this a little more seriously."

"Perhaps I should, General Manes, but it appears we are approaching a time when we will know nothing but seriousness. And until that time, I shall enjoy the lack thereof."

Manes shook his head in exasperation.

General Khik of the Rockhoppers spoke up. "I suggest this meeting be adjourned so we can prepare for the Great Gathering."

The others concurred and began to file out of the chamber.

Leepoh stood back, watching them pass through the exit. General Manes stepped in front of him. "General Leepoh, I understand some of what you went through on RHC 23. I lost one of my Kings during the capture of the human, but we need to stand together in this endeavor."

"Bah!" Leepoh exclaimed indignantly. "First off, I am sorry for the loss of the penguin. Second off, you have yet to see anything close to the carnage I witnessed on that island. Third off, you don't need to tell *me* about solidarity. Fourth off, standing together does not mean that we no longer have our individuality and identity. Fifth off, with that said, the latrine awaits me. And I am sure it will give me a warmer welcome than the one you accorded me."

A couple of other penguin generals snickered at Leepoh's comments as he walked off haughtily. Manes growled in frustration.

CHAPTER 36

Supreme Commander Liutites waddled up a sloped, curving corridor at the end of which was the entrance to the Imperial rookery. This was where the Royal Emperor chicks were hatched and fledged. Here, they were free from the struggle for survival on the ice fields that confronted their common Emperor cousins. Here as well, the chicks were raised and nurtured by the females alone. Unlike the "feral" Emperors, as the Royals called them, most of the chicks survived. After they reached six months of age, the chicks were put through a process of role searching and development.

First, the chicks were separated between male and female. The females were taken to a separate chamber where they were instructed in chick rearing and survival skills. The Royal Emperor Commanders assessed the males, however. The commanders judged them by their particular characteristics and decided in which manner they would best serve—whether it would be as an officer, a warrior, an elite guard, or something else entirely.

This day, Liutites was to give the final assessment of a group of three-year-olds who had just returned from a nearly two-year trial at sea. A formation of almost three hundred fifty Royal Emperor penguins stood motionless, their beaks held high in salute, awaiting the Supreme Commander's inspection. As Liutites passed through the lines of penguins, he was shadowed by four other commanders and two females. The females, by imperial regulations, were forbidden to hold rank.

At the conclusion of the inspection, one of the females approached Liutites. "What is your opinion, Supreme Commander?"

"You have done well, Mearna, as expected," he answered with a trace of unusual kindness in his voice.

Mearna puffed out her chest in a gesture of pride. Emperor penguins are usually indistinguishable between the sexes, but Mearna and the other Royal Emperor females had subtle white patches behind the eyes, giving them a somewhat softer appearance. "Thank you, Supreme Commander. Your praise is appreciated. Though, to be honest, the Overlord's offspring are natural leaders, which makes my tasks much easier and your decisions more difficult."

"Yes," Liutites said in a tone that could be interpreted as disgust or even jealousy. "Though I fear that this group's swimming abilities may be somewhat hampered by their more prodigious hands."

"Possibly, but they did survive the trials. Outside of that, the ancient Royal bloodline will be all the better equipped to fight our enemies."

"True," Liutites said while studying Mearna. "How are the other females proceeding with the weaponry?"

"All warriors will be equipped by tomorrow as planned."

"Good, good. Has there been any information on the missing Chinstrap? Has he come back here for a second look?"

"I doubt that even a Chinstrap would be fool enough to do that. Although with his flipper broken, I doubt that he would have left PIC. Have you checked the Chinstrap quarters? They may be attempting to hide him."

"Yes I have, and they're not hiding him. They do know that he is missing, however. And we can't interrogate the others without letting *them* know that *we* know he is missing. He was to be the final sacrifice to the Phocids before we spring our trap. And he knew where he was headed, making it all the more imperative that we find him."

"It's been a moon's time since he disappeared. Don't worry. I'm sure he's either dead or gone by now," she said, looking away from his hardened glare.

"Do I sound worried?" Liutites lashed out. "I am concerned—concerned that one insignificant Chinstrap managed to escape the elite guards unaided."

"Are you suggesting he had an accomplice to assist him in his escape?" Mearna asked with a touch of concern of her own.

"It's difficult to say. I think he was just fortunate, that's all. The elite guards overseeing him were our hatchlings and are unswerving in their loyalty." Liutites paused, watching Mearna then changed the subject. "The attack on the Phocids is crucial to the Overlord's plans, and it will take place as scheduled. If the Chinstrap is not found, we will have to find a suitable replacement."

"You sound like you already have one picked out."

"Several, but they are, for the time, unobtainable. It's our good fortune that there happens to be plenty of strangers in Pack Ice Command, and one or two of them just might have to become lost. I don't want to arouse any more suspicion among the Chinstraps."

"Shall I instruct the Kings to find one?"

"No," Liutites answered quickly. "Leave them out of it from this point on. If it becomes necessary, my personal guards will find one."

The two looked around the chamber and then back to each other, bowed their heads together affectionately, and exchanged the subtle clicking noises of their language.

"I must go and prepare for the gathering," Liutites said as he straightened up. "The human captive is to be put on exhibition during the event, and I want to make sure it is placid enough for display. Mearna," he said, nodding to her as he left.

"Liutites," she said back. Once she was sure that he had gone, she hurried into her personal chamber room.

CHAPTER 37

Lieutenant-General Lavour arrived back at Chinstrap quarters just as Captain Mevoule was lining up the penguins for final inspection. "Well done as always," Lavour told him.

"Thank you," Mevoule said, somewhat surprised by Lavour's chipper tone.

"Everything appears to be in order. Has General Devét been informed?"

"Yes, sir. Once he is ready, we will go to the auditorium."

"Good," Lavour said with a noticeable spryness in his voice as he overlooked the Chinstrap formation.

Mevoule took all he could of Lavour's changed demeanor and had to say something. "If you don't mind my saying, you seem to be in better spirits."

"Oh, that," Lavour said as if it were nothing. "I guess I just adjusted my thinking a bit. Maybe you were right."

Mevoule gave him a befuddled look. "And when did you come to this realization?"

"You said Trevot may have been insensitive to the plight of others. I still don't think he should have been reassigned. That was uncalled for. But after talking to some of the other members of the PDA, I realized just how fortunate we have been."

"How so?" asked Mevoule.

"Well, sure, we have lost some of our nesting grounds to the humans, but we have never really known the type of persecution others have had to endure—at least not on the same scale and definitely not in recent memory. So maybe it's time to bring that persecution of our comrades, our brothers and sisters, to an end."

"That's an interesting change of opinion, my friend."

"Just trying to keep up, I guess."

"I was wondering. You said you overheard something at Forward Command, something that bothered you when you were talking about Meuseaux. What was it?" Mevoule asked.

"Just talk," he said, once again uncertain of his friend's motives.

"What kind of talk?"

Lavour sighed, trying desperately to keep up his new enthusiastic attitude, but he was curious to see where this would lead. "Once, when I was going about my duties there, I overheard General Diutes mention something under his breath to a King that didn't seem right."

Mevoule waited for him to continue.

"I was a couple of meters away, so I couldn't hear it all," Lavour continued with trepidation. "They were talking about disciplining an Adélie and said something about giving him to the Phocids. When they caught sight of me, they quickly changed the subject."

Mevoule looked at him in silence for a moment. "They wouldn't do anything so barbaric, would they? I mean even General Diutes has limits to his madness," Mevoule said.

A shrill noise echoed throughout Pack Ice Command, ending any further discussion.

"That's it," Lavour said, happy to end the conversation. "The gathering is about to begin. Let's get everyone moving."

"Yes, sir," Captain Mevoule said as Lavour rushed to the head of the lines to join General Devét.

"All right, Chinstraps," announced Lavour. "Two columns. Complete silence. Move out!"

The two lines of Chinstraps snapped their heads in a unified salute and began to march to the Grand Auditorium for the Great Gathering of the clans.

CHAPTER 38

The Grand Auditorium was filled with representatives of nearly every penguin species on Earth.

The crested penguins—consisting of the Rockhoppers, the Macaroni, the Fiordland, the Snares Island, the Erect Crested, and the Royal Crested—occupied one side of the expansive room. Their bright yellow and orange head plumes, gave them the appearance of a field of spring flowers. On the opposite side were the Chinstraps, the Gentoo, the Blackfoot, the Adélie, the Magellanics, and a small contingent of the nearly extinct Yellow-eyed and Humboldt penguins. In the center were the Emperor and King penguins.

Not present were the Galapagos penguins, which could not brave the harsh conditions. The Overlord and Supreme Commander's servants, the Blue penguins, were absent but never too far away. Surrounding the crowd were one hundred elite Royal Emperor guards. They stood silent, motionless, and ever ready should they be required.

The Grand Auditorium was permeated with the azure glow common to PIC. Its ovoid ceiling demonstrated the unique design of penguin architecture. At the forefront was a large stage, which held the anticipatory attention of the multitudes. From center stage, the entire crowd could be seen. From the back of the Great Auditorium, rows of steps tapered downward toward the stage in stadium-like seating, to give each spectator a perfect view.

The mass of penguins grew silent when ten elite guards filed onto the stage and positioned themselves five to each side. Two additional guards came on stage, pushing a three-foot square block of ice. After positioning the block center stage, they joined the others.

The entire auditorium grew still. A door began to open at the rear of the stage. The seams of the doorway were barely visible as it slowly ground open to reveal a purple mist that emanated from the darkness beyond.

The block of ice suddenly exploded as gunfire flashed from behind it. In the wake of the heart-stopping blast, the Overlord slowly meandered through the darkened doorway, holding the still-smoking gun. He stood at center stage and waited for the nervous chatter to die down. Once silence returned, he gazed at the mass of penguins and held up the weapon. "This is the primary weapon of our enemy!" he bellowed. "It is called a gun. Some of you know its destructive power," he said, looking at the Rockhoppers. "Some of you will."

An elite guard came to his side and carefully took the weapon away. The Overlord observed the crowd in silence and let them draw their own conclusions about his statement.

"I welcome you to Pack Ice Command. I am Overlord Antaean." His voice echoed throughout the auditorium in a preternatural fashion. "For those of you who are unaware, I am descended from the ancient bloodline of Royal Emperor penguins."

The announcement caused a stir among the gathering. Lavour looked to the Gentoo and caught the eye of Leepoh, who gave him a dubious look.

"For over a thousand years the ancient bloodline has lain dormant, only to be reborn in this time of great peril and threat to penguin kind." The crowd rustled once more, but the Overlord continued. "Five hundred generations ago, the Ancients brought together clans to meet a threat to our survival during a period known to some of you as The Great Auk War. We were victorious against our adversary, and our seas and breeding grounds were secured. But now we face a new and more immediate threat to our survival—the humans!" he said with theatrical flair.

"The humans have wiped our ancient nemesis, the Great Auk, from the face of the Earth—rendering them extinct and relegating them to only a distant memory." His voice trailed away, and he bowed his head as if mourning the memory of a long-deceased friend. He paused overdramatically to let what he said sink into the minds of the assembly.

"The humans have been coming to our homes for nearly two hundred years. Many of our kind in the more northern regions have been brought to the edge of extinction. During this time, the humans have murdered hundreds of thousands, if not millions of us, in what can be described only as an attempt at genocide. They have taken us as food for themselves and for their servant beasts, the canines. They have killed us for trophies or for other obscene purposes, and they have even taken the guano on which many penguins depend for nesting. They have also taken our unborn for food. The humans are as loathsome as the Petrels. And in a most hideous act, they have used our bodies as fuel to power their flames."

A steady murmur of anger arose from the crowd, and Overlord Antaean watched the penguins' reaction with satisfaction. "Now the time of unification is upon us once again, as we have brought together all of the penguin clans of the world," he said into the again silent crowd. "The Emperors, the Kings, the Adélie, the Chinstraps, the Gentoo, the Magellanic, the Humboldt, the Blackfeet, the . . ."

"Blackfoot!" a particularly stout Blackfoot, also known as Jackass penguin, shouted imprudently.

The Overlord paused and then looked to one of the elite guards. The guard nodded then went to the offender, dragging him from the auditorium. Antaean gazed at the crowd and continued, "The Rockhoppers, the Macaroni, the Snares Island, the Erect Crested, the Fiordland, the Royal Crested, and the Yellow-eyed are here standing as one. Unfortunately, the Galapagos clan was unable to send representatives, but I have their assurance that they are united with us and will support and aid us in our endeavors."

"The attacks on our lives and our way of life are unacceptable. For those of us who nest here, where the humans scarcely tread, the threat is growing. The humans are coming here in greater numbers. Every year more and more come, and I have learned of a plan for a more permanent occupation on their part. It will be only a matter of time before they begin to persecute us here once again. This is the last great sanctuary of our kind, before we are all driven to extinction."

The Overlord stopped his speech and looked to his left. Supreme Commander Liutites came forward, followed by four elite guards. Behind the four guards, ten more followed, escorting the human prisoner to the stage. The presence of the prisoner drew a collective gasp from the surprised audience. The Overlord stared at his captive in a malevolent sneer.

Randy scanned the gathering, bewildered by what he saw. The strange assemblage reminded him of historical films in which a tyrannical dictator addressed an audience of fanatical followers. After being abruptly, and none too gently, awakened, he had been taken to an antechamber of the theater, and he'd had the opportunity to listen to the indecipherable torrent of clicks, whirs, and caws the Overlord communicated to the crowd.

On his way to the auditorium, the guards roughed him up to ensure his passivity. Liutites had made it perfectly clear that, if he made so much as one wrong move, he would be stripped of his clothing and thrown outside. There he would have just enough time to think about his inability to follow instructions before he froze to death. Randy harbored no doubt that the threats were not empty.

"Look here," Overlord Antaean commanded after the buzz of the multitudes died down. "This is the face of your enemy. It is an enemy that is deceptive, brutal and ruthless in its very nature. It possesses weapons of unimaginable power, and it will not hesitate to use these terrible weapons against us. But the humans are not invincible. They bleed the same as every living creature, and they can be destroyed."

"So I say to you now, my fellow penguins, that we, united as one in the Penguin Defense Alliance, shall cast these humans from our homes. We will not stand by as these murderous and treacherous beasts eliminate us from this world. We will not let them do to us as they did to the Great Auks. We will reclaim our seas and nesting grounds. And we will claim the seas far to the north, abandoned by our ancient and now extinct enemy. Our futures depend on this. Our lives and our very existence depend on this. We will destroy all those who intend to do us harm, and we will be victorious."

The crowd of penguins erupted into a wild cacophony of shrill calls, beating their flightless wings against their sides in a steady thrum. The exuberant birds lofted loose pinfeathers into the air in a maelstrom of white and gray.

Lavour joined Mevoule in the celebration, though somewhat less enthusiastically and more for show. Leepoh seemed to share Lavour's lack of enthusiasm. Nok stood silent and still.

Randy watched the celebration and was overcome with a sickening dread. He had put the pieces together. His capture, being paraded about and put on display, the charismatic leader, and the gathering of the different species confirmed that the penguins held no goodwill toward man. He knew that this was a pivotal moment in Earth's history. It was the beginning of an interspecies war. It was beyond survival of the fittest. It would be true war, and the world would never be the same. He knew as well, that these extraordinary penguins might have just hastened their own doom.

Randy's guards turned on him and began beating him without mercy. The beating elicited an excited response from the crowd. The guards pushed and shoved him back off stage where he found Liutites waiting for him.

"Your time has come, human," Liutites sneered at him. "Take him back to his cell," he barked in penguin to the guards. Liutites paused as if something had caught his attention. "Go now. I have to attend to something."

Leepoh watched as Randy was taken away. He was both troubled by the Overlord's plans and in awe of his ability to rouse the multitudes into mindless obedience. He spotted Lavour, who had stopped his conforming applause. The two exchanged haunted looks. They both knew that all of their lives had just changed forever.

The guards pushed and prodded Randy with vigor on his way back to his cell. He saw that the door had been left open with no guards watching over it. He thought about attempting to overpower his guards before entering the room, but a hard hit to his knees caused him to fall and quelled any such notion. He knew what was coming next, covered his head, and took the rap on his hands and curled into a fetal position as the guards beat him.

The guards finally grew tired of their game and left the room. Randy lay on the cold ground and watched the door close. The room went slightly darker. The bruised and battered man attempted to sit up but managed only to roll over. Hopelessness threatened to overcome him and he briefly considered killing the next penguin he saw. He knew that would mean certain and immediate death, not eventual death, as was likely. That also would mean that he would never see Gina again, and it was that one small hope that motivated him and kept him from doing something stupid.

He slowly found the strength to pull himself to his makeshift pallet. He looked around the dim room, and it dawned on him to call his penguin cellmate. "Meuseaux, you can come out now." He waited for the sound of shuffling webbed, clawed feet, but none was forthcoming.

Alarm overtook Randy, and he struggled to the empty drums. "Meuseaux, are you in here?" he asked, spinning the drum around. He realized that his friend was gone. His heart raced in panic, fearing for the little penguin's safety. He collapsed back onto his pallet and pulled his coverings over his head. With his mind sluggish from the most recent beatings, he finally comprehended that when he was taken away to the bizarre assembly, the Chinstrap must have taken the opportunity to escape. At least he hoped he had. "Good," he said in an exhausted whisper. "Good for you, Meuseaux. God speed, little friend."

CHAPTER 39

Corporal Meuseaux scampered down the corridor and toward the closest exit, hoping to escape PIC. While traveling toward his newfound hope of freedom, he briefly thought of trying to contact Lavour—who, he knew, was trustworthy. He wanted nothing more than to warn the others of the Supreme Commander's treachery and to try to convince Lavour to help gain Randy's freedom. His time was short, however, and he thought it would be best to go back to the nesting grounds and explain it all.

He'd heard the ruckus coming from the crowd and wondered what could have gotten the crowd so excited. Meuseaux encountered two elite guards dragging away one heavily protesting Blackfoot penguin, and he had to duck into a side passage to avoid being spotted. He shuddered when he heard the guards say they were throwing the unfortunate penguin down into the lower reaches. Nobody ever returned from there.

Meuseaux had been out of contact with the general population for nearly a month now. Although the announcement of the Great Gathering had been made after he went into hiding, he was able to piece together enough tidbits of announcements to guess what was taking place. As he traveled near the auditorium, he stooped and listened to some of the Overlord's speech and got the gist of what was to come. He figured the penguins were to go to war against the humans, and after what he had seen in the Royal

Emperor rookeries, the thought worried him.

While on cleaning duty, he had come upon an open passage that led to another that he had never before seen.

Curiosity got the better of him and he had to steal a peek. What he saw amazed and terrified him. He entered an enormous room, nearly the size of the rest of Pack Ice Command itself. Inside were thousands of Royal Emperor penguins, only larger than the others he had seen. They were larger even than the Supreme Commander. All had the grasping hands of the elite guards, and all had the golden head coloring of the Overlord.

They stood in ranks and held the staffs of the elite guards. They were going through a precision military exercise with the staffs, and each was in perfect sync with those next to it. The only non-conformity among them was in the staffs themselves. All had the toothed spear tips, but they were made of various materials. Some were made of what appeared to be whalebone, and others were made from a variety of items scavenged from human camps. All of the weapons did have one other thing in common; they appeared deadly in the firm grip of the warriors holding them.

Meuseaux crept further into the room, trying to stay out of sight by hiding in the shadows, and found another passage that led to the actual rookery. It was a quarter of the size of the room he had just left. Within were at least twenty thousand nests. The nests, or rather standing spots, since Emperors incubate the eggs by resting them on their feet, were all occupied by females with the familiar golden-topped head. He had no idea of what this all meant, but it didn't feel right.

He crept further in until he heard the voices of two penguins coming up behind him. One of the voices was distinctly male, the other female.

"With the Overlord's army nearly complete, we will be the most powerful clan ever assembled, and at last, all others will be our servants," one of them had said.

"But what of the Emperors—the 'feral' clans of the ice fields? They will not be so eager to be our servants," the female said.

"If they will not join, they will go the way of the Great Auks. I have a feeling, though, that they will conform to our way of thinking. Liutites will be pleased with this new . . ." The male Royal Emperor paused. "Hey!"

Meuseaux had been spotted. Unsure of what to do or where to go, he just stood in place, not thinking he had actually done anything wrong.

"Guards!" the Royal called out.

Meuseaux looked past the two penguins that raised the alarm and saw several elite guards rushing toward him. As the guards approached, he contemplated making a run for it but truly thought he had done nothing.

"What are you doing in here?" the female asked him.

"Cleaning duty. Only cleaning," Meuseaux stammered nervously.

"What did you hear?" she asked as the guards flanked the Chinstrap.

"Nothing, nothing at all," he lied unconvincingly.

The male looked him over. "Take him to Supreme Commander Liutites. He will deal with this intruder."

This announcement put a new fear into Meuseaux. Although he had never actually met the Supreme Commander, he had heard rumors of his harsh treatment of those who had broken rules, whether or not they knew the rules existed. "I didn't know this place was restricted!" he pleaded with the Royal Emperors as they dragged him away. "Please!" he continued to beg, struggling in the powerful grip of the guards. Ahead, he saw the form of Liutites filling the entryway that he had so unwisely entered.

The guards dragged Meuseaux closer as he struggled harder to break free of their grasp. One of the guards picked him up by his wing, twisted it and threw him the remaining distance between them and the Supreme Commander. The Chinstrap squawked out in pain as felt his flipper break from the guard's abuse. He lay on the floor as Liutites loomed over him like a statue of an ancient God.

"Chinstrap!" boomed Liutites's voice. "What were you doing in a restricted area?"

"I did not know this place was restricted, sir," Meuseaux said, struggling to his feet. "I was merely seeing to my cleaning duties, saw the open passage, and

thought there may be more to do in here."

Liutites eyed the Chinstrap with a hard glare. "Ignorance is no excuse."

"I am ignorant no longer, sir," Meuseaux said submissively, hoping his punishment by the guards would satisfy the Supreme Commander.

"That is, unfortunately, too late for you, Chinstrap. You are damaged now as well," Liutites said in mock apology. "Your purpose here is now at an end."

Meuseaux had a fleeting hope that the Supreme Commander meant he would be allowed to leave and return to his nesting ground. But his hope died quickly.

"Guards, see to it that this one is prepared for the Phocids."

"What?" Meuseaux cried. "Prepared for the Phocids? What does that mean?"

Liutites glared down at the wounded Meuseaux. "Be proud, Chinstrap. Be proud that your sacrifice will allow you one final opportunity to serve the greater good—that your death will not be without purpose. Guards, take him away!"

The guards followed their commander's orders and seized Meuseaux once again.

"No! I will heal," he screamed as he was dragged away.

He was taken down a back corridor, out of the general population's sight and through several secret passages. They came to a doorway, and when one of the guards let loose of Meuseaux to insert its staff into the keyhole, he saw his chance. Quickly and without hesitation, he stabbed his beak into the remaining guard's foot. The guard let out a pain-filled yowl, lost its grip on the reluctant sacrifice, and Meuseaux pulled away. The guards were not expecting such defiance from a Chinstrap and briefly hesitated, which allowed Meuseaux the time he needed to escape.

He had eventually found his way to the storage room but had the bad luck to get locked in. When the guards had come for Randy, they left the door open, and that had given Meuseaux a second chance at freedom.

After the guards passed by with the doomed Blackfoot, Meuseaux entered the corridor once again. He was still torn as to what he should do.

He desperately wanted to get a warning to Lavour but knew that would most likely be a fatal error. He adhered to his original plan and continued on his way.

The corporal carefully turned each corner of the presumably abandoned corridors as he traveled to the exit. At one point, he swore he heard a slight shuffling noise behind him. He quickly swung his head around but saw nothing. He walked a little further and a little slower and heard the noise again. He snapped his head around and again saw nothing. After rounding another corner, he came to a stop. Ahead, in the shadowy recesses of the hall, he saw a small dark form of a penguin. The form became still, as if trying not to be detected. He heard the noise come from behind him again and took a quick look. Nothing. When he looked back to the shadows, the dark figure had gone. He made up his mind that it was time to go, and quickly.

He heard the noise of excited penguin chatter in the halls behind him as the members of the gathering began to exit. He stopped, looked back, and then altered his plan. He decided to hide in the midst of the hundreds of penguins and hopefully contact another member of his company. He hoped the Supreme Commander would be less bold if he was in the presence of others. Meuseaux threw caution aside and began to run toward the crowd. As he rounded the next turn, he suddenly wished he hadn't. Supreme Commander Liutites was standing directly in his path, as if he had been expecting him.

"Well, look what I have found. It appears as if your escape has failed, Chinstrap. It was somewhat foolish of you not to keep going. Had you not turned back, you might have made it," Liutites scoffed.

"You won't get away with this," Meuseaux said with as much defiance as he could muster.

"You are in no position to make threats. Guards," the Supreme Commander said casually.

Meuseaux started to make the Chinstrap call of alarm but was stopped by a hard blow to the head. As he faded into unconsciousness, he had one last thought. *Someday, somehow, I will kill you, Liutites.*

CHAPTER 40

Supreme Commander Liutites entered the Overlord's chambers, particularly proud of his accomplishment in capturing Corporal Meuseaux.

As he approached the dais, the Overlord spoke first. "What is it Supreme Commander?"

"My lord, I have captured the escaped sacrifice," he announced with satisfaction.

"With the assistance of your spies, of course," Overlord Antaean said scathingly.

Liutites's pride in his capture diminished noticeably. "Yes, my lord."

"I feel the Phocids have been fed enough. Do you feel that they trust us?"

"As much as a beast of their nature can, my lord. They gather twice weekly to await an offering, and they will gather again tomorrow."

Antaean acted as if he were pondering the information Liutites gave him, but Liutites knew he had already contrived a plan to deal with the Phocids. Everything the Overlord did was a carefully laid-out scheme.

"Good. When they gather tomorrow, bring your Chinstrap, but also bring a full battalion of Royal Emperor warriors. Flank them, surround them, and kill them. We cannot have primitive beasts interfering with our plans. After they have been killed, have their corpses taken to Forward

Command Two for processing."

"Yes, my lord," Liutites said with a slightly renewed eagerness.

"And remember, Liutites. The war has already begun," Antaean admonished him while fixing him with a hard stare.

Liutites was unsure what that last comment meant, but he did know that it was unwise to question Antaean's cryptic remarks. "Yes, my lord."

After leaving the Overlord, Liutites immediately headed to the quarters of the elite guards and summoned ten of his best. "Captain, take the Chinstrap offering out the back passage and head to the Phocids without delay. Wait on the high point before the ice floe. Do not sacrifice him until I arrive. I am bringing a full battalion of warriors to eliminate our nemesis once and for all. Wait until we are in position, and on my signal, bring the sacrifice to the edge of the ice. A company of warriors will come in from the water behind the Phocids to cut off their escape. Are you clear on this, Captain?"

"Yes, sir."

"Are there any questions?"

"Yes, sir. Is the Chinstrap still to be sacrificed?"

"Yes, Captain, this is our most important offering yet. The Phocids must be distracted for us to spring our trap. Remember, Captain, this is the penguin who escaped from the elite guards once before. Do *not* let it happen again, or you will take its place. Do you understand?" Liutites asked in his usual threatening manner.

"Perfectly, sir," the captain of the guards said, snapping a high beak salute.

"Good. Now go. You haven't much time."

∧∧∧

Early the next morning, high-ranking officers of the Penguin Defense Alliance attended a meeting in what was known as the map room. The room was nondescript from the outside, lacking most of the etchings that designated various chambers around PIC. The arched doorway was marked by a single jagged line placed above the keyhole. The meaning was known only to those with the rank of general or higher. The doorway was closely guarded inside and out.

Supreme Commander Liutites stood at the head of a large table, or more an oblong block of ice, situated in the middle of the room. The top of the table consisted of a rough map of the entire continent of Antarctica and its surrounding and nearby islands. The map had colored representations of brown, black, and yellow mountains. It showed coastlines and human settlements, bases, and camps.

"These marks indicate where the humans are known to be," Liutites told the others while pointing to various spots on the map. "We will begin our assault from Forward Commands One through Five. The Chinstraps have committed two hundred thousand troops and will lead the attacks on the more populated regions. The Blackfoot, who are more adept at infiltration, will go in first and scout the areas to give us as much information as possible on their numbers and positioning. The Emperors, Kings, and Adélie will eliminate isolated bases and camps, indicated here," he said, pointing to several dots on the map. "The Gentoo," he said, looking at General Leepoh, "will attack their sea vessels and will be reinforced by the Magellanics." Liutites paused and looked around the room. "This is the ideal time to strike. Winter is nearly upon us, and the humans will be at their most vulnerable. All humans are to be considered hostile targets. We must attack swiftly and in force to eliminate their communication, to prevent them from escaping, and to keep them from warning others. I will be leaving shortly with a battalion of Royal Emperor warriors to remove the threat of the Phocids, which will assure us safe passage to the outlying islands and beyond."

The news of the Phocids caused a stir among the commanders.

"The Rockhoppers and Macaroni will be held in reserve for the time being to complement our forces as it becomes necessary. The remaining crested clans will return to their homes for defensive purposes, and they are to take targets of opportunity along the way. Once we have eradicated the humans from the mainland and surrounding islands, we will meet up with the Kings at the Sandwich Islands and move toward the Falklands. It is imperative that we secure the mainland by winter's end."

"Won't the humans send more to investigate the reasons for the lost contact?" Leepoh asked.

"In all likelihood they will, which is why it is necessary to complete the first phase by the end of the season. After the attacks on the islands, we will liberate the Humboldt from their oppressors as we continue to push up the Pacific coast. This will happen as we do the same on the Atlantic side as well. The Blackfoot will begin a limited assault on South Africa, and after we reach the Galapagos, we'll send messengers to the crested clans to begin their assault on New Zealand and other islands."

"Do we have enough resources to fight on so many fronts?" A Royal Crested general asked.

"Yes. Our goal is not necessarily to occupy these areas but to drive the humans away and give them pause should they think to return." Liutites hesitated for a moment as he looked at the commanders once more. "We will continue in this fashion until we reach the Northern lands, and then we shall colonize there."

"And what part will the Royal Emperors play in this?" Leepoh asked, never being one to shy away from asking audacious questions.

Liutites stared at Leepoh, unhappy with his boldness. "The Royal Emperors will defend the homeland."

"So they're not accompanying us on the journey northward?" Leepoh followed up.

Liutites stared at the impudent Gentoo. He was never one to appease anyone other than the Overlord and despised having to be cordial. The Overlord's plans, however, depended heavily on the participation of what were, in his opinion, the lesser clans. So he had to bear with it for the time being. "No. And it is for obvious reasons. Their swimming abilities are not up to the task of long journeys," he said, referring to their digit-tipped flippers. "The initial campaign, however, will involve as many as can be spared. A Royal Emperor Advisor will be assigned to every company at every front. They will relay messages to and from Pack Ice Command in an effort to revise strategy as the situations require."

"Why won't the field commanders have direct contact or control?" Leepoh continued to question.

Liutites clamped his beak down in an effort to remain calm, being unaccustomed to answering to subordinates. "They do, General. You are free to revise and improvise as needed. The Royal Emperor advisors are only a link to command so that we can deploy forces where they are needed and in a timely manner. This will avoid any extended debate or feelings of favoritism by the clans on troop deployment, which could cost unnecessary loss of penguin lives."

"Sounds sound, sir," Leepoh said rather blithely.

Liutites looked Leepoh over and took a noticeable breath of irritation. "Now if there are no more questions . . ." He paused with his eyes fixed on Leepoh. "Return to your respective quarters and await your orders. It begins tomorrow. Be prepared, and may the spirit of the Ancients be with you." Liutites returned the multitude of salutes and rushed off.

As the commanders began to file out, Leepoh stopped to examine the map. "I was wondering, is this map made of what I think it's made of?" he asked General Devét as he passed by.

Devét looked perplexed by the question. "If you mean guano, then yes."

"That's what I thought," Leepoh said while laughing.

"Why is that so amusing to you?"

"Because I believe it is entirely proper."

"And are we privy as to why you would think that?" Devét asked as he was joined by General Butiewy of the Blackfoot.

Leepoh presented the map with his flipper. "It complements this plan perfectly."

The comment elicited a laugh from Butiewy, but General Devét just shook his head and walked away.

"Some penguins just don't have a sense of humor," Leepoh said with mock indignation to no one in particular.

CHAPTER 41

Captain Mevoule walked down an empty corridor, stopping to check around every corner and looking back regularly to make sure he wasn't being followed. The corridor was dark and shadowy, as it was below the common area of PIC and received little of the reflective light. He stopped once again, double-checked the shadows, faced the wall, and made a barely audible clicking noise. After a few moments, an unseen door opened in front of him, and he hurried inside.

"Captain, come in," said a voice coming from a large shadowy penguin standing in the back corner. "Were you followed?"

"No," Mevoule said with assurance.

"Good. We must be cautious," the dark form slowly spoke.

There were others in the room as well, but they remained silent. Only their faint outlines could be seen, highlighted by a slowly dying lantern that emanated a flickering glow in the center of the room.

"There are spies within PIC. They have been watching you and Lavour," the silhouette informed him.

The news ruffled Mevoule. "I had heard rumors of them, but I didn't know they were watching me."

"Only because of your connections to Lavour," the shadow said. "What can you tell me about him? Do you believe he is with us, or do you think he will go the other way?"

"I still have a small doubt, but I believe he will be ready soon."

"He is too valuable an asset to lose," the shadow said.

"As was Trevot."

"That was unfortunate, but it could not be prevented on my part. That is why it is all the more important that you keep Lavour on the right path. We do not want him to disappear as well."

"He would be missed even more than Trevot."

"Yes, the Chinstraps admire him and look to him for guidance and understanding. How does he respond to your propaganda?"

"He's obviously uncomfortable with it," Mevoule answered quickly.

The shadow mulled over the response in silence. "Discontinue it. We want to be sure of his loyalty, not wrest it from him."

"He may no longer have a choice."

"Yes, the Overlord's plans are already in motion. The first attacks will begin soon. It is already arranged for you to stay here at PIC. You will fill Trevot's place. Lavour, however, might be sent to the front very soon. Liutites will see to that," the shadow said regretfully.

"Liutites doesn't like him or Chinstraps," Mevoule said with a hint of anger, feeling that Liutites seemed to take pleasure in singling out Chinstraps to detest.

"Liutites likes no one. He cares only for his own power." There was a hint of moroseness in the silhouette's voice. "Our time for discussion is at an end," it said abruptly. "There is one more thing before you go. Liutites's spies found Meuseaux, and he will be sacrificed later this morning as the final offering to the Phocids."

"Can it be stopped?" Mevoule asked in alarm. "Meuseaux is intelligent and resourceful. He would be a valuable asset."

"Unfortunately, no. It is impossible to get to him. He has seen too much and knows too much. Liutites would not alter his plans for any reason—simply out of pride, he wouldn't. But if Meuseaux is as resourceful as you say, he may yet save himself."

"We can only hope," Mevoule said, uncertain that Meuseaux would be able to cheat death a second time.

"Go now, before you are missed," the shadow told him.

Mevoule went to the door and looked back as the light clicked off. The door silently slid open, and Mevoule retraced his cautious trek back to the Chinstrap quarters.

^^^

"This is unacceptable!" Nok exclaimed excitedly to General Khik. "I am a member of the Rockhopper Defense Ministry. My priorities are to defend the Rockhoppers, not pursue some foolish idea of conquest." On hearing from the Rockhopper commander that General Khik requested the current contingent of Rockhoppers at PIC be assigned for support of the initial strike, Nok began furiously arguing with Khik about where his loyalties should lie.

"Captain Nok, please calm yourself," Khik said, only moderately calm himself.

"Do not try to placate me, Khik. When General Treeg learns of what has taken place here, he will see to it that you are relieved of command."

"And what do you think has taken place here, Nok?" he asked defensively.

"You volunteered our company in order to make yourself look good before the Royal Emperors," Nok said accusingly.

"I do not take orders from General Treeg. I am a member of the PDA first and the Defense Ministry second. Don't forget that it was the formation of the PDA that enabled your victory at RHC 23. Without the PDA, the Gentoo would not have felt compelled to come to your aid."

Nok thought about the statement for a minute but felt sure his friend, General Leepoh, would have come to his aid with or without the PDA. "I don't know how you do things at RHC 12, but we at RHC 23 do not commandeer another general's forces. Those forces were sent as a sign of good faith. By what right do you enlist them in open warfare without their approval?"

"You have faced the humans before, and I need your experience. Have you changed your feelings toward the humans? Does your fear of them diminish your hatred of them?"

Nok had had enough. He leapt feet forward and knocked Khik to the ground. He rushed toward Khik and stood over the general as he lay on the ground with his eyes wide in surprise and fear. "Until you've tasted the blood of a human, do not presume to lecture me on fear or hate. If you do not fear your enemy for what it is capable of and hate it because of those things, you are a fool. You, Khik, are a fool who will soon die because of your arrogance and stupidity."

Khik rolled over and pushed himself up. "That's why I need you, Captain Nok," he said placidly, trying not to provoke Nok again. "We on RHC 12 have had only one encounter with the humans in the past eight winters, and most of us were away on a hunt. You know them. You have the experience and the knowledge of how best to deal with them. I need you. We need you," he said, motioning to the other Rockhoppers, who were standing by silently as they watched the spectacle. "Whether you stay or don't stay, I have my orders from the Supreme Commander, and this group will perform its duty for the PDA. We would have a better chance of surviving this with your assistance."

Nok looked around the room and saw the eager but unsure looks of the Rockhoppers gathered around them. *They'll be slaughtered*, he thought to himself, realizing he couldn't turn his back on his fellow Rockhoppers, regardless of how he felt about the whole mess. "This does not mean that I agree with you or the Overlord," he relented. "I will do what I can. I do it for them but only for the time being."

"Thank you, Captain," said Khik with obvious relief. "You will be here no longer than our needs require."

"We shall see, General Khik. We shall see."

CHAPTER 42

From an icy blue ledge on an upper level of PIC, Lieutenant-General Lavour stood looking at the morning sun, quietly contemplating the orders he had received the night before. Command had informed him that he and a majority of the Chinstraps at PIC were to begin the grueling trek toward the human settlements. Now, just hours before he was to move out, he enjoyed his last few moments of repose.

The Blackfoot infiltrators had sent the necessary information on the humans, and all seemed to be in place. Lavour's forces were to join one hundred thousand other Chinstraps and twenty thousand Gentoo near Forward Command One. Once the main force conquered the human bases, they were to continue along the Antarctic Peninsula and, if all went well, meet up with the Royal Emperor, King, and Adélie forces to drive any remaining humans from the archipelagos. Only a small group of Chinstraps was to remain at Pack Ice Command, under the command of Mevoule, to serve as messengers and share in various other duties.

Lavour snorted at the irony. Mevoule, who was seemingly excited about the prospect of facing the humans, was staying behind while he had to go to the front. "Strange how fate works," he said quietly. "Well, once I reach the archipelagos, I might be able to see Lannera again," he hoped.

"Hello, Lavour," a voice from behind him said, snapping him out of his thoughts.

"Hello, Mevoule," he said without turning around.

"I thought I would find you here. Not many penguins know of this place."

"That's the reason I come here," Lavour said, trying not to sound annoyed.

The two stood in silence for a minute while looking out at the icy plains and distant mountains. "Everything changes now," Lavour said, breaking the silence.

"What does?" Mevoule asked.

"What changes?" Lavour asked in surprise. "Our lives, our future, everything. The penguins have known relative peace for a thousand years, and today it all comes to an end."

"Not all of the penguins have known that peace," Mevoule said to gauge his reaction.

"I know, and I know the humans are a threat. I just think this war will hasten our destruction. Many winters ago, the humans used to hunt the Chinstraps. But they've stopped, and our population has increased."

"You don't think our strength should be used to assist those who lack strength?"

"No, that's not what I mean," Lavour answered in frustration. "Think about this. If the Overlord's plans don't go according to his design, the humans will retaliate. Who will bear the brunt of their retaliation? We will. Because in their eyes, we'll be the face of the enemy," he said, alluding to the fact that the Chinstraps have the largest number of forces involved.

After a long pause, Mevoule looked at him. "There are others who feel as you do."

Lavour looked at his friend, feeling a little puzzled by his statement. "Do you, Mevoule?"

"Now is not the time," he said cryptically.

"When is the time?" Lavour asked, not sure of Mevoule's point. Mevoule's rhetoric for the past few weeks had planted a seed of distrust toward his friend, and his statement seemed to be contrary to all he had said.

"Lavour—Lieutenant-General Lavour—are you up there?" Leepoh's voice called from down the passage leading to the landing, ending Mevoule and Lavour's discussion. "Ah, there you are," the Gentoo said, looking between the two Chinstraps. "Am I interrupting something?"

"No," Mevoule said before Lavour could answer. "I was just leaving. And in answer to your question, Lavour, the time will be soon. Be safe, my friend."

"I will," Lavour said with a hint of sadness. The two friends exchanged looks, each for his own reason, then Mevoule left. Lavour turned his attention to Leepoh. "How did you find me here?"

"Hello to you too," Leepoh said none too seriously.

"I'm sorry. I'm a bit edgy. It's my first war, you know," Lavour said after realizing he had sounded a little rude to his new friend.

"Oh don't start molting on me. It's only my second, and I'm no more eager about it than you are."

"My reluctance shows, then?" Lavour asked, not wanting to appear cowardly.

"Don't worry about it. When I fought the humans for the first time, it was a quick decision. We had to act fast, or all of us would have been killed—if not that day, then soon after. Had I had time to think about it, I don't know if I would have been so eager. But as it stands, we did what we had to, and those particular humans got what they deserved."

Lavour looked away to the horizon. Lavour did have time to think about it. Leepoh had had his battle thrust upon him. Even if he had been unwilling, eventually he wouldn't have had a choice. "Do these humans deserve what they are about to receive?"

Now it was Leepoh's turn to look away. "I don't know. Maybe. I've been away from here far too long to pass any real judgment. The human prisoner—Randy, he calls himself—doesn't deserve misfortune, I think.

But do any of us truly deserve the misfortunes we are forced to endure?"

Lavour took a deep breath, feeling slightly more relaxed from the conversation. "Tell me. Are all Gentoo philosophers?"

"Bah! I just like to hear myself talk."

"So I've noticed," Lavour said straight, and Leepoh shot him a sideways look. "So why were you looking for me?"

"Oh, I forgot. It's time to get tipped. Your Sergeant Gereaux was looking for you when I asked for you. He told me where I might find you. And by the way, my company will be accompanying you."

"Well, that's some consolation. I could use someone with your experience nearby and could do with the distraction."

"Hah! Let's go get tipped, shall we?"

"All right. By the way, what do you mean by *getting tipped*?"

"Oh, you'll see."

Lavour gave him a dubious look and followed him down the hallway.

CHAPTER 43

Meuseaux lay on top of an upthrust of ice overlooking the spot where the seals gathered near the ocean's edge. Five hundred Leopard Seals were there already, squabbling with one another as they jockeyed for position to receive their free meal. He looked at the seals and wondered how many penguins had been sacrificed to make so many Phocids gather here. He remembered all of the so-called reassignments and wondered if they had met the same fate as he was about to meet. "The Royal Emperors are not our allies. They are our true enemies," he said quietly. "The others have to know . . . somehow."

"On your feet, Chinstrap. The time has come," the guard standing closest to him said.

Meuseaux dug his beak into the ice and pushed himself upright. "We're all members of the PDA. How can you take part in this?" he asked, not expecting an answer.

"Shut up and get moving," the guard barked, not disappointing Meuseaux's expectations.

"That's a lot of Phocids down there. I hope they don't mistake you for food as well."

"That is not your concern. Shut up and move."

Meuseaux was escorted along the icy crags by ten guards. They stopped several meters away from the noisy beasts. He looked around as he tried to figure a way out of his predicament and spotted the silhouette of a penguin against the low sun in the distance. "You have an audience," he said to a guard, hoping that would distract him. It didn't.

"The Phocids prefer to take their meals alive, but if you don't stop talking we'll disappoint them."

"Hmm, die now or die later? I'll choose later," he said sardonically.

"Wise choice. Get moving." The guard pointed his spear at Meuseaux.

Only a pair of guards escorted him closer to the hungry jaws of the seals. Meuseaux guessed they didn't want to lose any more than a couple of guards should the Phocids become anxious. They climbed an outcrop of ice and Meuseaux spotted several penguins opposite where he had seen the other silhouette. He looked to the water, where hundreds of icebergs could be seen. *No sense trying to escape to the sea. With my flipper, they'd catch me in a second.* He was trying desperately to work out an escape plan.

He looked back and saw hundreds of Royal Emperors marching toward the seals. He looked back at the water and spotted an unknown number of penguins porpoising their way in behind the Phocids. *Something is about to happen*, he thought. Meuseaux looked at one of his guards. "It's worth trying again," he said to him.

"What is?" the guard asked, sounding confused.

"This," Meuseaux said and quickly plunged his beak into the guard's foot. The guard let out a startled cry, and Meuseaux scrambled away from him. The guards gave chase, stabbing at the fleeing Chinstrap with their staffs. The Phocids spotted their meal taking flight, and their pursuit instinct was triggered.

Meuseaux climbed and ran as fast as he could. He heard the startled scream of one of his pursuers, stole a glance backwards, and saw that a seal had one of the guards in its jaws, shaking it furiously. The stolen glance caused Meuseaux to misstep and he fell to the ice, belly first. He quickly righted himself but looked up to find the other guard looming over him.

"There is no escape for you this time, Chinstrap," the guard said, raising his staff for a killing blow.

Meuseaux closed his eyes and braced for the impact, but it never came. He opened his eyes to see the guard's flipper in the firm grip of a Phocid's jaws. He watched the guard get dragged away screaming. With the remaining guards now focused on fending off the swarming Phocids, Meuseaux scrambled away.

He made it back to the ice juts and came face-to-face with hundreds of Royal Emperor warriors rushing toward him. They paid him no mind and instead began attacking the seals. Meuseaux moved farther away and looked back at the scene in amazement. He saw the swimmers coming ashore to block the Phocid's escape route. The battle was pitched, and the cries of dying penguins and seals alike filled the air.

The penguin warriors stabbed at the Phocids with their spears, and the Phocids gnashed at their attackers with their deadly teeth. Some of the seals turned back to escape to the sea, only to be met by the surrounding penguins who lunged at them with oddly glimmering beaks.

Meuseaux climbed a nearby slope and watched the spectacle as more warriors arrived to battle the Leopard Seals. He looked to the distance and saw five penguins watching the battle as well. A penguin in the middle of the group caught his attention, and Meuseaux knew by its form that it was Supreme Commander Liutites. The sight of Liutites pumped a renewed energy in Meuseaux, and he scurried off as fast as his legs could take him. Not wanting to tempt fate, he didn't look back. He had escaped.

^^^

Supreme Commander Liutites watched in disbelief as the fortunate Chinstrap escaped once again.

"Sir, shall I send a squad after him?" a Royal Emperor lieutenant asked.

Liutites continued to watch Meuseaux disappear into the horizon. "No, lieutenant, he is injured and has to travel overland. He will not last for long on his own. Stay focused on the task upon us. The battle is not yet won."

The battle between penguin and seal lasted for only another hour. For countless millennia, the Phocids had known the penguins only as a food source. When their prey fought back, the Phocids stood little chance. The rough and rugged ice was littered with the bodies of the combatants. The calls of the wounded warriors went unanswered.

"Supreme Commander, sir, how shall we treat the wounded?" the lieutenant asked.

"Leave them," Liutites answered harshly.

"Leave them, sir?"

Liutites fixed the lieutenant with a menacing stare. "If they are weak enough to fall victim to these mindless beasts, how do you think they would fare against the humans? If they are strong enough to find their way back to PIC, we will treat them. We have more pressing matters. We are to bring the bodies of the Phocids to the nearest Forward Command to be processed."

"Yes, sir," the other said, leaving to see to the task.

"And Lieutenant," Liutites added before he left. "Question my orders once more and your remains will be chumming the water."

"Y-Yes s-sir—understood," the lieutenant stammered then rushed away.

CHAPTER 44

Trevot fell to the ice from exhaustion. After just two days under the command of General Diutes, he felt like he was near his death. He wasn't. He was simply worn out. His last full sleep was at PIC. Diutes had put him on watch, patrol, or cleaning detail every minute he had been at Forward Command One. And now he was on a long-range scouting mission of no place in particular. He wanted desperately to sleep but knew he couldn't. If, by some chance, Diutes were to find out, he would receive another beating, like he had the night before, for falling asleep while on watch.

"Go home," he told himself, remembering what Lavour had said to him. And home was where he intended to go as soon as he got far enough away to do that. With a grim determination, he picked himself up and moved on. He climbed to the top of a mountain that overlooked the vast expanse of the Antarctic terrain. Behind him was the ice shelf where Forward Command lay. Far away to his left was Pack Ice Command, and ahead of him and beyond the mountains were the glacial plains. He decided that would be his chance for escape.

To save time and precious energy, he belly-slid down the frozen slope, quickly putting more distance between him and his tormentors. His plan was to head to the sea and then for home, but when he reached the bottom of the grade, he heard penguins calling in the distance. The sound sent a shiver through his heavily insulated body. It was the call of Emperor penguins.

He looked up the incline but decided against returning to the peak. If they hadn't seen him already, they definitely would if he were to go back. Trevot listened to the calls for any sign of alarm. There was none. The calls struck him as odd because they were using the Emperor language, not the universal penguin language the PDA used. Not being able to see the birds, he moved toward the next ridge in the hope of finding out what he was facing.

The noises were coming from just beyond the ridge, and he cautiously scrambled to the top and peered over. He saw a colony of Emperors nesting on an icy flat between two ridges. On closer inspection, he saw that none of them carried the golden plumes common to Royal Emperors. "Strange," he said and moved closer for a better view.

It was the breeding season for the Emperors, and they were busy pairing off into mates. Initially they paid him no mind. After a while, one of them spotted their voyeur. Trevot froze, not sure of what to do. The spotter, an older male, looked at him, clicked something to his mate, and began to waddle toward Trevot.

The Chinstrap didn't bother trying to run. There was nothing overtly threatening in the Emperor's demeanor, and they didn't seem to be part of the PDA.

When the Emperor arrived, he looked Trevot over. "You're a long way from home, aren't you?" he asked in a friendly voice.

"Huh?" Trevot asked in surprise at the Emperor's tone. The Royals, Kings, and few Emperors at PIC always spoke to him as if he were inferior. "Further than I'd like to be. Yes, sir," Trevot answered formally.

"Sir?" the Emperor snorted. "Am I to take it you are a member of the Penguin Defense Alliance? You don't need to call me sir. My name is—" and the Emperor made a series of whirs and clicks.

Trevot shook his head. "I'm sorry, but I couldn't possibly pronounce that."

The Emperor gave him an amused click.

Trevot saw these were not the Emperors that he was used to dealing with and felt more relaxed. "As far as being a member of the PDA, I'm not anymore. In fact, I'm trying to make my way home," he said, looking to the distance. "If you don't mind my asking, why are you out here and not at Pack Ice Command?"

The old Emperor studied him for a bit, as if trying to gauge his sincerity. "Not all of us hold to Antaean's ideals."

"I apologize," Trevot interrupted. "But who is Antaean?"

The Emperor snorted. "He is your Overlord. We have remained autonomous and free from the Overlord's reign. We hold true to the old ways—the ways of peace and freedom."

"Does Antaean know this?"

"Yes, but he doesn't know where we are. To avoid his detection, we no longer nest in the same area every season. If he were to find us, he would see to our destruction," he said with palpable bitterness.

Trevot listened in silence. He was not surprised by the accusations of brutality about the Overlord. He had experienced plenty of it while under the command of the Overlord's lackeys.

"Enough questions for now, my Chinstrap friend. Judging by your actions, I wouldn't think you were a spy. So how did you find your way out here—so far from where you're supposed to be?"

Trevot hesitated for a moment but decided that if these Emperors weren't what they appeared to be, it was too late to do anything about it now. "As I said, I'm leaving the PDA and trying to get back to my colony." He noticed the Emperor had not yet asked his name and decided that it was for the best.

"Since when does the PDA let one quit? And if you are headed home, I think you're headed in the wrong direction," the Emperor mused.

"Well, I'm not so much leaving as I am escaping. My commander—

no, my friend, back at PIC said if I felt threatened in any way by General Diutes, I . . ."

"General Diutes?" the Emperor interrupted. "Did you say *General* Diutes?"

Trevot wondered why that seemed to surprise the Emperor. "Yes," he answered hesitantly.

"So they put that monster in command. He would, wouldn't he? Now I am even more certain of our decision not to join them. Diutes is unstable at best. I would go so far as to say he is insane. You were lucky to escape him."

"I'm still not home, so I wouldn't count my chicks before they've hatched. You are right though. I believe he intended to kill me."

"Why would he want to kill you? Other than the fact that he enjoys such things."

"I believe it was on Liutites's orders. I was a bit outspoken on the direction the PDA is taking. I think the Overlord is planning to go to war with the humans," Trevot informed him.

The Emperor stared at Trevot in silent disbelief. "Fool," he finally said quietly. "That fool will cause the death of us all."

"I thought so as well," Trevot said in remorseful agreement.

"Thank you for this information, my Chinstrap friend."

"My name is . . ."

"Don't." The Emperor stopped him. "If I don't know your name, I can't give it."

Trevot nodded in agreement. He didn't want to do anything to put his new friends in jeopardy.

"Now I have to warn the others. You're welcome to stay and rest. You look like you could use it."

"I would appreciate it. I have a long journey ahead of me, and I'm already exhausted. But I've already put you at risk by lingering."

"Just a few hours, then," the Emperor told him kindly.

"Very well," Trevot said as they walked to the colony. "I wish all of the Emperors were like you."

"Most are. Antaean, Liutites, Diutes and the others are not *true* Emperors."

Trevot thought about what he meant by that statement and intended to ask about it, but the Emperor was busy talking to the others. Trevot was shown genuine hospitality by the colony as they led him to the center of their masses. Safe inside the group of warmer bodies, Trevot fell asleep almost immediately. He awoke several hours later, said his goodbyes to the Emperors, and headed off feeling refreshed, and with a new sense of hope and purpose.

CHAPTER 45

A combined force of five thousand Royal Emperor, King, and Adélie penguins marched across the landscape. They first attacked a research station that was under construction, where the humans' curiosity proved to be their undoing. They moved on and laid waste to several unsuspecting camps, suffering only five casualties during the fracases. They continued their march of conquest and destruction until they spotted a pair of treaded vehicles and a snowmobile in the distance.

King penguin, Colonel Kimmer, paced back and forth in front of the penguin line. "They see us," he said to a Royal Emperor advisor.

"Yes, sir."

"All right, then. We'll move in on them slowly at first until we reach charging range. Captain Seka."

"Yes, sir?" the Adélie Captain asked.

"Form your soldiers into ranks. Your troops have the benefit of more speed and will have to approach first. You will be followed by the Kings and eventually the Royals," he said, looking at the Royal Emperor advisor disdainfully. In all of the attacks so far, the Royal Emperors stayed to the rear, never putting themselves at risk. "Make sure they are all out of their vehicles before you engage. Remember, they trust us for now, and we don't want them to escape and warn other humans. We'll hold five hundred penguins in reserve. There don't appear to be many humans, so this should be over quickly. Now let's get moving."

^^^

Dan Alcorn threw open the door of his crawler, jumped down, and brought his binoculars to his eyes. "Lawrence, I think this is it."

Lawrence looked through his own binoculars. "I think you're right. I see two, maybe three different species." He pulled his radio free. "Okay, everyone, we've found them. Let's get together before we do anything else."

As they waited for the others to arrive, Lawrence studied the mass of penguins. "That's a lot of birds out there, Dan," he said with a hint of concern. "I think we're going to need more ammo."

"Yeah, I think you're right. I'll send Davis back for more. By the way, what are we going to do with all of the bodies?"

"Wait 'til everyone gets here, and we'll discuss a plan."

Lawrence waited until everyone had gathered around him before announcing his limited plan. "Okay, listen up. We'll focus on the bigger ones, as they're the easiest targets. Try not to kill too many of the smaller ones. We're going to have enough of a mess to clean up as it is. And if they're found, some damned naturalist might raise a stink, and we'll never get to our work. Honestly, I don't know what Vance was thinking. Remember, they probably still trust us, so you should be able to just walk right up on them."

"Davis," Dan said. "We're going to need more rounds, so take the snowmobile back to camp and get some. And while you're there, make sure Gina actually left. And hurry up about it."

"All right, all right. I'll be back," Davis said in his usual irritated tone. He climbed on the snowmobile and sped away.

"Okay, everyone, let's get to it," Lawrence said as if the whole thing was just a bother.

"What are they doing?" Jack asked no one in particular.

"I don't know. Maybe we spooked them," Dan answered.

Lawrence looked through his binoculars again and watched one of the smaller penguins as it hurried off and approached a larger one at the rear of the line. He continued to scan the lines of penguins and spotted something that surprised him. "Dan," he said casually. "Do penguins have metallic looking beaks?"

"No," Dan answered, somewhat alarmed. "Let me see." He grabbed the binoculars. He pulled the binoculars away, and looked at Lawrence. The two exchanged worried looks. "Damn it. This isn't how it was supposed to be. Maybe we should go back."

After a moment of deliberation, Lawrence shook his head. "No, let's get this over with. I don't feel like tracking them down again. Let's do it quickly. I'm freezing my butt off out here. Vance is going to owe us big time after this."

"Now what are they doing?" Lawrence asked as he spotted a hundred or more penguins split away from the main group.

"Look!" the resident geologist, David Cobb, said in alarm. "They're coming at us and in a hurry!"

"Okay, then. Fire away, men!" Dan announced as he brought his weapon up.

"Nice shooting, Dan," Jack shouted as Dan found his mark again and again. "But it looks like all we're doing is pissing them off."

Dan thought back to Randy's description of the penguins before he disappeared, and it didn't require much imagination to guess as to Randy's fate. "Shut up and shoot, Jack! I don't think these things are going to run away!"

As the penguins approached, Dan looked at Lawrence in horror, realizing what was about to happen. Lawrence returned the expression and fired another shot, dropping the nearest penguin. Dan ran out of ammo and nervously fumbled to replace the clip. The first penguin to reach him gave him a sharp peck to the leg. "Ow! Damn it!" he yelled as he kicked the bird away. He finally got his weapon loaded and dispatched his attacker as it struggled to right itself.

The penguins arrived in greater numbers and finally dropped their first victim.

"Jack!" Lawrence shouted as he watched him fall after being relentlessly pecked in the legs. Lawrence could do nothing but listen to the man's high-pitched scream as he died. Lawrence continued to shoot in increased desperation.

"We have to get the hell out of here!" Lawrence screamed over the din of squawking birds and gunfire. He turned and ran toward the crawlers, firing blindly into the mass until he had emptied his gun.

The Royal Emperors and Kings finally arrived and joined the fray. A man tripped over an Adélie as he tried to flee from the swarm. The Royals and Kings savagely attacked him. Dan saw the assault and fired his last round into the attackers. "Lance is down!" he shouted.

"It's too late. Leave him," Lawrence shouted as he tried to get away. The penguins surrounded him, forming an impenetrable wall of black. He swung his empty rifle, repeatedly clubbing the penguins as he desperately tried to pull his tattered legs free from the throng.

Lawrence screamed and flailed wildly as the penguins intensified their relentless attack. He knew he wasn't going to survive the ordeal, so he reached out and grabbed one of his assailants by the neck as he fell. He felt a satisfying crack as he snapped the penguin's neck before falling victim himself.

From the corner of his eye, Dan saw Lawrence go down and knew he was the last one standing. The penguins knew this as well and turned their attention to him. His legs were tattered, but he somehow found the strength to stay on his feet. He threw off his gloves and fished his last clip from his pocket. He saw his salvation in the form of the crawler just twenty feet ahead of him. He slammed the magazine into the rifle and brought it to bear on the birds.

The penguins ripped into his legs from behind. This time, instead of pecking, they buried their beaks into his flesh, anchoring themselves to him.

Dan struggled to stay on his feet. He poured gunfire into the penguins, but they were undaunted and pressed their advantage. He heard Davis's voice on his radio as he fell, but it didn't matter now. All that mattered to him now was the hope that it would be over quickly. In a less than a minute, it was.

^^^

After the fracas, the Royal Emperors strolled through the carnage, taking note of the losses.

"Good work today, advisor," one of Liutites's personal elite warriors commended another Royal. "We will report this to Pack Ice Command at once and have the necessary replacements sent immediately."

"Very good," the advisor replied, happy to take credit for the victory. "Now, if you will excuse me, we must rejoin Colonel Kimmer."

The penguins gathered into their groups and followed Kimmer's path, leaving the wounded behind, as the Supreme Commander had ordered.

CHAPTER 46

Davis brought his vehicle to a stop on a hill overlooking the base. He could see that the supply ship had gone. He also saw movement outside of the base. He looked through his binoculars and spotted Gina frantically loading and strapping supplies to the back of the remaining snowmobile. "What the hell does she think she's doing?" He grabbed his radio to report to Dan. "Dan, it looks like our little girl is being naughty. She didn't leave."

There was no reply.

"Dan, did you copy that? Lawrence, do *you* copy?" He still didn't get a response. "Damn it!" he swore, not knowing whether to deal with Gina or go back to find out why he couldn't reach the others. "Lawrence, if you can hear me, give me two clicks." He waited but heard nothing. "Well, if you can hear me, I'm going to deal with Gina before I come back."

Ferdinand Davis, lifelong flunky and thug for hire, reached inside his jacket and pulled his pistol free from its holster. He made sure it was loaded before sticking it in his coat pocket, and then he mounted the snowmobile and headed for camp.

Gina fastened down her load with rope and bungee, looked it over, and went back inside for one last look for anything she might have forgotten. She was supposed to be on the supply ship headed for Punta Arenas, Chile. After the others left, she lied to the captain, telling him Lawrence had changed his mind. The captain, in a hurry to get underway, didn't bother to argue the point and left without question.

Surprised at her good fortune, she decided to load up and head to the nearest American settlement, some seventy-five miles away. While it would've been more prudent of her to call for help, she was pressed for time and didn't know when the others would return. She packed as many supplies as the snowmobile and its sled trailer could carry. She intended to search for Randy along the way.

Confident she did indeed have everything she needed, she backed out of the supply room, turned down the hall, and was startled to find Davis casually leaning against the front door with his hands in his coat pockets.

"What are you doing here still? You were supposed to be on that ship," he said in a voice that was harsh even for him.

"I was running late and missed it. Besides, I didn't have a boarding pass," she nervously wisecracked.

"I'll ask you one more time," Davis said, not amused. "Why are you still here, and where are you going?"

Gina picked up on the menace in Davis's voice, which made her feel uneasy. "I'm going to find Randy," she told him defiantly.

"He's dead, Gina," he said without emotion.

"You don't know that. Nobody knows for sure."

"Dan, Lawrence, everybody thinks so."

"Then why are they out there looking for him?"

Davis responded only with silence.

Gina stared at the unfortunate-looking man, and suddenly she knew. "Oh my God—they're not even looking for him, are they? They lied."

"Think about it, Gina. It's been what? Over a week? He was alone with no shelter and in temperatures at minus sixty. What were his chances?" Davis asked, positioning himself in front of her.

"I don't care. I'm going anyway," she said and started to go past him.

Davis put his hand across the doorframe to block her path. "I'm sorry, but I can't let you do that."

"You don't have a choice," she said angrily and started forward again.

"No, Gina, *you* don't have a choice," Davis told her, pulling the gun from his pocket.

Gina stopped at the sight of the side arm. She was scared but also angry at the man's audacity. "What are you doing, Davis?"

"My job. I'm stopping you," he said evenly.

"With a gun—isn't that a little extreme?" she asked calmly, trying to keep the situation from escalating. She tried to think of a way out of her predicament, never taking her eye off of the gun pointed at her chest.

"You had your chance. If you would've just gotten on that boat like a good little girl, I wouldn't have to do this," he said, hardening his tone.

"What, Davis? Are you going to just shoot me?" she asked as panic crept into her voice. "This doesn't make sense. Who are you?"

"I protect the company's interests, and they're not interested in you anymore. So you're gonna have to disappear, just like that boyfriend of yours."

The implication of the statement made Gina's blood boil. "You *killed* him? You lousy piece of . . ."

"Calm down," Davis said forcefully, raising the gun so it was even with Gina's head. "I don't wanna have to make a mess in here, but if you don't step back I will. He just got lost, an unfortunate accident."

"Why are you doing this?" Gina asked, trying to stall, becoming more desperate.

Davis shook his troglodyte head in disbelief. "You know, for someone as educated as you are, you're not too bright. You could've just gotten on the boat and avoided all of this. Hell, they probably would've sent you a fat check to shut you up."

"Who would have? Why?" she asked, legitimately confused.

"If you really have to know, you and that photographer were here just as a front. A face of legitimacy is what Vance called it. Both he and Lawrence thought it would be a good idea to bring a wildlife photographer and climatice, or whatever the hell you're called, for show."

"Show for what?" Gina said, scared and frustrated at whatever he was getting at.

"My God, Gina, wake up. Do you really think a non-profit group could fund something like all of this?" he said, gesturing around the room. "We're here for the mining and drilling rights."

"Mining and *drilling*? There's no oil here. The geological surveys . . ."

"Are a lie. Do you honestly think anyone would spend all of this money just to find out why this frozen hell is melting?" he asked, sounding as if the thought of it was a joke.

"But there are treaties in place."

"That'll expire in less than twenty years, and we already have plans in motion to sidestep those treaties," he interrupted again. "There's enough oil, natural gas, coal, and minerals down here to make the rest of the world forget about the Middle East. It's enough to supply whatever country claims it for a hundred generations, and GT intends to be the contractor behind the supply." He leveled the gun at her once more. "So, in the interest of the company, I have to tie up some loose ends. The secret dies with you, Gina."

"Listen, I had no idea. I'll help with whatever you need," she said frantically, trying to find an angle to appeal to whatever twisted set of morals Davis held. "I can figure out weather patterns to help."

"Nice try," Davis said, cutting her off again. "You had your chance. We don't intend to lose out on trillions of dollars should your conscience get the best of you."

She figured if she *had* gotten on the ship, she probably would have ended up tossed into the icy Southern Ocean somewhere along the journey. At least this will be quicker. "I can't believe this," she said, feeling defeated.

A slight tapping noise came from near the front door, but the two of them ignored it.

"Well, you have about two minutes to wrap that pretty head of yours around it. Get moving," he said, motioning her to the door with his gun.

They both heard the taps again, only this time more distinct and coming from more than one place.

"What the hell is that noise?" Davis grumbled, becoming increasingly agitated. "Don't try anything," he warned and went to the door to investigate.

"What am I going try? You have the gun." Gina's sarcasm was lost on Davis.

He pulled open the door with a jerk and was surprised to find a King penguin standing on the step. "What the hell?" said Davis while looking at the equally surprised King. "Damn penguins. I've had just about enough of these things," he said, raising his pistol to fire.

Gina saw what he was about to do and reacted. "No!" she yelled as she lunged toward him, pushing his arm aside.

He missed the shot and the bullet exploded into the pre-fabricated wall beside the door. The King penguin flinched as pieces of debris sprayed him in the face. Davis spun around to line up a shot at Gina. The penguin looked between the two humans, and attacked. Davis screamed as the King's beak drove into his midsection. The man's screams were answered by a hundred penguins outside the door.

A second penguin, followed by a third, rushed through the door and joined in the fight. They stabbed madly at the man. Davis fired another shot, killing one of the attackers, but it was quickly replaced by three more. He tried to flee, but he was overpowered by the growing group.

Gina backed away and stood frozen in horror as Davis was brought down by the overwhelming assault. With an expression of terror, Davis fell forward and lost his grip on the gun. It slid across the floor and came to a rest at Gina's feet. Without hesitation, she grabbed the weapon.

"Help me, Gina. Kill them," Davis screamed, seeing that Gina had the gun.

She looked at him as the penguins pecked away and pinned him under their combined weight. She knew Davis had been ready to kill her before the penguins arrived. She read his horrified eyes, turned away, and sprinted down the hall. She heard him screaming as she turned the corner. Then she heard nothing else.

Gina slammed the door of the supply room behind her and leaned into the door, trying to catch her breath. She tried to regain her composure but was in complete disbelief at what she had witnessed. "Penguins. Why would penguins do this?" she asked, and her thoughts immediately turned to Randy. "Oh God, no, Randy." She slid to the floor, weakened by the thought of his having been killed by the animals he so adored. She thought about the horror he must have experienced when they turned on him, and she remembered the panicked sound of his voice as he pleaded for her to hurry.

Gina sat in silence, listening to the sound of a hundred clawed feet ambling around the base. Crashing and banging came from outside the door, sounding as if the penguins were demolishing everything as they searched for their next victim. "Do something," she told herself, trying to break the paralysis of fear. She got up and frantically began searching the room for something she could use. She found a nondescript box containing bullets and checked whether they were the right caliber. They were, and she stuffed them into her coat pocket.

"The snowmobile," she said as if it were a great epiphany. During her panic, she had forgotten why she was there. She looked at the small window, which was painted over and behind a storage rack. She knew she had to get to the vehicle but didn't know how with a hundred or more angry penguins milling around.

CHAPTER 47

"We should leave this human," Colonel Kimmer said to a Royal Emperor advisor who had come along.

"We can't do that. If it warns others, our plans will be ruined. Surprise is our advantage," the advisor informed him.

"I know, but this one spared my life. It could have killed several of us but didn't."

"No human life will be spared. Those are our orders, Colonel."

"Do not lecture me about orders. I know our part. You seem to have forgotten I was there when General Diutes decided to capture the human and not kill it," Kimmer said, trying to bite back his anger at the Royal Emperor's condescending tone.

"Are you suggesting we should capture it?"

Kimmer pondered the idea for a moment and thought of what General Diutes's reaction would be if he thought a subordinate was trying to equal or outdo him. He had seen Diutes's ruthlessness up close and decided he did not wish to be on the receiving end of it. "No," he said regretfully. "Find it and kill it. Honor dictates that I should not take part in the killing of one that spared me, so I shall wait outside."

The advisor looked around the room and saw that several of the penguins had stopped their rampage to watch the exchange. "You heard the colonel. Tear this place apart until you find that human!"

^^^

Gina heard the penguins just outside of the door and, after a temporary lull in destruction, it sounded as if they resumed with a renewed vigor. She looked up at the window and decided she could fit through with little trouble. She climbed up the shelving, being careful not to make too much noise, and scraped some of the paint away to look outside. She saw several penguins roaming about. "Crap," she exclaimed. She was discouraged but not hopeless. She searched the windowsill to find a way to open it, but in Antarctica, windows are not there to be opened.

She knew she couldn't break the window without giving herself away. Briefly, she considered opening the door, making a break for it, and shooting every black-and-white thing that crossed her path. But she thought about how fast Davis was brought down, and she quickly dismissed the idea. As if to emphasize that it was a bad idea, something hard slammed into the door. There was no other option now. It was the window or certain death.

Another crash against the flimsy door, followed by the sound of splintering wood, made Gina turn and look. She saw metal-covered beaks angrily pecking through the door. She threw over the racks and began to bang on the window. It was triple-layered tempered glass, and all she got for her efforts was a bruised hand. Another crack from the door and Gina saw a penguin head sticking through the opening. The penguin called out in alarm just before she kicked it in the head.

Gina climbed back to the window and started banging on it furiously. She looked out once more. She saw the penguins outside cock their heads and run to the front entrance in response to the alarm calls. She looked back and saw a penguin trying to squeeze through the widening hole. In a moment of clarity, she pulled out the gun and fired it at the penguin. She missed the target, but the marauders recoiled at the gunshot, buying some time.

She shot at the window and watched in satisfaction as the tempered glass cascaded down. A penguin popped through the now demolished door and slashed at her wildly. She dove out the window and landed face first, ignoring the stinging pain. She pocketed her weapon, quickly slid on her gloves, and bolted toward the snowmobile.

^^^

Kimmer stood outside, holding true to his honor by not partaking in the attack. He had been immersed in the Overlord's doctrine of hate as most of his kind had been, but the human had saved his life. He figured he owed it to the human to give it a chance to survive. He had heard the two gunshots and had ordered the remaining penguins to go in and assist their compatriots. Judging from the calls, they seemed to have found their quarry.

He heard a strange noise from off to his side, which was followed by the sound of heavy feet crunching through the ice and snow. He looked and saw the human prey running straight at him. "Clever," he said, admiring its tenacity. His admiration quickly turned to fear, however, when he realized that he had to face the human alone.

^^^

Gina ran toward her loaded-down snowmobile and saw a lone penguin standing near it. *A guard?* she thought. As crazy as it sounded, it wouldn't have surprised her after seeing the organized manner in which the penguins had attacked. She hesitated but decided she could surely keep one penguin at bay while she started her vehicle.

As she got closer, the penguin seemed nervous, but it made no aggressive move to stop her. She mounted the snowmobile and fumbled around, trying to start it while keeping an eye on the penguin. The penguin stood by, watching her cautiously. Gina noticed a blood smear on its white chest and assumed it was more than likely one of Davis' killers. She hoped it would kill Lawrence and Dan as well.

She finally got the vehicle started, pulled on a pair of goggles, and cinched her hood tight. She sped away.

CHAPTER 48

The Chinstrap corps led by Lieutenant-General Lavour, along with two divisions of Gentoo and Adélie, and a company each of Rockhoppers and Kings, amassed five kilometers away from Pack Ice Command to begin their march toward the human settlements. They were to attack at dawn.

"I don't like this," Lavour muttered to Leepoh.

Leepoh and Nok joined Lavour at the head of the march to pass the time on the long journey. "You don't like what?" Leepoh asked.

"Getting tipped."

Before leaving PIC, every penguin had been fitted with a piece of metal, which was affixed to the end of its beak for protection and for use as a weapon.

"The humans have hard heads," Nok informed him. "I saw a Rockhopper who cracked his beak on one of their skulls during our confrontation."

"But it's not very comfortable. I can't breathe right with it on."

"You'll appreciate it soon enough," Nok said.

The comment made the three of them go silent as they pondered the possible outcomes and their roles in the events being thrust upon them.

They traveled much of the long and arduous journey in silence. After many hours, they arrived. The sun had yet to rise. They stood just outside of their first target. Leepoh, who had returned to his division to see to his duties as the Gentoo commander came rushing back to Lavour, who had been rejoined by Nok.

"Two human ships left just before we got here, so that should make things a little easier," he told Lavour.

"How will that make it any easier?" Lavour, who was noticeably tense at the prospect of the upcoming assault, asked.

"Because a large number of them left with the ships," Leepoh answered.

Lavour took a deep breath. "Do you really think we can pull this off? Driving every human away, I mean."

Nok looked at Lavour. "I wouldn't worry about it. We have troops that number in the millions. The humans are spread out and at a disadvantage. They have no idea of what's about to happen. We won't have any problems," Nok said unassertively.

"You don't sound too convinced, yourself, Nok."

Nok averted his eyes. "Just allow me my delusions, will you?"

"How about you, Leepoh?" asked Lavour.

"The time has come, my friend. I will do my duty, if only to ensure the safety of as many as I can. Speaking of time, I have to go."

"Where now?" asked Nok.

"I am leading the assault at sea. The Blackfoot scouts informed me that every morning several small boats cruise the bay."

Lavour stared at Leepoh with uncertainty in his eyes.

Leepoh stared back at him. "I don't like this anymore than you do, but if I don't lead the assault, somebody else will, and I do have *some* experience. I don't want Gentoo to die because they weren't properly prepared. To that end, Lavour, we must comply."

Lavour studied his friend for a moment. "There you go philosophizing again."

"Hah!" Leepoh laughed.

"What sad times these are, when this is what we depend on for philosophy," Nok snorted, indicating Leepoh with his flipper.

"Bah! Now I have two to give me insults. What sad times indeed," Leepoh said with false hurt in his voice.

A Gentoo call broke up the trio's discussion. "Time for me to go," said Leepoh.

"Be safe," Lavour told him as he gave him a long look.

"You as well," he said to both Lavour and Nok and then hurried back to his division.

Several minutes later, led by General Leepoh, the Gentoo split away from the main force and headed toward the sea to begin the new phase of the war.

^^^

"We've spotted the Chinstrap, sir," a Royal Emperor announced to General Diutes.

"Be more specific, Sergeant. We now have two we are searching for," Diutes snapped in his customary angry tone.

"I apologize, sir. Trevot, I believe its name is. He was spotted near the ocean."

Diutes looked away, as if he could see the sea in the distance, making a sinister clicking as he thought. "Sergeant, send word to Supreme Commander Liutites that we have a defector, and request a company of warriors to deal with the problem."

"Yes, sir. Sir, may I ask a question?"

"It appears as if you have just done so, Sergeant, but you may ask another," Diutes said, unable to communicate with civility.

"Why do we need a full company of warriors to handle one Chinstrap?"

"It is not for a *single* Chinstrap. The Supreme Commander informed me that several of them are beginning to have *questionable* loyalties. The warriors will motivate them so that they will have no doubts as to where their loyalty should lie. Our Lieutenant Trevot is, most likely, headed to his nesting site." Diutes paused for dramatic effect. "The Royal Emperor warriors will be waiting."

CHAPTER 49

A twenty-foot sightseeing boat was cruising along the edge of the ice floes. It was one of several that, for those who could afford the privilege, provided tours of Antarctica's icy coast. It was the last voyage of the season. The approaching winter would make the weather too inhospitable for all but the rugged. The wealthy tourists were bundled in orange jackets with fur-lined hoods, looking for anything other than icebergs.

"This is ridiculous," a pompous man chided the boat's captain and tour guide. "We've been down here for a week and haven't seen a thing other than a seal. We can see that in any zoo back home. My wife and I are going to demand a full refund."

"Sir," the captain said in a placating voice, "you have seen many wondrous things during your stay here. You came here for sightseeing, and that is what we have been doing."

"I don't care about the *sights*. I promised my wife we would see penguins, and we have yet to see a single one," the man said belligerently.

"It is more than a little bit unusual," the captain conceded. "As a matter of fact, we're a bit alarmed by their absence. Perhaps the effects of global warming are disrupting the natural cycle."

"Don't give me that tree-hugging *global warming* nonsense. That's just a bunch of liberal, environmentalist hype, aimed at reducing corporate profits."

The captain just shook his head and peered through his binoculars with the hope of finding at least one group of penguins before they left for the winter. As he scanned the water, he saw the distinctive porpoising of swimming penguins. He held them in his sights a few seconds longer, and his shoulders slumped in relief at finally finding some. "Okay, everyone," he announced. "It looks as though our luck has changed. If you'll look off the port side, you should be able to see a large group of penguins swimming in our direction."

"Strangely convenient," the obnoxious man told his wife. "When I said I was going to demand a refund, the penguins showed up. What'd they do, release them from a cage?"

The captain ignored the man's asinine comment. "Get your cameras ready—they're almost upon us," he said as he tried muster up some enthusiasm. It had been a long season, with nary a penguin to be found. Most of the people who could pay the price of the excursions were just as pompous as the man and his wife. People expected wildlife to perform like circus animals.

About fifty meters from the boat, the penguins dove beneath the surface.

"Hey! Where'd they go?" one of the tourists asked.

They stared at the calm sea for half a minute.

"We didn't even get a picture," a disappointed passenger lamented.

"I don't know. But you have to remember that these are wild animals. They don't live according to our schedules," the captain said, checking the other side of the boat to see if they would surface there.

The water suddenly began to churn, and without warning, the penguins began to launch themselves over the side of the skiff. The passengers were at first surprised and confused. Then they were horrified when the penguins flew in from the depths and knocked a man over the side and into the near-frozen water. The tourist erupted into screams as the penguins began to stab at the crowd ferociously.

The obnoxious man stood frozen in horror as his wife fell under the attacks. He reached for her but was hit by the second wave of marauders and fell to the deck. A dozen or more penguins pounced on the fallen man and soon silenced his cries for help. The captain ignored his cries, struggling to stay on his feet himself. He desperately tried to make his way to the helm, kicking, grabbing, and throwing the diminutive beasts from the boat. He hoped to survive long enough to restart the engine and call for help.

Leepoh floated on the surface of the water, observing the mêlée. He spotted the man fighting his way through the throng toward the back of the boat. "What are they doing? Get him!" he said, knowing what the man was doing. The attack had gone relatively smoothly so far, but he didn't like the way it was headed. If the boat escaped, they would be hard pressed to catch it. The assault group was doing their best, but the small boat allowed them only so much room to fight.

Leepoh decided to take action. He quickly dove under the surface and swam with a burst of speed. He was unsure if he had enough distance to build up his speed to clear the low sides of the boat. As he shot through the water, he passed the body of one of their victims that had quickly died in the freezing ocean. He gave himself one final thrust with his powerful flippers, flew over the side of the boat, and hit the man square in the chest.

The captain stumbled backwards from the unexpected blow to the chest, and Leepoh fell backwards as well, stunned from hitting the man headfirst. The captain struggled to get up and reached for the handset of the radio to make a distress call. Leepoh shook his head, trying to clear his vision. The penguin saw what the captain was doing, lunged forward, and pecked him hard on the hand. When the peck failed to stop him, Leepoh grabbed the cord of the radio in his beak and ripped it from the console.

The surprised captain stared at Leepoh. With all the passengers now dead, the penguins turned their full attention on the remaining survivor. The captain appeared to give up and let himself fall backwards over the side of the boat and into the icy depths. He froze to death far faster than he would've died by being ravaged by penguins.

The battle was over, and Leepoh surveyed the carnage. "How many did we lose?" he asked the Gentoo sergeant.

"Five," the sergeant informed him.

Leepoh lowered his head and sighed. "All right, let's get going. We still have another one out there. And, Sergeant, see to it that the wounded get to shore. Notwithstanding the Supreme Commander's orders, *no one* gets left behind under my command."

"Yes, sir," the sergeant saluted and began to tend to the injured.

Leepoh looked away distantly and tried to shake off the dizzying effects of his head injury before he jumped back into the water.

CHAPTER 50

Leepoh arrived at the predetermined area to regroup with the main penguin strike force. Once at the area, he found an astonishing sight. The human settlement was completely overrun with penguins. The bodies of humans were strewn about the township. Some were trampled into the ground from thousands of the marauders treading on them.

Dead men were lying in the doorway of a church built in the distant past. Snowmobiles were overturned from humans having tried to drive through the masses, and a helicopter sat on its landing pad with its rotor slowly turning, its deceased pilot partially hanging out of the door. A dog barked and growled in the distance, followed by the calls of an undetermined number of penguins. The dog yelped, and silence once again returned. A trail of the dead led to the ramp of a ship still moored at the dock. The unfortunate victims never reached the safe haven they had hoped for.

From his vantage point on a hill overlooking the settlement, Leepoh spotted a Chinstrap and Rockhopper walking together amid the cloud of black and white. He knew at once that they were his two friends. He paid close attention to Lavour and could tell by his actions that his innocence had been lost, his soul sullied by the violence of warfare.

Leepoh slid down the hill on his stomach, got to his feet, and stumbled a bit from dizziness. "Hello, my friends," he said when they spotted him.

"Are you all right?" Nok asked when Leepoh swayed as he stood.

"Just have to watch where I land after coming from the water. How are you two doing?"

Lavour remained silent, so Nok answered. "We're alive. The battle was ferocious but relatively short. The humans were, of course, taken completely by surprise."

"It won't be that way for long. I understand humans have incredible communications devices that enable them to communicate over thousands of miles. If they used such devices, they won't be caught off guard again." Leepoh looked Lavour over and saw a smattering of blood on his white chest. "Are you all right, Lavour?"

Lavour just nodded.

"He lost one of his friends—Sergeant Gereaux. And he nearly lost his head attempting to save him," Nok answered in more detail for him. "One of the humans was fighting with some sort of weapon that had a blade on the end. My group had just arrived when I saw Gereaux go down. Lavour here rushed in, and the human took a swipe at him as well. Fortunately for Lavour, the human's aim was high, which allowed Lavour and about ten others to take it down."

"It was all so *horrific*," Lavour finally said. "The blood, the screams of the humans and penguins alike—then their beasts attacked as well."

"Beasts?" asked Leepoh, unsure of what he was referring to.

"Yes. They were like the Phocids, but with legs and hair."

"Dogs," Leepoh informed him.

"Well, the Overlord should have been more specific about what they were, because they're fast, and they killed several of us before we stopped them," Nok said with an obvious tone of resentment.

"We know now," Leepoh remarked.

"How did your assault go?" Nok asked.

"Quick, but I lost five Gentoo," Leepoh said remorsefully, not bothering to elaborate.

"How many were lost here?"

"So far the count is up to nearly two hundred. The last I heard the humans lost eighty-one. That's over two penguins to one human, and only one of them used a gun," Lavour said in a monotone. "At this rate, we'll usher in our own extinction."

A Royal Emperor advisor approached the trio while they stood talking. "Well done today, Lieutenant-General Lavour," the advisor commended. "Was your assault a success as well, General Leepoh?"

"If by *success*, you mean did we eliminate the humans, then yes," Leepoh said, continuing his efforts to annoy every Royal Emperor to which he spoke.

"Good. Very good," the Royal Emperor responded, oblivious to Leepoh's effort. "Return to your respective divisions. We are to wait here for one or two days, until we are issued new orders. Have your troops gather any human items that may be of use. A group from Forward Command One will be arriving to gather items for processing." The advisor turned away to leave.

"Excuse me." Leepoh stopped him. "Has there been any report from the other assault groups?"

"Our messengers are only just now reporting in. Colonel Kimmer's group and a few others have reported success. I'll know more at a later time."

After the advisor departed, Leepoh turned to the others. "I hope we head to sea soon."

"Why is that?" Lavour asked.

"When the humans figure out they can no longer communicate with any of their kind here, they'll investigate," Leepoh explained, uncharacteristically serious.

The others pondered what would happen when more humans arrived and learned of the fate of their kind. The sky began to grow dim from an approaching windstorm, which seemed to foreshadow their unclear future.

"Looks like a storm is coming. We'd better get to work," Nok said, and the three went their separate ways.

CHAPTER 51

Corporal Meuseaux trudged across the barren landscape. All the while, he kept an eye on the impending windstorm. A haze of gray in the distance was a telltale sign. It was going to be an intense storm. He knew if he didn't find shelter soon, he probably wouldn't survive the night.

He traveled on and fought to push his exhausted body against the increasingly strong wind. He knew the mountains were close, but his sight was limited by the blowing snow. As he pressed forward, he heard a strange sound from somewhere in the distance. He strained to hear it, but it disappeared in the gale. He continued on his way and heard it again, only this time it was steady and closer. It was not a natural sound. It sounded almost like a human machine.

Meuseaux stopped to listen and saw a faint light coming toward him. He quickly thought of his options. It was obviously a human, and his training at PIC had taught him that all humans were evil. This hadn't been his experience though. The captive, Randy, considered him his friend, and those he had seen at his nesting grounds had paid him little attention or watched him enthusiastically.

A brief lull in the wind gave Meuseaux a better view, and he made his decision. He thought the human might help him find shelter, and if the human were out here alone, then it might need help as well. The machine approached him rapidly, and when it came near, he began to wave his good flipper frantically, hoping to get the human's attention.

^^^

Gina had her confiscated snowmobile at full throttle, hoping soon to find someplace to pitch her tent and ride out the storm. She knew she didn't have much time and that she was running out of options. The windstorms of Antarctica could last for days, and she knew if she didn't get her tent up soon, she probably would never be able to survive the squall.

Through her frosty goggles and the blowing snow, she spotted a small dark figure ahead of her. She knew by the size of it that it could only be a penguin. She briefly entertained the thought of running it down but decided against it. As she got closer, she saw it do something she didn't expect. It began to wave its flipper as if it were trying to get her attention. She remembered the attack at the base and had no intention of stopping.

Gina eased off the throttle a touch when she came upon it, and the penguin began to wave even more frantically as she passed. She watched it as she went by and, in that moment of inattention, hit an unseen object. She tried to regain control but overcorrected, nearly flipped her vehicle, and was thrown off. She landed hard on her back and was dazed from the impact. Fortunately, the snowmobile didn't overturn and instead cruised to a stop just thirty meters away.

While trying to regain her senses, she saw the little penguin running toward her. She felt for the pistol in her coat pocket but left it inside. With her bulky gloves on, she couldn't fire it anyway. It was just one penguin, and she figured she could handle it if it did attack.

Meuseaux rushed to the accident. When he approached, Gina stood and backed away. He stood before her, looking up. "Are you all right?" he asked.

Gina shook her head, not believing what she was hearing. "I must've really hit my head."

"Iss your head all right?" Meuseaux asked her.

She looked at him in silence and surveyed her surroundings, thinking it was some kind of hoax. "Penguins can't talk," she assured herself, but she remembered that she had thought penguins didn't attack people either. "Um, yeah. I'm all right," she answered slowly and without confidence.

Meuseaux nodded. "Seek shelter. You, me not sssurvive we stay." He headed to the snowmobile.

Gina stood and watched skeptically as the Chinstrap hurried away. When Meuseaux reached the snowmobile, he turned back to her and waited. Unsure as to whether she was delusional or lying unconscious in the snow and dreaming this, she decided to see it through.

"Me go on machine, sso both seek shelter," Meuseaux asked when she arrived.

"You're real. I'm not dreaming this?"

Meuseaux tilted his head. "I do not know word dreaming," he told her.

Gina shook her head and decided that it wasn't a figment of her imagination. As if to emphasize the point, the lull in the storm ceased and the wind howled.

"We live, must go," Meuseaux urged her.

"Okay, whatever you say," Gina said as she mounted the snowmobile and restarted the engine. There was no time to contemplate the reality of the situation. If she didn't get out of the storm soon, the reality would be death.

Meuseaux looked back and forth, searching for a way on. Gina saw this, lifted him up, and placed him in front of her on the seat. "MMountain small away. Give uss hide from wind," he informed her.

Gina took a deep breath. "This can't be real," she mumbled and sped away to escape the rapidly deteriorating conditions.

CHAPTER 52

Trevot swam along the shore of the Antarctic Peninsula near his home and breeding ground. Several times along his journey, he had needed to seek a place to hide to avoid being spotted by passing groups of penguins. From a safe distance, he had watched many of the battles between the penguins and the humans. While at Forward Command, he had heard talk of the impending attack on the settlements but never imagined it would be on such a grand scale. He hoped that his home was safe from the carnage.

His home was a small strip of an island in the archipelagos. It was also the home of Lavour, Mevoule, Meuseaux and the rest of the Chinstrap company assigned to Pack Ice Command. He floated in the water just off shore and watched the others nearby. After escaping the brutality of General Diutes, crossing the harsh open land, and swimming for miles, he was home. He was exhausted, but home nonetheless.

He slowly paddled his way in and casually went ashore. As he stepped foot on the pebbly beach, a Chinstrap spotted him, and the welcoming calls erupted immediately. A crowd of Chinstraps rushed to greet him and rubbed their beaks against his in a show of welcome. Trevot looked at them happily. It had been a long time since he had looked at the faces of the colony he loved.

"Trevot!" a female called to him. It was Lannera, Lavour's mate. "It's good to see you home. Are the others coming as well? We've waited so long and have heard nothing."

"It's good to be home, but I'm afraid I am the only one who has returned for now," he said to her regretfully. He had lost his own mate—two seasons before—to the Leopard Seals and had not taken another.

"Oh," she said, disappointed. "But you're back, and that's cause for celebration," she continued, changing her tune.

"Don't celebrate too soon. I don't know whether you have heard, but the Overlord has begun a massive offensive against the humans. War has been thrust upon the penguins."

"Is Lavour involved?" Lannera asked with concern.

"I'm afraid he most likely is."

"How did it happen that you were sent home and nobody else?" Lannera asked.

Trevot hesitated, suddenly feeling guilty for being in the comforting safety of home while his friends were facing danger. "It's a long story, but the short of it is that somebody must have overheard me talking against the Royal Emperors and I was punished for it."

"Punished?" one of the others asked. "By whom and why? Since when can we not speak our mind?"

"It's the Emperors, or Royal Emperors, to be more specific. The Overlord has complete control over the PDA, and the Royal Emperors rule with a stone flipper. They are not to be trusted."

At hearing this, the crowd of Chinstraps began to chatter angrily among themselves. Trevot looked away from the others and, as if speaking the words had conjured the enemy, saw Royal Emperor warriors emerging from the sea, led by General Diutes. "Go!" he said to Lannera in alarm. "Go before it's too late!"

"I don't understand, Trevot. What's wrong with the Royal Emperors?" she asked.

"Just trust me, please," he urged her, with general approaching.

Diutes ambled his way to the Chinstraps and stared at Trevot with malice in his eyes. He was followed by a wall of warriors that blocked nearly every escape route. "Thank you, Lieutenant Trevot," he said, looking at him with his freakish red eye. "The Chinstraps are due for a lesson in loyalty, and I myself couldn't have found a better place for such a lesson. Isn't this the home of your company?"

"What do you want, Diutes? I quit the PDA. You no longer have any control over me," Trevot told him angrily.

"You are mistaken, Chinstrap," Diutes said with a twisted glee in his voice. "It is you who no longer has control over you."

"What are you talking about?" Trevot asked, confused by Diutes's insane babble.

"This colony has become a problem for the Overlord. There are too many dissidents. Between you, Meuseaux, and possibly Lieutenant-General Lavour, you might cause an insurrection, so it's time to cut off the problem at the head."

"You're insane," the now fearful Trevot exclaimed.

"Possibly, but who are you to judge? Troopers, kill them all."

"No," Trevot shouted and charged at Diutes with the full intent of plunging his beak into his chest. He leapt at Diutes, but the general slapped him aside with his powerful flipper. He struggled to clear his head and right himself but felt the full weight of Diutes on top of him. "You won't get away with this!" he said between gasping breaths.

"Who do you suppose will stop me, you? You won't live long enough to draw your next breath, Chinstrap."

Trevot looked to his left and saw Lannera taken down by the warriors. By crossing a narrow fjord between the island and the mainland, several more troops had arrived. They overtook the Chinstraps with overwhelming force. Trevot fought to free himself of Diutes's weight but didn't have the strength. He felt the searing pain of Diutes's beak plunge into his flesh, and his scream joined the terrified calls of his colony. Trevot's life faded away, leaving behind his hatred of General Diutes.

CHAPTER 53

Gina brushed the ice from her clothing and crawled inside the temporary refuge of her tent. She had made camp at the base of the mountains, having been guided there by the remarkable Chinstrap. She immediately began to rummage through one of her packs that crowded the small tent. She pulled out a small stove. In spite of the protection the mountains provided, the wind whipped at the tent at nearly sixty kilometers per hour, and with the temperature near negative fifty degrees Celsius, Gina found it difficult to light the stove.

After finally getting the stove to light, she opened her pack of provisions, put a small pot on the stove, and emptied a food pack into it. The food would not get hot, but it would eventually get warm enough to eat. Gina then turned her attention to the Chinstrap, who stood by the entrance, seemingly unsure of what to make of what Gina was doing. She stared at the Chinstrap for a while, not knowing how to start a conversation with a penguin. "I know you can talk, unless I'm imagining all of this," she said.

Meuseaux watched Gina as well. "Why do you doubt to believe me can talk? Me . . ." he paused to correct himself. "I . . . I am not without intelligence."

It wasn't a good start. This was her first conversation with the penguin, and Gina had insulted him. "I'm sorry. It's not that I think you're not intelligent. It's just that I didn't know penguins could speak my language.

So how smart are you?"

Meuseaux pondered the question. "Me . . . I do not know. How smart you?"

Gina was surprised by the penguin's retort. She thought about how she had found herself in her situation—duped by a corrupt corporation and nearly murdered. And she didn't even know what species of penguin was standing in her tent. To top it all off, she had let the man she loved face almost certain death. "All right," she conceded. "That was a tough question. So how about this one: how long have penguins been able to speak our language? Or are you the only one?"

"I am not only one. We learned human speak only little time. Do no things speak than humans and uss?"

Gina took a moment to decipher Meuseaux's question. "No, I don't think so. Other creatures can talk. A bird called a parrot can be trained to talk, but they more mimic. One can't have a true conversation with them. Do you have names as well?"

"Yess," Meuseaux plainly answered.

"Can I know yours?"

"Yess," Meuseaux answered again.

"What is it?" Gina asked, seeing that she would have to be more specific.

"It is Meuseaux."

"If you don't mind my saying so, that sounds very human."

"I do not mind. The names of uss came from the humans that first came here long time. They did not know we were hearing them."

Gina sat in silence as she thought about how many years people had been coming to this place. She knew humans influenced animal behavior, but usually it was in a negative way. She thought about the attack and decided to ask about the reason. "Why are penguins attacking people?" she asked hesitantly.

"Iss because uss are to make humans leave this home," Meuseaux answered, sounding almost embarrassed for his kind's behavior.

Gina took in the Chinstrap's statement, trying to wrap her head around a penguin revolt. "But why? Are we causing you problems?"

"Not uss. Otherss, they have not lived well. By being here, it make problems. I know that not your intent, but for some it iss," Meuseaux said in his straightforward manner.

"I understand," Gina told him. Her earlier suspicions had been correct. The penguins' behavior had indeed been affected by people. It was not just a long-term matter related to global warming or pollution. They had been affected in their thought process. Their evolutionary path had been irrevocably altered from man's very presence in this isolated habitat.

"Yess, some of you do. The other I spoke said sso as well."

Gina's heart lurched at hearing this. Her first thought was that it was Randy, but she knew that that would be too much to ask. "The other? You spoke to another?"

"Yess, it iss Overlord's and Supreme Commander's prisoner," Meuseaux told her.

Gina was confused. "I'm sorry, but did you say Overlord and Supreme Commander?"

"Yess."

"This is getting weirder by the second," she said to herself. "Do you know the prisoner's name?"

"Yess, he said I was his friend."

"What is his name?" Gina pressed, trying to remain patient and calm.

"Randy."

Gina jumped up with excitement at hearing his name, nearly knocking over the stove. "Are you sure? Is he all right?"

"Yess—do you know of him?"

"Yes! Yes, I do. He's the reason I'm out here. I'm searching for him," she said, barely able to contain her joy. "He's still alive, then?"

"He was when I go," Meuseaux said, understanding her excitement.

"What do you mean? Is he in danger?" she asked as her joy turned to fear.

"He iss, I know."

Gina remained silent for a minute as she thought about her options. She knew she had to get to Randy. That much was clear. But if the place where he was being held was full of the type of penguins that attacked the base, how could she save him once she got there? "We have to go to him. Can you take me to him?"

It was Meuseaux's turn to be silent.

Gina picked up on his hesitation. "You don't want to go there?"

"My in danger there," he said, then straightened. "But Randy is friend. I will lead you to him, though we cannot go until storm is over. It would not serve him if we were to die before."

During her excitement, Gina had completely forgotten the windstorm. "That's right. Then we'll leave as soon as it ends. Is it far from here?"

"I believe that it iss not far. For now, we must rest. We will need our strength when time comess."

Gina looked at the Chinstrap and admired his levelheadedness. "You're right. Hopefully the storm will be over soon."

"They are most time."

CHAPTER 54

Supreme Commander Liutites entered the Overlord's chamber, exhibiting a feeling of pride and near excitement, which was quite the opposite of his usual angry and stoic demeanor. He was not at ease, though; he never was when visiting Antaean. The only time he was ever at ease was in the company of Mearna. But now those times were few, relegated only to when they met for the business of the training and raising of the elite.

It had not always been this way. In the early days of the PDA, Liutites and Mearna had raised several chicks together, but with the founding of Pack Ice Command and its rookeries, more and more of his time became dedicated to Antaean's demands. Being of the Royal bloodline, he could not ignore his duty. Through cunning and sheer ruthlessness, he ascended to the rank of Supreme Commander. He guarded the title jealously, a title he would kill to defend. It was a title he had killed to defend

As Liutites approached, the Overlord's back was turned to him. He briefly considered attacking him and making his final ascent to become *the* most powerful penguin but dismissed the thought when the Overlord spoke. There would be another time.

"Supreme Commander, what information do you bring me?" the Overlord asked as he turned and fixed Liutites with a glare that seemed to read his thoughts.

"My lord," said Liutites with a high beak salute. "We have had phenomenal success in the attack on the humans. In just two days we have achieved a complete victory," he said proudly.

"The victory is far from complete, Supreme Commander," Antaean bellowed. "It is true that we have won a major battle. And with the onset of winter, the humans will be hard pressed to retaliate. But we must not rely on that alone."

"Yes, my lord," Liutites said with less enthusiasm.

"Yes to what, Liutites?" the Overlord inquired.

Liutites paused before answering. His thoughts had been on the victory and then on the Overlord's accusatory stare. He was merely agreeing with the Overlord to placate him. "Yes, you are correct to bring my error on my appraisal of victory to my attention. We must strike at the outlying islands immediately to keep the humans' attention away from the mainland."

Overlord Antaean eyed his subordinate briefly. "Very good, Supreme Commander. I believe a new group of elite warriors is now ready for combat. Have them reinforce the reclaimed coastline."

"Yes, my lord."

"You may order the attack on the surrounding islands immediately."

"Yes, my lord."

"Has the situation with Chinstraps been dealt with?"

"Yes, my lord—by General Diutes personally," Liutites answered, returning to his stoic behavior.

"Very good. I am pleased with your success in dealing with the Phocids. However, I am concerned about our sacrifice having escaped once again."

"Yes, my lord. He was resilient. But he was wounded and caught in the storm alone. I am sure he could not have survived," Liutites said but immediately regretted having offered his assessment of the Chinstrap's chances.

"Perhaps," Antaean said, turning his attention back to what he had been looking at when Liutites entered. "Supreme Commander, before you leave, come and look at my trophies."

Liutites waddled beside him and looked at the ghastly display of bare skulls.

"These are our enemies. Stripped of their identity, they are left only with what lies inside." Antaean turned his focus on Liutites. "It would be a shame to add a Royal Emperor skull to my collection, wouldn't it, Supreme Commander?"

Liutites stared back at the Overlord. He would have to be cautious in dealing with the Overlord. "Yes, my lord. It would be," he said, unflinching under the Overlord's gaze.

"Go and begin the campaign on the islands at once. You are dismissed," the Overlord said, sounding as if he had lost interest in the conversation.

Supreme Commander Liutites saluted and exited, eager to be free of the Overlord's company and feeling considerably less proud and excited.

CHAPTER 55

In the days since his first battle with the humans, Lavour had spent most of his time with Leepoh and Nok. Although nothing in his training while at PIC had prepared him for the violence and loss of dear friends, his time spent with his two odd companions had helped to ease his troubled mind.

A messenger from Forward Command approached the three as Leepoh rattled on about his typical nonsense.

"So the squid darts left, then right, thinking it can fool me. But it should have known better than to think it could fool a Gentoo with an empty stomach."

"Is there a point to this story?" an annoyed Nok asked Leepoh. "I have things to do, you know."

"Like what?" Leepoh asked.

"Breathe, for one. Your story has been so very riveting that I have been holding my breath for half the day in anticipation of its exciting conclusion," Nok answered.

"Hah!" Leepoh brayed out. "Now like I was saying, the squid . . ."

"Excuse me," the Chinstrap messenger interrupted Leepoh.

"Thank the Ancients," Nok said to Lavour as all three looked at the messenger. "We get a break from his incessant nattering."

"I am Corporal Mauntrüse from Forward Command. I have a message."

"Forward Command?" asked Lavour. "How is Lieutenant Trevot faring?"

"Trevot?" the corporal asked, trying to recall. "He has not been seen for several days. But that is not why I am here."

"I hope he followed my instructions," Lavour said to himself.

"Sir." The messenger interrupted Lavour's thoughts rather sternly.

"I apologize, Corporal. You have a message for me?"

"Yes, sir. We received word that the humans have mounted a small counterstrike."

"Well, that was to be expected. Tell me, Corporal Mauntrüse, what does that have to do with me?" Lavour asked suspiciously.

"They attacked your colony, sir."

"What?" Lavour asked in shock.

Leepoh and Nok came to Lavour's side.

"Were there survivors? Did any escape?" Lavour asked in a panic.

"No, sir. I'm sorry," Mauntrüse answered hesitantly.

Lavour's mind raced to make sense of what he was told.

"If it's any consolation, sir, a passing patrol of Royal Emperors heard the attack and killed the humans," the messenger said, not knowing what else to say.

"No," Lavour whispered as he looked at his two friends. "No."

Leepoh looked at the messenger. "Go now, Corporal. We'll take care of him."

"Yes, sir. One more thing," the messenger said quietly. "There is word that the island campaign will begin tomorrow."

"All right, Corporal, dismissed," Leepoh told him impatiently.

"We're here for you, Lavour," Nok, who knew the pain of loss, told him.

"I have to go," Lavour said despondently. "I have to see." He tried to go, but Leepoh stopped him.

"You don't want to do that, my friend. You don't want to see," Leepoh told him.

"I *have* to, Leepoh. Lannera was there. I have to know."

"Then we'll go with you," Nok told him as he looked to Leepoh for reassurance.

Lavour shook his head. "No. This is a Chinstrap matter. I'll bring those in my company who are from our colony."

"Are you sure you want to do this?" Leepoh asked with concern for Lavour.

"No, but I have to. My son was there as well." Lavour began walking toward the other Chinstraps but turned to look at Nok and Leepoh. "I'll be back," he said with uncertainty as to what he was about to face. He went to the others and informed them of the tragedy. One hundred Chinstraps joined Lavour in a race to the sea.

Leepoh and Nok watched the Chinstraps. "Do you think he'll be all right?" Nok asked Leepoh.

"No, he won't," Leepoh answered quietly.

CHAPTER 56

Lavour swam faster than he had ever swum in his life, leaving his Chinstrap followers in his contrails. He dove under large icebergs and flew over small ones, driving himself to the brink of exhaustion. He had no purpose in pushing himself to his limits other than an attempt to burn away the pain he felt. He didn't care about abandoning his post, about the war, the PDA, or Liutites; all of those things were trivial. All that mattered was reaching home.

He broke from the surface to see his home looming ahead of him and swam harder still, until, at last, he was there. He went ashore, catching his breath as the others arrived behind him. He was home, but what he saw was no longer home. Before him lay devastation. He didn't hear the happy calls of greeting or see the Chinstrap chicks scurrying alongside their parents. There was no joy or bliss. All he saw was death.

He walked through the nesting ground and found the young and the old, male and female, lying side by side. He saw the trampled nests. He silently searched for his Lannera among the carnage. The calls of sorrow began to fill the air as the Chinstraps discovered their deceased loved ones. Lavour saw his nesting site ahead, and his legs felt heavy, as though they were trying to prevent him from seeing what lay ahead.

He pressed forward and found Lannera, his life mate, lying lifeless and broken on the cold ground. Beside her was his nearly grown fledgling, lifeless as well. He stood in silence until his legs betrayed him. Weakened by his grief and no longer able to support his weight, he fell to the ground beside his family and began to weep.

From all around the Chinstrap nesting ground, the mournful cries of heartache and loss could be heard in a chorus of lamentation.

For nearly an hour, Lavour lay on the ground beside the bodies of his family until he finally found the strength, or the will, to stand. Not far from where he stood, he spotted two Royal Emperor warriors standing like silent sentinels. "Time for answers," he told himself and proceeded their way. A few steps away, he found the body of Trevot. His eyes were still open in a frozen expression of horror. "I told him to go home," Lavour whispered, looking at the wounds on his dead friend's chest. "I sent him to his death."

A tinge of anger began to well up inside Lavour as he approached the warriors. "I am Lieutenant-General Lavour. This was my colony. What can you tell me about what took place here?"

The two penguins exchanged looks. "The humans came here and attacked," one of them said. "We were on patrol not far from here when we heard the alarm calls. By the time we arrived it was already too late."

Lavour looked at the ground, trying to swallow his burgeoning hatred. "And what of the humans?"

"We killed them. One of them tried to escape, but we caught it and killed it. Their bodies have been taken to Forward Command for processing."

"Processing?" Lavour inquired.

"Yes, sir. Their bones are strong, and we can use them as weapons," the other said.

A few days, or even a few hours, before, the thought would have been abhorrent to Lavour, but no longer; he was glad to hear it. He stood in silence as he thought about what Lannera had faced in her final moments. Grief threatened to overcome him again, but a new feeling of hatred shored his strength. "Good," he said angrily. "Kill them with their own bones."

"Yes, sir, we will," the warriors said with assurance.

Lavour walked with a renewed purpose to the shore and called to his fellow Chinstraps. "Chinstraps," he cried out as they arrived. "Gather your strength and swallow your grief. Use it to fuel your hatred of our enemy. From this day on, we will show no mercy. We will return in kind what the humans have done to our families, what they have done to us, and what they have done to our home. The humans must pay. The humans must die."

The Chinstraps gave a united angry call in support of their commander, and Lavour led them to the sea, leaving their home behind forever.

The two Royal Emperors stood in the distance, watching the display with the satisfaction of a job well done.

CHAPTER 57

Gina had spent the past two days impatiently waiting out the windstorm. It was time well spent though. She had gotten to know her Chinstrap companion better—a lot better. She had helped him along with his grasp of the English language, and she was continually amazed by what Meuseaux told her about the penguins and their lives. He told all about Pack Ice Command, its command structure, and the Overlord. He warned her of the Supreme Commander and of what he knew of the war against the humans.

Gina was horrified by some of his tales. The penguins seemed almost human in that they seemed to share the same penchant for treachery and manipulation. To some degree, she understood the reason behind their insurrection. For years these creatures had been forced to endure hardships, and with the ban on mining in Antarctica about to be dissolved, this was a species on the brink. She knew by their actions that the penguins might have been hastening their own demise. She knew, as well, that man's stupidity and greed wouldn't allow another species to share the world if that species held land where obscene amounts of profit could be made.

As Gina and Meuseaux cruised across the frozen landscape, her thoughts turned to only one thing—rescuing Randy from the clutches of the evil Royal Emperors.

Meuseaux, who was riding nearly on Gina's lap and seemingly having a grand time, looked up at her and motioned for her to stop. Gina complied. "Pack Ice Command is not far from this point."

"That's great. So why are we stopping?"

"We must take shelter until night. As I told you, we must be secretive. I can get you in only if we are not seen."

Gina sighed impatiently from being so close yet having to wait further, but she appreciated the penguin's good sense. She was still trying to grasp the fact that the Chinstrap seemed to have the same intellect as most people she encountered, if not more. During their time together, not only did she learn about the penguins, but she also taught him about people and about the world. Meuseaux was remarkably astute. He remembered everything he was taught, and even his speech had begun to sound as if he had spoken English since birth. Although, because he had a beak and lacked lips, he had trouble pronouncing some words.

"Be patient, Gina. We are close and cannot take unnecessary risks. Soon you will be united with your mate."

"He's not my *mate*," she said sternly, but not overly so.

"So you have said," Meuseaux replied with a knowing voice.

Gina looked at the penguin and shook her head at his being able to discern her feelings toward Randy. "I guess we wait, then," she said, changing the subject. "I'll put up the tent." After climbing inside the shelter, she tried to get her mind off of Randy and the cold by asking more questions. "So, how *did* this Overlord come to power?"

"I do not know completely. He has always been since I was hatched. From what I have learned, it was prophesized."

"There are penguin prophecies?" asked Gina, surprised.

"Yes. Do people not have them?" he asked, confused at her surprise.

"Well, yeah," Gina said apologetically, not wanting to trivialize the penguins' belief system.

"It has been told since the Great Auk Wars that the Royal bloodline would come again in our time of need," he began.

"Wait a second," Gina interrupted. "The Auk Wars—are you talking about the bird that looks like a penguin?"

"Yes, the Great Auks. They inhabit the North."

"The Great Auks have been extinct for nearly a century now," she told him.

Meuseaux paused. "I did not know this. What is a century?"

"It's a hundred years, or winters as you call them. The Great Auks were hunted into extinction by man," she said hesitantly.

"That is unfortunate for the Great Auks," he said with slight indifference.

"Can you tell me about these wars?" Gina asked him, thoroughly intrigued.

"I know only sso much. The wars were two hundred winters. The Great Auks came to the south and my kind began to fall. A great leader was hatched, Theosidon. The clans became one, and the Great Auks were turned away. But many clans were lost during the war. Theosidon did not stop at driving the Great Auks away. He became like the enemy and pushed the clans north. Those who defied him were punished. The Elders of the clans became the Council of Thrace. They united against him and brought his end.

"The Royal Emperors were separated to prevent offspring, and they were soon gone. The penguins knew peace for a thousand winters, until the humans came. Our time of peace ended."

"I'm sorry," Gina said after hearing the tale.

"I am sorry a war has begun against your kind." Meuseaux returned the apology.

"We now have laws to prevent people from hunting you," she said.

"I remember. The Chinstraps have prospered because of it, but the same cannot be said for others."

There was a moment of silence between the two. Both of them knew that both penguins and humankind were doing things they shouldn't do.

"So how did the Overlord come into being if the bloodline ended?"

Gina continued.

"I know only stories. It iss said an egg was hidden. The egg wass in the ice and would hatch when the Ancients showed a sign. Twenty winters ago, a bright light was shown. A strange cloud appeared. The Elders knew it was the time."

"Eggs were found and were given over to be hatched. The Overlord was one of the eggss. What became of others, I do not know. But, there are rumors of them. Though thiss might be not true. The Overlord keeps secrets. What iss not a secret is he cannot swim too well. His flippers have claws like our feet."

"Did Theosidon have them as well?"

"No, I don't believe so. It was told that he was a powerful swimmer."

Gina looked at Meuseaux, feeling awed by the Chinstrap and his capacity for intelligence. "I think you should reassess the extent of your knowledge. You seem to know a lot."

"Talking of stories and rumors is not the same as truly knowing. To know these things I would have to have lived them," Meuseaux said sagely.

"The penguins must have encountered humans before those early times. The name Theosidon sounds remarkably human."

"Perhaps they did, but there are no tales of such an encounter."

Gina thought some of the names sounded Greek in origin. "What about Liutites? What's his story?"

"Liutites is more of a mystery. Again, all I know are rumors. It is said that he is the first hatched of the Overlord's offspring and he is next in line to become Overlord. He is a brutal leader, but just because he is the first offspring does not mean he would be second in command. Although he is big in his size, he does not have the claws of his father. He has made up for this difference with cruelness. Many challengers have died by his beak. I am fortunate to have escaped." Meuseaux went silent.

Gina watched him and sensed his uneasiness. "You just stick by me, and I'll protect you."

"Again, it is good to know that not all humans are as we have been told," he said. "It is near our time. Remember, the elite guards are not like other penguins you have encountered. They are very strong, agile, and quick. They carry weapons and there are many more than most penguins know exist, or so my unwise curiosity taught me."

Gina broke down the tent once again and watched the sun disappear into the horizon. "Are you ready?"

"Yes, I believe so. We can travel closer on your machine, but then we will walk. There is a little-known entrance I discovered while investigating PIC, but it is difficult to get to."

"Investigating? So your curiosity wasn't an isolated event?"

"Perhaps it wasn't," Meuseaux admitted coyly.

CHAPTER 58

When Lieutenant-General Lavour arrived back at the human settlement, his fury had not diminished. If anything, it had increased. He came ashore to find General Devét waiting for him. "General Devét, sir," he said, snapping to attention.

"Lavour, I came as quickly as I could after getting the message. I honestly don't know why they didn't inform me first. Were there any survivors?"

"No, sir, there were none," he said with precise military cadence.

"I am sorry. We can give you and your company a furlough for some time to deal with the loss," Devét told him softly.

Lavour stared at the general while considering his choices. After spending so much time at PIC, wanting nothing more than to go home, he was offered a break only after it was too late. He nearly lashed out at Devét for making the suggestion after the fact but reconsidered. All he wanted now was vengeance. "No, sir, I would prefer to stay."

"Very well. Are you sure about this?"

"Yes, sir. When do we begin the assault on the islands?" Lavour asked, devoid of emotion.

Devét studied Lavour for a moment. "We leave in the morning. The Chinstraps, along with the Kings, Gentoo, Magellanics, and Rockhoppers, will begin a campaign of island hopping, so to speak. We will proceed in this way until we reach the Falkland Islands. After we liberate those islands, our forces will split. Half will continue to make their way up the east coast of the Americas. The other half will do the same on the west coast. The western front will free the Humboldt from their oppressors along the way."

"What of the others—the crested and the Blackfoot," Lavour asked, trying to throw himself into his work to prevent his thoughts from lingering on the tragedy for too long.

"The Blackfoot will return to South Africa immediately to cause what disruptions they can with the limited resources they have. The crested clans will begin their assaults in their region at a time when called upon. Our own coastal journey will be a series of strike and fade attacks. We will hit the coastal settlements and disappear in random order—going north then back south, so that they will never know where we will strike next. By doing this, we hope to keep them off balance enough that they will ignore our homeland and seas." Devét concluded his extended synopsis and looked at Lavour for more questions.

"How long will we be attacking their coastal areas, and will we ever move inland?"

"We will continue to attack in this manner until we reach the Arctic—if it really exists," Devét added as a side note. The Northern Paradise had been fabled for so many generations. As sometimes happens with legends, many doubted it was real. "For obvious reasons, we will not strike inland. However, this does not rule out attacking along inlets and tributaries. Now is there anything else, Lieutenant-General?"

"No, sir, I am only eager to begin our campaign."

"Very well. We leave at first light."

Lavour stepped away from the general and spotted his two friends coming his way.

"Lavour," said Leepoh as he arrived, his mood somber. "I don't know what to say, except to ask how you are holding up."

"Everything has changed. The humans left no one. They are *all* dead," Lavour said, still lacking emotion.

"I am sorry, my friend."

"Any doubts I harbored about our cause have disappeared. I want nothing more than to see our enemy suffer," he said with a bit of hatred that seemed out of place on him.

"I understand your feelings and your want for revenge, but do me a favor." Nok interrupted the conversation.

"What would that be, Captain Nok?"

"I have been there myself. All of those whom I have cared for have been taken or affected by the humans in one way or another. Do not let it consume you. It can bring you to the point of your own destruction. You are a good penguin, Lavour. Don't let them kill your spirit as well."

"My spirit," Lavour snapped back. "My spirit is gone with my family. All that matters to me now is the death of these mindless beasts. If one penguin can truly make a difference, I will."

"All I'm trying to say is that I know what you're going through," Nok said calmly. "If it weren't for blind luck, I'd be dead too. I let my hatred control me to the point where I was out of control. Because of that, I watched my lifelong friend die."

Lavour lowered his head in resignation to Nok's point. He knew Nok had suffered repeated hardships and regretted snapping at him. "You're right. I know you're right. It's just that I can't get the images out of my mind. And it—I just—I hate them."

"Me as well, my friend. Me as well," Nok commiserated.

"And how about you, Leepoh?" asked Lavour.

"As Captain Nok can attest, I have no love for the humans. I have seen many penguins suffer at their hands. I have experienced that suffering myself," Leepoh said, continuing in his glum tone.

"In what way?" asked Nok, sounding surprised.

"One of my young was taken from me," Leepoh said, looking away.

Nok looked at his friend with compassion. "I had no idea."

"Bah," Leepoh replied, but not in his usual jovial way. "It was a long time ago, and this is the time for Lavour's mourning."

Lavour looked away then back at Leepoh. "No, Leepoh, we're in this together. It would be selfish of me to think that my woes are any more important than yours. Besides, it might help me to get a better understanding of things to get your perspective."

"You are an admirable penguin, Lavour. Selfish is not a word that should ever be used in the same breath as your name," Leepoh told him, and Lavour looked at the ground in humility. "My son's name was Mee'oni. He was our fourth hatchling and our last. He hatched with a lame foot, but we took care of him. We brought him food long after the age when other chicks fledge, and he was my constant companion. He would sit near the sea and wait for me to return from feeding runs. But he would always stay far enough away from the shore to avoid the seals." He paused and looked away. "He wouldn't just wait for me for the meal, but to greet me as well. He was a kind and sincere penguin."

"One day, when we were retuning and trying to get past those forsaken seals, I heard him calling out to me from somewhere far away. I disregarded the seals, raced to the shore as fast as I could, and found my mate in a panic. '*The humans took our Mee'oni,*' she cried. The humans had come while I was gone. They weren't the hunters. They were the watchers, like Randy." Leepoh paused for minute, as if lost in thought. "Anyway, my mate pointed to a boat that was taking him away. I ran to the water, but by this time the others had already come ashore, and the seals were on the beach. It was impossible to alert the other Gentoo, and the seals blocked my every path. No matter which way I went, they were there. I couldn't get past them and I watched helplessly as the humans reached their ship and took my Mee'oni from me."

Nok and Lavour were silent as Leepoh told his agonizing tale. "And what of your mate? Where is she?" asked Lavour.

Leepoh lowered his head. "For months we waited and hoped for his return. We hoped that maybe the humans were doing something to help his condition and that they would return him. It was a foolish way of thinking, but it's not like when you lose a hatchling to a seal or something else. When that happens, there's finality to it. Its heart wrenching, but you know it's over. You know your hatchling has moved on to the Great Sea. We knew these humans weren't like the raiders. They didn't kill anyone. So we waited and hoped."

"After many seasons, my mate—Tanaea was her name—she . . ." Leepoh stopped for a second, closing his eyes. "I think she just gave up. One morning, she just walked to the sea. The seals were there." Leepoh stopped for breath. "She didn't even try to get away."

"I am so sorry, Leepoh," Nok told him.

"Don't be sorry, my friend. All things have purpose, though at times we can't see. After that, I heard rumors of the PDA. I left my colony and joined. I still have hope that he is not gone forever, that he is safe somewhere. But until I know, the humans will pay for their transgressions against us," Leepoh said, looking from Nok to Lavour. "So, yes, I also hate them."

CHAPTER 59

The moonlit landscape silhouetted Gina and Meuseaux's shadowy forms as they scampered across the ice. They were headed for the huge ice monoliths. Within lay the penguin stronghold of Pack Ice Command. The two clambered over rugged and jagged ice, juts, and fissures until they reached an unassuming hole.

"This is it," Meuseaux proclaimed.

"What is? This is?" Gina reacted on seeing the hole, which was barely wider than she was.

"Yes. It is an old entryway. I believe it was used when PIC was first constructed. It is little known now. It was abandoned when larger, more efficient entryways were constructed."

"Where does it lead to?" Gina asked while she cautiously peered into the darkness.

"To the levels below PIC. I will go first. A penguin will be far less suspicious if we are to be discovered. Bring only what is necessary. Your light is needed. Pack Ice Command is dark at night, and the lower levels are especially so. I will call to you if it is safe. Listen carefully. It will be a quiet call," Meuseaux instructed her.

"Okay," she said, unsure as to what she was about to embark on. "I'll send my pack down first, and then I'll follow." Before she left the camp, she had packed only the items required to survive in the event she and Randy couldn't make it back to the snowmobile.

"One more thing," Meuseaux said to her. "You may want to go feet first. It is a quick trip to the bottom."

"What?" Gina asked, suddenly becoming alarmed. "What do you mean by quick?" Meuseaux jumped into the hole without bothering to answer and vanished into the abyss.

Gina stood alone in the darkness, straining to hear any call from below. She began to feel vulnerable. She wondered if this were a trap. These penguins were clever, after all. She dismissed the idea. The Chinstrap had already had ample opportunities to betray her but hadn't done so. She had no choice. She had to trust the little fellow.

After what felt like an eternity but actually was only a couple of minutes, Gina heard Meuseaux's faint call coming from somewhere below. She took off her pack and, feeling a little insecure at sending her necessities down a hole, let it go. She waited for a minute and then put her feet in the hole. "Here goes nothing," she said and let go to the force of gravity.

The drop was fast. Sliding down the hole on smooth ice, Gina pinned her arms to her chest. She hit a small bump, grazed the top of the tube and suppressed a scream. The tube began a gradual upward slope, which slowed her speed. She was spit out at the bottom and landed hard with a soft groan.

Meuseaux was by her side immediately. "Quiet," he told her.

She struggled to get her bearings in the darkness and stooped next to Meuseaux. "You didn't tell me about the sudden stop," she whispered to him. She wasn't sure how a penguin laughed, but she swore that's what she heard.

"Your pack iss lying behind you," he told her.

"You can see in here? Because I can't see a thing."

"No, I only know because it hit me."

"Oh, sorry about that," she said as she felt for her pack. She removed her cumbersome outer gloves, unzipped her pack, and pulled out her flashlight and gun. "At least it's a little warmer in here," she said as she clicked on the light. "Wow," she whispered at her first look at the large, oval-shaped, cavernous room. It was devoid of almost everything, including the etchings on the walls that one saw elsewhere. She scanned the area with her light and saw only a few small rounded stalactites here and there. "What is this place?"

"I am unsure what its function was. I only know it has been abandoned. For what reason, I do not know."

"What's with the piles of junk over there?" she asked, spotting a few piles of old timber, metal, and other refuse hidden in the dark recesses.

"Penguins gather what we can to make use of it. Your junk is sometimes our tools."

Gina looked around and marveled at the penguins' resourcefulness. In a land without any *natural* resources, they took advantage of the waste left behind by years of explorers, researchers, whalers and the like. It occurred to her that, in part, these penguins are a creation of man's presence here. Would they have had the ability to build such a place if man had never come here? Would they have ever reorganized into a collective society? Humankind's impact was obvious to her. These once peace-loving creatures were now forever changed.

Gina knew something else—the source of the great light on the island that Meuseaux mentioned. Over twenty years before, a nuclear device was detonated by an unknown country near Antarctica. The test was never admitted to by any government. That may have been the reason behind the Royal Emperors' reappearance. And it could explain the mutations in their Overlord that Meuseaux had described. The thought of it weighed heavily on Gina's mind. Gina could do nothing about that or the events that were unfolding. There was only one thing she *could* do something about; she could find the man she cared for.

Gina focused on the task at hand, turning to her guide and asking, "Where do we go from here?"

"Thiss way. We must be cautious. I have heard rumorss of outcasts living in these lower levelss," Meuseaux said, leading the way, his nerves showing by dragging his S's again. "You should take a piece of that long, round wood. We may need it." He indicated a six-foot-long, two-inch-diameter pole lying on the ground.

"What for?" asked Gina, wondering whether he expected her to use it as a weapon against the outcast.

"To unlock the doors, of course," he told her as if she should have known.

"Oh, of course," Gina said sarcastically.

CHAPTER 60

Supreme Commander Liutites's eyes opened suddenly. He was awoken by a Blue penguin standing in front of him, chattering nervously. "Are you sure?" he asked with alarm.

The Blue answered in the affirmative with a quick chirp.

"Very well, you have done well. Now go and keep me updated on their whereabouts. I will go to the Overlord at once."

The Blue Fairy penguin quickly exited through a small crevice in the wall of Liutites's chamber.

Liutites gave his low-frequency click to alert his elite guards to meet him on his way to the Overlord's chamber. He exited his quarters and was joined by two warriors. The three marched down the corridor and were joined by four more. The Supreme Commander's entourage grew until, by the time he reached the outer door of the Overlord's chamber, there were sixteen.

His group included four elite commandos, who were a new breed of Royal Emperor. The commandos were more powerfully built than the other warriors or troopers. They no longer had the residual fatty layer designed to protect and incubate eggs. Their flippers were jointed and more defined. They were not swimmers. These commandos were completely terrestrial and built for one thing—combat.

When Liutites entered the chamber, he found it crowded with guards and warriors.

"Liutites, come before me," Antaean boomed.

The Supreme Commander became slightly nervous at the Overlord's tone. "Yes, my lord?"

"It appears as though Corporal Meuseaux was not taken by the storm, as you predicted. In fact, he has allied himself with our enemy," the Overlord said accusingly.

"Yes, my lord. He appears to have found assistance."

"I am not interested in excuses. They must be captured."

"Yes, my lord, we will act at once," Liutites said with conviction.

"No, you will not, Supreme Commander," Antaean corrected.

"But, my lord, the human—"

"Is here to save the other human." The Overlord finished the sentence for him. "This is the one that Colonel Kimmer let escape. Send word to General Diutes that Kimmer is to be executed at once."

"That will not sit well with the Order of the Kings, my lord."

"Order of Kings be damned, I *will not* tolerate failure," the Overlord said, glaring at Liutites.

The Supreme Commander bowed his head in submission. "Yes, my lord." Liutites knew he was fortunate that Antaean had not ordered his execution as well. *Let him try it*, he thought defiantly.

"If the Kings have an issue with my commands, let them speak to me directly," the Overlord said, threateningly. "Put the guards who are watching the human on alert. I am sure that, with our resilient Chinstrap as its guide, this human will find its way to its companion. We will lay a trap and capture the three of them together. All but the Royal elite are to be confined to their quarters unless needed."

A Blue hurried into the chamber and began its chattering.

Antaean nodded at the little penguin and looked to Liutites. "Go now. They have already exited the lower reaches. Once we have them, you may do with the Chinstrap as you wish."

"Yes, my lord. He has already caused me more problems than his life is worth."

"Do not underestimate this human. It appears to be quite cunning as well," the Overlord warned.

CHAPTER 61

After making their way out of the lower region of PIC, Gina and Meuseaux began walking up a gradually sloping corridor. "This place is amazing," Gina whispered. "Your ingenuity is astonishing."

"I did not build it, nor did I take part," Meuseaux said.

"Huh?" Gina said, puzzled as well until she realized what he meant. "Not just *your* ingenuity, but the penguins as a whole," she clarified.

"I understand. Forgive me. I still get confused with your language."

"That's all right. I sometimes do too. And I've been speaking it my whole life. So don't—Hey!" she said suddenly, catching a fleeting glimpse of something small disappearing in the shadows ahead. "What was that?"

"What was what?" Meuseaux asked, becoming more alert. "I did not see."

Gina waved her light back and forth, trying to spot what she thought she saw. "I don't know. It looked like a small penguin, but it was quick. I didn't get a good look at it."

Meuseaux stood silent and still. "We should be cautious. Perhaps our presence here is known."

The thought didn't sit well with Gina. She definitely didn't want any more surprises. She put her pole in the straps of her pack and pulled out her pistol.

The pair resumed their walk in silence. When they reached the point where she had caught the glimpse of something, she shined her light near the ground and found a small opening. "There, what's that?"

Meuseaux inspected the hole. "It is for air, I believe."

"Ventilation, huh? I swear I saw something here."

"I do not know of any clans who are ssso small as to fit in such a place. A chick, perhaps. But only the Royal Emperors have rookeries here, and they are well protected. I do not believe a Royal chick could have gotten lost."

"Hum," Gina said thoughtfully. "Maybe my eyes are playing tricks on me."

"Your eyes have their own will?" Meuseaux asked, confused again.

Gina snorted a laugh. "No, it's just an expression. It means you think you see something that's not there."

Meuseaux nodded. "Just because I do not know of any penguins so small does not mean they do not exist. I have heard rumors of the Overlord's spies. I assumed it was meant that they were one of our own. Maybe you spotted one of those spies."

"I hope you're wrong. When we find Randy, he should be able to tell us more. He knows more about penguins than anyone I know—though obviously not as much as he thought," she sniffed a laugh.

A few meters further along the passage, the pair came to their first door.

"Beyond this doorway is the feeding area," Meuseaux informed Gina. "Beyond that is a side passage that will lead us to where I last saw Randy. You will no longer require your light, and we must be quiet from this point on. Most penguins should be asleep, but the guards patrol the halls at night."

"So this pole will open the door?" Gina asked as she drew the stick and put the flashlight in her pack.

"Yesss, insert it into the hole."

"Won't it make noise?" she asked warily.

"Yes it will, but it is unavoidable."

She inserted the pole in the keyhole and the door began to open slowly. It made a loud scraping noise, like a stone door in an ancient tomb, which the quiet corridor amplified. Gina cringed at the sound. Once the silence resumed, Gina had a thought. "How did you get around this place if you couldn't open the doors?" she whispered to Meuseaux.

"There are other passages, but they are too small for you. We should go," he said as he peered down the dim passageway.

They traveled down the empty passage until Meuseaux stopped. "It is unusually quiet here, even for the night. Be alert for a trap."

"Great," she said, gripping her weapon.

They travelled from hall to hall and room to room, passed by the food troughs, from which Meuseaux stole a quick snack, and finally exited through a smaller arched opening. "We are nearly there," Meuseaux said quietly. "If our presence is known, this is where they will be waiting. Be prepared."

Gina gripped her staff firmly with one hand and rested her other hand on the gun in her pocket as they crept down the passage. They came to an intersection, and Meuseaux turned to her. "This is it—to the right and at the end of the corridor."

"Okay," said Gina, her hands becoming moist with perspiration.

"I will go first. If there *are* guards, you will have to move quickly to render them unable to call an alarm," the Chinstrap explained and then bolted down the passage without giving Gina a chance to ask questions or object.

Gina peeked around the corner and saw Meuseaux disappear around a curve. She followed his path, and as she rounded the next curve, she saw Meuseaux engaged in a very tense conversation with two exceptionally large penguins. "Oh my God," she said at the sight. "Those things are *huge*." She saw that the two guards had their spears pointed at Meuseaux as he slowly backed away.

Gina didn't give herself time to think; she grabbed her staff in a firm two-handed grip and charged forward. She had never actually fought anyone or anything in her entire life, but she had seen enough movies to get the gist of it and was fit enough to pack a punch. She reached the guards in a full sprint and drew her stick back to get a full swing at the closest one. As she swung her weapon downward, the guard brought its own up and absorbed the brunt of the attack.

The guard retaliated with a strike of its own, and Gina nearly lost her grip on her weapon as she blocked the surprisingly powerful counterattack. She switched her grip on the makeshift weapon, sliding her hands apart from each other into something resembling a *bōjutsu* fighting style.

The second guard smacked her across her shoulder with a blow that caught her by surprise. The force made her weight shift forward, and she locked staffs with the first guard, looking him in the eye. She used her forward momentum to shove the guard away and blindly swung backwards at the attacker. The guard tried to bring its staff up to block but was out of position and Gina landed a lucky hit across its beak, which sent it spinning away, squealing in agony.

With Gina's attention diverted, the first guard attacked again, lunging with his spear tip. Gina parried the attack and landed a quick snap to the left side of the guard's head, following with a second, more powerful shot to the right. The guard fell to the ground. Her satisfaction with that attack was short-lived as the second guard landed a hard blow to the side of her leg. She fell to one knee and braced for the second strike she knew would be coming. Meuseaux, who had stayed out of the fray until that point, charged in and stabbed his beak into the guard's mid-section. The attack knocked the guard back a step, which gave Gina a chance to recover.

The infuriated guard turned his attention to his diminutive attacker and swatted Meuseaux away with his powerful flipper, sending Meuseaux flailing against the wall. The brief moment of distraction was what Gina needed. She jabbed the end of her staff into the guard's side, causing it to drop its spear. She followed up with a tremendous two-handed swing across the guard's head and the guard fell to the floor, motionless. She turned and spotted the first guard struggling to get up. She attacked with an overhead strike to the back of its neck, dropping it to the ground as well.

With the guards dispatched, she went to Meuseaux and helped him to his feet. "Are you all right?"

"Yes, I will be," he answered. "And you—you are a powerful warrior. I am happy that you are my ally," he said with admiration.

"I had help." In spite of Meuseaux's forewarning, she hadn't expected the penguin guards' strength and quickness. She made a mental note never again to underestimate her opponent.

"Quickly," said Meuseaux, "insert your staff into the hole and break it off. Hurry, before more arrive."

Gina found the keyhole, inserted the butt end of the staff, and pulled down with all of her weight to break it off. The door to Randy's holding cell ground slowly downward, and Meuseaux rushed in before it had completely opened. Gina looked around the dimly lit room and spotted Randy as he crept from beneath his pallet.

Randy rubbed his eyes. "Meuseaux, is that you?"

"Yes, it is me. Stand up. We must go. We haven't much time."

"What do you mean?" he asked as he stood and stretched. "How did you get past the guards?"

"He had a little help," Gina said casually from the doorway.

"Gina?" Randy said through a whisper. "Gina!" he shouted when he realized it was indeed her. He went to her and grabbed her in a tight embrace.

"Randy," she sighed in relief. "Are you okay?"

"I am now. How did you find me? I never thought I'd see you again."

"They said you were dead, but I knew you weren't. And Davis tried to stop me." She rambled as her emotions began to pour out. Randy took hold of her and kissed her. When they parted, they looked into each other's eyes and knew they felt the same for one another.

"I have fish breath," Randy said with a beaming smile.

"I don't care," Gina said and kissed him again.

Meuseaux, who had found Randy's bucket of icefish, looked up at the two of them. "You can mate later. Now we must go."

"We are *not* mating," Gina said, shaking her head.

"Have you been teaching him how to talk?" Randy asked.

"Sort of. Why?"

"He sounds like you. You know, sarcastic."

Gina smiled, happy to hear his playfulness. "Nice, *strawberry*. Now let's get out of this place."

The three stepped outside of Randy's dungeon, happy to be leaving, but their joy was quashed. Ten meters in front of them stood a dozen Royal Emperors with their spears at the ready. The formation parted, and Supreme Commander Liutites stepped forward.

"Liutites," Meuseaux spit out with venom.

"It's the Supreme Commander," Randy said, leaning into Gina.

"It appears as if I have obtained another prize for the Overlord," Liutites hissed from beside his forward most guards. "And I have one for myself," he continued. His eyes shifted to Meuseaux.

Meuseaux stood firmly under the Supreme Commander's glare at first, but just to be safe, he scooted beside Gina.

"You humans are a pathetic breed. Did you really think you could escape our stronghold?" Liutites sneered.

"Well, the thought did occur to me," Randy remarked.

"It is even more unfortunate for you," said Liutites, looking at Randy. "You were to be left alive as a hostage should your kind have been so unwise as to attack this place. Now, both of your heads will decorate the Overlord's chamber. As for you, Chinstrap, your time is coming to an end, but you will learn the meaning of agony before I send you to meet your ancestors."

While Liutites continued to promise pain and suffering, Gina put her hand in her pocket and nudged Randy. "Get ready," she whispered.

Randy slowly reached down and picked up one of the fallen guards' spears. "You know what, penguin?" he said to Liutites, who snapped his head toward him. "I don't care too much for your attitude," he said with false bravado, drawing the Supreme Commander's attention.

Liutites spotted the spear in Randy's hand. "Insolence coming from insignificance is meaningless. But I see that you wish to die with honor in combat."

"You're mistaken, Liutites," Gina said. "It's you who is about to die."

Liutites stared daggers at the two. "Guards, kill them."

Gina drew her weapon and pointed it directly at Liutites.

The Supreme Commander's eyes went wide in surprise and fear.

Gina squeezed the trigger, but it didn't budge. "Damn it!" she exclaimed, remembering she had set the safety.

Liutites took the moment's reprieve and ducked behind the guards. "Attack. Kill them!" he yelled.

The first penguin moved toward the three. Gina released the safety and fired. The elite guard flew backwards, spraying its blood on those nearest it. The surprised penguins looked at their fallen comrade, hissed and charged. Gina fired two more shots, dropping two more, which gave the others pause.

"He's getting away!" Randy yelled, pointing at Liutites sliding on his stomach back down the corridor as fast as he could.

Three more penguins made a move and Gina dispatched them all.

"Liutites does not matter. We must go before more arrive," Meuseaux shouted in his best English.

"I agree," Gina said.

Seven guards remained, including three commandos, and they advanced together. Gina began to fire repeatedly, killing four and grazing one. The grazed warrior stumbled over one of the dead, landing face first. Randy took advantage, lunged forward, and drove his spear into the penguin's back. Gina took aim at the two remaining commandos. She pulled the trigger, but the gun was empty.

"Randy," she said, trying to remain calm.

"Don't tell me you're out," Randy said. "Do you have more?"

"In my pack," Gina whispered. She observed that the penguins appeared to have figured out something was wrong with her weapon. "I don't think there's time."

The two remaining penguins began to advance slowly, unsure about the weapon that killed their companions. Gina waved the gun at them and they came to a halt. The sound of several more warriors could be heard coming from down the corridor.

"We must do something," Meuseaux said nervously. "If we are captured, we will die."

"I know," Gina snapped as Randy's nearly frostbitten hands fumbled with the zipper on the pack. "Too late," she said, seeing the end of the corridor fill with very angry penguins.

Randy gave up on unzipping the pack and picked up his spear. Gina pocketed her gun and grabbed a spear.

"Get behind us, Meuseaux," Randy told him. "Are you ready for this?" he asked Gina.

Gina nodded and looked at Randy. "I love you."

Randy looked at her and smiled. "So do I."

Gina shook her head and snorted a half laugh. "You're an *ass*."

The warriors began to move.

CHAPTER 62

"What was that?" Mevoule asked in alarm as gunfire interrupted his sleep. Nervous chatter began to sound throughout the Chinstrap quarters. Wide awake, Mevoule went to the entrance to the quarters. "Stay here and stay calm. Let me find out what's happening," he said to the twenty-five remaining Chinstraps. With the others away, he was left to act as the commanding officer of the small group.

Mevoule stepped into the hallway as several elite warriors passed by. "What's going on? Is there an invasion?" he asked.

"Stay in your quarters, Chinstrap," the Royal Emperor grumbled, brushing Mevoule aside and nearly knocking him off his feet.

More gunshots echoed from somewhere within PIC. Mevoule became more concerned. "I'll be back. Sergeant Bevior, you're in charge until I return. If anyone should ask as to my whereabouts, tell them," he paused, unsure about instructing a subordinate to lie for him. "Tell them you don't know. Understood?"

The sergeant acknowledged the command, and Mevoule set off. More gunshots rang out, which gave him pause about what he was doing. In spite of his apprehension, he continued. There was only one place to find out what was happening, but going there posed a risk. As another column of soldiers passed by, Mevoule jumped back into his quarters. He slid out and followed the group at a safe distance.

After the warriors disappeared around a corner, Mevoule scampered into a crossway and peered out the other side. Seeing it was clear, he entered the adjoining passageway. He moved quickly along the curved hallway. From behind him, he heard the familiar sound of clawed feet scratching on the ice floor. It was more warriors, and he picked up his pace. Just ahead of him was the passage he needed, but he had been spotted.

"You there!" a warrior shouted.

Mevoule ignored the penguin and dove into the darkened passage. He heard the warriors just outside the entryway and pressed his body, stomach first, against a corner in the darkness, exposing only his black back in hopes of camouflaging himself.

"It went in here," the warrior said to its commander.

"What did? I didn't see—" More gunfire erupted, cutting off the commander's words. A barely audible warble filled the air. "The Supreme Commander needs reinforcements. Let's go."

"But there was someone here," the other hissed.

"Forget it. It was probably a Blue. Now move out," the captain ordered.

The warrior peeked into the darkness, made a long clicking sound, then abruptly turned away to follow the others.

Mevoule let out a long-held breath, stepped away from the wall, and thanked the Ancients for his good fortune. He continued along the dark corridor, wondering what the warrior meant by a 'blue.'

"Get in here," a hushed voice said to him from a doorway when he reached his destination. Mevoule quickly obeyed. Once the door closed, flickering light silhouetted a pair of large penguins. "What are you doing here, Mevoule?" one of the forms asked.

"I heard the gunfire and thought now may be the time," Mevoule answered.

"Unfortunately, no," one of the shadows said. "We do not yet have the resources available to us."

"Oh," Mevoule said, disappointed in the answer. "Where are the others, and where is she?"

"She is in the rookery and is unable to free herself. The others will be here soon."

"Well, then, what's going on? Have the humans discovered Pack Ice Command and attacked, as they did to my colony?" Mevoule asked with obvious bitterness. After hearing of the attack on his colony, he rethought his part in future events, but he was told to wait before he passed judgment. He wasn't sure what that meant, but the clandestine group with which he associated himself had not led him astray as of yet. But that still did nothing for the pain of loss.

"There is only one human, and it is neither attacking nor invading. It is attempting a rescue of the other," a shadow said. "A very resilient Chinstrap is guiding it."

"It intends to rescue the prisoner, then? Is this Chinstrap who I think it might be?" Mevoule asked.

"Yes, it is a rescue, and yes, it is Meuseaux."

"I thought as much." Mevoule sighed in relief at verifying that another of his colony had survived. "How is this rescue proceeding?"

"We are not sure yet. Although, by the sound of it, not well."

Two large penguins entered the room from the back. It was the female, followed by a Royal Emperor elite guard. Mevoule hissed in warning and alarm. "So, I have been betrayed," he accused them angrily.

"No! Mevoule, no," the female told him calmly.

Mevoule was scared and confused. "Then what is that doing here?" he demanded, indicating the guard.

"This is Ceocilus. He is my own hatchling and acts as my bodyguard."

Mevoule said nothing. He was confused by this penguin having laid a Royal Emperor egg.

Responding to Mevoule's obvious confusion, the female said, "Some things are better left unknown to you for now, Mevoule. Suffice it to say, his loyalty to us is unwavering."

Mevoule didn't say anything. He only nodded.

"It is good that you came, however," the female continued. "We need your help."

"What is it?" he asked, eager to get away from the Royal Emperor guard, regardless of where its loyalties may lie.

"The rescue of the human is not going well. It is imperative that it escape. This human is the Overlord's bargaining stone should the humans attack PIC. If it were to escape, it would put the Overlord in a position of significantly less power."

"How can *I* help?" he asked, unsure of what a Chinstrap could do in this situation.

"Go with Ceocilus to the passage where the humans and Meuseaux are trapped. Ceocilus will open a side doorway, and you will lead them to here. From here they will be shown a little-known exit."

Mevoule began to object. He didn't trust Ceocilus and he had no desire to go anywhere alone with him.

"There is no time for questions. Meuseaux will need someone he trusts to lead him to safety. It is fortunate that you took the initiative to come here," she told him. "Perhaps the Spirits of the Ancients are truly with us. You *must* go now."

Without further question, Mevoule followed Ceocilus from the room.

^^^

Gina and Randy stood with their spears pointing forward and at the ready. Meuseaux did as instructed and stepped behind the two humans. There was little he could do against so many larger opponents. He would fight to the end. He knew that much, but he also knew it was best to leave the fighting to the bigger and stronger humans until it was necessary for him to join the fight.

The Royal Emperor soldiers moved slowly and cautiously, gauging their adversaries. After realizing the gun no longer was a threat, they began to move with more speed. The elite commandos led. They hopped over their slain comrades without trepidation.

As the trio braced themselves for the onslaught, something caught Meuseaux's eye. To his left he noticed several small fissures in the wall. The fissures turned into deeper lines, and a door suddenly slid open. Meuseaux hissed a warning, expecting an attack from the unseen passage, but what he saw surprised him even more than a sneak attack.

"Meuseaux," Captain Mevoule said as he made his appearance. "This way if you want to live."

Meuseaux didn't hesitate. "The humans as well?" he asked.

"Yes, now!" Mevoule demanded.

"Gina, Randy, this way!" he told the humans, who were focused on the oncoming attack.

The two turned and traded an astonished glance. Disbelieving their good fortune, they dashed into the dark room. The warriors were only feet away when the door slid shut.

Once inside the room, Gina threw off her pack and began to fumble around to find her light. Randy turned on his small light and spared her the trouble. The two of them looked at Meuseaux, then at Mevoule, while Gina reloaded her gun. "Since we're not dead, I take it this is a friend of yours?" Gina asked, locking the new ammo clip in place.

"He saved us, so I believe that he is." Since his ordeal, Meuseaux had learned not to fully trust anyone inside PIC. "His name is Mevoule."

"Good to meet you," Randy said.

"Greer—gerr . . . sssaluta—hello," Mevoule finally said, giving up on trying to say greetings and salutations.

"And who is that?" Gina asked as Randy shined his light on the imposing Royal Emperor standing in the shadows.

Meuseaux, who had been distracted by Mevoule, immediately hissed a warning.

"Don't be alarmed," Mevoule urged him. "He is an ally. Without his help you would already be dead—or worse."

Meuseaux listened to his logic and lowered his defenses, slightly. "Who is he?" he asked warily.

"A friend—I will tell you what I know later, but now we must go. We will show you a way out where you won't be seen," Mevoule told him and began to walk away.

Meuseaux didn't argue and told his human companions to follow.

"Are you sure about this?" Gina asked Meuseaux.

"No," he answered quickly. "But it is better than our previous circumstances."

"You know . . ." Randy said to Gina as they began to follow, "that's a pretty smart penguin there."

"You don't know the half of it."

The sound of spears or beaks, or both, scraping against the door motivated the group to pick up their pace, and they hurried down the long, dark passage.

CHAPTER 63

Supreme Commander Liutites flew backwards, landed on his back, and slid to a stop against one of the Overlord's trophy pillars. "This is unacceptable!" Overlord Antaean shouted at the fallen Supreme Commander. "How did you let this happen?" Antaean thundered.

Liutites tried to shake his dazed head clear, rolled onto his stomach, and pushed himself up with the aid of his beak. He glared at Antaean with hatred for striking him like a common penguin. "They had assistance, *my lord*," he said deliberately.

The Overlord returned his glare. "From whom do you think they received this *assistance?*" he asked with wickedness in his voice.

Perhaps from a future ally, Liutites thought. *One that could help me destroy you.* "We do not know as of yet, my lord. They were not seen."

"Are you telling me that there are enemies within my fortress, *other* than those you let escape?"

"They have not escaped, my lord. And yes, that is the only way they could have avoided the warriors. Somebody has constructed a secret tunnel network right under *our* beaks." Liutites emphasized the word *our* to put some of the blame on Antaean as well.

"I want them found!" the Overlord lashed out. "Search the entire compound. Everyone is suspect, especially the Chinstraps." The Overlord called the Blue penguin spies into his chamber.

About a dozen Blues entered immediately, chittering nervously. The Overlord gazed down as one of the diminutive Blues approached him and snapped a high beak salute with its little head. Antaean continued to gaze down at the penguin, letting a tense silence fill the room. He struck with unexpected speed for a penguin of his size and pierced the spy through its chest. He raised his head back up with the penguin dangling from his beak. He shook his head violently and the lifeless body of the Blue flew across the room and landed in a crumpled heap near the entrance.

"Let that be a lesson to the rest of you," the Overlord growled at the remaining tiny penguins, who had gathered in a tight group for safety. "I will not tolerate further incompetence. Find who is responsible for giving aid to the humans before your usefulness to me comes to an end!"

Liutites watched the little Blue penguins scatter and bolt from the chamber. He cared little for anyone or anything, other than his own ascendancy. However, the Blues were his eyes and ears, and their loyalty was unquestionable. He secretly began to plot a way for the Overlord's fit of rage to be used to his advantage.

"Supreme Commander!" the Overlord bellowed, bringing Liutites out of his pensiveness.

He slowly turned to his leader. "Yes, my lord?"

"Go to the quarters of the Chinstraps. Find out if anything is amiss, and bring Captain Mevoule to me. I will give him a test of loyalty." Liutites turned to leave, and the Overlord added a remark. "Two of my personal guards will accompany you."

Liutites stopped, and his blood went cold as he wondered what the Overlord might know of his desires. "Yes, my lord," he said, adding the salute he'd failed to give when he first started to leave. The two guards came to his side, and he exited the Overlord's chambers somewhat less confident of his plans to overthrow Antaean.

CHAPTER 64

"Where are you leading us?" Meuseaux asked Captain Mevoule as they entered another secret passage. It was the third such passage they had taken since escaping the attack. Their return trip to the clandestine hideout was taking longer than expected; every exit from the adjoining passages had been blocked by Royal Emperor elite guards, and they were quickly running out of options. Eventually they were going to have to make a break across one of the corridors.

"Before I answer your question, let me ask you one," Mevoule replied. "I take it by your actions tonight that you have no love for the PDA?"

"For the penguins of the Alliance I do, just not for the Royal Emperors. They tried to feed me to the Phocids," Meuseaux answered bitterly.

"Yes, I know about that. It has happened to many penguins: Chinstrap, Adélie, Gentoo, and even some Emperor and Kings who did not agree with the Overlord's policies. I'm sorry we couldn't help you or prevent it," Mevoule said with regret.

"When you say 'we,' whom do you mean?"

Mevoule paused, remembering the events that led him to the group. "After I had suffered some *abuses* by the Supreme Commander several months ago—"

"Yes, I remember," Meuseaux interrupted. "You didn't seem too upset by it as I recall."

"Yes," said Mevoule, "soon after my *discipline*, I was sought out by a secret . . . organization that feels the same as we do about the state of affairs under the Overlord's rule. They asked me what I just asked you. Our hope is to one day change the way things are, to make the PDA truly equal for all penguins. But with the Overlord's war, our task has become more difficult."

"What about our colony? There were many who were against the Royals from the beginning." Meuseaux exclaimed, excited at the prospect of ending the Royal Emperors' reign.

Mevoule lowered his head and looked away. "You didn't hear? Of course you didn't. How could you?"

"Hear what?" Meuseaux asked with a feeling of dread overcoming him. When Mevoule didn't answer right away, Meuseaux became more agitated. "What is it?"

"A couple of days after the start of the war, apparently a group of humans retaliated."

"And . . ." Meuseaux said, becoming impatient.

"Our colony was destroyed," Mevoule said, looking him in the eyes.

Meuseaux became rigid and then lowered himself to his tail, staring at Mevoule in shock. "Survivors?"

Mevoule shook his head. "Only those of us who were away at PIC or on the front are left."

Meuseaux sat to gather the strength that had suddenly left him and then turned to look at Randy and Gina.

Mevoule stepped between Meuseaux and the humans. "Meuseaux, there's more."

Meuseaux looked at Mevoule with the hurt plain in his eyes. "What more can there be? The humans have killed our families and our friends."

"I was told not to pass judgment until we have all the facts and that all is not as it appears."

"I don't understand."

"Neither do I. But I think there must be something more to the attack than we know. Remember, these humans fought to protect you."

Meuseaux took a deep breath and tried to push the thought of his colony's demise from his mind and focus on what needed to be done.

"We *must* be going," Ceocilus told the group.

The cast gathered together and Ceocilus opened the next door. As the door opened, they spotted a tiny penguin standing on the other side. The Blue turned toward them and let out a shriek of alarm.

"The Overlord's spies!" shouted Ceocilus as the little penguin began to run away. "Stop it!"

Meuseaux quickly translated Ceocilus's words to Gina and Randy, and the five of them gave chase to the fleeing informant.

Gina moved ahead of the pack of pursuers and saw that the penguin was headed toward a small opening in the wall. "Oh no you don't," she said and dove at the bird, grabbing hold of it just before it reached the gap. "Gotcha!" she said, holding it firmly in her grasp as it squirmed to try to free itself.

"Silence it!" Ceocilus said when he arrived.

Gina clamped the penguins beak shut, silencing the struggling bird.

Meuseaux and Mevoule looked at the writhing bird. "It's so small. Is it a fledgling?" Meuseaux asked, never having seen a Blue Fairy penguin before.

"No, it's not a fledgling," Randy said. "You've never seen this kind?"

"Most have not," Ceocilus said with surprising articulation. "These are the Overlord and Supreme Commander's spies. Very few know of their existence. It must be killed."

"No!" Randy shouted, surprising even himself. "These penguins are threatened."

"What are they?" Mevoule asked, and Meuseaux interpreted for him.

"They have a few names, but they're commonly called Blue penguins. They come from a place called New Zealand and the southern part of

Australia."

"Still, we must kill it. It has seen me and will betray me to the Overlord," Ceocilus demanded.

"I won't let you kill it," Randy asserted as he took the penguin from Gina.

"Then it is your responsibility. If it escapes your grasp, I will present you both to the Overlord myself," Ceocilus threatened them.

Randy nodded. "I understand," he said, accepting the burden.

They entered another passage and the humans had to duck under the rough-hewn ceiling. Ceocilus jabbed his spear into an unseen keyhole and turned to the others. "This is where I leave you," he said as the door opened to reveal a faint light from somewhere within. "Follow this passage. It will take you to where you need to be. Morning will come soon. You must hurry."

"Thank you for your help," Gina told the Royal Emperor.

Another doorway opened, and the Royal Empress called to Mevoule. Meuseaux spotted her, called out in alarm and ducked behind Gina and Randy for protection.

"Don't be alarmed," said Mevoule, trying to calm him.

"I know her. She is the consort of Liutites! She betrayed me to him!" he said angrily. Meuseaux remembered too well the events of that day and remembered as well that she was an integral part of what took place in the rookery.

Mevoule turned to her. "Is this true?" he asked, stepping back to Meuseaux's side.

Judging by their tense body language and nervous chatter, Gina sensed something was wrong and drew her gun.

"That is not necessary," the Empress told Gina and then looked at Mevoule.

Gina wasn't convinced and kept her weapon trained on the large female.

"Mevoule, there are certain things that I cannot reveal to you for the safety of us all. Meuseaux is correct in his accusations. I am Mearna, *the consort to the Supreme Commander*," she said with disdain, "but I had little choice. That is all I can tell you for now."

Mevoule remained silent for half a minute. He looked at Meuseaux, who still hid behind the pair of humans. "She's had plenty of opportunities to betray us. We have to trust her. There's no other choice," he finally said.

"I know in light of how things appear, this may sound suspicious, but Liutites is on his way to your quarters to see you," Mearna informed him.

"Why would he want to see me?" he asked in alarm.

"It was on the Overlord's behest. But you *must* hurry back. Ceocilus has returned to escort you."

"But he'll suspect me. Maybe I should leave with the others," he said in a panic.

"No," she said quickly. "If Liutites truly suspects that you took part in this and you're gone, he will punish all the remaining Chinstraps from your colony. You and Ceocilus return after Liutites. Tell him you spotted the humans passing by and sought the help of Ceocilus. In other words . . . lie. Ceocilus will back your story."

After a moment's hesitation, Mevoule said goodbye to his friend and began to leave. Gina lowered her weapon.

"If Liutites does not believe either of you, we will see to it that you are safe," Mearna added.

Mevoule nodded in response and turned back to Meuseaux. "Be safe, my friend."

"You as well," Meuseaux told him, foregoing the usual penguin blessing.

With Mevoule gone, Mearna turned her attention to Randy and the Blue he was holding. "Do you know what you hold?"

"A Blue penguin and, I believe, a spy," Randy answered matter-of-factly.

"Why has it been allowed to live? If it were to get free, it—"

"I have no intention of letting it go, but I will not kill this penguin," he said to her with defiance.

Mearna studied Randy with a mix of irritation in his stubbornness and respect for his unwillingness to kill the Blue showing in her eyes. "Very well, but you must take it with you. Speaking of such things, a guide will show you to the exit. This way." She indicated a door at the back of the room.

The two humans and Meuseaux decided it was indeed time to leave, but before leaving, Meuseaux stopped and turned to Mearna. "If you truly oppose the Overlord's rule and you knew what my fate would be, why did you let them take me?"

Mearna bowed her head. "I am sorry, Meuseaux. With Liutites and the others watching over, there was little I could do. However, once you escaped, we saw to it that you found your way to safety in the storage room. We had planned to rescue you, but the arrival of the human prisoner prevented us. Moreover, if I were to have gone to you myself, I doubt that you would have trusted me."

Meuseaux let out a deep sigh. It all seemed plausible, but like Mevoule, he was wary of her, regardless of her explanation. "I too am sorry. I'm sorry that you find yourself in such a position."

Mearna didn't reply at first. She lowered her head in embarrassment at the Chinstrap's remark. "I wonder if others see me in that light."

Randy, Gina, Meuseaux, and the Blue captive made their way out of Pack Ice Command without further incident, reached the snowmobile undetected, and sped on their way in hope of survival and freedom.

CHAPTER 65

Under a gray sky, hundreds of thousands of penguins amassed near the ever-thickening pack ice. A distant plume of smoke could be seen emanating from the wreckage of a helicopter the humans had sent to investigate the mysterious communication outage across the whole of Antarctica. The pilot and investigation team had landed among the throngs of penguins, oblivious to the danger. Some of the team had been armed, but they had little to no effect on the thousands of penguins, hell bent on destruction. The pilot had made it back to the chopper and even got it off the ground before a few penguin stowaways attacked. The chopper spun out of control and crashed in a fiery explosion against the icy, rocky terrain.

With the smoke as his backdrop, General Diutes stood before a group of fifty penguin leaders. Leepoh, Lavour, and Nok stood together in the crowd. They were becoming inseparable; their bond of friendship became tighter with the shared experiences of loss and the accompanying heartache. For the time being, Lavour pushed aside his burgeoning hatred toward Liutites in exchange for the opportunity for revenge against the humans.

Diutes began to speak, and his red eye seemed to flare as his passion for killing revealed itself. "Our home is once again ours. Any attempt by the humans to reclaim it will result in their death. Now, we will turn our attention to the Falkland Islands. The Kings have already begun their assault on the South Georgia and Sandwich Islands, and there are preliminary reports of incredible success there. We have received reports from the Magellanics at the Falklands that the human warships have left their ports and are presently headed on a southward course. We presume they are headed here. Those ships were our biggest obstacle to taking the islands. Now, the islands are vulnerable."

"The Magellanic, King, Gentoo, and Rockhopper forces already on the islands will position themselves for the coming attack and await our arrival. They will attack from the interior as we attack from the sea. The humans' largest settlement will be our primary objective. We will draw their remaining military out from their base and overwhelm them with our numbers. There are approximately three thousand humans on the islands. That is nearly four hundred penguins to every one human."

"The anticipated time from invasion to conquest is six days. After completion, you will regroup, leave an occupying force, and swim around the cape to begin the northward press along the Pacific coastline. You will then liberate the Humboldt from the human oppressors. Remember," said Diutes as he gazed at every penguin commander, "all human vessels are a target. If you can clear the sides of their boats, do so and eliminate the humans within. As the Chinstraps can attest," the general said, looking at Lavour, "the humans are merciless."

Lavour broke eye contact with Diutes and looked to the ground.

"We *must* free our kin," Diutes continued, "and press northward to the paradise that awaits us. Go now. Show no mercy and bring a reign of terror upon the humans!" On his closing remark, General Diutes spread his flippers wide for dramatic effect, and the penguin commanders dispersed.

"This is it," Lavour said to Leepoh while milling around the crowd.

"I believe you are correct. This is definitely *it*," Leepoh said jocularly, but not overly so. "Say—if there's time, how about if I show you and Nok my old nesting ground while we're there? It's not far away."

"I'd like that. I'd like that very much," Lavour said distantly.

Leepoh watched Lavour for a moment. "What's wrong?"

Lavour's eyes were fixed on Diutes, who was returning his stare. "Nothing. Just nerves," he answered. Lavour didn't like the way Diutes was looking at him. He had the look of someone who knew something. Something others didn't know.

"That's expected," Leepoh said, following Lavour's gaze. "What do you say we go hunting for humans?"

Lavour turned from Diutes. "Death to the humans?"

"Death to the humans," Nok said with modest eagerness.

"Death to the humans," Leepoh followed with similar enthusiasm.

Lavour looked back at General Diutes. "Yeah, death to them all," he said, distracted once again. "Well, my friends," Lavour said, turning back to them. "I'll see you at the islands." He nodded his head in farewell and rushed off to join his company.

"What was all of that about?" Nok asked after Lavour had gone.

Leepoh watched Lavour then looked back at Diutes, who was still watching the Chinstrap. "I believe he's not sure who his enemy is."

"The humans," said Nok assertively. "Of that we should have no doubt."

Leepoh looked down at Nok. "That much we know for sure."

CHAPTER 66

In the township of Stanley on the Falkland Islands, rows of brightly colored rooftops of red and green lined the streets. It is the capital of the British colony. Cheerful gardens with ceramic figures enhanced vibrantly painted homes and businesses that, in turn, contrasted with the brilliant blue sky. A landscape of rolling green hills and low mountains in the background added to the feeling of a quiet paradise, despite its violent history.

Two middle-aged men strolled along the waterfront, headed to one of Stanley's many pubs. "The Navy sure did pull out of here in a hurry. I wonder what's happening," one of the men said, more by way of making idle conversation than out of genuine curiosity.

"You didn't hear it from me, but I heard it had something to do with that news report," the other said.

"What report?"

"Jeez, Allen, don't you pay attention to the world around you?"

"Well, Leonard, when my pint goes dry I pay attention."

"That's a fine time," the man said, shaking his head. "The report where they said they lost all contact with everyone in Antarctica."

"Everyone?" asked Allen apathetically.

"*Everyone.*"

As the two men continued on their way, forty or more Magellanic penguins scurried across the roadway in front of them.

"That's a bit odd. I've never seen the buggers do that before," Leonard said.

"Do what before?" Allen asked, more focused on reaching the pub than watching the penguins.

"You really are quite astute, Allen," Leonard said bitingly. "When was the last time you seen fifty penguins traipsing about town . . . together?" he asked, adding the last bit of information for his slow-minded friend.

"Yeah, it looks like they're headed inland."

Surprised at his friend's off-handed but insightful observation, Leonard came to a stop. A couple of steps later, Allen followed suit.

"You know they say animals can sense danger before it happens," Leonard said.

"Who are *they*?" Allen asked, not caring either way.

Leonard ignored the question. "What d'ya say we have a look at where they're headed?"

The other man contemplated it for moment. "Nah, it'll keep 'til we have that pint."

Leonard watched as the penguins disappeared into the rows of houses. He didn't want to expend the effort anyhow. He really wanted a drink too, despite his righteous indignation at Allen's one-mindedness. "Yeah, it'll keep," he said, and then they themselves disappeared into the nearest pub.

^^^

Five miles off the coast of the Falklands, the penguin strike force gathered and awaited the order to begin the attack. Along their journey they had taken several of the "attacks of opportunity" that General Diutes had urged against unfortunate fishing trawlers. The poor souls aboard the vessels obviously never saw them coming and never had the chance to make distress calls.

A Chinstrap messenger swam up to a King penguin and, after a brief exchange, the Chinstrap swam back into the ranks.

The King penguin, Commander Kiley, summoned the other penguin leaders and, after they arrived, conveyed the information he had received. "I have just received word that the Magellanics are finally in position on the hills behind the settlements. A separate assault force has arrived at the human military compound, and it will attempt an infiltration by inconspicuous means. It is of the utmost importance that the infiltration team keeps the military occupied. If they join in the fray, we will suffer heavy losses."

"The key targets will be the populated areas and the airfield. For those of you who do not know what an airfield is, it is an area where the humans keep their flying vessels. Again, if they are allowed to take flight, they could inflict heavy damage. Our plan is to strike hard and fast. Our goal is to quickly overwhelm them, be done with it, and move on. Remember, we do not want to get involved in a prolonged engagement. If there are not any questions—" he paused to look at the faces of bobbing penguins in the surf "—good. You know what to do. May the Ancients be at our sides."

Lavour swam up alongside Leepoh. "Are you ready for this?" he asked nervously.

"Bah! I'm *ready* to go home," Leepoh said, seeming unusually upset.

Lavour looked at Leepoh with concern. "Is something wrong?"

Leepoh lifted his head and looked to the sky, as if he was lost in thought. Something *was* wrong, but he couldn't pinpoint what that something might be. Ever since they left Antarctica, he had been troubled by something. He knew Lavour had felt it too, but whatever it was, it remained elusive, like a squid just out of reach. He shuddered at the thought of not catching a squid. "I don't know—*is* there something wrong?"

Lavour stared at the Gentoo in silence. "I don't know," he answered, pulling his eyes away. "Let's take care of this, and afterwards we'll see if we can figure it out."

Nok swam in a circle around the others, nervously looking toward the islands. "What are we trying to figure out?"

"If we knew we wouldn't have to figure it out. Would we?" Leepoh remarked.

Nok let out a derisive snort. "Leave it to a Gentoo to not know what he's trying to know."

"You sound like a Gentoo," Lavour cracked.

Nok growled. "I've been told worse. Not much worse, mind you. But worse nonetheless."

The order to form ranks sounded over the bickering penguins and howling wind. The three companions exchanged looks of concern. No one spoke. They went their separate ways hoping tomorrow would come.

CHAPTER 67

Commander Boulét and Lieutenant-General Lavour reached land and immediately began to survey the area for targets and threats while the Chinstraps came ashore.

"There!" Commander Boulét shouted, spotting a group of humans standing in the road. "Attack!"

Swarms of penguins rushed from the shore toward their first targets, who stood watching them in curiosity. At first, the people were confused by the penguins' odd behavior. Then, as the penguins advanced with greater urgency, the humans began to back away and run. Their flight was too late. The penguins were already on them, and they began to stab and slash at the shocked people. Screams of pain and horror filled the once quiet air. The sheer number of birds prevented their victims from escaping, and their screams fell silent.

The commotion drew the attention of more people. They came out of houses and shops and beheld the unbelievable. Thousands of penguins filled the narrow roadways. The onlookers were brought out of their dumbfounded haze when the Chinstraps turned on them. Most made it back inside, but those who were too slow to realize their peril were quickly eliminated.

"Watch out. To your left!" Lavour shouted when a man threw open his front door and brought a shotgun to bear on the invaders. A single blast from the weapon dropped two Chinstraps. The man pumped the shotgun and fired again.

"Kill it!" Commander Boulét ordered, and the penguins rushed forward to carry out the command even as the man continued to pour pellets into their ranks. The man backed inside and slammed his door shut, halting their advance. The penguins began to peck at the door with ferocity.

Two shots rang out from a second story window, and a Chinstrap dropped to the ground in front of Lavour. "Find a way inside that shelter, and eliminate that human," he said, pointing with his flipper. The sound of breaking glass was heard over the cacophony of squawking invaders, and penguins began to leap through the breech. "That's it. Through those," Lavour ordered.

Hordes of penguins started to pour through the broken windows, and sporadic gunfire erupted inside the building, followed by the shouting of men and women as the penguins overtook them. The gunfire from the second story window abruptly ceased, and the window exploded as the sniper leapt from his vantage point in a desperate attempt to escape. The blanket of penguins beneath the window broke the man's fall. The surprised birds threw off their shock and took off in pursuit of the man who had somehow managed not to break his legs.

The sloping main road had become slick with blood by the time Lavour arrived. "We're getting slaughtered this way. Take the side paths and go between their shelters. Go around them and then surround them." Bullets sprayed asphalt in Lavour's face and he quickly ran behind a house and down an alleyway with a trail of gunfire following him. A door flew open in front of him, and five people dashed out with a swarm of Chinstraps on their tail.

Four of the five humans sprinted down the alleyway, and Lavour leapt at the fifth, driving his beak into the surprised man's stomach. The human, a large male, fell backwards, and Lavour pounced again, only this time he was met with a fist to his body. Lavour flew back into the brick façade of the house across the alley. Before he could clear his head, the man stood up and delivered a solid kick to Lavour, which sent him spinning down the alley. The man held on to his wounded stomach and turned to run but was met by more Chinstraps.

A human female's voice screamed from the end of the alley, and the man yelled for her to go as he was brought down. Angered by the kick, Lavour joined the attack and began pecking at the man—tentatively at first but then with more vigor. As the man lay dying beneath him, Lavour followed the direction of his eyes as he reached out for the still screaming woman. The man's body went limp and Lavour hopped off, looking at the woman as she lowered her head. At another human's urging, she ran away.

Lavour stood motionless, frozen in his thoughts, remembering Lannera. He looked down at the departed man and made the connection that it must have been his mate that he had urged away. These humans weren't the ones who had wiped out his colony. Maybe they were guilty as a species for the atrocities, but maybe they weren't. A sickly feeling arose within him and his stomach lurched.

All around him, the chaos of battle raged; penguins and humans alike screamed out in pain, fear, confusion, anger, and death. But for Lavour, the world was silent. He remained motionless, his thoughts fixed on his deceased loved ones and those who had died defending them.

A Chinstrap fell to the ground beside him, its body bloodied and torn from a gunshot. He thought back to the scene at his nesting ground and the bodies of the dead. Try as he might, he couldn't shake the visions of home. There was something he missed.. A ball of flame shot from the doorway of the house across the alley, followed by several flaming Chinstraps. But he stood transfixed by the dead man and penguin.

"Lavour!" a distant-sounding voice called out to him. He didn't respond. "Lavour!" He heard it, but it sounded as if it was coming from a fading dream.

"Lieutenant-General Lavour—are you all right?"

When, through his fugue, he finally realized someone was talking to him, he turned his head toward the voice.

"Lavour, can you hear me?"

"General Leepoh?" Lavour asked, coming out of his haze.

"Are you all right? Are you injured?" Leepoh asked, concerned with Lavour's discombobulated state.

"Yes. I mean, no. I mean I just got kicked around a bit. Why are you already here?" he asked the Gentoo once reality caught up with him again.

"Reinforcements. The Rockhoppers are on their way too."

A bullet ricocheted off the nearby wall, and they pressed against the opposite wall for cover.

"There's a human on top of that shelter, and we can't get to it," Leepoh told Lavour.

Still aching from the beating he had received, Lavour took a deep breath, grimaced in pain, and peeked around the wall at the shooter. He ducked back for cover as another shot sent chunks of flying debris. He lowered his head in resignation while looking at the dead man in the alley.

Leepoh followed Lavour's gaze to the dead man and then to the bloodstains on Lavour's white feathers. "Can you go on?"

Lavour pressed his beak shut firmly. Regardless of how he was beginning to feel about the war, he was determined to do his part to ensure the safety of as many penguins as he could. He let cold detachment overcome him once again and repressed his doubt for the time being. "I have an idea," he said while looking at the burning building across from him. "Chinstraps!" he barked out, wincing in pain as he did.

A dozen Chinstraps and two Gentoo rushed to him and stood front and center. More Chinstraps followed while gunshots peppered the ground near them as they ran. One penguin called out after getting hit then fell to the ground. "No!" Leepoh yelled, but Lavour acted like it didn't faze him.

"Listen to me," Lavour ordered. "Grab whatever you're able to find that can hold fire. Take the fire to the shelter the human is on and burn it. We'll get it off of there one way or another." Lavour finished up by looking at Leepoh.

"Sounds sound," Leepoh said and then looked at one of the Gentoo. "You, tell the others to protect these Chinstraps at all costs. If one goes down, one of us will take its place."

The bullets ceased while the rooftop shooter was distracted by targets on the other side of the house. The penguins seized the moment and rushed to the burning building, picking up bits of wooden debris. The squad carried the fire across the street and reached the shooter's house without incident. They rushed through an opened doorway, and soon, draperies and furniture burst into flame. The penguin arsonists rushed from the burning house, and the shooter turned his unwanted attention back to them.

The shooter managed to drop two penguins before the bullets abruptly ceased. With the house already fully engulfed, the man was faced with the choice of being burned alive or fleeing through a crowd of killers; he chose the latter. He climbed to a second story balcony, stopped to fire a few more shots, and leapt over the railing. He fought hard for several seconds, but the mob quickly overtook him.

CHAPTER 68

"What are we waiting for?" Captain Nok asked General Leepoh.

Nok and the rest of the Rockhoppers had arrived on the tail end of the conquest of the Falklands. They were called in from their reserve position to occupy the town of Port Louis. But when they arrived there wasn't much left to occupy, so they swam around the island to meet up with the main strike force.

Structures were burning throughout Stanley, and there was not a human to be seen. If there were any survivors, they would not be so for much longer. The invasion had gone off far more expediently and quickly than planned. Although not strangers to unexpected attacks, the islanders were solidly defeated within hours, not days, as the penguin leaders had anticipated.

The key to the penguins' overwhelming success was the Magellanics' victory at the military base near Mt. Pleasant. Nearly a week before the invasion, the Magellanic commander, T'Cuh-ka, had learned that the Falkland Islands were to be liberated. His troops had burrowed tirelessly to gain a point of entry to the base. Their hard work had paid off handsomely, and the garrison was routed.

The day's victory was not without a cost, however. Over six thousand penguins had been lost, and nearly double that number had been wounded.

Many of those casualties had been suffered by the Magellanics at Mt. Pleasant, which didn't set well with Commander T'Cuh-ka.

The Magellanics of the Falklands stood just two feet tall. They had a black horseshoe stripe and a smattering of spots on their chest with pink skin showing around their eyes. At first they had been reluctant to join the Penguin Defense Alliance. They had enjoyed many years of peaceful living among the humans. There were dissidents who remembered tales of the old times. They told about the humans colonizing the island and relentlessly hunting and persecuting the penguins. But by and large, the majority of the population was not opposed to the humans.

The Magellanics had heard accounts of the atrocities that occurred in other places, but that was a long way from their breeding grounds. They remained happily isolated until a group of Magellanics arrived from another island to seek shelter. They had abandoned their own burrows after poachers had persecuted them. The stories from the newcomers soon spread throughout the Magellanic community, and opinions about the humans and their benevolence slowly began to shift.

Ambassadors from the newly founded Penguin Defense Alliance urged the Magellanics to become members, but the fiercely independent penguins remained reluctant. Then, after a group of intoxicated humans raided their burrows and stole several eggs, the devastated penguins formed a guild of leaders to address the situation. Even then, it was decided that they would not join the PDA. Most did not want to be subject to the Overlord's increasingly powerful rule. They resolved to defend their nest more aggressively to continue to avoid falling under Pack Ice Command's authority.

For several breeding cycles there were no further problems from the humans. But all of that changed when a large group of penguins were traveling across a roadway and a car headed in their direction. The penguins thought nothing of it; the local motorists always yielded the right of way to the birds, but not this time. The car, which was traveling at a high rate of speed, plowed through the procession. The penguins were shocked but thought it was an accident. But the car turned around and ran through them a second time, and the passenger threw an empty liquor bottle at them. Laughter from within vehicle could be heard as they sped away. It was obviously not an accident. The bottle struck T'Cuh-ka, and hatred for the humans was born.

Not long after that incident, the dead bodies of several Magellanics began to wash ashore; all of them had died a mysterious death. T'Cuh-ka urged the guild to join the PDA. They agreed and T'Cuh-ka was elevated to the rank of Commander.

"We are *waiting* for Commander T'Cuh-ka to arrive. He's the authority on the islands, and Commander Boulét thought it would be fitting for him to be here for the final battle against the human remnants," Leepoh explained to the impatient Nok.

"I say we should attack now and not give them any opportunity to regroup," Nok said angrily. He was not truly angry; he was fearful and anxious. After witnessing the scale and ferocity of the battles, Captain Nok was eager for the assault to end.

When he first arrived on shore, he was appalled by the carnage. Human bodies lay in the streets, outside of homes or businesses, in gardens, in fields, and on the beach. For every dead human, there were, at the very least, five dead penguins. The sight was horrific, but that wasn't what concerned the Rockhopper. It was the fact that this was just a small taste of what lay ahead. Also, the fact was not lost on him that these islands were sparsely populated, and the humans had been caught completely off guard. The penguins would not be so lucky in the future.

"I'm not going to disagree with you, my friend, but Boulét said the orders came from PIC."

"I still say we should attack now. Look at them. They're planning their defenses as we speak. This will cost us additional casualties."

"I know. Lavour and I both agreed on that. But we're not in charge here, are we?"

Nok looked at Leepoh in silence for moment before continuing. "Speaking of Lavour, where is he? Did he make it?"

"Yes, he's fine. He took a beating, but he'll be fine. He took a squad to a place they call Sea Lion Island. There are supposed to be some humans there."

"Are you all right?" Nok asked.

Leepoh looked at Nok, who was staring at him curiously. "Bah!" he finally let out. "I am now." General Leepoh had kept his emotions distant and buried since the loss of his loved ones, but Nok's genuine concern for him made him realize that he truly had a friend, and probably one in Lavour as well. He had *called* them friends before, but now he meant it. If he could have smiled, he would've done so at the thought and at knowing he had friends. "There's T'Cuh-ka now," Leepoh said, seeing a company of Magellanics appear on a hill to his right.

"Good—we need to finish this before any humans return."

"Once they investigate Antarctica I'm sure they'll be preoccupied. Be ready. It looks like the commander is."

"Right—I'd better get back. After we leave this place, I'll take you to a place near home where the squid gather."

"A Rockhopper secret?" asked Leepoh, who suddenly felt hunger for the first time all day.

"A well-guarded one at that. You just make sure you stick around to see it," Nok told him, as if the motivation of boundless squid would make Leepoh extra cautious.

"You can count on it," Leepoh assured him.

"Count on what? I only have two flippers."

"Hah! I see my influence on you has been too great."

"Hah!" Nok said, mocking Leepoh's characteristic laugh, and then he ran off to join the other Rockhoppers. As he made his way back, an odd sound came from the distance, and he stopped to look around for the source. He spotted Leepoh, who was doing the same and ran back to him. "Do you hear that? What is it?"

Leepoh craned his neck as he listened. "It is death."

The sound of jet engines could be heard bearing in from the south, burning at full throttle. Penguins who had heard stories of the human war that had taken place here years earlier had been told of destruction the flying killing machines could deliver. General Leepoh knew there was no time to waste and issued the attack order at once. Commander T'Cuh-ka, also, heard the fighters and followed Leepoh's lead, foregoing any speech on final victory. The combined forces of the PDA bore down on the last of the human survivors.

CHAPTER 69

The surviving humans attempted to make their escape in an assortment of automobiles. Finding the roads blocked by thousands of penguins coming at them in every direction, they abandoned their flight and formed a wagon circle with the cars. They gathered in the interior, bearing a few guns, axes, and other weapons, intent on making their last stand.

Leepoh flinched under the sound of Harrier jets as they flew overhead. He watched them make a tight turn and head back toward them. He didn't like the looks of what was happening and briefly considered ordering a full retreat, but after thinking about the sacrifices already made by the penguins, it didn't seem prudent to go away with anything less than a full victory. After a moment of hesitation, he joined the attack, running headlong at the remaining humans' defenses.

"Over the top," Commander Boulét ordered his Chinstraps. One of the shooters stopped firing to reload. The penguins took advantage of the break and piled on top of one another to clamber over the top of the vehicle. The first were met by the swing of an axe by a gun-less defender, but more took their fallen comrades' place and breeched the defenses. The man who was attempting to reload his weapon panicked and dropped his shells. Several Chinstraps pounced on him.

The British Harriers hovered over the battlefield on their angling thrusters and with a 30mm cannon, capable of firing 1,700 rounds per minute, they began to unleash hell upon the penguins. The powerful guns literally tore the defenseless birds apart, killing them by the dozen. One of the fighters fired a missile into the rear of the penguin lines and left a crater where once a hundred or more penguins stood.

The penguins began to breech the makeshift redoubt in greater numbers and engaged the humans in hand-to-beak combat. The close-quartered fighting rendered the guns useless as the humans were unable bring their weapons to bear. They had the strength, but the penguins had the numbers.

"Kill them all!" Boulét ordered after finding his way to the roof of a car. He was confident they would achieve a victory, but with the rest of the force getting pounded by the jet fighters, he was eager to make a retreat.

A final shot from melee found Boulet, tearing away his flipper and sending him flailing to the ground.

Leepoh watched as Commander Boulét fell. Despite the sight, he moved closer to the human fortification. He checked on the Chinstrap Commander, who was still alive, and then moved to the nearest car. The calls and screams of both men and penguin could be heard over the thunderous roar of jet engines and cannon fire. The human gunfire had all but ceased, but with the Harriers relentlessly attacking the marauding birds, they couldn't muster enough attackers at one time to deliver the killing blow.

"We need to attack in unison—not separately," said General Leepoh, who saw that their current tactics were ineffectual against the determined defenders. "Swarm them," he commanded.

Two of the three jet fighters, exhausted of ammo, began to hover close to the ground on their powerful thrusters and scatter the penguins. Then all three suddenly lifted up and tore into the sky. The confused penguins looked around, decided this was their chance and began to rush the defenses. Captain Nok and the Rockhoppers led the charge. The Kings, Magellanics, Chinstraps, and Gentoo followed.

"Very good," Leepoh said to himself and then gave himself a running start to try to get enough speed to be able leap to the hood of one of the cars.

The reason for the sudden departure of the fighters then made itself apparent. Two missiles slammed into the ground, followed by six more fighters racing in from the north, spraying the field with cannon fire.

Leepoh shook his head to try to clear the dizzying effects of the blasts' concussions and opened his eyes to see the Rockhoppers sprinting through the clouds of dust and smoke and hopping onto the cars. Captain Nok had fallen behind the group after the blasts and was rushing forward to join the fracas when a second volley of missiles hit behind him. Leepoh watched in horror as he saw his friend launched into the air. "No!" he screamed and ran to where Nok had landed in a crumpled heap.

Leepoh approached his friend cautiously, afraid of what he would find. "Captain Nok," he said. "Can you hear me, Nok?"

Captain Nok was motionless, his eyes closed.

The Rockhopper reserves attacked the last of the human defenders with zeal and ferocity, fully intent on ending the fiasco once and for all. The windows of the cars shattered under the fury of the reinforced penguin beaks, and the penguins attacked their occupants from all sides. The last human on the main Falkland Islands was felled.

CHAPTER 70

Lieutenant-General Lavour and his mixed squad of Chinstrap, Gentoo, Magellanic, and King penguins scurried up the beach and toward the lone homestead of Sea Lion Island. As the penguins made their way to the home, they were startled by the screaming of jet engines passing low overhead. All twenty-five members of the squad stopped to watch the spectacle, except Lavour, who was watching the house instead. He had spotted a man stepping out onto the porch. The man had spotted them and quickly closed the door, which Lavour found odd. He didn't think the man would know they were a threat. *He knows,* Lavour thought.

Within seconds of the jets passing overhead, the muted sounds of explosions were heard coming from the Falkland main islands. The squad began to fidget. Lavour looked at his nervous squad then back to the house. Something bothered him about the assault, and he had to make a decision on whether to continue.

"We have to go back. Something has gone wrong. The human military shouldn't be here," Lavour said.

"But what about the house?" a Gentoo asked.

"If their military knows, they know."

"Shouldn't we make sure?" the Gentoo asked further.

"No," said Lavour, slightly impatient. "If the humans are already striking back with such force, our plans change. We need to get back for new orders."

"Then we abandon our orders here?"

"I am in command here, Sergeant. I will give the orders and you will follow them. Do you understand?" Lavour snapped with authority, finally having had enough of the Gentoo's impudence.

"Yes, sir, sorry, sir," the reprimanded Gentoo said while lowering his head.

Lavour sighed. He didn't like losing his patience, but he had to maintain a structure of command in the face of this insanity. "Get the squad back to the sea. If I'm not mistaken, these aerial attacks should induce a retreat on our part. I think this shelter is already vacated. Nevertheless, I'll do a quick recon and rejoin you at sea. Our priorities have changed. Regroup with the others."

"Yes, sir," the Gentoo acknowledged and happily snapped a salute. Even after being scolded by Lavour, the Gentoo sergeant was happy to do his bidding. Lavour had that effect on penguins, and others were beginning to take notice.

After watching his squad depart, Lavour turned back toward the house and began to creep forward, wary of what he might find. He reached the surrounding fence and slipped through the white painted palings, moving ever closer. He stopped on the spacious front porch, investigated his surroundings, and noticed the front door slightly ajar. He took a deep breath and, with his head, pushed the door, which made a loud squeak. He jumped back and pressed his body against the outer wall.

After a few moments, he regained his nerve and eased inside. He heard hurried footsteps coming from the hallway on the other side of the room he had entered and stopped. "Why am I doing this?" he asked himself quietly. But when he couldn't answer himself, he pressed on.

Lavour walked slowly to where the footfalls had come from and cautiously peered down the hall. He caught a fleeting glimpse of motion near the end of the hall and froze again. He heard whispers coming from a room near the end of the hall, followed by more footsteps and a loud creak. He crept to the room and stood at the door, staring at it. He still wasn't sure why he was doing this, only that he felt compelled. He hesitated a second longer and then nudged the door. To his surprise, the door swung open easily. He expected that his time on Earth was at an end.

The man Lavour had seen entering the house earlier was standing before him with a shotgun trained directly at him. To his right, a woman stood holding a large kitchen knife; behind them were two young girls, one of whom was climbing down into a storm cellar.

"No!" Lavour blurted in human. "Don't shoot!"

The woman let out a startled gasp, dropped the knife, and covered her mouth in shock. The man stood upright from his firing posture, equally shocked. He looked at the penguin as if it were a freakish abomination or a demon-possessed entity and drew his weapon once more.

"Please don't. I saved your lives," Lavour pleaded and braced for death.

"What do you mean?" the woman asked as she picked up her knife and pushed down on her husband's gun barrel.

"What are you doing? This is a penguin. Penguins don't talk, or shouldn't. And they shouldn't be killing people," said the husband angrily. "There's something wrong with it."

"But they *can* talk, Papa," one of the little girls said from behind him.

"And they can kill as well."

"I apologize," Lavour interjected. "I know that is not nearly enough. We were sent on a mission to destroy this shelter, but I sent the others away."

"Don't," said the woman who sensed her husband was ready to pull the trigger.

"This thing is a freak of nature and should be destroyed immediately," the man said, but he still didn't fire.

"Please, no. If I do not return, they will search for me; and the others are not as—as merciful. They will be relentless."

"We can hide in the cellar. Get back, girls," said the man as he brought his weapon up to firing position.

Lavour watched the man and the way he protected his children and then thought about what he would have done had he been there when the humans attacked his colony. He knew he would have done the same thing and would have defended his family to the last. "Do what you must. I will make myself accountable for my kind's actions," said Lavour while lowering his head. And that was it; that was why he had come to this house. He felt a certain amount of guilt for his actions and the actions of the penguins in general, regardless of his feelings about his colony's death at the hands of the humans. He knew now that no amount of revenge would ever change what had happened and that this war was largely inexcusable.

"Is that why you came here?" the woman asked.

"That *and* I wanted to show that we are not all what you have been shown." He thought about what he had just said, *not all what you have been shown,* and for some reason the phrase stuck in his head, like a piece of a puzzle that didn't quite fit. The click of the shotgun brought Lavour out of his thoughts and back to the reality of his current situation. He closed his eyes and waited for the inevitable. But to his surprise, it never came.

"Get out of here, beast," the man said and ushered his family down into the cellar without another word spoken.

Amazed at his good fortune, Lavour made his way outside and to the sea. He dreaded going back to the other islands and seeing the carnage there. His mind, once again, turned to his dead colony and then to the dead he witnessed at the battle. They didn't match up. The bodies of the dead penguins here were ravaged and torn. Those back home looked more as if they were—stabbed. Like stabs from a . . . *That would be too much,* he thought. *Too much even for someone as twisted as Diutes or Liutites.* There had to be another explanation.

CHAPTER 71

"To the sea," Commander T'Cuh-ka ordered the disoriented penguins. "It's our only hope!"

After the penguins dispatched the remaining humans, the planes stepped up the ferocity of their attacks and pounded the penguin-filled landscape with everything they had. The penguin warriors were being destroyed by the hundreds, and the sea was their only hope of escape.

"We'll regroup on RHC 23. Pass it through the ranks. Go, go," T'Cuh-ka shouted to a Chinstrap captain and then fell into step with the crowd of stampeding penguins, fleeing for their lives.

The penguins scattered, leaving behind the dead and wounded. All hope of occupation and a penguin safe haven was abandoned. Every last penguin was charging toward the Atlantic except for one; Leepoh remained behind, standing over the fallen Nok and pleading for him to wake up. "Come on, Nok," he yelled. "Don't you die—not now—not after all we've been through."

A group of Gentoo rushed past. "General Leepoh, we have to leave now!" one of them beseeched him.

"No," Leepoh barked back over the sound of continual explosions. "I'm not leaving without my friend."

The Gentoo looked at Leepoh and then at Nok. "We're regrouping on RHC 23," he said and ran to catch up with the rest of his group.

Leepoh watched the Gentoo disappear into the swirling dust and then looked back to his friend. "Don't you leave me too," he said as he lowered his head in despair.

"Do you *never* stop talking?" a quiet voice said.

Leepoh found Nok's red eyes staring back at him. "Hah!" he blurted out, followed by a string of relieved jubilant laughter. "Napping on the job, were you?" he jibed. "Let's go. We have to get out of this place."

Although he was still groggy, Captain Nok rolled onto to his belly and struggled to push himself upright, determined not to show any signs of weakness in front of Leepoh, which he knew would lead to more ribbing. Nevertheless, he accepted a helpful nudge from the Gentoo as he stood on his shaky legs.

"Can you make it? We're going to regroup back home," Leepoh informed him.

"What? Why? I thought we won," the still-disoriented Nok said.

"It was . . . short-lived." The sound of more jets approaching left no need for further explanation, and the two penguins started to head to the closest shore.

One of the Harriers had exhausted its supply of ammunition and set down just beyond the circle of cars. The hundreds of escaping penguins altered their path at seeing the devilish machination land in front of them. The pilot opened his canopy and began firing with his sidearm, killing penguins at random. A second fighter set down as well and followed suit. With the engines powered down and the other fighters churning the water with their 30mm cannons, the battlefield was awash in the cacophony of squawking, frightened penguins running for their lives.

Nok and Leepoh made their way from the battlefield and came across Commander Boulét, who was minus one flipper and standing wobbly.

"Come on, Commander," Nok told him.

Commander Boulét didn't move. Instead he stood and stared at the fighter jets that had landed in the field.

"We have to go. Now," Nok urged him.

Boulét looked at Nok and Leepoh. "No, I can't make it. I can't swim." The badly wounded Chinstrap commander lowered his head in resignation to his fate.

Nok and Leepoh exchanged knowing looks. "May the spirit of the Ancients be at your side," Leepoh blessed Boulét.

"Soon I will be with them. Go, find safety and fight another day." Commander Boulét, intent on fighting until he drew his last breath, stumbled toward the jets.

Nok and Leepoh watched him as long as prudence allowed and then continued to the sea. They dove into the water, frothy from thousands of fleeing penguins, well away from still-attacking humans.

^^^

"Lieutenant-General Lavour, let's go," a Chinstrap called to Lavour near the ocean's edge as he returned from Sea lion Island. "We have to evacuate."

"What happened here?" Lavour asked, even though he already had an idea. He knew the humans had retaliated, but he didn't know the extent of the destruction.

"The humans are annihilating us, sir. Their flying weapons have slaughtered thousands already," the Chinstrap continued.

"We have to regroup," said Lavour.

"We already are regrouping, sir," the Chinstrap told him as they swam on the surface of the waves. "RHC 23. A Magellanic told us before they left for the mainland."

"All right, then. Wait—what do you mean by 'left for the mainland'?" Lavour asked in surprise after realizing what the Chinstrap had said.

"Commander T'Cuh-ka has withdrawn his forces from the PDA, sir," the Chinstrap informed him.

Lavour shook his head in disbelief at first but then didn't really blame the Magellanic commander; after the day's debacle, he and his group no longer had a home. "Well, best of luck to them," he said as still more jets tore in from the south. "We had better leave while we can."

The sounds of explosions on the islands urged Lavour and the others to pick up their pace. They soon caught up with the tail end of first members of the exodus, consisting of those who were exhausted from the fighting or struggling from being wounded. Lavour desperately wanted to do something to help the injured, but nothing could be done. The injured grouped together for safety but would eventually succumb to their fate.

CHAPTER 72

Gina, Randy, Meuseaux and the incessantly protesting Blue Penguin arrived back at the GT base just as another powerful windstorm swept in. They had traveled for nearly a full day after leaving Pack Ice Command, stopping only to swaddle themselves in spare dry clothing that Gina had had the foresight to bring, and for Meuseaux's frequent restroom breaks. After several such stops, Randy decided there were worse things in the world than having penguin guano in one's lap, and they made no more stops.

On arriving, they found the savagely pecked and frozen body of Ferdinand Davis lying in the open doorway.

"My God," said Randy. "What happened?"

"Don't be too horrified. That man tried to kill me," Gina informed him. Through all of the excitement, if that was what it was called, she realized she had forgotten to mention that their employer had nearly murdered her.

Randy stood, looking at Gina, obviously stunned by her revelation. He looked down at Davis' body. "Did you . . ."

"No, of course not," said Gina in feigned offense at the suggestion. Though she doubted she was capable of killing another human being, she did know she felt no remorse for leaving him to his fate at the beaks of the penguins. "I'll tell you all about it, but first let's get his body outside and try to get this door closed."

Randy hesitated and stared at the body. "Okay," was all he managed to spit out.

After placing the body well away from the camp and covering it as well as they could, they came back inside and managed to get the door closed with a surprisingly tight seal. Gina looked around the room and at the amount of damage the marauders had caused. "This place is a mess."

"Yeah, it is. So why would Davis want to kill you?" Randy asked.

Meuseaux seemed to pick up on the seriousness of the mood. "I will try to learn the Blue penguin language," he said, and quickly exited the room.

Gina stood an overturned chair upright and sat down in it wearily. Randy looked around the room and followed suit. She took a deep breath, knowing Randy was concerned with what had happened to her and that he wasn't going to let it go. She couldn't blame him; if someone she cared about revealed he had almost been murdered, she knew she would press until she got answers.

"After you went missing," Gina started, "we searched for you and only found your camera and a dead penguin. It wasn't much to go on."

"Do you still have my camera?" Randy joked.

"Anyway," said Gina, ignoring the question, "they downloaded the pictures and, of course, everyone was amazed. But then Dan—I think it was—said I'd have to sign a nondisclosure agreement. I think this was after he said he had spoken to Vance about sending me home."

"Wait a sec. Why would they want you to sign a nondisclosure?" Randy interrupted.

"They fed me a load of bull about their getting credit for the discovery."

"That *does* sounds like a load of bull," Randy agreed.

"Yeah," said Gina while standing up from the suddenly uncomfortable chair. "They all left, supposedly to search for you, and instructed me that I had to leave and needed to be on the last ship home. I took the opportunity to load up and start my own search. I didn't want to give up on you just yet," she said as she looked at Randy then quickly turned away. "*Any*-ways, that was when Davis returned and I found out the real reason for their, or our, being here."

Randy looked at Gina expectantly. "Which was?" he prompted when further explanation wasn't forthcoming.

"Oil, mining, you name it—GT has their hands in it."

"I knew something didn't feel right about this trip. It felt . . . *odd,* right from the start. I mean, it was just too easy to get on. They came to *me.* I should have known better; because nobody does that." He stopped talking and looked at Gina. "Then again, it hasn't been *all* bad."

Gina almost seemed to blush, but not quite, and quickly went back to the subject. "The bottom line was they didn't trust me not to say anything about the penguins and I guess it was important enough to kill me over. Davis said something about not wanting to let any environmentalists know about the penguins. He told me Dan and the others were out hunting them down instead of looking for you. There's more, but to be honest, I'm exhausted and I really could use some sleep." Gina began to walk down the hallway and Randy followed.

"Yeah, me too." Randy stretched and let out a heavy breath. "So I take it that's Davis's gun you have?"

"None other," Gina quipped as she tried to make heads or tails of the sleeping quarters.

"Something still doesn't add up, or maybe I'm too tired to make any sense of this."

Gina nodded in agreement as they returned to the front room. "It looks like we may have some time on our hands to make sense of it, unless you know how to repair this. I'm pretty sure Dan and the others had the sat phones" said Gina while indicating the thoroughly trashed communications equipment.

The two surveyed the interior of the base and exchanged tired looks but decided to forego their much-needed sleep in order to clean up the mess. As they rummaged through the amazing amount of damage the penguins had caused, Randy watched Gina out of the corner of his eye. "So how *did* you get away from Davis?"

"I was wondering when you'd get to that," remarked Gina. "Ironically, a penguin saved me."

Randy gave her a dubious look.

"Davis was about to shoot me when the attack came. The penguins came through the door. He raised the gun to shoot them. I knocked his hand up, and he fired and missed. The penguins attacked and killed him. Hand me that," she said, pointing to a cylinder of oatmeal on the floor. "He dropped the gun and I grabbed it."

Gina got a distant look in her eyes as she recalled the event, and Randy didn't prod her anymore about Davis's death. "How did they save you?" he asked instead.

"I'm not sure, but I think the leader realized I had saved its life and held back from attacking just long enough for me to get away."

"This is all really . . . overwhelming," said Randy. "An army of killer, talking penguins—my employer leaving me for dead and trying to kill you—me falling in love with you . . ." he said nonchalantly and with a half-cocked smile while pretending to busy himself with some canned foods.

Gina stepped close to Randy, pulled him by his jacket collar, closed her eyes, and kissed him. She slowly opened her eyes, looked at him, and spoke softly. "You really do smell, you know."

Randy opened his eyes, as if being brought from sleep. "Actually, college girl, I stink, and you can smell my stink."

"Let me be more specific. You have an odor about you . . . and I love you too," Gina said with her own half smile.

Corporal Meuseaux scurried into the room, saw the two humans, and tried to ease away.

"What's going on, Meuseaux?" Randy asked.

"I apologize. I did not mean to interrupt your mating ritual once again."

Gina shook her head in amusement. "We're not *mating*, Meuseaux."

The Chinstrap looked at Gina curiously. "If you insist," he said.

"You see how you corrupted this poor penguin?" Gina said to Randy, who threw up his hands in a show of innocence.

"There are several dead penguins in the rear of your dwellings and I was wondering if you could remove them. It is quite unpleasant," Meuseaux said more seriously.

"Oh, I am so sorry about that. They were trying to kill me. I had to defend myself," Gina explained.

Randy immediately walked down the hall to investigate.

"There is no need to apologize. To survive is why we live," Meuseaux told her and followed Randy.

After the two humans removed the bodies, they collapsed onto the sofa in the main room. "Any luck with the Blue?" Gina asked Meuseaux.

"Luck?" the Chinstrap asked.

"I mean did you make any progress in learning its language?" she corrected herself, remembering the Chinstrap had trouble with vernacular, slang, and double entendres.

"Not much of it," said Meuseaux. "I think it understands we mean no harm."

"Trust is good," Gina said while looking at the Blue penguin. She shook her head as she became lost in thought. For years, the penguins had been hunted and, in some places, still were. They were driven from their homes, polluted, and poisoned. Their hunting waters were overfished, and they were pushed to the edge of extinction. She wondered had people known how intelligent they were, if they would have still done what they did. Would things have been different? *Probably not*, she thought.

They were unassuming creatures. No one knew they were also vengeful. She remembered her earlier conversation with the Chinstrap. He had told her that the penguins had learned by watching the humans—killers studying those who were studying them. Now they were fighting back and, knowing what she did, Gina did not blame them. However, she did not wish them success.

The sound of Randy's soft snoring roused her from her thoughts, and she focused on Meuseaux through her bleary eyes. "Will you do something for me, Meuseaux?"

"Anything—you saved me, and I am in your debt," Meuseaux answered proudly.

"You saved me as well. So we're even. Just remember that not all humans are evil. If Randy and I don't survive—or even if we do—remember that."

"I know that, and I will always know that," he said.

Gina watched the little Chinstrap as her eyelids grew heavy. Despite all the trouble the past few days had presented her, she drifted away into a contented sleep.

CHAPTER 73

The remnants of the defeated Penguin Defense Alliance began to trickle onto the north shore of RHC 23 near Gentoo Rise. They came in slowly at first but then in greater numbers. Most were exhausted, many were wounded and all were demoralized. To make matters worse they had to fight their way through hungry Sea Lions as they approached the island. But the penguins were becoming experienced warriors. After they had killed two of the seals, the others seemed to decide the meal wasn't worth the effort and let the penguins be.

Lavour, Leepoh and Nok swam together in the midst of the group, with Lavour remaining stoic and unresponsive to most of Leepoh's attempts at humor. Undeterred, the Gentoo continued to seek his Chinstrap friend's support for many of the insults Leepoh lavished on Nok, receiving only a subtle nod for his efforts.

"Lantot is really going to have a hard time with this," Leepoh told Nok and Lavour as they floated offshore and waited for the masses to thin out before going ashore.

"He'll be all right—as long as no one talks to him," said Nok mockingly.

"Who is Lantot?" asked Lavour, finally joining the conversation.

"Oh, now he has something to say, not while we spent the last few days swimming," Leepoh said, nodding at Nok.

"Don't get me involved in your idiocy," Nok replied, turning toward

Lavour.

"Bah! Rockhoppers," Leepoh snorted, focusing his attention back on Lavour. "Lantot is the Elder of the Gentoo colony here. He's a little *flippy*, as he would say, but he's a kind and caring old penguin."

"After you meet him, I'll take you to my colony and show you the warrens and the Defense Ministry," Nok chimed in.

"Hey," said Leepoh. "What about me?"

"What about you?" Nok asked with feigned irritation.

"I haven't seen it either—at least not inside."

"Yes, I know, but we are selective as to the type of penguin we let in."

Leepoh stared at his friends in silence as they shared a much-needed chuckle at his expense. "We should get to shore, where I can find someone who appreciates my company," he said flatly.

After a minute of silence, Leepoh popped his head up in alarm and the others followed suit.

"What is it?" asked Lavour.

"There's a ship nearby," Nok said, tilting his head to hear. "It's just off the shore between Petral Landing and Black Sand Beach. Let's go."

"You four, come with us," Lavour said to the penguins closest to them.

The three raced ahead of the others toward a group of coastal sea stacks where hundreds of seabirds roosted, giving the structures their name. They surfaced near a converted trawler drifting in the current.

Leepoh swam closer with Lavour, Nok and the others following his lead.

"It's not making any noise," Nok said, looking up examining the sides.

Leepoh swam below the boat while the others waited. "It's not tethered to the seafloor like others I've seen."

"There doesn't appear to be any men on it. As far as I can see, that is," Lavour said.

"Well, there's only one way to find out," Leepoh said. "We'll send the Rockhopper on board to get a looky."

"Wait! What? I'm not going on there alone," Nok protested.

"Don't get your crest in a knot, I'm joking," Leepoh said. He turned to Lavour. "So much for Rockhopper bravado, eh."

Lavour didn't take the bait.

Leepoh studied the sides of the trawler. "We can clear that. We've done it before. What about you, Lavour?"

Lavour gave him a sideways glance. "I've cleared higher icebergs. Of course I can."

The group wasted no time in diving deep to gain the speed needed to clear the sides. Six of them successfully landed on the deck, the seventh slapped against the hull. Leepoh hopped on a step and looked over the edge, spotting the Gentoo who mistimed his leap. "You need to jump higher than that."

Nok shook his head. "I think he might've figured that out on his own."

"I'm just trying to be helpful," Leepoh said, his voice becoming hushed as he looked at the deserted deck. "Nobody's here."

On closer inspection Nok spotted something and ran to it. The others followed, coming up behind him. "No, no, no," he said, standing over the body of a dead Rockhopper. "This is Teesek. She's the daughter of a member of the Tribunal."

"It appears your marauders have returned," Lavour said, hopping past Nok and Leepoh. "We need to see if there are any survivors on board."

"Come on, Nok. There's nothing we can do for her now," Leepoh said, following Lavour up two steps and along a narrow walkway beside the cabin. He turned to the three others. "You go up the far side. And be careful."

By the time they reached Lavour, he had already entered an open door leading to the galley. Their first sight was the body of a badly mangled human. Deep gashes in man's throat and face told them the Rockhoppers had made certain their prey was dead. Farther in they found several more dead Rockhoppers. They examined each for signs of life. Finding none, they made their through another door, kept open by the leg of another dead man.

"I think we can say we know what happened here," Lavour said. He walked across the hall and stepped onto the bridge.

Leepoh watched Lavour curiously as he followed him. "You seem a little bolder than before. Are you all right?"

Lavour walked over to another dead penguin, carefully stepping around the thoroughly damaged remains of a man. "I've seen and experienced enough over the past two moons to feel both fearless and terrified. I guess I'm stuck somewhere in the middle at the moment." He made his way back over the threshold, back into hall. "I don't think we're going to find anything else here. Or at least nothing alive.

Leepoh looked at Nok and let out a snort. It pained him to see Lavour in his current state. One of Lavour's greatest qualities was his empathy, and he would hate to see him lose that part of himself. Leepoh, trailed by Nok, followed Lavour out on the deck.

Nok stood staring at the dead Rockhopper. He sighed. "I guess we should head to shore now."

Leepoh was about to answer when he heard a faraway sound. His body stiffened. He looked around and ran to the bow for a better view of the shore.

"What is it?" Lavour asked, struggling to keep his footing on the wet deck.

"Wait," Leepoh said. He lowered and cocked his head. "There."

"I heard it too," Nok said.

"It's a Gentoo distress call. We need—" Leepoh stopped talking. Over the howling wind he heard the faint crackle of distant gunfire. "There are men on the island. Let's go!" He dove overboard before Nok and Lavour could say a word.

∧∧∧

The three lunged forward and dove under the crowd of penguins still trying to get ashore. On reaching the shallows, they sprang up and out of the water, nudging the others out of the way. Finally, they came to the coarse sand.

Leepoh came to a quick stop when he reached the bottom of Gentoo Rise. "No," he let out. "No, no, no, no!"

Nok and Lavour traded glances, and then looked to their friend. "Leepoh," said Lavour at seeing the horror in his eyes.

Leepoh ignored his friend and sprinted up Gentoo Rise. He saw the bodies of Gentoo and stopped to check each for a sign of life. All the while, he took notice of the telltale signs of gunshot wounds or worse. Among them all, he found one survivor. "Tanty," he said with relief.

She stood before Leepoh with her eyes glazed over from shock. "Leepoh?" she asked, confused.

"Yes, Tanty, it's me. Are you injured? What happened?"

"I don't think I'm hurt," she said, unsure. "It was the humans. They came and—" She paused to get her thoughts straight. "They were near the ship of the ones who came before. The ones we killed. They attacked before we could mount a defense. With so many gone to war, we couldn't—we didn't have a chance."

"Where are they now? Leepoh asked in barely controlled anger.

"The Rockhoppers came to our aid and attacked their ship."

Nok and Lavour arrived as the Gentoo explained the situation.

"They could not return to their ship and were driven inland. That's all I know," Tanty finished. She sounded exhausted, as if telling the brief tale took all of her effort.

"Where is Lantot?" asked Leepoh with a feeling of dread.

Tanty lowered her head and then looked to the top of the rise, and Leepoh understood. Leepoh sat back to take the weight of more loss off his weakened legs. He lowered his head in lament at the loss of his friend. After several minutes of sitting in silence, he turned to his two companions. "Commander Boulét is dead. Commander T'Cuh-ka has abandoned us.

Commander Kiley has yet to arrive. Therefore, for the time being, I am assuming command. Lavour, you are now the commander. Captain Nok?"

"Yes, sir," Nok said, snapping to attention.

"Go with our new commander. Commander Lavour, it might be a difficult task, but see if you can rouse the troops. They're tired and their spirit is broken. But night will be falling soon, and I don't want these humans to see another dawn." Leepoh turned toward the summit of the rise. "Come and see me after you have rallied the troops. I have to pay my respects to a kind and gentle friend."

Nok waited on Lavour, who hesitated. A moment later the newly appointed Commander Lavour nodded and began the march toward the beach.

Leepoh watched Lavour for another half minute. Satisfied, he ascended Gentoo Rise and found the tattered body of Lantot on the summit. He tried not to think of what the phobic Elder had gone through in his final moments while watching his beloved colony being destroyed by the barbaric humans. Lantot deserved a better end than this, he thought. Lantot's grizzled old pinfeathers blew slightly and took flight in the wind as Leepoh stood over him. Of all the death he had seen that day, this made his heart ache worst of all. He reached down with his beak, closed the lids of the departed Elder's eyes, and said his farewell. "Rest easy, old penguin, and take your place at the Ancients' side."

From the top of the rise, Leepoh could just make out the throngs of Rockhoppers who appeared to be corralling their quarry. "Time to go," he told himself. As he turned to face the sea, he was surprised to find thousands of penguins—Chinstrap, Rockhopper, King, Macaroni, and Gentoo—marching up the rise behind Commander Lavour and Captain Nok.

"The troops are ready, sir," Nok said with a hint of dramatic flair that was uniquely his own.

General Leepoh gazed down at the masses and spoke. "Our fight is not over, fellow penguins. *These* humans on *this* island are our *true* enemies. Leave nothing of their flesh intact. Let the scavengers quarrel over what remains." Leepoh turned to Nok. "Captain, lead the way."

Nok turned his head in surprise and then puffed his chest proudly as he faced the crowd. "Death to the humans!" he shouted. He threw a quick glance at Lavour and Leepoh as the penguins answered his call. He then led the charge toward the surrounded humans.

As the thunder of thousands of webbed feet passed by, Leepoh looked at Lavour. "How did you get them to rise up once more?" he asked.

"I just told them the day is not lost, that we can still achieve a victory. And few other words." Lavour answered without a thought about his accomplishment of getting the demoralized and exhausted penguins up to fight once again.

"Hmm." Leepoh snorted as he studied the Chinstrap. "The masses like you, Lavour. You're one of them."

Lavour turned away. "If you say so, General." He began to follow the mass of penguins, but stopped. "Will you be joining us?"

Leepoh surveyed the devastation of Gentoo Rise. He nodded without looking at Lavour. "I believe I will. There's nothing left for me to do here."

CHAPTER 74

Upon arriving at the scene, Lavour spotted six men standing atop the remains of an ancient sea stack, shooting, kicking, and beating away the persistent Rockhoppers. He immediately ordered the reinforcements to join the assault and the gunfire intensified briefly. He cringed each time a penguin fell, but the men had to be dealt with. If they found some way off the island, all penguins nesting here would die.

Each time a penguin, almost always a Rockhopper, surmounted the two meter tall rocks, they would get kicked off or shot. The battle was quickly turning into a stalemate and the blue sky was quickly turning transforming to dark. Lavour watched as an older man, with a substantial paunch, stared toward the beach. The commander followed his gaze and spotted two zodiacs, tethered on the beach. "It's going to make a break for the boats."

"What?" Leepoh yelled over the cacophony of shouting birds.

"The humans, they're going to go for their boats. They can outrun us. We'll have to cut off their escape."

Leepoh looked and spotted the boats as well. "I think you're right."

Lavour called for Captain Nok, who ran to him immediately. "Nok, send half of the forces to the beach over there." He pointed with his flipper.

"But the battle is here, sir," Nok replied.

"True, but they're going to try to get to their boats. It's getting dark and they're desperate. Now, get to it, my friend."

"Yessir," Nok said and quickly went about following his orders.

Lavour saw the human jerk when he caught sight of the penguins moving toward the boats. What the man did next was completely unexpected. The corpulent man hit another man in the back of the head with his rifle, knocking him off the perch; shot two others, and when the two remaining noticed what was happening, he punched one in face, and shot the other.

The penguins quickly pounced on the unwilling sacrifices. With the penguins distracted, the man scurried off the rocks and made a dash for freedom.

"These creatures are disgusting," Lavour said. "How can they just turn on their own kind like that?"

"I have to believe they're not all like that," Leepoh said. "For my son's sake at least."

"Let's hope not," Lavour said. "C'mon, let's finish this."

Leepoh barked out orders and the penguins gave chase to the escaping man.

The sun was fading as the man made his desperate flight. Seeing that his path was about to be cut off, the man turned toward the rocky and tusset-grass-filled slope where Manuel and the others had met their end.

He stumbled over a tuft of grass and landed hard on the ground. He quickly righted himself, but the penguins were nearly on him. The rocky cliffs of the Rockhopper Defense Ministry loomed ahead of him, and hundreds of Rockhoppers came bounding down the craggy cliff face toward him.

The man stopped. Caught between the cliffs and thousands of penguins, there was nowhere left to run. Completely surrounded, he attempted to turn the gun on himself. But the penguins got to him first. The man screamed out as the mob of vengeful birds overtook him.

"Everyone, take a piece," Nok commanded as he stabbed his beak into the fallen poacher. "Leave nothing of this creature!"

The Penguin Defense Alliance did Captain Nok one better and trod over the poacher's body after they pecked at it. When the attack ended, a scavenger would have been hard pressed to find a meal. Countless thousands of penguin feet trampled the dead man, leaving nothing more than an indistinguishable stain in the earth.

Nok came to where Lavour and Leepoh stood, sat down, taking a deep breath. "Can we stop now? I'm really tired."

"Of course we can," Lavour said. "You did great today. I think a promotion may be in order."

Nok was too exhausted to show any signs of pride.

"You did well today, Commander," Leepoh said. "This is what the Alliance was meant to do. We should protect, not invade."

"If only the Royals saw it that way," Lavour added. "Changes need to be made."

Leepoh regarded Lavour for a moment. "And I think I know just the penguin to do it. As a matter of fact, I think that today, on this island, I am witnessing the *true* rise of the penguins."

More from Rockhopper Books

Rise of the Penguins Saga

Rise of the Penguins
Book 1

The Warlord, The
Warrior, The War
Book 2

Crosscurrents
Book 3

Whispers of Shadows
Book 4

The Royal Creed
Order of Kings
Book 5

The Great Auk War
Book 6
(coming soon)